Benz

No one c~~~~
No one.

Jillian felt her control snap. "This was a mistake. I should have let you take me to court. I could have told the judge how you asked me to marry you and didn't have the guts to tell me in person that you'd changed your mind. What kind of example is that for a boy?"

Trevor's whole body tightened. "We're going to get past this, Jillian." He raised his voice slightly. "Right now."

Her gaze flew to his face.

"Say what you have to say," he continued harshly. "All of it. Hit me if it will make you feel better, but get that damn poison out of your system. I've paid for what I did, Jill. More than you can ever imagine...."

"We've both made mistakes. I hurt you badly, I know that. But how do you think I feel, knowing you deliberately denied me my son?"

Dear Reader:

Once again, Silhouette Intimate Moments has put together a very special month for you, with the sort of exciting yet always romantic plots you've come to expect from us.

A couple of books this month deserve special mention because their heroes are a bit different from the usual. In *Full Circle*, Paula Detmer Riggs gives us Trevor Markus, a man with a hidden past that threatens to destroy all his hopes for the future. I think your heart will beat a little faster and you may even find tears in your eyes as you discover the secret Trevor has spent years protecting—the secret that may separate him forever from the only woman he's ever loved.

New author Ann Williams brings us another very different hero in her first book, *Devil in Disguise*. "Nick" is a puzzle when he first appears, a mystery man with no memory of his past. Only two things about him are clear: he's the key to the troubles that have begun plaguing tiny Fate, Texas—and he's the most sensuous and appealing man rancher Caitlin Barratt has ever met.

I'd love to hear from you after you've read these books—or any of our other Intimate Moments, including this month's other selections, from Mary Anne Wilson and Sibylle Garrett. Please feel free to write to me with your comments at any time.

Sincerely,

Leslie J. Wainger
Senior Editor
Silhouette Books
300 E. 42nd Street
New York, NY 10017

Paula
Detmer Riggs

Full Circle

Silhouette Intimate Moments

Published by Silhouette Books New York

America's Publisher of Contemporary Romance

SILHOUETTE BOOKS
300 East 42nd St., New York, N.Y. 10017

ISBN: 0-373-07303-8

First Silhouette Books printing September 1989

Printed in the U.S.A.

Books by Paula Detmer Riggs

Silhouette Intimate Moments

Beautiful Dreamer #183
Fantasy Man #226
Suspicious Minds #250
Desperate Measures #283
Full Circle #303

PAULA DETMER RIGGS

discovers material for her writing in her varied life experiences. During her first five years of marriage to a naval officer, she lived in nineteen different locations on the West Coast, gaining familiarity with places as diverse as San Diego and Seattle. While working at a historical site in San Diego she wrote, directed and narrated fashion shows and became fascinated with the early history of California.

She writes romances because "I think we all need an escape from the high-tech pressures that face us every day, and I believe in happy endings. Isn't that why we keep trying, in spite of all the roadblocks and disappointments along the way?"

For Alex

Chapter 1

The Clayton High School band swung into a rousing rendition of the "Washington Post March" as Jillian Anderson, high heels clattering and long auburn hair flying, bounded up the steps of the bunting-draped platform.

The four other members of the town council had already arrived and were gathered around the podium in the center of the stage, their eyes trained in her direction. Jillian could almost hear their collective sigh of relief as she hurried across the rough boards.

From below the platform, where most of the spectators were bunched, she heard the shouts of the crowd egging her on.

"Yeah, Jillian."

"Go get 'em, Mayor."

With a sunny but slightly breathless smile, she dropped her speech and her purse onto the nearest folding chair and returned the friendly waves of her neighbors.

"Whew, that was much too close," she managed between ragged breaths as she joined the others. Her wide green eyes sparkled as she glanced down at her watch. "Two minutes to spare."

The ceremony was scheduled to begin at ten, and she'd jogged in a narrow skirt and heels most of the distance from the parking lot outside the fence in order to make it on time.

Her cheeks tingled from the brisk September wind, and her sun-streaked auburn bob, unruly even on the best of days, tumbled wildly over the trim collar of her tailored blue blazer, framing her face with exotic color.

The three men on the welcoming committee exchanged pained looks, and Jillian hid a smile. In the 142 years since the town had been founded by two survivors of the Donner Party, Clayton, California, had never had a woman mayor—until now.

Three years ago she'd been elected by a landslide. At the time, she'd promised to bring increased employment to the economically depressed area, and today she was keeping that promise.

Wilderness Horizons, a drug treatment facility based in Seattle, was opening its newest unit on a twenty-five-acre plot outside of town, and nearly forty-five local citizens were starting new jobs there this morning.

The town was celebrating, and Jillian was scheduled to give the first speech.

"Here, have a program," said the only other woman on the stage. "Wouldn't you know, they just arrived from the printer an hour ago? Talk about small-town casual."

Adrian Franklin was the town's only doctor and Jillian's best friend. She was a small pretty woman with short dark brown hair, snapping black eyes and a mischievous sense of humor.

Jillian laughed and used the program as a fan. "I feel as though I've been circling the parking lot for days," she told Adrian with a quick look over her shoulder.

The newly renovated grounds were packed with casually dressed visitors, with more streaming past the uniformed guard at the gate. Family groups on blankets dotted the wide open space under the flagpole, while others clustered along the edges of the swimming pool and spilled over onto the volleyball court.

"I know what you mean," Adrian replied, tossing her long straight bangs away from her face. "My Jeep's crammed into a spot better suited to a bicycle. It's a good thing the people from Horizons are coming by helicopter. Clayton is definitely not set up to handle a crowd this size."

"Don't talk about crowds, Addie. You know how nervous I get when I have to speak in public. Every time I stand in front of a microphone I'm absolutely convinced that I'm going to open my mouth and gibberish will come out."

Adrian laughed. "Not you, Jill. You're never at a loss for words."

"That comes from living with a teenager. You learn to think on your feet."

Jillian leaned against the rough two-by-four railing and lifted her face to the sky. The sun was hidden by the thick overhanging clouds, and the cool breeze carried a hint of winter. To the west the green slopes of the Sierra Nevada slanted sharply upward to disappear into the gray fog. It was a gloomy day for a celebration, but no one seemed to mind.

Adrian looked around. "Where *is* Jason?"

Jillian's face softened into a dimpled smile as she thought about her son. He was a small miniature of her, with his flyaway red hair and pale freckled skin, but in many ways he was different, too. Jason was far too stubborn for his own good, she admitted, and impossibly quick-tempered, just as his father had been.

"He's at home," she told Adrian with a quick smile. "Said he had homework."

"Good kid."

Jillian laughed. "Actually I think he was afraid I'd embarrass him. He's at that awkward age where he hates to admit that he even has a mother. You know, when girls are calling at every hour of the day and night, and a pimple is an occasion for panic."

Adrian groaned. "How well I remember."

"Don't we all! I was known as 'Jill the Giraffe' until my weight caught up with my height."

Adrian clucked her tongue. "I was 'Old Thunder Thighs.'" She glanced down at her trim form. "They're still there, lurking, waiting for that extra bite of chocolate."

As they shared a laugh, Jillian's idle gaze dropped to the chairs placed directly in front of the podium. Seated there were the boys, fifty in number, who were going to be living at Horizons for the next six months, sentenced by the courts to the strict high-security facility as a last resort.

All were hard-core drug addicts, and most had been arrested more than once. At the moment, each boy wore the sullen look of a half-grown kid forced to be where he didn't want to be.

Even the counselors, dressed as casually as the boys, looked uneasy, as though they were equally uncomfortable. Was something wrong? she wondered, frowning. Something she as mayor should know? Her gaze traced the line of faces again, then stopped abruptly at the last boy.

A ragged open area segregated the group from the rest of the spectators, and at each side of the empty space stood an armed deputy sheriff.

"For God's sake, Mel, are you crazy?" she exclaimed, whirling to lock gazes with a giant of a man wearing the olive drab uniform of the Clayton County sheriff. "You're deliberately humiliating those boys, and I won't have it. It's wrong, and it's cruel."

The loose flesh above the sheriff's tight khaki collar reddened, sending streaks of dusky color along his pugnacious jaw. "Full-fledged hoodlums," he exclaimed in an overly loud voice. "That's what they are, rotten little bastards, all of them. And our tax dollars are supporting them."

"Mel, we've been over this a dozen times," Jillian said with barely concealed impatience. "Wilderness Horizons is a private corporation. Your tax money is safe."

Mirrored in the lenses of his sunglasses, her oval face was pink with outrage, and below her swooping auburn brows, her jade-colored eyes seethed with angry gold sparks.

Stay calm, Jill, she told herself firmly, taking a slow breath. The last thing the town needed at this moment was an ugly scene. Today was supposed to be a happy time for all of them—including the boys sitting in front of her.

"If it'll make you feel better, Sheriff," she told him, instinctively slipping into the same quiet but firm tone she'd once used as a Navy nurse to control belligerent patients twice her size, "I'll assume responsibility for their behavior."

"Sure, you say that now, Jillian," Mel Cobb shot back sarcastically after a moment's hesitation, "but what happens when one of these *boys* gets loose and goes on a rampage? Maybe even rips off your precious Sierra Pharmacy for money or drugs? How're you going to feel then?"

Jillian ignored the sarcasm. "Move the deputies, Mel. Right now."

Cobb gave her a long, tight-lipped look, then spun on his heel and stalked toward the steps.

The two deputies were quickly dispatched to take up other posts in the area, and Jillian breathed a sigh of relief. Mel had good credentials, in spite of a reputation for using force where it wasn't always necessary, and he'd accepted the minimal salary that was all Clayton could afford to pay. Otherwise the town would never have hired him.

"You should have gone out with the guy when he asked you. At least once, anyway," Adrian teased in a low voice. "You know what they say about a man scorned."

"Please, Addie," Jillian told her friend in a long-suffering tone. "Not today."

Adrian's answer was forestalled by a sudden blinding light cocooning the platform.

Two yards away a stocky man in a safari jacket and shorts hefted a minicam to his shoulder, then approached slowly, panning the platform from left to right. Behind him came a young black man in jeans and a sweatshirt carrying a light bar and sound equipment.

The PBS series *Focus*, a popular monthly documentary on health and safety in the eighties, was doing a feature on Horizons' innovative program of combining military survival training with conventional methods to treat chemical dependency.

"Here they come," Adrian exclaimed, clutching Jillian's arm and glancing upward.

The noise of rotor blades thundered in Jillian's ears as a sleek red-and-white helicopter cleared the needle-sharp tops of the tallest pines and settled gently onto the ground. A cloud of red dust billowed upward, and the leaves of the hardwood trees rustled overhead.

Orrie Hughes and Rick Garcia, the other two members of the town council, came to stand behind her. The sheriff returned to the platform and stood alone, a dark scowl on his face.

"This is the most exciting thing that's happened in this ol' town since Hans Baumgartner tried to make beer in his basement and blew out all the windows in his house," Orrie muttered close to her ear.

Jillian chuckled and glanced over her shoulder. Orrie, eighty-three and still working every day in his barbershop, was dressed in a suit for the first time in her memory.

"When was that, Orrie?" she asked with a grin.

"Oh, after the war. Nineteen twenty. Twenty-one, some-place in there."

An excited buzz rose from the spectators, punctuated by the shrill shouts of excited children, most of whom had never been this close to a helicopter before.

As she straightened the collar of her white silk blouse and buttoned the dark blue jacket, Jillian struggled against a queasy feeling of déjà vu. During the Vietnam War she'd seen too many Medevac helicopters carrying too many dead or dying men to enjoy the sight of another one.

"Horizons is obviously not lacking for money," Adrian told her with a grin as the rotors began to slow.

"Actually," Jillian said absently, "the parent corporation is one of the most profitable in the health care field. I checked them out before I opened negotiations, just to be safe."

Suddenly the helicopter door slid open. Three passengers, two men dressed in conservative dark suits and a tall blond woman in beige silk, stepped out into the bright light and be-gan walking toward the platform, ducking their heads against the down draft from the slowly spiraling blades.

Jillian recognized the woman as Robin Bessaman, the exec-utive director of Wilderness Horizons with whom she'd been negotiating the terms of the lease. She didn't know the men.

The band swung into another march, and Jillian absently tapped her foot along with the pounding rhythm. Quickly she ran through her speech in her head. This was going to be a great day for Clayton.

"Now that's what I call a *good*-looking man," Adrian mut-tered at her side.

"You always were a sucker for a guy with a beard, Addie."

"Uh-uh. I mean the other one, the tough-looking type with the dynamite shoulders and the don't-mess-with-me swagger."

"Control yourself, Doctor," Jillian teased, peering through the swirling dust. "He's probably Horizons' accountant."

"No way. I tell you, Jill, if he's carrying anything but mus-cle under that Brooks Brothers suit, it's more likely to be a gun than a calculator."

Jillian's pulse tripped as her gaze fastened on the shadowed features of the husky, ramrod-straight man in a gray three-piece suit bringing up the rear. He was bigger than most men she knew, with the shoulders of a lumberjack and long, powerful-looking legs, and he walked with a rolling gait that suggested a barely restrained impatience. Or, she admitted reluctantly, danger. This time Adrian wasn't far off the mark.

The dust began to settle, and she got her first good look at his face. His features were strongly carved, with angular lines and shadows adding to the aura of danger surrounding him. His mouth, slanted now into a controlled white grin, looked hard, as though smiling was something he rarely did. His eyes—

Jillian gasped. Oh, my God. No! It couldn't be.

Only one man had eyes like that, intense, passionate copper eyes that looked almost black when he was aroused. Eyes that had once bathed every inch of her naked body with fire.

"Trevor."

His name shuddered from the darkest part of her memory where she'd fought so hard to bury it.

The air around her thinned, making it hard to breathe, and she blindly groped for the back of the nearest chair. This couldn't be happening, she thought. Not when her life was finally in order, and her wounds were healed.

Her hands were shaking as she ripped open the program Adrian had given her and quickly scanned the names of the guests. He was listed under the executive committee.

Trevor Madison Markus, Chairman of the Board and Founder of Wilderness Horizons. The black letters wavered in front of her eyes, mocking her. She crushed the program between her hands and let it fall to the stage as she stared past the empty chairs toward the steps.

The crisp, sandy blond hair was now a solid gunmetal gray, and the years had added muscle and power to his whipcord frame, but his face was even more ruggedly handsome than she remembered—if that were possible.

Than she remembered . . .

It had taken years of hard work, years of missing him and crying for him, years of lying awake, lonely and aching, but she'd pushed him out of her mind and her heart.

Jillian glanced around hastily, filled with a sudden powerful urge to run. Robin Bessaman had never mentioned his name. Not once, even though she'd spoken highly of the Horizons Board on occasion.

Jillian's heart began to pound and her breath shortened, coming in irregular intervals that hurt her chest. She bit the inside of her lip so hard she tasted blood.

"Jill, are you all right?" Adrian's voice had lost its teasing lilt. "Your face is as white as your blouse."

"I . . . yes, I'm fine. I missed breakfast, that's all."

Jillian glanced back toward the steps. The television lights caught her, and her cheeks burned. She was onstage, held in the spotlight of the camera, her every expression monitored. She was trapped.

At the edge of the stage, Robin paused, an anticipatory smile on her face. As soon as she caught sight of Jillian, her smile broadened, and she waved. Before Jillian could react, the woman had turned back to direct a remark to the two men behind her.

Trevor's head came up abruptly, and his grin faded. As his copper gaze locked with Jillian's, he paled, and his shoulders jerked. He looked like a man who'd just been blindsided by a knockout punch.

His lips moved stiffly, forming her name. The years telescoped, and she felt again the pressure of that hard mouth on hers. Trevor's mouth.

His wide, warm lips had tasted hers with bold masculine relish, each kiss more demanding than the last, until he had only to smile in that special half challenging, half beguiling way, and she'd shivered helplessly in anticipation.

She shivered now, and something barbed and cutting twisted inside her. Once she'd loved the way his lips had smiled against hers. Once she'd loved *him*. But he hadn't loved her.

Robin hurried across the platform, her hand extended eagerly. "This is a terrific welcome, Mayor. I couldn't be more grateful."

"Clayton prides itself on its neighborliness," Jillian managed to get out, her voice unnaturally flat. Inside, her stomach was tumbling violently, and her mouth was dry. "I'm sure everyone here is as pleased as I am to welcome Horizons."

The two men approached, with the leaner, bearded man slightly in the rear. Jillian felt the bloodless chill on her cheeks as she turned to greet them. She concentrated on breathing normally.

Her welcoming gaze included both men, but in her mind she saw only Trevor. The strong, square face, the quizzical lines bracketing his quiet, surprisingly sensual mouth, the slight cleft in his stubborn chin. And the bleak, shuttered look in his eyes.

Robin introduced her to Trevor first, adding with pride in her voice, "Trev doesn't usually attend opening ceremonies, but since Clayton Horizons is our twentieth unit, he's made an exception."

"How nice for us," Jillian murmured, watching his thick sandy lashes lift until those deep-set eyes were resting intently on hers. Something powerful and unreadable shifted in the midnight pupils, tugging at her. *Anguish.* The thought came, then was banished from her mind in the instant it took him to blink.

Ignoring the shiver of uneasiness that shot down her backbone, she fixed a cool smile on her face and extended her hand. Because he was a guest of the town, she would be polite.

"Hello, Trevor," she said in a voice that sounded perfectly calm. "It's been a long time."

His shadowed gaze fell to her small hand. "Yes, a long time." His grip was warm and strong. Too strong. He was hurting her, but she refused to show it.

He cleared his throat. "It's...good to see you again...Jill."

"Is it?"

"Yes. I've thought about you over the years...wondered what happened to you." His voice deepened, grew husky, more intimate.

"Really?" She tugged her hand from his, but the skin still stung where his long fingers had crushed hers. His touch still had the power to shake her.

A muscle worked along his strong jaw. "Yes, really. But I see that you don't believe me." His mouth twisted down at one corner. "Maybe I don't even blame you. I was a bastard."

Shock shuddered through her. Abruptly she wrenched her gaze away from the eyes that had haunted her dreams for too many years. She wouldn't remember, she told herself, balling the hand that he'd held into a fist. It hurt too much.

"Trev?" Robin's pleased smile slipped, and a look of concern replaced the warmth in her eyes.

"You give the speech today, Rob," Trevor said in a clipped, husky tone. "You're better at it than I am, anyway."

Abruptly he unbuttoned his coat and shoved his hands into the pockets of his trousers. Jillian recognized the unconscious gesture of masculine insecurity, and she felt a sharp stab of satisfaction. He might have stunned her into silence, but Trevor Markus wasn't as confident as he appeared.

"Excuse me," he said curtly.

He moved past them to greet the others on the platform, and Jillian suppressed a sigh of relief as she turned her attention to the bearded man waiting patiently for an introduction.

He was tall, almost as tall as Trevor, with a rangy build and intelligent gray eyes. Robin introduced him as Dr. Henry Stoneson, the director of Clayton Horizons.

Jillian summoned a polite smile. "Dr. Stoneson."

"Call me Hank," he said in a lazy West Texas drawl as they shook hands. She estimated his age at forty-five, give or take a few years.

"I'm Jillian."

"That's an ... unusual name."

Suddenly she had a strong but totally inexplicable conviction that this man knew her or, rather, knew exactly what she was feeling. But that was impossible. She was very good at hiding her feelings. She'd had to be.

Involuntarily she glanced toward Trevor, who'd moved to the rail and was talking with one of the counselors who'd been sitting with the boys. He stood rigidly, tension written in every powerful line of his long body, and his hand gripped the railing so tightly that the knuckles poked white against the bronzed skin.

If she didn't know better, she would have sworn that Trevor had been hurt by her indifferent welcome. But that was a fool's perception. A man had to love a woman before she could hurt him. And Trevor had never loved her.

Suppressing a shiver, she turned away and briskly introduced the other members of the council to the two visitors. There was a flurry of handshaking and polite conversation while the band pounded out the last verse of the march.

As soon as the last notes died away, Jillian stepped up to the podium and switched on the microphone. The others on the platform took their seats, and the crowd settled down.

Directly below her, the cameraman from PBS prowled the area, expertly framing his shots as Jillian smiled warmly at her fellow citizens. The knot in her stomach pulled tighter.

She took a deep breath, praying silently for control, then began to speak. "Ladies and gentlemen, honored guests..."

Jillian spoke the words she'd practiced by rote. Her speech was short and optimistic, laying out all the reasons why the town was welcoming its new neighbors.

"...and we all remember what this town was like four years ago, when Pacific Timber declared bankruptcy and closed their doors. Families were uprooted, homes went into foreclosure, people were scared. But this town, all of you, fought back. You didn't give up. And so today we celebrate a new beginning, a second chance for all of us...."

When she finished, the crowd applauded and whistled, and she waved her thanks. When the applause began to slacken, she quickly introduced Robin Bessaman, then sat down next to Adrian.

From the corner of her eye she saw Trevor sitting across the aisle. His spine was pressed against the back of the metal folding chair back, and his long legs were fully extended in front of him.

His eyes were focused on Robin's back, but his expression was stiffly remote, as though his thoughts were far away. As she watched, his hand slowly tightened into a fist against his heavily muscled thigh, and he lowered his head as though in prayer.

Jillian dropped her gaze to the unpainted planks beneath her feet. Slowly she slid her burgundy pumps backward and tucked them under her chair. Letting Robin's perfectly modulated voice flow over her, she studied the tracks her soles had made in the fine layer of dust covering the bare boards.

Footprints in the sand, she thought. No matter how deep, they were only temporary. Sooner or later the tracks would be swept away—like the promises Trevor had once made her.

Jillian drew in a deep breath of air that smelled of pine and threatening rain. Overhead, the large, jagged leaves of a sycamore shuddered in the brisk wind, twisting and turning on their fragile stems.

The trees outside the big military hospital in Tokyo that summer had been a vivid green. Jillian had loved to sit by the window in the nurses' lounge and watch a pair of little brown birds tend their newly hatched nestling.

The baby, undersized and feeble, had fought hard to survive, but one gloomy July dawn she'd found him lying crumpled and lifeless in the tiny nest.

Like so many of the critically wounded men in her ward, he'd lost the fight to live.

But Trevor had won, against all odds.

The sound of Robin's voice faded as Jillian's thoughts spun backward....

* * *

"His name's Markus," the burly corpsman tossed over his shoulder as he positioned the bed carefully against the wall in the small cubicle.

The patient was a big man, with long legs that stretched to the end of the hospital bed, and muscular shoulders that were almost as wide as the pillow. He'd been in surgery for nearly seven hours, and his face was pasty white and lined with pain. "Doc says he probably won't make it through the night."

Jillian quickly scanned the chart. His first name was Trevor, and he was twenty-nine. In six days he'd be thirty, she realized. If he lived.

He was a lieutenant commander in the Navy, a pilot assigned to the carrier *Ranger* which was operating in the South China Sea. His crippled jet had run out of fuel only seconds before he was to land, and the plane had hit the deck instead of the sea. The crash landing had shattered his legs and crushed his spine, but because his fuel tanks had been bone-dry, the plane hadn't exploded on impact. Somehow he'd survived, critically injured and near death, one more wounded Naval officer to add to a lengthening list.

The evac hospital had struggled to stabilize his vital signs and, as soon as he'd been out of immediate danger, had immobilized him for the trip to Tokyo, where the surgeons had worked to save his legs and reconstruct his spine. Most of his body was now encased in plaster, and he had months of almost total immobility ahead of him.

"He's not dead yet," Jillian muttered at the weary-looking corpsman. Together they studied the ashen face half buried in the pillow. The man's nose had been broken in the crash, and one eye was purple and swollen shut. His short sandy hair was damp and matted with sweat.

"Guy looks tough," the enlisted man said with an edge to his voice. "Maybe he *will* make it." He gave Jillian a sympathetic nod and left the room.

An hour later the unconscious pilot started thrashing and moaning in pain as he tried to pull the IV needle from his wide, bronzed forearm.

"Easy, Commander," Jillian murmured, preparing a syringe. The doctor had ordered the maximum dosage of morphine every four hours if he needed it, but she had a feeling it wasn't going to be enough.

As she plunged a needle into his arm, he opened his eyes, blinking in the light. His eyes, deep-set and framed in dark blond lashes, were a startling shade of brown that was almost copper. At the corners, deep weather lines were etched into the tanned skin, and his brows were boldly defined and sun-bleached blond.

"Am I home?" His voice was a ragged whisper, a dark sound of agony.

"No, Commander, not yet. You're in Tokyo, in the hospital." Jillian wiped the sweat from his brow with a cool cloth.

He blinked up at her, trying to smile. "You . . . have a nice face."

Under several days' growth of whiskers, he had the look of a practiced flirt, a hotshot pilot who knew he was irresistible to women. She'd met her fill of Navy flyers just like him in every officers' club from Newport to Subic Bay.

But there was more than conceit in the pain-filled eyes that stared up at her with such intensity, much more. There was intelligence and humor and tough resilience that gave her hope. Maybe the corpsman was right. Maybe he wouldn't die.

"I bet you say that to all the girls," she said with a teasing grin.

His thick crescent lashes drooped, then raised. "No, just you. Who . . . are . . . you?"

Each word was an effort, and Jillian moved closer. The man was in for a rough time, rougher than he could even imagine. She made her voice light and cheerful, trying to distract him from the pain. "My name is Jillian. I'm your nurse."

"Pretty name," he whispered through stiff lips. His hand groped for hers, and she slid her fingers over his, holding his strong brown hand while the morphine worked its way through his veins to numb the screaming nerve endings. He tried not to groan, but the pain was too much for him. He twisted his head on the pillow, trying to escape the agony.

"Hang on to me," she told him, squeezing his hand. "Hold on, Trevor."

His hand crushed hers, but she didn't cry out. His breathing was harsh, and his eyes were tortured.

"Don't . . . leave me," he whispered through parched lips. "Don't let go. I can make it if you don't let go."

* * *

A burst of applause shattered Jillian's inner privacy, jerking her back to the present with a heart-pounding start. She heard the rumble of conversation from the others on the platform and the buzz of the crowd. The band was playing again, and children were laughing. Robin had finished, and the ceremony was over.

She stood.

Trevor came up to her before she could escape.

Without thinking, she moistened her parched lips with the tip of her tongue, and a tiny flare of something hot came and went in his black pupils. Once he'd looked at her just that way before he'd pulled her down for a heated kiss.

"I liked your speech," he said quietly.

She had the oddest feeling that Trevor was holding back, restraining himself in some way. But that was patently ridiculous, she told herself. There had never been *anything* restrained about Trevor Markus.

"Thank you," she said primly, glancing around. The others were all gathered near the steps, where the TV director was interviewing Hank Stoneson.

"I especially liked the part about a second chance."

"Did you?"

"Very much." There was a tense pause, one that seemed to throb between them. "I believe in second chances, too." He glanced down the lean length of his body. "As you can see."

Jillian didn't want to see the solid muscles and rangy sinew that were barely gentled by the civilized pinstripes. She didn't want to measure his length against hers. She didn't want to know where his thighs would press her, where her breasts would touch his chest. She didn't want to know... anything.

"I'm glad to see that you've completely recovered," she said with a chilly nod, preparing to excuse herself. She was shaking so hard inside that she felt as though she would shatter.

"You told me that I would." A glimmer of a smile came and went in the warm copper between his thick lashes.

She gave him an impersonal smile, the kind she reserved for visiting politicians. "At least I was right about some things."

He glanced around, impatience written on his face. "Look, Jill, I know we need to talk, but—".

"No."

He seemed not to have heard her. "Any time you say, any place. You set the terms."

Somewhere deep inside, scar tissue tore away, leaving her raw and unprotected. No terms, she thought wildly. Not for this man.

Her heart began to pound furiously, and her stomach lurched. She needed air; she needed to escape.

"There's nothing to talk about, Mr. Markus. You're an honored guest of this town. As mayor, I'm your hostess. Otherwise, I can assure you that I wouldn't have stayed on the same platform with you for more than the second or two it would have taken to find the stairs." She lifted her chin and met his copper gaze defiantly. "I hope I've made myself perfectly clear."

One side of his sensual, hard mouth lifted in a half mocking, half amused smile. She remembered that smile. The first time she'd seen it, he'd been trying to get her into his bed.

"In other words, get lost."

"I couldn't have put it better myself."

His eyes narrowed only a fraction at the corners, but Jillian noticed, just as she noticed the immediate prickles of warning dotting her skin. This man wasn't used to being crossed.

"Suppose, as an *honored* guest, I ask for a personal escort?"

He was at least five inches taller than she was, and she had to tilt her head to look at him. She hated the advantage it gave him.

"I'm sure one of the men on the council would be happy to oblige," she murmured politely.

"I want you."

For an instant Jillian couldn't move. Echoes of the past bore down on her, nearly smothering her.

I want you, Jill. For now. For always. But always had lasted less than seven months.

"Sorry," she said in a cool, steady voice that cost her dearly. "I'm not available."

She turned and walked away from him.

She felt sick.

Chapter 2

"Jill, wait up."

Jillian turned around to find Adrian struggling to keep her heels from sinking into the sun dried ground as she hurried across the littered clearing.

"What's your hurry?" Adrian asked, taking a quick puff of the cigarette she'd lighted the moment the speeches were over.

"I thought you were going to quit," Jillian said, waving the smoke away from her face.

"I am—soon. And stop evading my question. Where are you running off to?"

Jillian stifled a sigh. She'd just spent the past twenty minutes responding to the exuberant compliments of her neighbors. Her throat was parched, the muscles of her face ached from smiling, and her head was beginning to throb. She wanted to go home, but she had one more thing to do: help Hank Stoneson plant a tree.

"I'm not running. I thought I'd grab a glass of cider before I have to do the honors, that's all."

She glanced across the wide expanse of sunburned lawn toward the rear of the administration building, where a group of local citizens lined the large concrete patio. In a central area, a California redwood tree almost six feet tall, its roots balled in burlap, stood to one side of a mound of red dirt. From nearly every branch fluttered a bright yellow ribbon.

According to Robin, every unit of Horizon had such a tree. Trevor had planted the first one nearly ten years ago at the first facility in Seattle. It was a symbol of a new life for each boy who walked through the gate.

"Oh, yeah. I forgot about the tree." Adrian frowned briefly, then brightened. "Listen, I was thinking, how about meeting Peter and me for a drink when we're done here? He has a friend who—"

"Stop!" Jillian held up her hand and scowled. "No more blind dates. I'm still trying to get over the last guy. Remember him? The one who was into alfalfa sprouts and past life regression?" She sighed. "I'm having enough trouble with the life I have right now, thank you very much."

She began walking toward the patio, and Adrian was forced to fall in step or be left behind. The crowd was slowly dispersing, some ambling toward the patio, others heading for the far end of the compound, where members of the Ladies Aid Society of the Community Church were setting out a potluck buffet.

"You're too picky for your own good, Jill. Besides, Pete's friend is an attorney and very good-looking."

Jillian made a face. "That's not the point," she said in the placid, reasonable tone that she usually reserved for her son's more difficult moments. "My conscience tells me I should open the pharmacy for a few hours this afternoon in case anyone needs a prescription filled. You may not have noticed, but I *am* the only pharmacist in town."

Adrian's sleek black brows arched. "I've noticed. I've *also* noticed that you've been as nervous as a cat since you shook hands with one Trevor Markus, who just happens to have the kind of body bachelor ladies like me fantasize about while soaking in a bubble bath." A sly look brightened her black eyes as she puffed on her cigarette, then blew out a stream of smoke. "Dare I hope you've finally met a man who's gotten through that thick armor of yours?"

Armor?

Triple-tested and double-thick, Jillian thought as she sidestepped a discarded paper cup. Guaranteed to keep her safe against charming and selfish men who wanted only the pleasure they could strip from her body before moving on.

"For heaven's sake, Addie, you make me sound like some kind of man hater," she groused. "I'm just...particular, that's all."

"Now that's an understatement if I ever heard one." Adrian clucked her tongue in mock despair. "How many men have there been in your life since you moved here ten years ago?"

Jillian's voice sharpened. "How should I know? I don't make a mark on a scorecard every time I have a date."

"Just when *was* your last date?"

Jillian sighed. Adrian was beginning to get on her nerves. "Last New Year's Eve, the Fourth of July, I can't remember. I have other things to think about, Addie."

"Like what?"

She let her impatience hurry her speech. "Like making a living, heading the town council, taking care of my son, minor things like that."

She increased her pace, her long legs taking one step while Adrian, shorter by at least six inches, was forced to take two. "And for your information, Doctor, I'm not nervous."

Adrian detoured to a nearby trash receptacle, where she ground the butt of her cigarette against the metal barrel before discarding it.

"The autocratic Mr. Markus was nervous, too," she said as she fell in step again. "It wasn't obvious, I grant you, but the awareness was definitely there, around the jaw and in the set of those drop-dead shoulders, especially when he looked at you—and he looked at you a lot. I tell you, Jill, the man had the look of a patient facing major surgery. I've seen it dozens of times."

Jillian snorted in disgust. "That's a great analogy, Addie, comparing me to major surgery. Thanks a lot."

Adrian rolled her eyes. "You know what I mean. The man was shocked clear down to his spit-shined loafers."

"So? Maybe he was expecting the mayor to be a man."

Without seeming to, Jillian searched the area for Trevor's tall silhouette. He was standing alone near the rear entrance to the administration building, one arm braced against the large concrete post supporting the latticework overhang.

He'd removed his suit coat, and the sleeves of his pale blue shirt were rolled to the middle of his forearms. He had large, square hands and sailor's wrists, supple and thick and heavily veined where they widened into the oak-hard muscles of his arms.

She remembered the play of those corded muscles against the white sheet when he'd gripped her hand. He'd had a big man's wariness about his own strength, and he'd tried not to squeeze too tightly. But sometimes he hadn't been able to help himself, he'd needed her so desperately.

So many times, late at night as she'd sat next to him, watching him toss and turn restlessly in a drug-induced sleep, she'd tried to imagine what it would be like to stand in the shelter of his long, powerful arms, to be cradled against his chest, to hear the strong beat of his heart, to rest her head on his wide shoulder, listening to the quiet resonance of his breathing.

She inhaled slowly, fighting an irrational urge to walk into those arms and pillow her head on his shoulder. Once, he would have welcomed her....

Jillian glanced up to find Adrian looking at her as though she were some puzzling diagnostic case.

"C'mon," Jillian told her in a forced breezy tone, "we've got fifteen minutes. I'll buy you some cider at the VFW stand, and you can tell me your latest escapades with the handsome Professor Peter Morrow."

Trevor Markus braced his spine against the rough redwood siding of the building behind him and watched the two women sipping cider by the small red, white and blue stand.

He was sweating, even though the sun was hidden behind a fat gray thunderhead and a sharp breeze was blowing from the north. Inhaling the familiar scent of threatening rain, he shifted from one large foot to the other, trying to ease the knotted muscles of his lower back.

He should have worn his brace, but he hated the damn thing. It was hot and stiff and itched like the very devil.

He *should* have stayed home, that was what he should have done. He couldn't remember the last time he'd sat for more than a few minutes on the deck of his Belleview house.

Damn it, he'd bought the place because it had a fantastic view of Lake Washington, a view he rarely saw.

When he was home, he spent most of his time in his den, working on the latest project for Markus Engineering International, and it was usually dark by the time he finished. Most nights he ate his dinner at his desk, soaked for twenty minutes in the Jacuzzi, then fell into bed.

He ran his hand down the rough post. The ache in his back was beginning to get worse. It was always bad when he was tense.

He needed a drink, he thought grimly. A double Scotch. Or even one of Hank's foul-tasting cigars. Anything to keep from jumping out of his skin.

He hadn't been this edgy for years, not since he'd sunk every dime he'd saved into the civil engineering firm he'd founded a few years before he'd started Horizons.

His hand clenched against the post. The last time he'd seen Jillian Anderson, she'd been walking alongside the stretcher, trying to smile through her tears as he was taken to the Medevac plane.

The dope they'd pumped into him so that he could stand the twelve-hour trip back to the States had made him drowsy, but he'd forced himself to stay awake, struggling to burn her face into his memory. The face of his personal angel.

Nurse Jillian Anderson, he thought. His Jillian.

A thousand times over the years he'd told himself that he would never see her again. When he'd walked out on her, he was full of anger, full of self-hatred and resentment. Against the Navy, against the war, against her, for making him want things he couldn't have.

It had taken months, years, before he'd been able to think about that time in his life without wanting to put his fist through the nearest wall.

He'd been a bastard, all right, and she had every right to resent him. He'd treated her as badly as a man can treat a woman. She knew it and, God help him, so did he.

But he'd changed. He wasn't the same man who'd left her. It had taken him years to find the courage to look at himself in the mirror when he shaved, really look. Even now, he wasn't sure he liked what he saw.

But at least now he could sleep most nights without waking up drenched with sweat and guilt.

He still thought of her. He always would. But over the years she'd become more like an unattainable dream than a real woman. And as long as she'd remained only a memory, he'd been able to live with himself. At least most of the time.

But now, suddenly, when he'd least expected it, she was standing only a few feet away, so achingly lovely that it hurt to look at her. He had only to cross a few feet of concrete to be able to touch her, to feel again that soft, pliant body move sensually beneath his palm.

But he didn't move, didn't try to close the distance between them. He'd forfeited that right a long time ago, a right he knew he'd never have again.

His left hand clenched, the hard edges of his closely clipped nails digging into his palm. He welcomed the pain, even sought it. He needed something, anything, to distract him from the memories Jillian's presence aroused, terrible, accusing memories that had tortured him for months, even years, before he'd wrestled them into oblivion.

But this was a different Jillian, he realized as he watched her closely. The pixie cap of bright curls that used to smell of jasmine was now a thick mane of sun-washed waves, shimmering in the light and so soft-looking they begged to be touched. And her body... Trevor inhaled slowly, fighting the rush of raw need that flared in his loins. Once she'd been willowy, her hips scarcely wider than her tiny waist, and her breasts had been small perfect globes that barely filled his palms. But now, even sheathed in some kind of plain blue suit, her body had a ripeness that was sending his male radar into alarm status.

Damn, he thought. Why hadn't she grown fat or wrinkled? Why had she become even more desirable in her thirties than she'd been at twenty-one?

It didn't seem possible that she was thirty-six. And yet he knew that she'd celebrated her birthday in August, just as he knew that she loved chocolate and rum punch ice cream. And that she loved to be kissed behind her ears, and tickled behind her knees.

God, Trevor thought. He had to stop thinking like this. There'd been no spark of interest in her eyes, no nostalgia, nothing but cool rejection. Not that he could blame her, he admitted with a silent sigh.

No matter how hard he'd tried, he'd never been able to forgive himself for hurting her so terribly.

A familiar restlessness tightened the muscles of his thighs, and he shifted his feet. He needed to burn off the scorching tension that was lashing him.

He allowed himself to look at her again. She was explaining something to the woman with her, gesturing gracefully in the air with her left hand. There was no wedding band on her finger, no jewelry at all.

Over and over he'd told himself that she would marry, would have children and be happy, far happier than he could have made her.

"I want babies, Trev," she'd said with a dreamy smile that last night before he'd been evacuated to the States. "Lots and lots of babies, with your eyes. I want a house in the mountains, where we can hear the birds sing in the morning outside our window. And I want to make love in the thick green grass."

He remembered that she'd frowned then, thinking of the terrible suffering she'd seen every day at the huge hospital. "We'll be so happy, so normal," she'd vowed. "No more pain. No more problems."

Oh, Jill, he thought, closing his eyes to blot out her lovely profile. I wanted to give you all those things. I swear I did.

Instead, he'd buried it all: Vietnam, the endless months in the hospital, Jillian. It had been the only way to put his life back together again.

Flexing his shoulders in an attempt to ease the growing tightness, Trevor looked out over the crowd gathering along the edge of the patio. He'd been the one to okay this facility after Robin had done all the preliminary work.

The lease hadn't been signed when he'd seen it. If it had been, if he'd seen Jillian's signature at the bottom, there would have been no way in hell that he would have okayed this site. No damn way at all.

Hank Stoneson looked first at his watch, then at Jillian, who was standing a few feet away, listening to Adrian and Robin talk about the health problems a chronic drug user faced.

"Ready, Ms. Mayor?" he drawled softly, drawing her gaze.

"Ready, Dr. Stoneson."

"Then let's get this sucker planted."

Hank took her arm and led her over to the tree, where a shiny new shovel adorned with a big yellow bow was propped against the root ball.

"I promise to make this as painless as possible," he told her with a crooked smile that didn't alter the somber, watchful look in his cool gray eyes.

With his rangy loose-hipped walk and laconic way of speaking, Hank reminded Jillian of the heroes in the grainy black-and-white Westerns she'd watched on TV as a child.

"Please don't worry about me, Hank," she said equably. "I'm stronger than I look."

She felt a surge of satisfaction as his eyes suddenly warmed. His head dipped slightly as a slow grin slashed white against his beard. "Yes, ma'am, I do believe you are at that."

Jillian had the distinct impression that her words had pleased him. Even stronger was the feeling that she'd met this man before—or that he'd met her. She relaxed slightly and tried to ignore the butterflies in her stomach.

The crew from PBS fanned out to bracket the area surrounding the tree. The cameraman adjusted his lens, then nodded to his assistant, who turned on the lights and sound.

"Okay, y'all, gather round," Hank drawled, his voice raised to carry over the chatter of the crowd. He waited until the noise subsided and most of the faces were turned toward him. "What we have here is a *Sequoia sempervirens*, better known as a coast redwood." He fingered a branch. "Pretty, isn't it? And this is where it comes from." He reached into the pocket of his coat and pulled out a small pinecone. He held it up for everyone to see. It was barely an inch in diameter. "Hard to believe that a tree that grows as tall and strong as this one will can start from something so small, but it does."

Without warning he tossed the cone to one of the Horizon residents in the front row. Sullen and pale, the teenage boy was smaller than the others and painfully awkward, but he managed to keep the cone from falling.

"This pinecone is like a second chance. Plant it, nurture it with hard work and determination, and it grows. One day at a time."

Hank had a droll, relaxed manner that was entertaining as well as informative, and as he told about Horizons' program, the party attitude of the crowd added to the upbeat mood.

Jillian, waiting to toss a shovelful of dirt into the hole, idly studied the faces surrounding them. The crowd was much smaller now, but it was still sizable, and most of the spectators were smiling.

She noticed Trevor immediately. Taller than most, he was standing to one side, with another group of inmates. There was a tense, almost rigid set to his shoulders, and his jaw was tight. Suddenly, as though her gaze had touched him, he turned to look at her.

He was a stranger, and yet, oddly, he was terribly familiar. The rugged masculine features were the same, the strong almost square chin with a hint of a cleft, the large straight nose, the hollowed cheeks that were now seamed with harsh lines, all terribly familiar. It was the eyes that had changed.

Still strangely hypnotic, the bronzed copper no longer held a boyish exuberance for life. There was experience trapped there, and a deep brooding sadness that caught Jillian off guard.

As she watched him, his eyes darkened, then became completely blank, and his thick lashes lowered, shutting her out.

Flushing, she jerked her gaze away. She shouldn't have touched him, she knew now, shouldn't have let him wrap his large warm hand around hers.

She could still feel the warmth of his hand against hers. She'd never forgotten the way his hands had caressed her, seduced her, thrilled her.

He'd made love to her exactly six times, always with his legs sheathed in plaster. She'd never been able to feel his legs entwining with hers, never felt the power and the tension in those heavy thighs, never felt his thighs slide against hers.

Clenching her teeth, she pretended to concentrate on Hank's words. But in her mind she was hearing Trevor's voice, low like Hank's, but more resonant and filled with a raw masculine hesitancy that had stunned her. . . .

"Marry me, Jill, as soon as I can walk down the aisle with you." Trevor lifted her fingers to his lips and kissed the tips. "Say yes, angel. Say you'll marry me."

"Yes, yes, yes!"

He laughed and pulled her down against his chest for a long, bone-tingling kiss that left them both breathless.

It was the night before Trevor was being shipped back to the States to begin a lengthy and difficult course of therapy for his legs, and they'd just made love.

"Oh, Trevor, I love you so much," she whispered, wanting to go home with him so badly that she ached with it. "I couldn't stand it if I lost you."

Her hushed voice broke, and she bit her lip. Her happiness was like a fragile bubble, suspended in midair. Now that she'd found him, she didn't think she could face life without him.

During the months of his difficult convalescence he'd pursued her relentlessly, taking advantage of every moment she'd spent by his bedside to tease seductively, using his husky voice and his expressive eyes to do what his body couldn't.

But it was during the quiet time they spent alone that he'd won her heart. Terrified that he would spend the rest of his days in a wheelchair, he'd been moody and introspective and vulnerable, sharing his fears with her, along with his deeply buried hopes. She'd seen the real Trevor Markus during those hours, the sensitive, sometimes insecure man behind the devilish facade.

Jillian had convinced him that he would recover. Perhaps he would never fly again, or race his twelve-meter yacht on Puget Sound with his father and brother, but he would certainly walk. He'd believed her, finally, and after that had begun to make rapid progress.

In spite of the lack of privacy and the hard, unyielding casts that restricted Trevor's movement, they'd become lovers. It was always in the middle of the night, when the other men were sleeping, and it hadn't been easy. But Jillian's fellow nurses had helped, moving Trevor's bed to a private room as soon as one became available. Whenever the door was closed, no one intruded.

"You won't lose me," Trevor said with the careless note of arrogance that she'd first hated and then come to love, just as she'd come to love him.

He tugged her closer until he could lightly trace the curve of her lower lip with a long, blunt finger. Lying across his chest, she could feel the heat from his body flowing through the starched cotton of her uniform to warm her breasts.

Jillian allowed her body to soften against his. Her hands cupped his hard shoulders, and her skin tingled as she slid her palms along the hard ridge of his collarbone. His skin was warm and slightly damp, and the muscles below were hard and sharply defined.

Trevor inhaled swiftly as her hands threaded into his thick sandy hair. He kissed her hungrily, probing with his tongue, arousing her with the rough tip against hers. He tasted of chocolate, and his lips were hot.

He slid his hand to the back of her neck, and his fingers massaged the sensitive spot under her hairline. His kiss became hot and insistent, and she met his arrogant demand with a demand of her own.

His hand tangled in her short curls, and she could feel the pads of his blunt fingers pushing against her scalp. His breathing quickened and grew slightly more raspy.

She felt her own pulse trip into a faster rhythm. Boldly she slid the tip of her tongue along his lips, and they parted instantly. He'd taught her to be unrestrained, to unleash the wild sensuality inside her that was as vibrant as her hair.

A hot, sweet urgency began building inside her, and she tempted his tongue with hers. He groaned hoarsely and met her thrust with one of his own.

Tiny beads of sweat erupted on his broad forehead, and he began to caress her back with long, fevered strokes.

Under the sheet draped between his plaster-sheathed legs he was becoming aroused, exciting her as no man had ever excited her before. Jillian was ready, more than ready.

This was Trevor, the man she loved more than her life, the man who loved her.

"It's all set, angel," he said in a tortured voice. "Christmas Eve, on the grounds of the Royal Hawaiian, at sunset. You bring the minister and the witnesses, and I'll bring the champagne."

A tiny dimple appeared at the corner of her soft, full mouth. "And the flowers," she teased. "Don't forget the flowers. Red roses, lots and lots of red roses."

The breeze brushed a long, soft tendril of hair across Jillian's face, and she blinked. Trevor's resonant laugh had once shivered down her spine, like that strong north wind she remembered as she pushed the thick curl into place again.

"Red roses for my angel. I promise," he'd said then, and she'd believed him.

She'd believed everything he told her, until it was too late.

Jillian lifted her head, catching the chilled breeze on her cheek. She was no longer that young nurse, and she no longer believed in love, at least not the kind that Trevor had offered.

She shifted her gaze to Hank's intense face. He sounded as though he was almost finished. And then she could leave.

"...and thank God, most of you good people will never have to live with a ticking bomb in your belly, reminding you every minute, every second, that one slip will send you spinning back into a nightmare that ends only in death.''

Hank shoved one hand in his pocket and surveyed the crowd. ''The guys here aren't asking for your sympathy, and they'll have to earn your respect, but we *are* asking for a chance to show you that we can be good neighbors.''

A ripple of sound ran through the crowd, and the spectators began to applaud. Applauding with them, Jillian felt a flow of pride at the spontaneous outpouring of support. These were good people, generous and kind, and she prayed she hadn't done them a disservice by bringing Horizons to their close-knit community.

Hank grinned and held up his hands. ''Thank you very much. The boys and I appreciate the welcome. And now, if Mayor Anderson will help me, we'll put this fine tree in the ground.''

Jillian's smile felt stiff as she took the shovel from Hank's hands. Two of the residents came forward and lifted the tree into the hole.

''Give it your best shot,'' Hank said as he took a step backward.

She nodded and looked up at the crowd. Unerringly her gaze found Trevor's.

He looked sad, as though he'd just lost something precious. But that was impossible, she told herself with bitter scorn. He was probably as impatient for this to end as she was.

Mentally giving herself a shake, she shoved the pointed end of the spade into the mound of rust-colored dirt. The impact stung her hand, but in some strange way the pain felt good.

''Good job,'' Hank said as she tossed the dirt into the hole. The pellets of clay rattled like hail against the sturdy trunk, and the crowd cheered.

Hank took the shovel from her, duplicated her effort, then raised the shovel above his head. ''Let's hear it for Horizons number twenty,'' he shouted, and the boys began applauding. The crowd joined in.

''Thanks again, Jillian,'' Hank said, suddenly serious as the crowd closed around them. ''I hope we're going to be friends.''

''Me, too,'' Jillian said, smiling into his kind eyes.

They were engulfed by well-wishers, and Jillian turned away, politely acknowledging the congratulations of her fellow citizens as she angled across the patio toward the open space. She'd turned the corner of the building and was starting across the open area when she heard a shout behind her.

"Jillian, wait up!"

What now? she thought, recognizing the sheriff's strident call. She turned around, then sighed. It was Mel all right, red-faced and scowling and heading directly toward her.

"I *warned* you, Jillian," he said in a loud, angry voice as he reached her side. "I warned all of you, but none of you bleeding hearts would listen to me."

Jillian's heart began to pound. "That's enough, Mel. You're making a scene."

"Damn right I am! This town needs to wise up, and the sooner the better." The loose skin below his chin shook violently as he bobbed his head accusingly. "Grady Hendricks, you know, Ralph's son, the one who works here in security, just told me. One of those damn hoodlums is missing. Escaped, doing God only knows what right now."

"Calm down, Mel. You're overreacting."

"Overreacting, hell! You're the one who said we could trust these people. You're the one who ramrodded this through the council. Okay, fine, but now we have a problem, and I want you to call an emergency meeting of the council to discuss this."

Conscious of the stares and whispers directed their way, she counted to five, then said in neutral tone, "Tomorrow, Mel. If we find we really have a problem."

"We have a problem, all right, and I'm beginning to think it's you. What did these guys do, pay you to let them take over PacTimber's lease?" His voice quivered with disgust as he grabbed her arm.

A searing pain shot into her shoulder, and she tried to twist away. She'd never seen Mel out of control like this.

"Sheriff Cobb!"

The deep voice came from behind and carried the steel of command. Jillian inhaled sharply as Cobb's fingers bit into her arm like the jaws of a vice. "Let her go—*now!*"

The sheriff dropped her arm as though it were a glowing poker, and Jillian spun around, her eyes snapping indignantly. Trevor stood a shadow's length away, his copper eyes trained like twin howitzers on the sheriff's face.

"Now look here, Markus—" the sheriff began in strident anger, only to close his mouth with a snap as Trevor took a deliberate step toward him.

"No, you look here, Sheriff," he said in a quiet voice that hissed past Jillian's stony face like the wind of a mortar shell. "As I see it, you've made two mistakes. Number one, you jumped to the wrong conclusion because you're so damn prejudiced against these boys, you didn't wait to hear the whole story."

Jillian stood rooted to the ground. The Trevor she remembered had been a charming flirt, even a bawdy tease on occasion, but he'd never projected this kind of raw male power, never exuded such potent menace. Flustered, she wondered what kind of a life he'd led during the years since then to change him so drastically.

"What the hell do you mean, wrong conclusion?" Cobb demanded. "The kid is gone, escaped. As soon as I can get some men together, we're going out after him."

"The boy was lost," Trevor said in an even voice. "He'd been following some deer tracks and he got confused. One of the counselors just brought him back. They tell me he never left the grounds."

Mel glared at him, his mouth working, but before he could say another word, Trevor moved closer until his flat torso was only inches from Cobb's fat belly.

Jillian held her breath. She should stop this, but suddenly she was powerless to move.

"And number two," Trevor continued softly, "you took out your anger on someone who doesn't deserve it. That's not what I call smart."

Cobb blanched, and his voice shook as he took an awkward step backward, his heel crunching against a discarded candy wrapper. "Don't threaten me, mister. Your money doesn't mean anything here."

"I don't need money to bring you down, Cobb. Take off that badge, and I'll show you I mean what I say."

The two men locked glances, and the air seemed to crackle around them. Jillian stood in frozen disbelief, her heavy bag clutched to her breast like a shield.

Trevor and Mel were about the same height. The sheriff had the advantage in weight, but Trevor had more powerful shoulders and, Jillian noted as though from a great distance, the sinewy look of superb conditioning under the trim vest and pleated trousers.

Nearby the buzz of curiosity swelled. Mel's mouth opened and closed like a catfish scavenging on a lake bottom, and his watery eyes bulged wildly.

"This is only round one, Markus. Sooner or later one of those rotten kids will step over the line, and I'll be waiting."

He tugged the bill of his cap another inch closer to his blond brows and turned on his heel, stomping across the tennis court toward the parking lot, his gun slapping his fat thigh.

The comments of the crowd swirled around Jillian's head, and she struggled to keep her temper in check. Her breath came in short bursts, and her cheeks were burning as she trained her angry gaze on Trevor's bronzed face.

"Don't ever do that to me again!" she said in a harsh whisper.

Her hushed voice was shaking more from reaction than anger, but Trevor couldn't know that. She lifted her chin and glared at him, her back teeth grinding together.

Trevor stared at her. "Do what?" he asked quietly, his face coolly impassive. "Keep that bigoted ape from pawing you?" He jammed his hands into the pockets of his trousers and shifted his weight. His spine was rigid.

Jillian drew a long stream of air into her lungs. The smell of rain had grown stronger, and the clouds above were now swollen and black.

"Mel Cobb's a bully, and he blusters a lot, but he wouldn't deliberately hurt anyone."

Trevor's unruly brows drew together. "Oh, sure, that's why you were trying to get away from him."

"I was trying to get away from him because I don't like anyone touching me without my permission."

"Take a look at your arm tomorrow, and then tell me he didn't hurt you."

Jillian resisted the urge to rub the bruised skin. Trevor was right, but she would never admit it. And the longer she stood talking with him, she realized grimly, the more she was risking.

"Let's just forget it, okay? I'm glad your... your inmate is back safely."

His lips tightened. "We call them residents."

Jillian nodded. "Sorry, I'll remember that. And now, if you'll excuse me..."

With a scowl she turned away, fighting to keep the memory of this man locked away where it had been for so long. She wouldn't allow herself to remember how he'd touched her so long ago, how his big hand had searched and found all the tender, sensitive spots that had given her so much pleasure. How he'd pleasured her heart and her soul even more deeply.

"I'm sorry, Jill."

Shock shot through every curve and angle of her body. Slowly she turned to look at him. His face was as hard as the granite slope beyond the tree line, and his eyes carried no hint of his feelings.

"Sorry for what? For embarrassing me? For walking out on me fifteen years ago? What are you sorry for, Trevor?"

She swallowed the angry tears that scalded the back of her tongue, tears that were as bitter and poisonous as her thoughts.

"I'm sorry for hurting you, Jill. Fifteen minutes ago *and* fifteen years ago."

Jillian's stomach heaved. "Deftly put, Trevor. You have a real way with words."

One corner of his mouth curled downward. "But you're not impressed."

"I doubt there's anything in this world that you could say or do that would impress me."

Her eyes smoldered as she glared at him, and a tight pressure gripped her chest painfully. No, she wouldn't remember. She wouldn't.

"Goodbye, Trevor."

"Don't go."

Before she could escape, Trevor crossed the distance between them until he was standing between her and the rest of the clearing. Jillian was startled to see that her mouth just reached his strong brown throat. She had only to move forward a few inches and her lips could brush the clean line of his jaw.

Chagrin burned in her blood as she jerked back a step. What was she thinking? This man had once hurt her so terribly that she'd wanted to die. She took another stumbling step backward.

Trevor's eyes darkened to mahogany as he watched her retreat, and a tiny muscle spasmed next to the taut corner of his mouth. "You look great, Jill," he said in a husky voice. "Very elegant. But then, you always were beautiful."

Trevor watched her skin turn so white that he wondered if there could be any blood left in her face. She was angry, and bitter as hell. He'd never seen her eyes so dark, not even when they'd made love.

Suddenly, irrationally, irresistibly, he wanted to kiss that soft, angry mouth. He wanted to hold her, to feel her warmth just one more time against his chest. This time he wanted to feel all of her against him. This time he wanted to be the strong one. This time he wanted to take care of her, this one time.

"Jillian," he began in a husky tone, then faltered. Suddenly he didn't know what to say. He'd been so sure he would never see her again. So damn sure.

He reached for her, his big hand folding gently over her shoulder. With a harsh cry, she wrenched away.

"Don't touch me!" she said desperately, backing toward the side of the building. "I don't want you to touch me."

She hadn't been prepared for the wild spurt of raw desire that had shot through her. This hot urgency was more than she could handle.

"You used to like me to touch you. Remember?" His eyes warmed, and his voice dropped into a rough whisper. "You used to stretch like a cat and beg me to pet you. And then you'd make that sexy growling sound in your throat when I found all the right places."

Jillian's mouth went dry. She couldn't seem to think. She couldn't seem to move. A breathless pleasure filled her lungs, and the same warm tingling that Trevor had always excited in her slowly spread through her body.

"I don't remember," she said woodenly. But she did. Dear God, she did!

She took another step backward, feeling the rough redwood siding of the building snag her skirt. She was trapped.

"This is pointless," she said, tightening her grip on the smooth leather of her bag. She had to get away from him.

"Jill, listen—"

She refused to let him finish. "You don't care a thing about me, and I certainly don't care about you."

His jaw jerked, as though she'd slapped him. "Maybe you don't care about me, Jill, but I . . . care about you. I always have."

Trevor knew that he should let her go. But even as he told himself to turn around and walk away, he couldn't leave her.

Not yet. Not until he'd said the words he should have said fifteen years ago.

Absently he massaged the knotted muscles of his neck. He was stalling, trying to find the courage to look her in the eye without flinching, but it was harder than he'd thought it would be. Just do it, he told himself angrily. He straightened his shoulders, gritting his teeth against the hot flare of pain in his lower back. "Jillian, about Hawaii—"

"No! I don't want to talk about that, ever."

Her anguished cry was like a razor slash across his spine. For the first time he saw the scorching contempt in her eyes, along with the raw pain that had been hidden behind the indifference. A heaviness gripped his chest, and he inhaled deeply, trying to fill the void inside. Payback time, Markus, he thought. With interest. One more debt he had to pay, just as he'd been paying for years.

"I never meant to hurt you, Jill."

Jillian forced herself to ignore the grave lines of suffering around his eyes. "You made your point quite adequately. You didn't want to get married. You didn't want me. Fine. I accept that. Now let's drop it." Her chin jerked upward as she made herself breathe in and out slowly.

Trevor stared down at the sparse grass beneath his feet. What had he expected from her? Absolution? A second chance? Damn, he thought in vicious self-contempt. It hurt. Even after all these years, it still hurt like hell to know he could never have her.

All of a sudden he felt terribly tired, and his back screamed for relief. He nodded curtly, accepting her rejection. "Goodbye, Jill. It was . . . good to see you again."

He turned away, only to smash into a skinny redheaded kid carrying a skateboard. "Whoa, there . . . !" Grunting, the boy bounced off his chest, and the skateboard went flying, tumbling sideways to land upside down on the grass.

Trevor was furious with himself. He couldn't even make a graceful exit.

The kid was all arms and legs, with a long skinny torso and restless feet. He looked to be about twelve or thirteen, the same age as Trevor's brother's son.

He wrapped his hand over the boy's bony shoulder and looked into his pale, freckled face. "Sorry, son," he said tersely. "I didn't see you coming. Are you okay?"

The boy shook off his hand and pushed his dark glasses more firmly against the bridge of his nose.

"Yeah, I'm okay." His voice cracked, and color flooded his cheeks.

Trevor hid a smile. The kid sounded as though he was going to have a deep voice someday, but right now it was changing. He remembered those awkward days very well. He hoped this kid's father could help him through the agony of puberty as patiently as his father had helped him and his brothers.

The boy turned his attention to Jillian, ignoring Trevor completely. "Some of the guys are going over to Truckee to play video games, and I want to go along, if that's okay with you, Mom."

Mom?

Trevor froze. He'd always known there would be other men. Hadn't he told himself over and over that she would find someone else? That she would marry and have children? She'd wanted four—or was it five? He'd forced himself to forget a long time ago.

He kept his expression carefully neutral as Jillian brushed a damp red curl away from the boy's freckled forehead. He didn't want to think about the man who'd fathered her son. But he knew that he would, often. And that he would envy him.

"This is Jason, my son," she said calmly, her low voice soft with pride. In her eyes Trevor saw the same loving glow that had once been there for him alone.

He nodded, not trusting himself to speak yet. His stomach burned, and his throat felt as though it had been scalded. So this is regret, he thought numbly as he extended his hand toward Jillian's son. Funny. It had never hurt quite so much before.

"Hello, Jason," he said in a voice that sounded like a stranger's. "I'm Trevor, an old friend of your mom's."

The boy shook his hand halfheartedly, clearly uninterested.

"How 'bout it, Mom?" he asked, ignoring Trevor again.

Jillian took a tighter grip on her purse. "Who's driving?"

"Mike Cobb."

"Jase, he's had two tickets—"

"I know, but he's learned his lesson. Besides, his dad said he'd pull his license if he gets another one."

Jillian hesitated. Mike Cobb had lived with his mother in Los Angeles until six months ago, when she'd sent him to live with

Mel. He was sixteen, big for his age, and far too wild for her peace of mind. But Jason liked him, and she'd always trusted her son to pick his own friends.

"It's okay with me, but I want you back before dark. Tell Mike you won't be allowed to go with him again if you're late." Jillian felt Trevor's eyes on her, and she had to force herself to smile at her son.

"Killer! Thanks, Mom." The laces of his high-topped sneakers flapped around his bony ankles as Jason walked over to retrieve his skateboard. As he bent over, the dark glasses slid from his nose and dangled from a cord strung around his neck. He paused, squinting toward the swimming pool, where a group of friends were horsing around, poking one another and laughing.

Suddenly, before Jillian could move, he spun around and looked directly at them. In the light his eyes were a clear, startling copper.

She held her breath as a gray tinge spread under Trevor's dark tan. He looked stunned, his face frozen into a mask of disbelief.

Trevor's mind went blank, and he felt a savage pain twist his gut. It was the same feeling he'd had just before his F-14 had smashed into the deck.

"My God, Jillian," he whispered hoarsely. "How could you?"

Chapter 3

For an instant Jillian couldn't speak. She'd been so sure this moment would never have to happen.

Of course Trevor was shocked, she told herself as she hugged her purse against her stomach. Any man would be when suddenly faced with a part of himself. But the shock would soon pass, just as the shock of his rejection had.

Forcing life into her wooden features, she gave Jason a quick hug. "Be home for dinner, okay?"

"Are you sure you want me to go?" His brow puckered as he stared at Trevor's stony expression. "I can wait."

"No, it's okay. Have fun."

The boy hesitated for an instant, then pushed his dark glasses back onto his nose, spun around and took off at a run, his shirttail flapping. He didn't look back.

Trevor watched the boy until he disappeared into the crowd. A son, he thought, fighting the numbness of shock. Dear sweet God, I have a son. He ran a shaky hand down his jaw and turned to look at Jillian. His heart was thundering in his ears, and his skin felt clammy. He had to clear his voice twice before he could speak.

"I didn't know, Jill," he said harshly. "I swear I didn't know."

Jillian's jaw tightened until her ears hurt. Surely he didn't think that made his desertion forgivable.

"Jason's the surprise I had for you in Hawaii, the one I mentioned in my letters." Her voice thinned. "Or maybe you don't remember."

Remember? Trevor thought in a blazing surge of raw pain. He'd read those letters so often that the paper had worn thin and the writing had faded.

"But why did you . . . wait to tell me?"

"I'd planned to tell you as soon as I knew for sure," she answered truthfully. "I'd even written the letter, but I tore it up. I wanted you to be able to concentrate on your therapy without worrying about a pregnant fiancée."

Jillian was pleased to hear the lack of emotion in her voice. She'd done her screaming years ago, in private, sitting hunched over on a windswept beach, her tears mingling with the spindrift.

Trevor glanced up at the clouds above as though searching for an answer. Or an escape. "There's nothing I can say that would be enough," he whispered hoarsely as he dropped his gaze to her face. "Except—thank you."

Jillian forced herself to ignore the stark agony that settled in his eyes. She slung her purse over her shoulder. The crowd was clustering around the buffet table, and she and Trevor were alone at the side of the main building.

"I really don't expect you to say anything, Trevor. Not after all these years. Life goes on, and mine has gone on just fine, so you needn't feel any responsibility for me *or* my son." She lifted her chin. "Now, if you'll excuse me, I have things to do." She started to turn away, only to have Trevor stop her with a painful tug on her forearm.

"You can't just walk away, Jill. We have things to talk about." In spite of the pain in his eyes, his voice was edged with granite.

"Why can't I? You did."

Trevor's lips whitened. "What do you want me to say, Jillian? That I was a bastard? I've already said I was, and I meant it." His deep voice roughened. "Some things I can change, and I have, but there isn't one blasted thing I can do to change the past. I can only live in the present. And right now, today, I want to become a part of Jason's life. Whatever it takes, I'll do."

"No!"

The word was torn from her throat before she thought. She pressed shaking fingers against her lips to stop the trembling. She had to stay cool. She had to think.

"Yes, Jillian." His lips thinned. "As Jason's father, I have a right to be a part of his life."

"Rights, Trevor? You have no rights. None at all." Her voice vibrated with anger, and her hands shook uncontrollably.

"Don't push me, Jill. I've already said I was sorry. I screwed up, yes, but now I intend to make things right the best way I can. *Any* way that I can."

Jillian fought to control her temper. How dare he? she thought, her breath hissing past her dry lips.

"We don't need you to make things right, Trevor. Jason and I are doing great without you. He's happy here. I make a good living. We have friends. We don't need you." She glanced toward the front gate. Jason's bright head was a small speck in the jumble of spectators moving toward the exit.

"Look at me, Jill." Trevor's voice was husky. He waited until she reluctantly shifted her gaze to his face. "I'm forty-six years old, and I don't know the first thing about being a father. Hell, I'm still having trouble dealing with the fact that I *am* one. But I can't just walk away and pretend my son doesn't exist. I've walked away from too many problems in my life."

Jillian stared at him. Was that what she'd been to him? A problem? She banished the thought, but not the sick feeling in her stomach.

"What you do or don't do in your life is not my concern, Trevor," she told him. "But Jason is. And he's very happy the way he is. I can't see any advantage in changing things."

Trevor's eyes narrowed. "I won't accept that, Jill. Every boy needs a father."

"There's more to being a father than merely performing a physical act, Trevor. It requires hard work and commitment and a lot of staying power."

His chin jerked. "Did it ever occur to you that I might have changed? That maybe I've paid for what I did to you?"

She stared at him in disbelief. "If you've paid," she said slowly, her voice throbbing with conviction, "it wasn't nearly enough."

His jaw tightened for an instant, then relaxed, as though he were making a conscious effort to restrain himself. "What do you want me to say, Jill? That I've regretted every day I've had to live without you? That I would give everything I own to be able to live that Christmas Eve again? That I've never stopped loving you? Is that what you want to hear?''

Jillian was very close to tears. She didn't want his lies, his excuses, his apologies.

"I don't want to hear anything from you, Trevor. Except goodbye.''

He ran his blunt fingers through the pewter hair above his ear. "You're determined to hate me, aren't you?''

"Wrong. I don't feel anything for you.''

He exhaled slowly. "Then it shouldn't be difficult for you to let me become a part of our son's life.''

The chill in the air had seeped into Jillian's bones, and she repressed a shiver. "He's not *our* son," she told Trevor with that same chill in her voice. "He's mine. He doesn't know about you, and I don't intend to tell him.''

Trevor heard the ring of finality in her tone, and he felt sick inside. This wasn't the sweetly adoring woman he'd loved so fiercely in Tokyo. This woman was fiery and passionate and willing to scratch and claw to protect her child from a man she despised. But he knew only one way to fight—no holds barred. And this was a fight he had to win.

"I can take you to court, Jillian. I don't want to do that, but it's up to you.'' His voice was silky soft and edged with regret. "I have enough money to hire the best family law attorneys in the country.''

Jillian felt as though she'd been kicked in the stomach. Even blindsided and off guard, Trevor sounded as though he intended to fight, just as he'd once fought for his life.

"I'm not afraid of you," she lied. "There's no way you can prove Jason's your son. Legally his father is a man named William Paul White.''

Trevor's nostrils flared. "The hell he is!''

Jillian lifted her chin. Nausea was climbing from her stomach into her throat. "He was a patient in the hospital the same time you were, a good and decent man. And it's his name I put on Jason's birth certificate. He's dead now, and there's no way you can prove he wasn't my child's father.''

Pain ripped along Trevor's backbone, and he inhaled sharply. This wasn't the indifference she claimed to feel toward him. This was hatred, raw, bitter hatred. He knew all about that kind of bitterness. He'd lived with it for a long time.

"I'll find a way," he said with forced calm. "There are things you can't change—the color of his eyes, his blood type."

"I'm not stupid, Trevor. Bill White's blood type is the same as yours. And he had brown eyes, maybe not exactly the same color as Jason's, but close enough."

Trevor's jaw clenched. "Then I'll find something else to use. I'm not giving up. I've always wanted a child, more than you can know. And it hurt a lot when I thought I would never have one. I'm tired of hurting." His voice took on a steely edge. "Hate me if you have to, Jillian, but I won't let you keep me away from my son."

"Never! I'll never give you access to Jason."

She spun on her heel and walked away, moving with mechanical stiffness. Tonight, when she was alone, she would let herself feel. But right now she welcomed the icy numbness spreading through her. It would insulate her against the crippling pain of hating this man.

Trevor watched her until she disappeared into the crowd. Rolling his shoulders back carefully, he looked blindly up at the trees. His eyes stung with remorse, and he closed them convulsively. He had more to pay for than he'd thought. Much, much more.

But no matter what he did, no matter what he gave her, no matter how humbly he begged for forgiveness, it wouldn't be enough.

A son. Jillian had given him a son, a good-looking kid, with her hair and his eyes. Markus eyes.

Suddenly, in his mind's eye, he saw her as she must have been in Hawaii, the tawny skin of her belly swollen with his child, her vibrant green eyes filled with happiness, waiting to surprise him. She would have been so lovely. . . .

"Damn," he whispered, feeling the sting of moisture on his cheeks. The storm was coming closer.

I love you, and I miss you, and I can't wait to feel you next to me. All of you, my dearest Trevor. You are my strength when things get so awful here that I want to run and run and run. You're strong and brave and honorable. And you are my future. My husband. The father of those red-headed little sailors you keep talking about.

He knew the words by heart. She'd written them in the last letter she'd sent him from Tokyo.

Trevor bowed his head and shoved his hands into his pockets. Strong. Brave. Honorable. In the end, he'd been none of those things. And she'd been the one to suffer. No wonder she hated him. But she couldn't hate him any more than he hated himself. Not then, and not now.

Above his head, thunder clapped and the storm broke, pelting his face with cold, hard raindrops. Trevor uttered a harsh oath and glanced toward the helicopter. That damn pilot better be ready to go as soon as the ceiling lifts, he thought, striding stiffly toward the patio. He couldn't wait to get the hell out of this place.

The bell over the door jangled a loud warning, and Jillian looked up to see Adrian ambling into the pharmacy. She was dressed in satin shorts and a loose-fitting tank top, and her pink running shoes were covered with red dust.

Jillian felt a pang of guilt. Tomorrow, she told herself firmly, she'd haul her bicycle out of the shed and put some miles on it before the weather turned cold.

Adrian slid onto a stool in front of the marble soda counter and gave Jillian a curious look. "What are you doing here? I thought Darcy minded the store on Sunday."

"She does, usually. But she's nursing a bad cold. I told her I'd cover today."

Jillian shoved the newspaper she'd been reading aside and reached for a glass. "You want diet soda or water?" she asked as she filled the glass with ice.

"Water, please. And a hot fudge sundae. With everything." Adrian glanced down at her full hips, scowled briefly, then shrugged. Jillian laughed.

"You're something, Addie. You jog for miles every day, and then you pork out on ice cream."

Adrian unwound the sweat-stained bandanna from her forehead and wiped her wet face. Her shiny brown hair was damp and curled around her ears.

"Yeah, I know. I've created the perfect balance."

Jillian filled the glass, and Adrian took it from her hand. She gulped noisily until it was empty, then put it on the counter. "Be sure to give me lots of crumbles," she ordered, reaching into an inside pocket of her running shorts for a crumpled package of cigarettes and a lighter. She started to light up.

"Ahem."

Adrian froze. "What?" she asked guilelessly.

Jillian pointed the ice cream dipper toward a big red sign taped to the large mirror in a carved oak frame behind her. "'Thank you for not smoking,'" she read aloud, slowly. "That means you, Dr. Franklin who, I might add, ought to know better."

Adrian grumbled under her breath, but she put the cigarettes away. "Why do I sometimes feel as though you're my mother?"

"Because someone has to take care of you, Addie, since you do such a bad job of it yourself."

"Hey, I'm a big girl. Thirty-seven on my next birthday."

"If you're around to celebrate." Jillian scowled. "You drive too fast in that rattletrap Jeep of yours, you go hang gliding, for heaven's sake, and you won't eat anything that isn't loaded with preservatives."

She piled whipped cream over the dripping chocolate, plopped a cherry on the top and plunked the concoction down in front of Adrian with a loud thud.

"I'm going for the burn," Adrian said as she picked up her spoon and dug in. "Isn't that what we're supposed to do?"

"We're *supposed* to exercise some good old common sense."

"Hmm. Is that what you were doing when you let Trevor, as in gorgeous, sexy and rich, Markus hit on you yesterday? Being sensible?" She shoved a heaping spoonful into her mouth and watched Jillian with innocent blandness.

"*What?*" Jillian stared at her friend in consternation. Adrian's black eyes sparkled with impish delight.

"It's all over town. I heard it twice at church this morning, and again when I stopped to chat with Orrie Hughes outside the Mother Lode Inn."

"Oh, for heaven's sake," Jillian muttered, pouring herself another cup of coffee. Absently she reached for her third doughnut. "We were just . . . chatting."

"According to Jason, the aforementioned Mr. Markus was putting the make on you."

Jillian's throat tightened, and she nearly choked on a mouthful of glazed dough. She swallowed convulsively, then stared anxiously at Adrian. "He...talked to you about Trevor?"

"Trevor, is it?" Adrian grinned, but her amusement faded when she saw the strained expression on Jillian's face. "Jill, what's wrong? You look green around the edges."

Jillian sighed. "I feel a little green. I didn't get much sleep last night."

She sat down on the step stool she kept behind the bar and rested her elbows on the polished marble. This was home. This was reality, not a man with copper eyes and a short memory.

Jillian glanced around the long, narrow pharmacy. She loved the high ceilings with the ornate, hand-carved moldings and the tall, skinny windows that let in enough light on a sunny day to save her a tidy sum on electricity.

The thick wooden shelves were fully stocked, with the sundry items nicely displayed in neat multicolored rows and stacks of sale items at each end. The air smelled of cough syrup and fresh lemons in the summer, and pine boughs and cider in the winter.

Cheerful scenes of the Sierra, grizzled sourdoughs with their mules, trappers with their long rifles, mothers in their sunbonnets, had been painted on one wall, and Jillian had had the murals cleaned and restored to pristine brightness. The rustic reminders of a less complicated time had never failed to raise her spirits whenever she looked at them—until now.

Jillian stared down at the scarred travertine. She hated Formica. It was so cold and utilitarian. But marble had life and warmth and, most important, permanence.

Her gaze slid involuntarily to the folded newspaper. "Have you seen the paper this morning?" she asked glumly.

"If you mean, did I see the picture of you and Trevor Markus, I did," Adrian said mildly, sneaking a look at Jillian over her spoon. "You look terrific. He looks as though he'd just been struck by lightning."

The *Clayton Clarion* had featured the opening of Wilderness Horizons on the front page. Alongside a photo of Jillian and Trevor shaking hands was a short profile of Horizons' founder, briefly describing his exemplary Naval career as well as his professional credits.

The two corporations that he'd founded, Markus Engineering International and Wilderness Horizons, had been widely acclaimed for the high percentage of handicapped and ex-offenders each employed, and Trevor himself had been cited for his humanitarian efforts in the field of drug abuse and veterans' rights.

But the man behind the public face, Jillian had read, kept a very low profile. He'd conceived the original idea of combining drug treatment with the survival skills taught by the military, and he'd provided the money to open the first unit but, according to the sources cited, he left the running of Horizons to the people he hired.

Other personal details were sketchy. He had never been married, lived in an upscale community near Seattle, where his family was socially prominent, and rarely gave interviews.

I could give you such a scoop, Jillian thought with a silent wince as she pushed her coffee cup to one side. She was down to the dregs, and it tasted like floor sweepings.

Already this morning she had received half a dozen calls congratulating her on her farsightedness in attracting such a quality addition as Wilderness Horizons to Clayton's small business community.

The irony was wonderful, she thought. Clayton gained jobs, while the mayor who'd solicited them might lose her son.

Suddenly she wanted to lay her head on the cool counter and bawl. She hadn't felt so alone in years.

"This was just what I needed, Jill," Adrian said with a sigh of greedy satisfaction. "Now I can skip lunch."

She scraped the spoon around the edge of the glass, then savored the last of the gooey mess. Her expression was one of sublime pleasure, the kind only a true lover of ice cream can produce. She licked the spoon, then dropped it reluctantly into the glass.

"What did you think of the story on, uh, Trevor?" Jillian asked in a neutral tone.

"What's to think? The man is the catch of the century. Of two centuries. If he'd even glanced my way, I'd already be scheming to get him into my net. But alas..." She rolled her eyes, then reached for the paper and unfolded it. "Obviously the gentleman prefers redheads."

Jillian threw Adrian a fond look. Shortly after Jillian had taken over the pharmacy, Adrian had come to her with a prescription. It had been written by a doctor in San Francisco and called for one of the newer antiseizure drugs. Jillian was the only person in Clayton who knew that the bubbly doctor was an epileptic.

It had taken time for their friendship to develop. Both were intensely private people in spite of their congenial public facades. But over the years, at a casual picnic supper on the deck of Jillian's apartment or an occasional brunch at Adrian's redwood-and-glass nest, they'd gradually shared bits and pieces of their personal history.

Jillian had told Adrian of her struggle to combine a nursing career with the demands of raising a toddler, and of her ultimate decision to resign her Navy commission and return to college for a degree in pharmacy in order to have more time for her son.

In turn, Adrian had regaled Jillian with tales of her escapades in medical school, where she'd been known as a terrible practical joker and a dedicated flirt who was really a Puritan underneath the tantalizing bravado.

It had been just two years ago that Jillian had discovered that the kinship she felt with Adrian went deeper than she'd suspected. Adrian had been jilted by a fellow medical student, who'd broken their engagement less than a week after she'd told him about her epilepsy.

"I was so sure it wouldn't make a damn bit of difference," she'd told Jillian with a bitter smile. "He loved me, you see."

Adrian had stopped believing in love after that. She'd had lots of boyfriends, and even the occasional lover, but whenever a man became serious, she broke it off. She would never marry.

Jillian glanced down at the blurred newsprint. The article on Trevor had shaken her more than she wanted to admit. This was not the man whom she'd scorned all those years. This was not the man who, as she'd repeatedly told herself, wasn't fit to be Jason's father.

But maybe the story had been exaggerated. Or slanted for the best effect. She was enough of a realist to understand journalistic license. And public relations. A lot of corporations paid millions every year to generate favorable press releases.

"Addie, what did Jason really say about Trevor?" she asked in a voice that sounded alien to her ears.

Jason hadn't mentioned Trevor to her at all. And during dinner last night, when she'd casually explained that she'd known Mr. Markus during the war, he'd simply stared at her as though he couldn't understand why she was bothering to tell him something so unimportant.

Adrian glanced up from the photograph on the front page. "Just what I told you. We met in the parking lot, and he told me that this big tough-looking dude was putting the make on his mom, and did I think he should stick around? Naturally I told him no." She paused, then glanced quickly down at the paper. "I take it that you weren't terribly receptive?"

"Not very, no." She hesitated, then added softly, "Trevor Markus is Jason's father."

"Dear God!" Adrian looked stunned. "But...but you said...on Jase's medical records his father is listed as deceased."

Jillian bit her lip, then sighed. "Trevor didn't know about Jason. I...was afraid that, if by some remote chance, he ever found out that he had a son, he might try to...to take him."

"You parted badly?" Adrian's tone was sympathetic. She knew all about bad endings.

"You might say that, yes." Jillian's tone was extremely dry.

She stood up quickly and went over to lock the front door and flip the sign dangling in the window to Closed. She returned to the counter, but she was too nervous to sit. Grabbing a clean white cloth and a bottle of glass cleaner, she began to wipe the already spotless marble.

"Trevor wants to be part of Jason's life."

"And you don't want him to be."

"No. I never want to see him again."

Adrian gave Jillian a thoughtful look. "Why do I think there's more to it than that?"

Jillian sighed. "Because there is. He...threatened to take me to court if I refuse to let him see Jase." Her voice wobbled. "I'm scared, Adrian. If he fights me, I could lose."

"Would you like to talk about it?"

Jillian hesitated.

Why not? she thought after a moment's reflection. Adrian was her best friend and, in spite of her eccentricities, very clearheaded. Maybe Addie could help her figure out a way to keep Jason safe.

She returned the spray bottle and cloth to the shelf under the counter and opened the small refrigerator.

She took out a bottle of white wine and carefully eased out the cork, then reached behind her for a single glass. Adrian didn't drink because of the powerful drug she was forced to take daily to control her seizures.

"I need a little Dutch courage," Jillian said with a tight smile. "I've never told anyone what happened after I left Tokyo."

She splashed a generous measure into the glass, and shimmering droplets of Chablis scattered over the counter.

"You told me that you were stationed in Bethesda when Jase was born."

"I was, but before that I was on maternity leave. I flew from Tokyo to Hawaii, where I'd reserved a suite at the Royal Hawaiian. The bridal suite."

Absently Jillian mopped up the spill, then took a sip of Chablis. The wine was cold on her tongue and tasted like half-ripe apricots. "You sure you want to hear this? It's not pretty, and I'd hate to spoil your day off."

Adrian lifted her brows. "Only if you want to tell me about it, Jill. I know all about ghosts."

"Ghosts. I guess that's about it."

Slowly, in a voice so quiet Adrian had to lean forward to hear clearly, Jillian told her everything that had happened, beginning with the moment when Trevor had looked up at her that first morning and ending with a description of her anguish on the day he'd been shipped back to the States.

"He was the bravest man I'd ever met," she said simply in conclusion. "His doctor told me he'd never had a patient fight so hard against such impossible odds."

Adrian looked down at her hands. "Back injuries are the worst, I know. And so are multiple fractures. I've had patients beg for another shot barely an hour after the last one."

Jillian nodded. "It was rough. And parts of his therapy were just as bad. They had to stretch the scar tissue in his legs, and sometimes he passed out from the pain. He didn't tell me that, but his therapist did. I called her once, when I hadn't heard from him for over a week, and she filled me in."

The other woman nodded. "You said you were to be married at Christmas after your tour of duty in Tokyo was over. What happened?"

Jillian took another sip, then held the glass tightly and stared into the clear liquid as though it were a window into her past.

"As I said, we'd set the date for Christmas Eve. I'd made all the arrangements...."

* * *

The temperature was in the high eighties. Jillian stood at the window overlooking the Pacific and grinned at the thought.

Christmas on the farm in southern Ohio had meant a roaring fire and hot chocolate and warm sweaters. Many times over the years she'd had to wade through knee-deep snow on Christmas morning to reach the barn in order to do her chores.

This Christmas she'd be having both sunshine and snow in the space of a few days.

In two days, after a brief stopover in Seattle to meet his parents, Trevor intended to take her to Canada for their honeymoon, to a small inn he knew up north.

He was tired of sunshine, he'd written in his last letter from San Diego, which had reached her in Tokyo a week ago. He wanted to be snowed in with her, just the two of them in front of a fire.

"I need to see you in the firelight, angel. I need to kiss you and touch you and bury myself so deeply inside you that I won't be able to think of anything but you."

Soon, my love, she thought, as she shifted her gaze to the flower-bedecked grotto at the far end of the grounds. The florist had done a beautiful job, transforming the small rock garden into a romantic wedding bower.

The chaplain was due in twenty minutes, and the witnesses, the bubbly, deeply tanned night clerk and her fiancé, were having drinks in the bar by the beach.

Jillian hugged her belly, a blissful smile forming slowly on her lips. She'd been in Hawaii for four days, and most of that time she'd spent lying in the sun, working on her tan. She'd also found time to find a black lace nightie cut on the bias to accommodate her swollen stomach.

"It's gorgeous and very sexy, baby. I can't wait for your daddy to see it," she whispered, caressing her belly. The satin of her ivory maternity dress was erotically smooth against her palm, and her heart began to pound.

She wouldn't allow herself to believe that Trevor would find her unattractive. She was carrying his baby, and all pregnant women were beautiful. Hadn't he told her that once during one of their long nocturnal talks?

Trevor had written that he loved surprises, and she fervently prayed he would love this one as much as she did. As though reading her mind, the baby kicked hard. He was so strong and energetic that she'd already decided she was carrying a small replica of his daddy.

"Yes, I know, baby. I probably should have told him, but he sounded so down." Especially in the past few months.

His letters had become shorter, with fewer references to the future. Bachelor jitters, she told herself. She'd had a few pre-nuptial nerves herself, especially in the past few days, when the baby had become so active. She was beginning to feel like a lumpy blimp.

Jillian glanced at her watch. Trevor's plane had landed nearly an hour ago. She'd wanted to meet him at the airport, but he'd insisted she wait for him in the bridal suite. He didn't want to jinx their future happiness by seeing his bride before the wedding.

A sudden knock at the door startled her. He was here!

Jillian wet her lips and hastily patted her rebellious curls into place. Taking a slow, deep breath, she smiled down at her tummy, then walked quickly to the door and flung it open.

Her joyous smile faded when she saw the bellman. He was carrying a huge bouquet of long-stemmed roses at arm's length. His white beachboy smile was nearly obscured by the crimson blossoms.

"Flowers for Ensign Anderson, ma'am."

"Uh, th-thank you. Put them on the table, please."

He walked by her, and Jillian stuck her head out the door. She looked up and down the corridor, but there was no sign of Trevor.

The bellman refused a tip. "It's been taken care of, ma'am."

"Mahalo," she said self-consciously, thanking him, and he gave her another good-natured grin.

She waited until he'd closed the door behind him, then crossed the room to snatch up the small white card she'd seen buried among the velvet buds.

The writing was in Trevor's familiar slashing backhand, and the ink was black. Several words had been smeared.

It's no good, Jill. I tried, you'll never know how hard. But I don't want to get married, not ever. Find someone else, someone who wants to settle down, someone who can love you the way you deserve to be loved. Forget about me, just as I intend to forget about you.

For a long time Jillian simply stared at the terse lines. This was a joke. A horrible joke.

But the handwriting was his. She would recognize it anywhere. And if it was his handwriting . . .

Hastily she glanced at the florist's name on the envelope, then raced to the phone. Her fingers shook as she dialed information, and her voice was so unsteady that she could barely get the name out when the operator answered.

It took some persuasion, but the florist finally admitted that a tall sandy-haired man on crutches had purchased the flowers less than an hour ago. He'd paid extra to have them delivered on time.

"I hope you enjoy them, ma'am," the woman added cheerily. "The gentleman was most anxious that you receive them by four. Something about a wedding that he was unable to attend?"

Jillian dropped the phone onto the desk. The florist's tinny voice called out sharply several times before it was replaced by the abrupt sound of the dial tone.

"No, please, no," she whispered, an icy numbness beginning to spread through her. "Not Trevor. He wouldn't do this to me. He wouldn't."

Suddenly another knock sounded on the door. "I knew it," she whispered, her breath coming quickly. "It was all a mistake."

She flew across the room, her hands pressed against her belly protectively. Her heart was racing so fast that she felt light-headed as she threw open the door. "Darling—"

The young chaplain's cheerful smile faltered as Jillian grabbed the edge of the door and stared at him. "Is something wrong?" he asked anxiously.

Jillian didn't answer. The man's tanned features began to waver, then blur at the edges. And then they faded to black.

For the first time in her life Jillian had fainted.

Jillian drained her wineglass and set it carefully on the counter.

"I woke up on the bed. The chaplain had called a doctor and then the manager. None of them seemed to know what to do."

"It's a wonder you didn't go into premature labor," Adrian said in a quiet voice. For the first time since Jillian had met her, there was no animation in Adrian's face.

"I know. The doctor gave me a mild sedative, nothing that would hurt the baby, and I slept until the next morning. When I looked out the window, the flowers and the white carpet were gone. Everything was gone."

"And Trevor? What happened to him?"

Jillian felt a chill. Chewing on her lip, she slowly rolled the sleeves of her plaid cotton shirt down to her wrists and carefully buttoned the cuffs.

"It took me a day or two to sort it out, but I finally decided I had to tell him about the baby. He had a right to know."

Adrian nodded but said nothing.

Jillian hesitated, then went on with her story. She might as well tell it all.

"Trevor had been staying in an apartment near Balboa Hospital for several weeks after he'd been reassigned there as an outpatient. He was still undergoing therapy on his legs, and there was one more minor operation still to be done on his spine. So I went to his place, but he'd moved without leaving a forwarding address."

Her throat burned with unwanted tears, and she tried to swallow them away.

"I was desperate, so I went to the hospital. Trevor's therapist was on vacation, and the orthopedic ward charge nurse was noncommittal, until I showed her my Navy ID. As soon as she saw my name, she broke into a big smile. Commander Markus had left something for me, she told me. A package."

Jillian's brief laugh carried no humor. "I couldn't wait. I ripped it open in the car right there in the parking lot." Her voice faltered, and she stopped. She couldn't go on.

Adrian rubbed a spot from the marble with a corner of her bandanna. "If you'd rather not tell me, I understand, Jill. I can see this is hard for you."

Jillian's lips slanted into a bitter smile. "Actually, it feels good to let it out."

Adrian hesitated, then asked softly, "What was in the package?"

"Letters. Stacks of them. Every one I'd ever written him. And the pictures I'd sent him before my pregnancy had begun to show. He was telling me that he no longer wanted them—because he no longer wanted me."

"The bastard," Adrian whispered softly, wiping tears from her lashes with the back of her small hand. "I can't believe he's the same man I just read about, or the man I met on the podium. He has a nice face. And kind eyes, maybe even a little sad, like a man who's suffered a great loss."

Jillian refused to acknowledge her similar thoughts. Trevor was a great actor. Once he'd even convinced her that he loved her.

"Believe it," she said tersely.

Adrian looked concerned. "What reason did you give Jason for your not being married?"

Jillian sighed. "He thinks his father is a man named William White who died a hero before our wedding, and that's what he's always going to think."

Adrian gave her a thoughtful look. "Are you sure that's wise, Jill? Trevor's bound to come back here occasionally, maybe even spend a few days now and then. He could find Jason anytime he wanted. One wrong word and Jason would find out that you've been lying to him. He . . . he might never get over it, Jill. Kids are very vulnerable when it comes to things like that."

The icy hand of raw fear tightened around Jillian's lungs until she thought she would suffocate. Adrian was right. Clayton was only a matter of hours from Seattle by plane. And nearly everyone knew her—and Jason.

"Trevor won't be back," she said, praying she was right. "At least not to see me—or Jason. Once he's back in Seattle and over the shock, he'll realize that a half-grown son who thinks he's dead and a woman who hates him aren't worth his trouble."

"I thought you said he promised to fight for Jason."

Jillian snorted. "Trevor's good at making promises, but he's rotten at keeping them. I tell you, Addie, he won't be back."

"Well, I won't argue with you," Adrian said as she slipped off the stool and picked up her bandanna. "But, from what I saw of Trevor Markus, if he does come back, you'd better be prepared for the fight of your life."

Chapter 4

Jillian was restless after Adrian left. She kept thinking of Trevor, and the way he'd looked when she'd told him his name wasn't on Jason's birth certificate.

He'd appeared to be angry, certainly, and hurt, but she'd also seen disappointment cross his face, as though he'd expected more of her.

"He has no right to judge me," she muttered fiercely as she paced up and down the aisles.

Jillian stopped in front of a display of baby products, a smile playing over her face as she fingered a soft flannel sleeper adorned with laughing pink and blue teddy bears.

She'd bought Jason his first teddy bear at the airport in Cincinnati when she'd flown back to Ohio to tell her parents about the baby on the way.

The visit had been a nightmare.

Her stepfather had been quietly furious, pacing the shadowed parlor in the old-fashioned farmhouse with angry, lumbering strides.

Her mother had cried quietly, sending Jillian reproachful looks from sad, faded eyes.

"I won't have it, Jillian," Reuben Anderson had said in his nasal Ohio twang. "I raised you right, since you were three. I

gave you my name, and it's a proud one. I won't have some
playboy pilot throwing dirt on it. I'll get me a lawyer, or a
shotgun, I don't care which, and make him do the right thing
by you and the child.''

Jillian had been appalled and very frightened. Reuben was
an obstinate man with very strict ideas of right and wrong.
He'd meant to do what he'd threatened, no matter how much
he might embarrass her or risk the welfare of her baby.

So when he'd demanded the man's name, in desperation
she'd given him the name of a patient who'd died.

As her due date grew closer, she'd been terrified that her
stepfather would somehow discover her deception and carry out
his threat. For days she worried that Trevor would suddenly
appear, demanding her baby.

Now, from the perspective of years, she realized she'd been
slightly irrational in those final months of her pregnancy.

She'd been very sick toward the end, and the last weeks had
been passed in a daze of weariness and worry. She'd been terrified when her obstetrician had ordered her into the hospital
almost six weeks before her due date.

Jason had nearly died during the difficult delivery, and Jillian, struggling to bring Trevor's child into the world, had
called his name over and over until her voice had sunk to an
inaudible whisper. Afterward, she'd sobbed helplessly when
they'd taken Jason from her arms, even though it was to put
him into an incubator in order to save him.

Jillian crushed the soft flannel sleeper in her hand and
blinked at the hot tears pressing her lids. Her shoulders slumped
as she stared down at the smooth, worn boards that bore the
scars of countless heels.

From the instant her tiny redheaded son had wrapped his
stubby fingers around hers, she'd been filled with so much love
that she'd been shaking with it.

He'd been helpless and trusting and precious, a wonderful
little person who needed her. As she'd kissed his soft, sweet
head, she'd vowed that nothing would ever hurt this child. All
the love that Trevor had rejected, all the caring that he'd
scorned, she would give to his son.

Her son.

''Why did he have to come here now?'' she muttered, stalking up the aisle to the glass-lined cage where she kept the pre-

scription drugs. Opening the safe, she took out her Class Two ledger and sat down at her cluttered desk.

She'd forgotten him, she told herself as she opened the log. She'd gotten on with her life. She didn't want to think about things that might have been. She didn't want to open old wounds. It hurt too much.

Jillian's hands shook as she reached for her pen. She was thirty-six now, not twenty-one. She was no longer at the mercy of her emotions. *She* was in charge of her life, not her hormones, or some half-remembered love that had died long ago.

Right? she asked her reflection in the glass door of an old drug cabinet where she kept her reference books.

The tall, unsmiling, auburn-haired woman who stared back at her didn't look very convinced.

"See you later, Mom. I'm going to Mike's house to study." Jason thundered through the living room, his books under one arm. Dinner was over, and Jillian was tidying the kitchen.

"Be home by nine," Jillian called after him. "Remember, you have a test tomorrow. You need your rest."

The slamming of the screen door was her only answer.

Sighing, Jillian poured a glass of iced tea and sat down at the table under the open window. Jason had been oddly silent during dinner. He'd played with his food and stared down at his plate, answering her cheerful attempts at conversation with monosyllables.

He'd behaved so strangely that she'd felt his forehead to make sure he wasn't feverish. His skin felt normal to the touch, but his freckles had stood out in stark relief, as though he were paler than usual. And he'd drunk three full glasses of water with his meal.

If he was still behaving strangely tomorrow, she decided, she'd call Adrian and take him in for a checkup. Having made her decision, she felt better, and she let her mind wander. It had been a long and difficult week, and she was bone tired.

Idly she stared down at the town square. Main Street was quiet. Not much was happening. Nothing much ever happened on a Sunday in Clayton, unless it was ski season. Then the snow bunnies would descend on the town in parka-clad waves, stopping for hot chocolate or brandy on their way back to their nine-to-five weekdays in the cities down the mountain.

Trevor had been a skier. They'd talked about it once, about the way he and his brothers would race down the steepest slopes, shouting insults at one another. As the eldest, he'd invariably won, until his youngest brother, Tim, cadged lessons from a family friend who was also a former alpine champion. After that, Tim had whipped his big brother on every run. Trevor had been nineteen that season, and it had been the first time he'd ever lost at anything.

"I sulked for days," he'd told her with a self-conscious smile. "And then I decided that I'd better take a few lessons myself. Then, if Timmy beat me, I could live with it, knowing I'd done everything I could to win."

Everything he could to win.

Jillian ran her finger through the condensation on her glass. Trevor had fought hard for his life, too, fought to win against terrible odds. The compound fractures in his legs had become infected. For days he'd been delirious, racked by fever. During her off duty hours she'd stayed with him, sponging his hot face with cool water, holding his hand, talking to him, and she'd heard his disjointed remorse over the unavoidable pain his bombs and missiles had caused. Under the playboy facade Trevor had gradually shown himself to be a very caring man.

Jillian shut her eyes convulsively. She didn't want to relive that time. She'd locked those four months they'd had together in some deep dark place at the back of her brain and refused to let the memories escape.

But what she'd told Addie was right. Maybe it was better to face the ghosts. Maybe, after all these years, the memories had lost the power to hurt. In any event, she'd better find out. Otherwise, she would be helpless to control her feelings if Trevor surprised her and showed up again.

And she had to be in control. If she showed the slightest sign of weakness, Trevor would start calling the shots. That was the kind of man he was.

Quickly, before she could change her mind, she left the table and went into her bedroom. From the top shelf of her closet she took a small wooden box. Shaking, she placed the box in the middle of her bed and piled pillows against the headboard. She kicked off her sandals and settled back.

Her hands were shaking and her palms were damp as she opened the dusty lid. Inside were two packets of letters. The ones tied with red satin ribbon were the ones Trevor had written to her. The other packet was thicker in spite of the air mail stationery. These were the letters he'd left behind. Her letters to him.

Her heart began to pound as she slipped the rubber band from the packet and sorted through the flimsy envelopes. They were all there but the last one, the long, loving letter she'd written just before she'd left Tokyo. She'd timed it so that Trevor would receive it just before he left San Diego.

She'd poured all of her love and loneliness into those two pages. She'd told him all the things she loved about him. And she'd told him of her dreams for their future together.

Rapidly she checked one more time. The last postmark was December twelfth. But she'd mailed her last letter on the fifteenth, nine days before her wedding day. She remembered distinctly.

He must have torn it up, she thought as she neatly rebundled the letters and slipped the rubber band over the thick pile. Or tossed it out. Either way, it didn't matter.

Besides, she'd simply been stalling, looking for a letter whose contents she knew by heart. It was Trevor's letters that she needed to read. Trevor's words.

Her fingers were clumsy as she untied the knot in the ribbon and lifted the first letter from the packet. Her name was written in large, bold script, with imperious capitals that commanded attention.

The paper rattled as she unfolded the single page. The first time she'd read these words she'd cried. She took a deep breath and began to read.

My Angel:
   I did it, by God! I finally made it all the way to the end of the blasted corridor without falling on my can. I used the canes, of course, but I walked, Jill. I really walked!
   Denise—my therapist, remember?—was so excited she cried. Okay, so maybe you were right after all. Maybe she wasn't really a Gestapo agent in a former life. Anyway sweetheart, I'm feeling pretty good tonight. Tired as hell, but missing you so much.
   I wish you were here right now to crawl in beside me. I want to make love to you so badly I'm hard just thinking about you. Remember the first time, angel? Remember—

Jillian couldn't go on. The poignant words were too blurred by tears for her to see. Fighting back the sobs, she dropped the letter onto the quilt and folded her arms over her stomach. She remembered. Oh, God, how she remembered!

"I look like a damn lizard," Trevor grumbled, straining his neck to look down at his chest. It was late, nearly midnight, and they were alone behind the closed door of Trevor's room.

That afternoon the doctor had removed the cast from his torso. After thirteen weeks in plaster his skin was covered with a crusty layer of dried skin.

Jillian laughed. "You are pretty scaly, at that." She tipped the bottle of lotion into her hand and poured out a generous measure. "Now, lie still and let me work this in."

"Not until I get my kiss." His eyes glowed as he gazed up at her.

The dim light over the bed turned his thick hair to gold, and his lashes cast dark spiky shadows on his cheeks. Jillian felt her heart swell with love as she leaned forward to brush her lips over his.

Instantly his mouth firmed under hers and became hungry. One large hand cupped the back of her head, while the other framed her jaw. "Angel. I want you so much," he whispered before taking her lips again. This time he wasn't gentle. This time he demanded.

Pleasure shot through her as his tongue slipped past her lips. The raspy surface was exciting as it abraded the inside of her mouth, and he tasted sweet.

She could feel the tension in him, and the heat. A faint musky smell mingled with the cherry scent of the lotion, exciting her. He wanted her just as much as she wanted him. She wrapped her hands around his shoulders, feeling the lotion go from her palms to his skin. It felt good, like a sweet, sensual lubrication.

He growled deep in his throat, then let her go. "You're better than any pill," he said with a crooked smile. His gaunt cheeks were flushed, and a vein throbbed violently in his temple. A faint sheen of moisture glistened on his forehead, and he was breathing hard.

Jillian felt the muscles of her face soften into a smile. "A kiss every four hours, you mean?"

"At least." He wiped his brow with his hand and let his forearm rest there, as though he were in pain.

"It's worth thinking about, anyway."

"That's about all I can do," he grumbled as she began massaging his shoulders. "The doctors tell me to be patient, but I feel like a damn eunuch."

"Don't worry. Your body just needs time to heal, that's all," she whispered soothingly. His arousal came swiftly whenever he touched her, but it never lasted.

He sighed and rested his forearm over his eyes to block out the light.

His skin was warm and tough against her palms, and his chest was covered with a fine layer of golden hair. Her fingertips burrowed tiny tracks in the silky thatch, and the lotion turned the gold to brown.

His nipples were tiny flat pebbles, darker than the rest of his skin, and when she touched them they hardened instantly and turned white. Her palms began to tingle, and heat shot up her arm. It felt so good to touch him, to feel his muscles, still hard despite being unused for so long, contract under her fingertips.

She loved the massive lines of his chest and the powerful slant of his shoulders. Beneath the stubborn jaw, he had a strong neck, the kind a woman liked to nuzzle. His tan had faded, but his skin had regained much of the healthy color it had lost.

He was a male animal in his prime, vibrant and virile, in spite of his temporary incapacity.

She poured more lotion, warming it for several seconds in her palms. Then, slowly massaging in gentle circles, she moved down his ribbed torso, feeling the hard slab of muscle that tightened into granite as she pressed.

A thin curling line of golden hair led her lower, and she began to warm inside. Beneath the sheet Trevor was naked. The sheet had been pulled to his waist, and she slowly slid it toward his hips.

Her fingers tangled in the triangle of coarse, tightly curled blond hair below his hard abdomen.

Trevor groaned, and his breath became shallow. Jillian froze, her palms flat against him. His hands covered hers, and he exerted a gentle pressure.

"Don't stop, angel," he whispered, his eyes closed. "I feel alive. For the first time since I hit that damn deck, I feel like a man again."

He was aroused, but this time his arousal didn't disappear as quickly as it had come.

Jillian fought back tears. His face was taut, his brows drawn, his lips compressed. Deep lines bracketed his mouth, lines she knew would never completely disappear, even when he'd recovered. They'd been too harshly imprinted by the fever and pain—and fear.

She felt the tears glisten in her eyes, and she tried to blink them away.

"Hey, don't cry, angel," Trevor said huskily, capturing her hands and rubbing his thumbs over her wrists. "I don't ever want you to cry. If I could, I'd take all the bad things out of your life forever."

The gentle friction was nearly unbearable, and she inhaled sharply. "I'm crying because I'm happy. You make me so happy, Trevor. Just being with you makes all the bad things disappear."

She saw the flush of embarrassment touch his cheeks. He had trouble talking about this feelings. Or hers. But she would be patient. The tenderness was there inside him. She'd felt it in his touch and seen it in his smile.

Trevor's gaze fell to the bulge between his legs. "I'm afraid to move. I think I might explode." His grin was lopsided and tinged with humor, but his eyes were turbulent and intense—and filled with harsh male frustration. "God, I want you," he whispered with a groan, but he made no move to pull her toward him. "But that door doesn't lock."

Jillian's heart swelled with love. In spite of his need to prove he could still perform as a man, he was leaving the decision up to her. If she were caught making love to a patient, she would be court-martialed.

"Maybe I can do something about that," she whispered, leaning forward to kiss the slanted edge of his mouth. "I'll ask Bev to see we're not disturbed. That is, if you think you can stand the strain."

Her breasts brushed his chest, and he inhaled swiftly. "I want you so damn much I can stand anything to have you."

Jillian kissed him, then hurried into the corridor. Beverly Sons was flipping through a patient's chart when Jillian beckoned to her. "Trevor and I need some privacy, okay?"

Bev's blue eyes twinkled with understanding. "No problem. It's quiet tonight." She grinned. "Give the big hunk a kiss for me."

Jillian blushed and nodded happily before she returned quietly to the room she'd just left. "All taken care of, sir," she said with a snappy salute.

"Come here, Ensign," he said with a growl, and she hurried eagerly across the room.

His arms closed around her, and he hugged her against his chest. She could feel his heart pounding beneath her, and there was desperation in the cadence of his breathing.

"I was afraid you wouldn't come back," he said thickly. "I thought sure you'd have second thoughts."

"Never. I know a good thing when it's offered."

His laugh was a throaty rumble that sent chills down her spine. She smiled against his neck and trailed her hands down the hard muscles of his upper arms. Slowly she pushed upward until he was holding her loosely.

His eyes held hers as she reached up to turn off the light. A silvery glow from the outside lights turned the room to velvet gray, making it seem warmer somehow, and more intimate, as though they were the only two people in the huge, sterile building.

"Let me go a minute, darling," she whispered.

A tiny frown appeared between his dusty blond brows, but he obeyed, and she slid off the bed. With eyes that seemed to glow, he watched her intently.

Jillian felt a deep shiver of love as she slowly untied the waistband of her loose-fitting surgical scrubs. She started to pull the smock free, but he stopped her with a growl.

"Let me."

Trevor's hand shook as he tugged the top from the pants. She hesitated, then straightened quickly and pulled the smock over her head.

She gasped as his hand slid up her rib cage to cup her breast. Her bra was mostly lace and fell away easily as his fingers found the front opening.

Trevor's breath was raspy and urgent, and his eyes were on fire as he watched her step out of the baggy trousers. She stood before him, a trembling smile on her lips as he bathed her in a reverent gaze.

"My fantasies were never this good," he said in a harsh whisper as she slowly removed her silky panties. He reached out and took them from her hand, then tucked them under his pillow. "I've imagined you doing this a hundred times in my mind, but you're even more perfect than I thought."

Slowly she leaned closer. His face tightened with strain as he moved slowly, twisting at the waist until he was on his side at the edge of the mattress. He bracketed her rib cage with his hands, then slid his palms down the curve of her hip.

"You're perfect, angel," he whispered. "Your skin is like cognac on the tongue, so smooth and hot."

Jillian held her breath as his fingers dipped lower. She threaded one hand in his thick hair while the other stroked his hard back. She was afraid to move, afraid to breathe. She wanted him desperately, but she didn't want to cause him any more pain.

His eyes were narrow golden-brown slits as he stroked her with slow absorption, his hard fingers trailing along her inner thighs.

It took some ingenuity, and caused him to inhale sharply against the pain, but Trevor finally maneuvered himself so that he could bury his face against her belly. His breath was hot on her skin as he wrapped his arms around the curve of her hips and pulled her closer.

His tongue trailed long, lazy circles around her navel, dipping into the tiny folds of her belly button to lap her skin. His lips were soft and insistent as he moved lower, licking her into glistening wetness.

"Such a sweet taste," he murmured against her. "I've been so hungry."

Instantly on fire, she buried her fingers in the ragged thickness of his hair and held on. She'd never felt such glorious urgency, such intense longing. Under his tongue, her nerve endings began to flutter in involuntary reaction. He was taking control of her body, exciting sensations in the sensitive receptors that made her shiver.

Suddenly he groaned. "I can't wait," he said in a tortured voice. "Baby, now, please, before I disappoint us both."

Slowly he eased onto his back again. His eyes never left hers as she carefully knelt beside him. His teeth bared, he began breathing in short, raspy bursts as she slid the sheet away from his body.

Both his legs were encased in plaster from his hips to his toes and elevated slightly on pillows. Careful not to jostle him, she straddled his imprisoned hips, bracing her weight on her shins. The plaster casts were hard and rough under her buttocks as her skin brushed against them, and the sheet was slick and cool beneath her knees.

He was ready, his arousal standing between them, hot and hard and swollen. She saw the violent hunger in his eyes and heard the desperate urgency in his breathing.

"Now, angel. Don't wait. Let me feel you."

Heat flooded her face, and her heart thundered as she gently guided him into her. He filled her with throbbing heat.

He groaned and tossed his head from side to side on the pillow, gritting his teeth. He was trying to hold back.

Moaning, she eased forward until she was resting against his wide chest. She slid her arms under his and pressed her face into the moist hollow of his shoulder. Tremors shook him as she began to move, slowly at first, and then, as the fiery heat built inside her, faster and faster, until he was heaving under her.

And then, just when she knew she had to stop or explode, his muscles went rigid beneath her, and his fingers tightened convulsively in her hair. His clenched jaw muffled his groan of release, but she could feel the explosive shower inside bathing her with delicious heat. Her surrender came immediately as wave after wave of pleasure rolled through her.

Trevor wrapped his arms tightly around her and gasped for air. "My angel," he whispered in a hoarse soft voice. "Don't ever leave me. I couldn't stand it if you left me."

Jillian stared blindly at the letter in her hand and started to sob. Hot tears splashed on the thin paper, turning the ink to black pools. "But you left *me*," she whispered, crushing the letter to her heart. "And I still don't know why."

Jillian raised her head to the ceiling, and the tears dripped down her cheeks. She hadn't cried for Trevor in years. Not since the night she'd taken his Academy ring from the chain around her neck, wrapped it in tissue and put it away.

Slowly she let her gaze drop. The ring was still there, a pink wad in the corner of the small box, but she didn't touch it. Instead, sitting cross-legged on the quilt, her tears wetting the flimsy pages, she read his letters one by one. The words weren't eloquent. Sometimes they were funny, but more often they were angry and filled with terrible frustration and loneliness. Still, they were Trevor's words, and she could almost hear him speaking them to her. Her tear-filled gaze dropped to the last lines of the final letter.

I know I'm not the greatest when it comes to words, angel. I've never been in love before, and I'm not sure I tell you the things you want to hear. But that doesn't mean I don't feel them.

Sometimes I wake up in the middle of the night, and I'm so scared of the hard things ahead of me, I'm sick, but then I see your face and hear your voice, and I'm okay again.

You're my lifeline, Jill, and my hope. You're the best thing that ever happened to me. And even if I sometimes let you down, or if I hurt you or disappoint you, always remember that I'm not perfect, but I do love you.

Jillian was filled with such a sense of loss that it nearly strangled her. She pressed the thin paper against her breast and squeezed her eyes tightly shut.

She rocked back and forth on the mattress, Trevor's letters piled around her. "Why, Trevor?" she pleaded through trembling lips. "Why did you do this to us?"

Her only answer was silence.

Sometime after midnight Jillian awakened suddenly, her heart pounding. Something was wrong. She sat up and listened. Adrenaline pumped violently through her system, making it difficult to breathe.

The door to her bedroom was open, and light streamed along the hall. But she'd turned out the light when she'd gone to bed, just as she'd always done.

The sound was coming from the bathroom at the end of the hall. It was a gasping, retching sound that sent shivers up her backbone.

"Jason," she cried in a strangled voice as she tossed off the sheet and reached for her robe. Without bothering with slippers, she ran down the hall, her robe billowing behind her.

Jason was bent over the toilet, his skinny shoulders heaving violently. It took Jillian a moment to realize he was fully dressed.

"Baby, what is it? Are you sick?" She bent over him, her hand against the sweat-dampened curls at the nape of his neck.

He moaned and shook his head. The worst appeared to be over, and he sat back on his haunches. His face was white, and he was sweating.

Jillian flushed the toilet, then wetted a cloth and gently wiped his face. The freckles stood out starkly against his pale skin, and his lips were gray.

"I'm calling Addie," she said, anxiously feeling his forehead. He still wasn't feverish, but he must have picked up some kind of intestinal bug.

"No, Mom," he protested in a slurred voice. "Don't call Dr. Franklin."

A sour odor wrinkled her nostrils, and she pressed her fingers against her nose and mouth as though to block out the smell. "Why not?" she asked quietly, already knowing the answer. Jason was drunk.

His shoulders slumped, and he hung his head. "Don't need a doctor," he muttered, his eyes blinking rapidly. His shoulders swayed back and forth in a jerky, disjointed rhythm, and he was breathing loudly through his nose.

Jillian pressed a hand to her stomach. Now she was feeling sick, as sick as her son had been. "You've been drinking."

Jason shook his head, then groaned. He hung on to the bowl to steady himself.

Jillian bit her lip. The first thing she had to do was get him back into his room. Maybe by then she would have figured out what to do. "Here, sweetie, let me help you up."

He was heavier than he looked, and his legs were rubbery. His arm was heavy on her shoulder, and he staggered as he moved, but she managed to get him into the bedroom. He collapsed on his rumpled bed, and Jillian sat on the edge of the mattress, trying to catch her breath. Jason was already snoring.

She shivered uncontrollably as she looked down at her disheveled son. He'd been a handful as a toddler and a rambunctious little boy. But he'd never been a bad kid. He'd never lied or taken something that didn't belong to him, and his grades, until recently, had always been good.

"So what do I do now?" she muttered under her breath as she hugged herself in a futile effort to stop the violent trembling. Nothing came to her.

Sighing, she shook Jason awake again. "Talk to me, Jase. What's this all about?" His eyes blinked rapidly, and he groaned. Jillian refused to let him sink back into sleep. "I want an answer, Jason."

"It's a club, Mom." He licked his lips. "Mike Cobb and a bunch of other guys and me. We had some champagne to celebrate our first meeting."

Jillian scowled. "A club? You mean, like a fraternity."

Jason's smile beamed crookedly. "Yeah, that's it. A fra-fraternity."

"But isn't that against school policy?"

"Who cares about the dumb school?" he said in slurred derision. "Besides, we meet after school in Mike's garage. Sheriff Cobb says it's okay as long as we don't play the music too loud."

Jillian refused to be blackmailed. Mel Cobb wasn't her idea of a model parent. "Who else is in this club?"

Her tone was sharp, and Jason's brow puckered. Slowly, his voice wavering, he listed the names. The other boys were from good families, and Jillian had known most of them for as long as she'd lived in Clayton.

She bit her lip. The idea of a club seemed harmless enough. In fact, it might even be a positive thing, especially now, when Jason seemed to be having so much trouble making the transition to high school. And all kids Jason's age experimented with alcohol, sooner or later. All the books and magazines said so. She just wouldn't let it go any further.

"There can't be any more drinking, Jason," she said sternly. "You hear me?"

Solemnly he nodded. Some of the color was beginning to come back into his cheeks, and his eyes had lost their wild sheen. "I promise, Mom. It was a stupid thing to do, anyway. I didn't even like the taste." His bloodless lips curved into a tentative smile, and Jillian melted.

This was her son, her baby. Of course he knew better. Jason had always had good sense. She hugged him tightly. He was caught in limbo, this half man, half boy. But he would be fine. She had no doubt at all.

Jillian helped him strip to his shorts, and he slid beneath the covers. He gave her a sweet smile, then snuggled his cheek against the pillow. His red hair was a bright halo around his long, narrow face, and his features were slack with tiredness. He was asleep in seconds.

His body was long, his bones large, with the promise of sturdy strength. He had big wrists and enormous feet. Like his father. And like Trevor, Jason had a smile that seemed to reflect the sun whenever it flashed.

The first time she'd seen that endearing, lopsided grin on Jason's small face she'd cried. It had hurt so much, knowing that Trevor would never stand hand in hand with her next to his son's crib and listen to the sweet, soft breathing. That he would never nuzzle his face against a chubby little neck that smelled of baby powder. That he would never hear his little boy laugh or say his first imperious words or mutter to himself in cheerful toddler nonsense.

Jillian's lips began to tremble, and her throat closed up. It had been Trevor's fault that he'd missed those rare and wonderful moments.

And she'd made it up to Jason for not having a father. She was sure of it.

"I love you, sweetie," she said, smoothing the frown from his brow. "And I won't ever let him take you away from me, I promise."

Chapter 5

Jason perched on the side of Jillian's desk and fiddled with the 1850s ore sample she used as a paperweight. His foot tapped restlessly against the worn floor, and he looked bored.

It was Saturday, the day Jillian spent in the mayor's office in the town hall. It was also the day Jason received his allowance.

"Could I have a little extra this week, Mom?" he asked as she pulled out her wallet. "Darcy and I did a good job washing the windows."

Darcy Hammond was a young mother of four and one of the workers laid off when PacTimber had gone into receivership. Jillian had hired her to clerk in the store on weekends and Wednesdays.

Every Saturday morning Jason helped Darcy clean the store before it opened, and Jillian paid him the same hourly wage as she paid her helper.

"Why do you need extra?" she asked, pulling out some bills. For the past two weeks, since the night she'd found him drunk in the bathroom, Jason had been moody and withdrawn. Guilt, Jillian had told herself. She'd decided to let him work through his feelings in his own way.

Jason's gaze slid sideways to meet hers. "It's my turn to bring the drinks to the club meeting this afternoon."

At her abrupt frown, he added quickly, "Cokes, Mom. Just Cokes. And some chips and things."

Jillian relaxed. She and the other mothers of the club members had agreed to monitor the boys' activities. If the boys drank again or got into trouble of any kind, the mothers would insist the club be disbanded. She hadn't spoken with Mel Cobb. It would have been a waste of time.

Slowly she counted out his wages, then added three dollars more and laid the money on the cluttered desk. Absently she riffled through the remaining bills. "One of these days I'm going to have to get some reading glasses," she muttered in disgust. "Or learn to count."

"Something wrong?"

"No, I just thought I had more money in this sorry old wallet than I have."

For days, since the dedication ceremony, in fact, she'd been horrendously absentminded. Twice she'd misplaced her truck keys, and just last week she'd found a carbon copy of a prescription for codeine she couldn't remember filling. The name of the patient was unfamiliar, but she'd initialed the bottom, just as the state required, and tucked the copy into the ledger, just as she always did.

Jason crumpled the bills in his freckled fist and reached down for his skateboard, which was propped against her desk. "Thanks, Mom. I'm outta here," he said in a rush.

"Sweetie, wait. I need to talk with you about something."

A wary look crowded into Jason's eyes, and his brow furrowed. He held the board in front of him, wheels out. "What about?"

Jillian masked her irritation. She was determined to keep the fragile peace between them. She couldn't stand it when Jason withdrew from her.

"Nothing serious. It's just that Mr. Sizemore called this morning while you were downstairs with Darcy. He really could use you on the team again this year."

The wariness left his eyes, and he grinned. "Ah, Mom, I told you, I'm tired of soccer. I just don't want to play anymore."

"But you've always loved to play. I don't understand why you say you're tired of it."

He lifted one shoulder in a familiar gesture of impatience. "I got better things to do with my Saturdays, that's all. And I might go out for basketball this winter, if I grow a little more. Mike's dad says I'm real good."

Jillian started to brush the matted hair from his forehead, but he jerked away and stood up. A quick hurt shot through her. He didn't want her to touch him anymore.

"Jase, I think you're spending too much time with Mike and not enough time with your other friends. I haven't seen Scott Sizemore around the house since the beginning of summer."

"Scott's a dork." His eyes carried a sneer, and he began to prowl the room, too restless to sit still.

"Jason! Scotty's a very nice boy. And you always said he was your best friend."

"Well, he's not anymore. He's not any fun. Nobody at school likes him."

Jillian leaned back in her chair and tried to keep her rising frustration out of her voice. "By nobody, I suppose you mean Mike?" When Jason didn't answer, she sat forward and gave him a pleading look. "Jase, what's wrong? You've been in a terrible mood since . . . since the opening of Horizons."

She tried to see what he was thinking behind the thick brushes of his lashes, but in the bright morning light his wide pupils conveyed only sullen impatience.

"I'm fine, Mom. I just have a lot on my mind, you know?" he declared emphatically, his lips twisting into a boyish smile that looked forced.

"No, I don't know. That's why I'm asking. You've always told me what's on your mind, but lately every time I try to talk with you, you clam up or find something you have to do."

Jason's brows pulled together in a rebellious frown. "I'm almost fifteen, Mom," he said in a petulant tone that she'd never heard before. "I can handle my own life."

"I know that, Jase. But I'm worried about you."

"I'm too old for that." The petulance had been replaced by anger. "You keep thinking I'm still a kid. It's time you started trusting me more."

Jillian sighed. She wasn't going to win this round. "We'll talk about this later," she said, beckoning him closer. "Give me a kiss, and you can go."

Jason hesitated, then came forward to give her an awkward kiss on the cheek. Then, as though he were terribly embarrassed, he spun around and hurried toward the door.

"Be home by six," she shouted after him.

"Six-thirty," he shouted back as he propelled his board down the deserted corridor. The wheels clattered loudly on the linoleum, and Jillian winced.

Thank God all the offices are closed on the weekend, she thought as she slumped back in the worn leather chair and stared at the ceiling. She closed her eyes and tried to relax, but she was as jumpy as her son.

Since the night she read Trevor's letters she'd been waging an inner battle. Part of her wanted to let go of the past, to forgive Trevor and let him become a part of Jason's life if that was what he wanted, but another part, the vulnerable young woman who'd been so badly scarred, refused to trust him.

What if he decided that an occasional visit wasn't enough? What if he wanted Jason to live with him part-time in Seattle? What if he wanted custody?

No, she thought quickly. She couldn't risk it. She couldn't bear the thought of someone else rearing her son, not even his father. She would fight if she had to. She would—

Suddenly the phone buzzed. Sighing, Jillian reached for the receiver. She was used to these Saturday calls. It was the only time when her constituents could be sure of her undivided attention.

"Jillian Anderson. May I help you?"

Absently she ran a hand through her curly hair. She'd spent an extra half hour in front of the mirror earlier, trying to tame the rebellious thickness into a more sophisticated style, but as soon as she'd stepped outside, the brisk morning breeze had ruined all her hard work.

"Jill, it's Addie. He's here!"

Jillian sat bolt upright and gripped the receiver more tightly. Inside the prickly denim of her tight new jeans, her thighs clenched painfully against the leather seat as she pushed the soles of her sneakers against the floor.

"You mean—Trevor?"

"Yes. I'm at Ray's Service. I saw him go by when I was gassing up the Jeep. He's driving a maroon Jaguar convertible with Washington plates. I know it's him."

Adrenaline poured into Jillian's veins, jolting her heart into a furious pace and spreading a sick feeling in her stomach. "I'm not ready," she said, more to herself than Adrian. Her free hand worried the open collar of her blouse, crushing the emerald silk against her nervous palm.

"I think it's a good sign that he's come back, Jill."

"Are you crazy, Addie? I told you that was the last thing I wanted."

There was a brief pause. "At least give him a chance to make amends to you and Jase. You might regret it if you don't."

Jillian swiveled around to gaze out the window. The town square bustled with Saturday shoppers, and traffic was heavy on the surrounding streets. But there was no sign of a maroon Jaguar, and no sign of Trevor.

She blew a slow stream of air toward her bangs, and some of the tightness eased from her muscles. "Maybe he's not even coming into town." Jillian searched the area below. There was still no sign of a man with Trevor's distinctive swagger. He could have taken the left fork at the crossroads toward Horizons.

"True. I imagine you'll find out soon enough." Jillian heard the sound of a sigh before Adrian added in a sympathetic tone, "For what it's worth, good luck. I'll be at the clinic until seven if you need a friendly ear."

"Thanks. And thanks for the warning."

"*De nada.*"

Adrian hung up, and Jillian slowly replaced the receiver, her gaze still searching the streets. A strange feeling of excitement leaped to life inside her, and her cheeks grew uncomfortably warm.

Trevor *had* come back.

"I'm impressed, Madam Mayor. You have a very efficient early warning system." The voice was raspy and deep and terribly familiar.

Jillian swiveled around so fast that she nearly overbalanced. Trevor was standing in the doorway, one hand braced against the doorjamb, the other holding a manila folder. There was the barest suggestion of masculine amusement in the crooked slant of his hard lips.

"You're not welcome here, Trevor," she said flatly.

"So you said. I was hoping you'd changed your mind."

She'd heard that husky note of resignation in his voice before. It was the tone he'd used when he was bracing to accept the pain of some necessary procedure during his recovery.

She shoved aside the illogical feeling of guilt that rose inside her. "I'll never change my mind about you, Trevor. Never."

He said nothing, only watched her with those fathomless eyes that changed color along with his mood. This morning they were a deep russet and unreadable. But the knuckles of his hand whitened as though he'd suddenly pushed hard against the wooden jamb.

She remembered the strength in that hand. And the gentleness.

But Trevor didn't look gentle. He looked tough and rangy and, in the faded blue work shirt and tight, wear-softened jeans, slightly uncivilized, like the burly, hard-living men from the lumber company who used to take over the town on Saturday night.

He had to be at least six-three, she realized as she measured his lean length against the door, and all muscle, but there was more than rugged masculine strength in his raw-boned frame. There was an air of restless magnetism about him that frightened her.

Heat surged into her cheeks, and her palms began to sweat. The mountain air seemed suddenly thinner somehow, as though Trevor's big powerful body had pushed most of the oxygen from the room.

"What do you want, Trevor? This is my day to catch up on my paperwork, and I'm behind."

"What are you offering?" he asked in a neutral tone.

"A polite goodbye." She shifted her gaze toward the empty corridor behind the massive triangle of his torso. "Have a nice day."

"I'm trying, but you're making it very difficult." A wry, lopsided grin creased his cheeks and crinkled his eyes, but Jillian ignored his devilish charm.

She had a fleeting impression that nothing would be too difficult for this man if he really set his mind on it. Or if it was something he really wanted.

Like being a part of his son's life.

She pressed her thighs together tightly and sat up straighter. "You didn't answer my question," she persisted. "Why are you here?"

"To claim my rights as Jason's father."

The teasing light left Trevor's eyes. He dropped his arm and walked toward her. In the close confines of her office she saw that his swaggering gait was the result of a slight but recognizable limp, as though one of his legs was slightly shorter than the other.

With a flip of his powerful wrist he tossed the folder onto the blotter in front of her. There was a deadly stillness about him that she'd never noticed before.

"What's that?" she demanded, glaring at him.

"Open it and see."

Jillian's hand began to shake as she did as he ordered.

"Oh, no," she whispered in horror as she saw the cold, impersonal lines of the deposition on top. Hastily she spread the other pages out in front of her. There were four in all, properly witnessed and notarized, sworn statements testifying that Ensign Jillian Louise Anderson and Lieutenant Commander Trevor Madison Markus had once been lovers.

There were also copies of Jason's birth certificate and a death certificate showing that Lieutenant William Paul White had died ten months and fifteen days before her son was born.

The name of the law firm was unfamiliar, but the stationery was a thick vellum, and the letterhead had been engraved instead of printed. He'd obviously carried out his threat to hire the best.

"The private investigator I hired hasn't found all of the nurses who were assigned to the surgical wing at the same time you were there, but the four who've been interviewed by my attorney so far were all quite cooperative—and talkative. They remembered you very well, Jill. And me." His voice roughened. "And our love affair. It's all there, how you pulled strings to get me assigned to a private room, how you asked them to insure our privacy after lights out." One side of his mouth slanted into a bitter smile. "It doesn't take much imagination to fill in the blanks. Any judge would be able to do it easily."

She raised stricken eyes to his. "You make it seem so tawdry." Her voice choked. "It wasn't like that. It wasn't. You're not being fair."

A harsh tension tightened the planes of his face into a stark mask, and under the soft material of his shirt, his muscles clenched until they seemed forged from steel. "You put another man's name where mine should be. How fair was that?"

"You know why I had to do that," she cried. "You didn't want to be a husband. I had no reason to think you'd want to be a father."

Trevor ran a hand through his hair. Except for the color, the coarse thickness was very much like Jason's, hard to tame and inclined to curl at the ends if it got too long.

"You're right," he said in a rough voice. "I walked away from you, and I've never looked back. Is that what you want me to say?"

"Yes, because it's true. You didn't even leave a forwarding address."

His hands balled into fists at his sides, then slowly uncurled, as though he were consciously controlling himself. "Jill, listen to me. I wasn't in any shape to take care of a wife. I was having trouble taking care of myself in those days." A tiny muscle jerked in his rugged jaw. "But if I'd known about Jason, I swear I would have tried. I wouldn't have let you face that alone."

"It's too late." Her fingers trembled as they pressed against her throat. For some strange reason it had hurt to say those words.

"For you and me, maybe, but Jason is still my son, and I intend to be there for him as I should have been from the first." A flicker of pain darkened his eyes for an instant before his thick lashes lowered. "Hate me if you have to, Jill, but I love my son, and I want him to know that. And as quickly as possible. We've already lost too much time."

Jillian turned to ice. Inside, she began to shiver violently, and her palms felt frozen. "And if I refuse?"

Something raw and powerfully potent simmered in his eyes. "Then I'll show these sworn statements to a judge."

"You . . . you wouldn't!" Jillian pressed her hand to her stomach. A sick dread was rapidly replacing the empty chill.

His skin paled, but his eyes remained hard. "I will if I have to, Jill. I don't like playing dirty, but you made the rules. Jason's the only son I'll ever have, and I'm not going to give him up."

The blood drained from her face in a rush, and she felt light-headed. Tiny pinpricks of light wavered in front of her eyes before she managed to clear her head. "If you do this, I'll never forgive you."

He absorbed the venom in her words with a stiff shrug. "I've never expected your forgiveness, Jill." His voice was flat, without any emotion at all.

She bit her lip. "What if Jason decides he doesn't want you in his life? Then what?"

He flexed his shoulders as though his back had suddenly given him pain. "I never think past today, Jill. If he makes that decision, I'll deal with it then."

Jillian's gaze dropped to the papers in front of her. She could hire an attorney and fight to deny Trevor access. Maybe she would win, maybe she wouldn't. But Jason would be the one to suffer if these affidavits were read in open court.

Her gaze absently noted the signatures, signatures she'd seen hundreds of times on hundreds of patient charts. Sally and Bev. Pat and Barbara.

They'd been young, just out of nursing school, like her. Every day they'd dealt with terrible suffering, just as she had. They'd been allies as well as friends, fighting desperately to keep their horribly wounded patients alive. Too many times they'd lost, but sometimes they'd won. And after every victory, they'd cried together in joy and relief.

Romance had been as rare as a laugh in the wards where they'd worked. So when she and Trevor had fallen in love, the other nurses had been willing conspirators. Helping the lovers escape the stark reality of the war for a time had been their own private expression of hope in that bleak world of suffering and death.

In spite of the terrible things around her, when she'd been with Trevor, she'd been so happy...and so foolish.

Her hand shook as she collected the papers he'd brought and shoved them into the folder. "Here's your evidence," she said stiffly, shoving the folder toward him. "You've made your point."

"It doesn't have to be this way, Jill," Trevor said as he moved forward and took the papers from her trembling hand. He sounded bone weary and very bitter, like a man who'd just run a gruelling race the best way he knew how and lost.

"Oh, yes, it does. You made certain of that when you came here with your tidy little file."

Trevor glanced up at the ceiling, his expression thunderous. "What the hell was I supposed to do?" he said with explosive anger. "If I walked away and let you keep me out of Jason's life, you'd think I didn't care, just the way you think I didn't care about you fifteen years ago. A man can't win with you, lady." He ran a hand through his hair again, this time in a savage gesture of restraint, and glared at her.

"That's right," she shot back. "So give up. Let me alone."

"Like hell I will! I have a lot to prove to you, and I'll be damned if I'll give up until I do." He looked furious, but there was a hint of something that looked like pleading in his eyes.

"Please leave now," she said in a stiff voice that contained the last of her strength. "I think we've said just about all there is to be said."

He exhaled slowly. "Not quite. You haven't given me your answer."

His stormy gaze shifted to the framed picture of Jason on her desk, and Jillian lifted a weary hand in surrender. She would never publicly expose Jason to the damning words in that folder, and Trevor knew it. It was one more reason to hate him.

"I'll talk to Jason tonight. If he wants to meet you, I won't stand in his way. That's the best I can do."

Emotions raced swiftly through his narrowed eyes, emotions she could neither read nor understand. He lifted his shoulders in a shrug that conveyed barely contained impatience.

"You can reach me at Horizons. I've...rearranged my schedule so that I can manage some vacation time. I intend to spend it with Jason." His deceptively low tone carried a strange combination of deep sadness and warning.

She folded her hands over her stomach as though to protect the tiny life that was no longer there. "I'll call you."

The harsh lines of his face, first put there by his months in the hospital, seemed deeper as he gave her a brief smile. "Good. I'll be waiting."

"Don't hold your breath."

He stared at her in stony silence for a moment longer, then tucked the folder under his arm and walked away from her.

The streetlight outside her kitchen window began to glow with an eerie orange brightness. Seated across from Jason at the table, Jillian rested her chin in her palm and watched a flock of birds flying eastward in ragged formation.

It was dusk, and the sun had fallen below the horizon, leaving bloody streaks in the dark sky. The air was oppressively hot, and there was going to be a full moon. A lovers' moon.

Ignoring the sudden tremor that shook her, Jillian shifted her gaze to the peaks in the distance. Somewhere between her and those jagged mountains, Trevor was waiting for her call.

She'd tried all afternoon to find the right words to tell Jason the truth about his father, but all the words she'd chosen had sounded stilted and defensive.

No, that wasn't the reason she was stalling. Admit it, Jill, she said silently. You're scared. No, more like terrified.

Trevor was rich. He traveled by helicopter and wore suits that cost more than she made in a month. His life was exciting and glamorous, just the kind of life a young boy would find irresistible.

What if Jason suddenly decided he'd had enough of his mother's quiet ways? What if he decided he wanted to live with his father in Seattle? She'd survived the loss of one person she'd loved desperately. How could she possibly survive the loss of another?

"Mom? Didn't you hear me?"

"What?" She blinked across the table. Jason had finished his dinner and was folding his napkin in the careful way she'd taught him.

"I asked if I could be excused?"

Jason pushed back his chair and started to rise. He looked as though he'd gained back a few of the pounds he'd lost over the past few months of summer vacation.

Jillian put her hand on his arm to stop him. "Not yet. There's . . . something I need to discuss with you."

Jason's thin chest heaved in a sigh. "Mom, I already told you I don't want to play soccer." His face was a curious mixture of teenage rebelliousness and adult exasperation.

Poor baby, she thought, aching for him. He wants to act grown up, but he's not sure how.

"Well?" He sounded impatient.

Jillian bit her lip, then glanced at the folded newspaper that was tucked into the basket under the window where she kept her magazines. "First, I want you to read something, then we'll . . . talk." She cleared the table, making a space.

Jason's pale brow furrowed, and apprehension crept into his eyes. "What's with you tonight, Mom? You're acting funny."

She forced a smile as she unfolded the two-week-old *Clarion* in front of him, pointing to the article beside the pictures of Trevor and herself. "Read this."

Grumbling under his breath, Jason bent his head and began to read.

Jillian ran her wet palms along the sides of her jeans. The hard seams hurt her skin, but she welcomed the pain. She could handle that kind of pain.

"Okay, I've read it. So what?" Jason sat back and looked at her. It was almost as though he were daring her to tell him something he didn't want to hear.

"What . . . what do you think? About Trevor Markus, I mean."

Jason shrugged disinterestedly. "Says here he's some kind of all-American hero. So what?"

He was edgy, she could see it.

Jillian ached to go to him, to wrap her arms around his thin body and hold him close. She would do anything to keep him from being hurt. *Anything*. But right now she had to get through this.

"I met Trevor when he was a patient in the hospital in Tokyo. You remember, when I was a Navy nurse?"

He nodded, his expression becoming more wary with every second that passed.

"He was a Navy pilot. He, uh, was very badly hurt, and it was four months before they could evacuate him to the Navy hospital in San Diego." She wet her dry lips. "We fell in love."

Her voice choked, and she had to stop. Her heart was pounding so hard that she felt faint, and her hands were clammy with nervous sweat.

The words had to be said, and she had to say them. But now, suddenly, she knew she'd been wrong, terribly, selfishly wrong, in denying her son his true heritage. She had only to look into his bewildered copper eyes to realize the dreadful wrong she'd done him. And Trevor. Whatever his failings, Trevor was Jason's father. Jason was their son, a part of each of them.

Oh, baby, I'm so sorry, she cried silently. Shaking, she took a deep breath, then said softly, "Trevor Markus is your father."

Jason's jaw dropped, then snapped shut. He went white and then red beneath the golden freckles. "You . . . you said my father was dead. Every time I'd ask you about him, you said he was dead." His voice rose to a shrill protest as he jumped to his feet. He moved a few jerky paces away from her, then stood frozen, staring at her, his eyes wild. "You said my father's name was William White. You said he was killed before you could get married."

"I had my reasons—"

"Yeah, sure." Jason flung out his arm in an awkward, jerky arc. "You're always preaching at me to tell the truth, but you've been lying to me all this time. *Lying!*" He gulped, then moved backward, his feet tangling in the laces of his sneakers. He grabbed the chair and righted himself awkwardly, like a clumsy puppy.

"I don't care who that guy is," he shouted, his voice breaking into a cracking falsetto. "I don't care if he's some kind of damn war hero, or how much money he has. Just keep him away from me. I don't need another parent nagging at me all the time."

Jillian held out a hand beseechingly. "Sweetie, listen, it's not like you think. Trevor and I had a . . . a misunderstanding before I could tell him about you. He didn't know I was going to have a baby. I—"

"So why didn't you just tell me that, huh, Mom? Why the big story that he died in the war?"

"Because I . . . thought it would be easier if you thought he was dead."

Jason looked as though he wanted to cry, but he whirled around and headed for his room. "So let him stay dead. I don't need him."

Jillian stood motionless, one hand clutching the back of the chair where her son had sat. The remnants of their dinner were still on the table, and a mournful country-and-western ballad was playing softly from the radio at the far end of the narrow kitchen. Suddenly Jason's door slammed, and she winced. Half a second later his stereo screeched a metallic guitar riff at top volume.

She hurried into the living room to close the front windows. She could stand the noise just this once. In fact, the discord was a welcome distraction. Maybe if she could summon enough irritation at the dreadful sounds, she might not feel the guilt quite so much.

Moving mechanically she went into the kitchen and began to run water into the sink. Washing dishes was usually Jason's job, but tonight she would manage without him. She'd always known her son had inherited his father's temper as well as his eyes, but Jason had never exploded as violently as this before. And never at her.

Her shoulders sagged with the weight of her own guilt. She'd deserved his anger. She'd let her own pain override her responsibility to her child. She'd been weak when she should have been strong. She'd let him down.

Oh, Trevor, she thought in deep anguish, how could we have made such a terrible mess of things?

The dish she was holding slipped from her hand and fell to the floor. Shards of thick china hit her bare ankles, leaving a bloody smear of tiny cuts. Her fingers were clumsy as she picked up the pieces one by one. She managed to get even the smallest bits.

It's too late, she thought numbly, staring at the pile of shattered crockery in her palm. Too late to pick up the pieces.

Suddenly she wished with all her heart that it wasn't.

Chapter 6

The night was too quiet. Sometime after midnight the crickets had stopped chirping, and now the leaves hung limp and quiet above his head.

Trevor leaned against the rough bark of a towering white oak and listened to the sound of his own breathing. He felt acutely uncomfortable, as though his skin were stretched too tautly over his bones, and, in his veins, his blood burned like hot lead.

"Damn," he muttered into the moonlit glade. "I haven't felt this wired in years."

A heavy tightness tugged at his belly as he stared at the sky. The stars looked close enough to touch, but no matter how high he climbed, they would always be beyond his reach.

Like Jillian.

He rubbed his jaw with a tired hand. No matter what he did for her now, it would never be enough. Never! She'd given him the greatest gift a woman can give a man, his child, and she wanted nothing from him in return. No, he thought with a silent, bitter chuckle, that wasn't quite true. She wanted him to disappear from her life. Again.

And that was the one thing he couldn't do.

If she'd asked him for anything else, *anything*, he would have worked like a son of a gun to give it to her, but he couldn't walk away again. Not from his son.

His son.

He was still having trouble dealing with the idea of being a father. He'd always wanted children, but over the years, he'd gradually come to terms with not having them.

Sometimes, as he'd watched his brother, Brian, and his sister-in-law, Mary Rose, struggle to raise their two sons, he'd told himself it was just as well that he had none. It had been exhausting work from what he'd seen, and sometimes Mary Rose had been at the end of her emotional strength.

But she'd had the luxury of a husband to help her, a man who loved her and provided a nice home, so that she'd been able to stay home with her boys. And when they'd occasionally become discipline problems, Brian had been there to take charge.

Jillian had had to do it all. For fourteen long years she'd handled more than any woman should have to handle, and from what he'd been able to discover, she'd managed damn well.

He was proud of her, for what it was worth. And he respected her more than any woman he'd ever known. She had guts and determination and a hell of a lot of strength. He had a feeling he was just beginning to find out how much.

Trevor shoved his hands in the pockets of his khaki shorts and stared at the lonely shadows crossing the large open area between him and the main building. Once she'd been a part of him. The best part. She had made him believe in himself in those terrible days when he didn't know if he would ever be a whole man again.

It had been her voice that he'd loved first. Soft and slightly husky, as though she'd just emerged from a deep sleep, her voice had soothed and cajoled and rebuked him. Listening to her, fighting with her, flirting with her, had kept him alive.

When he'd discovered he'd fallen in love with her, it had terrified him. He'd fought it, telling himself he was horny. That she was available. That he would forget her when he left Tokyo, just as he'd always forgotten the current lady in his bed when he left a duty station.

But somehow Jillian had gotten inside him. When she was with him, he felt ... complete. Whole. Ready to take on the world, or at least six grinding months of therapy. She'd given him her strength when he'd needed it, and her love when he'd needed that even more.

When she'd been holding his hand, the pain had been bearable. When she kissed him, he forgot the long, hard road ahead. And when, in the last few weeks before he'd been shipped home, she'd given him her love and her body, he'd felt like the luckiest man in the universe.

After he'd left her, he'd told himself over and over that he'd saved her from a terrible life with a man who would have eventually destroyed her spirit and taken the joy from her eyes. He'd made his decision, and he'd learned to live with it, but strangely, it hurt to come face-to-face with the woman she'd become without him.

Damn, he thought. He had to stop thinking that way. Jillian had her life, and he had his. That was the way it had to be.

But they both loved Jason. Their son.

With an unfamiliar sense of apprehension, Trevor allowed his thoughts to turn to the boy who was a large question mark in his head. Would he be like him, or more like Jillian? Would he feel resentment toward a man who'd never even known he was alive? Would Jason hate him the way his mother did?

Slowly he rubbed his tired cheeks. His whisker stubble felt as rough as the bark against his bare shoulders.

Fifteen years ago Jillian's skin had felt like fine porcelain under his fingers and had been burnished lightly with golden freckles. Once he'd teased her about the tiny specks that dotted the swell of her breasts. Once his tongue had moistened every one until her skin had glowed.

Trevor glanced down at his bare chest. She'd felt so tiny, so delicate, lying in his arms, so very precious. And yet he'd wanted her with a ravenous hunger that he hadn't been able to drive out of his system.

His body hardened instantly as he thought about the creamy silkiness of those long, graceful legs. He wanted to feel those legs between his. He wanted to stroke and pet her until she was wet and ready for him.

Ten minutes ago he'd left his bed drenched in sweat, the vividly erotic dream he'd been having still throbbing in his head. A few more minutes and he would have disgraced himself as badly as a teenager.

And he still wanted her. Every time he saw her, he wanted her more. But he'd learned a long time ago that wanting and having were often different things.

He muttered a vicious obscenity into the heavy silence, but it didn't help.

The familiar pressure inside him would build and build until it was a terrible ache. He had to move, to work off the tightness. He had to get Jillian out of his head.

He pushed himself away from the tree and headed for the pool. He would swim laps until his legs burned and he couldn't lift his arms. Maybe then the tension would let go, and he could sleep again.

And maybe, if his body was exhausted, he wouldn't dream of a redheaded temptress with sultry green eyes who hated him. Maybe, if his mind was numbed by fatigue, he wouldn't be tortured by memories of all the years he'd thrown away.

Maybe then he could find a way to make peace with a woman he wanted and could never have.

Jillian paced. Back and forth she walked, her bare feet leaving a rut in the plush area rug covering the middle of her living room. Her hands were crossed over her belly, and her face was drawn and pale.

It was nearly dawn, and she'd awakened with the birds. Her body was exhausted, but her mind wouldn't let her rest.

She couldn't stop thinking of Trevor. Over the years, when she'd thought of him at all, it had been with bitterness and hatred, and he'd deserved it.

But now she found she couldn't seem to sustain that anger. Yesterday she'd been furious at the way he'd forced her hand, but today she had to admit she would have done the same thing in his place. She would have used any weapon, resorted to any tactic, to get her son if he'd been denied to her.

The haunting sound of church bells slowly penetrated the deep gray fog that surrounded her. Six-thirty, she realized, time for the early service at the Community Church.

Framed in the open window, the tip of the white steeple was barely visible through the treetops, but it was there, solid and enduring. Slowly, feeling the leaden weight of indecision, she crossed to the window and looked south. Adrian's new clinic was nestled in the tall pines, and beyond the long, low building Miracle Lake glistened in the dawn light.

The early settlers had believed that the icy water pouring out of the mountains during the spring thaw had restorative powers. As soon as the snow had left the ground, they'd jammed the sandy beaches, shivering and hopeful, to wade into the clear water. A display in the *Clarion* office chronicled the claims of miraculous cures of ills ranging from anemia to yaws.

Jillian pushed her toes into the rough nap of the rug. That was what she needed now, she thought, a miracle, a way to erase her mistake and let her start over with her son. Except that miracles happened only in legends and fairy tales.

A gust of pine-scented breeze ruffled the lacy curtain and brushed her bare skin. The air was already warm and heavy, suggesting another muggy Indian summer day. She hugged herself and slumped back against the wall by the window.

She loved Jason so much that it frightened her. She wanted to wrap him in so much love that he would never feel pain.

But now, face-to-face with her son's anger and Trevor's persistence, she found herself doubting her motives. Had she, by denying his parentage, actually been seeking a subtle revenge on the man who'd hurt her so badly, a revenge so complete it would instead hurt the child he'd given her?

She felt the tears clog her throat, and she lifted her gaze to the ceiling. Whatever she and Trevor had once had together was past. But from that love had come a precious and perfect child. He was a part of both of them, maybe the best part. And nothing she could do would ever change that.

Quickly, before she could change her mind, she hurried into the kitchen and picked up the phone. When the night receptionist at Horizons answered, she nearly hung up. Her heart was pounding furiously, and her fingers were stiff on the receiver. "Trevor Markus, please."

"Mr. Markus is in the guest bungalow. I'll ring."

"Thank you."

The phone rang and rang, but there was no answer. A bitter disappointment shot through her. He'd left without waiting for her call.

"Markus."

His voice was rusty from sleep, and she shivered helplessly at the sensual promise of that deep masculine gruffness.

"This is Jillian. I told you I'd call."

There was a brief silence. "Uh, what time is it?"

She could almost see the sensual sweep of his thick lashes as he blinked himself awake. "Almost seven. I'm sorry if I woke you. I can call back, if you prefer."

"No, that's . . . okay. Just give me a minute to wake up."

She inhaled very slowly, willing her body to relax, but the sleep-slurred voice stirred her imagination irresistibly. Involuntarily she glanced down at the thin cotton gown that barely covered her thighs. It had been a hot night. No doubt Trevor had worn very little to bed.

In the hospital he'd slept in the nude. Even with air-conditioning, the east wing had been unbearably hot in the summertime. Most nights, even when she hadn't been on duty, she'd gone to his room in the early hours to exchange his sweat-soaked pillowcase for a crisp new one.

Sometimes he'd awakened then, his eyes heavy with drug-induced sleep, and he'd pull her down for a hard, demanding kiss. His voice had been husky then, too, and thick with desire.

Jillian gripped the receiver even tighter against her ear. She discovered she was holding her breath, and exhaled the trapped air in a nervous stream.

"How . . . are you?" he asked in a still-husky voice. She heard the rustle of bedclothes and the sound of his whiskers scraping against the phone.

"Fine," she lied. "And you?"

His chuckle was throaty and oddly infectious. "I think I'm suffering from culture shock. It's too quiet in this place."

"We like it," she said stiffly.

Her teeth ground together as she glanced around her cozy, pine-paneled kitchen. The copper pans hanging above the stove glinted in the light streaming over her shoulder, and the bright green leaves of the creeping Charlie on the baker's rack had a healthy sheen. It was homey and comfortable and no doubt completely alien to the fast-lane life he must lead.

His heavy sigh whispered into her ear. "I'm not criticizing, Jill. I was just trying to make a joke. Sorry."

"I . . . morning is not my best time," she said with a reluctant trace of apology. "Especially since I've been up most of the night." While he'd been dead asleep, she thought with a sudden pang of bitterness.

"Is something wrong?" he asked quickly. "You're not sick?"

At heart, yes, she thought. "No, just hot. Our apartment isn't air-conditioned."

"Well, maybe this heat wave will break soon."

"Maybe."

Jillian stifled a sigh. They were like two boxers in a ring, circling cautiously, each waiting for the other to throw the first punch. She stood up straighter and glanced toward the shimmering mirror that was Miracle Lake. "I, uh, called to invite you to a picnic. I've done some thinking, and I think that would be the best way for you and Jason to get to know each other."

There was a faint sound, as though Trevor had inhaled suddenly. "A picnic? You mean with paper plates and fried chicken—and ants?" His voice carried a murmur of caution, as though he didn't quite trust his hearing—or her.

"I'm not sure about the ants," she said, a strange and definitely unwanted excitement curling through her.

"Hmm, no ants. Sounds challenging." His velvet voice was low with amusement, and Jillian felt an answering smile shiver the corners of her mouth.

Instantly she twisted the smile into a frown. "I'll expect you at eleven-thirty," she said curtly. "My apartment is above the pharmacy. When you get to the center of town, you can't miss it. I'm right on the square." She heard a faint sound that could have been a sigh whisper into her ear.

"I know where the pharmacy is. Yesterday, when I drove into town, I went there first. The woman behind the counter gave me directions to the town hall."

She ignored the mention of their last meeting. The memory of her anger and frustration was too raw. "Use the outside steps in the back. They lead directly to our apartment."

"No problem. I'll be there at eleven-thirty."

Jillian glanced toward the hall. There was no sound from Jason's room. "There's something you should know before you come," she said quietly.

"What's that?" Suddenly there was a wary edge to his voice that hadn't been there before.

"Jason is pretty upset."

"About me?"

She hesitated. It was tempting to put the blame on Trevor, but she couldn't make herself do it. She'd been the one to tell the lies that now entwined the three of them.

"No, about me. He's angry because I lied to him."

Jason's door opened suddenly, and then the door to the bathroom clicked shut. Jason was up.

"Trevor, I can't talk now," she added hastily before he could say anything more. "I'll see you later, okay?"

"Okay." There was a pause. "Jill, about Jason, we'll handle it."

He hung up before she could answer.

Five hours later Jillian was pacing again, but this time she was angry. Trevor was nearly half an hour late.

Jason was in his room, where he'd gone after eating his breakfast in sullen silence. His eyes had been shadowed and his skin sallow, as though he'd gotten little sleep. He'd flatly refused to go on the picnic.

Her mother's instinct had told her to go slowly, so she'd simply excused him from the table and suggested he go back to bed for a few hours. Obediently he'd gone to his room, but his stereo had been blasting since he'd left her, one loud, raucous song after another.

Let's see how Trevor handles this, she thought grimly, pausing to look out the window for the fifth time in the past twenty minutes. Her breath whistled through her parted lips as she froze. Trevor was standing at the edge of the square, putting money in the parking meter.

As she watched, he ran a large, sun-browned hand through his hair, releasing the rebellious cowlicks and ruining the neat part. The sun caught the sandy blond mixed with the gray, making him look more like the man she remembered. From above, his shoulders looked enormous in the tight blue polo shirt, and his bare arms were deeply tanned and bulged with the kind of firm muscle that can only be built up with years of hard work.

Her skin prickled at the back of her neck, and her breath shortened. All too well, she knew his shoulders would be solid, with a thin layer of fat to round the hard masculine edges. And the lean torso that tapered into the band of his jeans would be ridged and corded and furred with soft blond hair in all the right places where a man should be rough to the touch.

An arrow of swift, primitive desire darted down her spine to bury its point deep inside her, and a warm, fluid feeling of tension spread outward, taunting her.

Phantom feelings, she told herself with a bitter silent laugh, like a man who's lost a leg but swears he feels his toes. Her body was simply remembering the feel of that hard masculinity long after it had been taken away from her forever.

She pressed her fingertips against the window frame, but the painted wood was too hot to touch. Snatching her hand away, she watched him, like a bullfighter sizing up the deadly animal across the arena.

The furious pounding of her heart was loud in her ears, and her mouth was dry. She was experiencing all of the physical manifestations of alarm, she noted, licking her lips. If asked, she could describe them in stark, clinical detail, but that didn't help. She was frightened, and excited, and nervous. And she hated the feeling.

She edged closer to the window. His head was bent, and he was staring down at the concrete beneath his dark blue running shoes. There was a stark, even lonely look to him that puzzled her.

What's he waiting for? she thought, tapping her foot impatiently. Why doesn't he just come up? Surely he wasn't trying to work up his courage, and yet, that was exactly what it seemed like.

But it was inconceivable to her that he could be nervous. Trevor had hurtled off the deck of a carrier at bone-jarring speed, flown into enemy fire and returned to that tiny gray speck in the ocean countless times.

As she watched, he lifted his head and stared directly at her. She stumbled backward quickly, but not before his shoulders had jerked in surprise.

"Great going, Jill," she muttered in irritation.

Jillian licked her dry lips as she heard him slowly climb the outside steps leading to the second-story balcony. Her front door was open, with only the screen door between her and Trevor. She saw him before he saw her.

His expression was somber, but there was a tightness along his jaw and a faint narrowing around his eyes. It was a look of gritty determination, and it was definitely unsettling.

"Hi," he said as she answered his knock. "Sorry I'm late. I had an overseas call from my crew chief in Thailand. I tried to call to let you know, but the phone was busy."

He tried to comb some order into his tousled hair with his hand. He didn't succeed.

"Uh, I guess Jason is using the extension in his room," she said, making a mental note to speak with her son. He was supposed to confine his conversations to the evening hours.

Silently, fighting a sudden moment of doubt, Jillian opened the door and stepped back. She resisted the urge to wipe her palms on her white cotton playsuit. It's the heat, she told herself absently as Trevor walked into her living room like a man with a mission.

He took a few steps, then turned and looked around. "Nice place," he said with a brief smile. "Homey."

Her house was like her, Trevor thought. Comfortable and warm and uncluttered, with nice, big furniture that looked as if it could take his weight. And he liked the colors, beige and brown, with some green here and there. They were restful and soothing, like the hills around the town.

The muffled sound of screaming guitars filled the sudden silence, and Jillian jerked her gaze toward the door leading to the hall.

"Sounds like Jason likes metal," Trevor said with a pained grin.

"Unfortunately." She felt an answering grin curve her lips. "It all sounds like noise to me."

"It did to me, too, until one of my nephews made me listen to his entire collection. I nearly went deaf, but I can now recognize a few of the groups, if I'm pushed." He glanced toward the sound of the screeching tones. "Most of the guys in treatment like that stuff, too."

Jillian frowned. "Great," she muttered, wincing as the throbbing sound smashed against her spine like a punishing fist.

"It helps, sometimes, especially in the first few weeks, when they're still half strung out. Takes their minds off their screaming nerves."

She nodded. He was so close that she could smell his aftershave, a dark musky scent that excited her senses. It was like Trevor himself, arrogant, and slightly dangerous.

He looked around, his gaze coming to rest on the bright orange cooler by the door. "Uh, are you ready? I only had one dime, and the meter said twelve minutes, even on Sunday."

Jillian had to raise her voice to be heard over the music. "Jason has refused to go." There was a husky note in her voice that startled her, and she cleared her throat. "I tried to talk to him, but he just turned up his music and ignored me. He can be very stubborn sometimes."

Trevor's grin was fleeting. "Like his dad."

"Yes."

More than once she'd countered his stubborn resistance with melting kisses. It had become a game, one that they'd both relished. Suddenly the solid oak floor felt unsteady under her feet, and she groped for the back of the wing chair beside her.

Her toes curled tightly in her thin-soled sandals, and her leg muscles strained against her skin as she slid her hand over the quilted chintz.

Trevor ran his tongue along his bottom lip. "Uh, you said he was upset?"

"I shouldn't have lied to him," she admitted in a thin voice. "But I just wanted to protect him. I thought I was doing the right thing."

She stared at the rug beneath her sandals. A shadow fell across her toes as Trevor moved closer. His shoes were scuffed and well-worn on the sides, and the laces were knotted and frayed. Like Jason's.

"Jill, don't do this to yourself. Take it from a guy who knows, regret is a heavy burden to carry, and it doesn't change anything."

Slowly she raised her head to look at him. A stiff sadness strained the edges of his smile, and his eyes were shadowed. She sensed he was telling the truth, and a part of her, the woman who'd once loved him, grieved for what might have been. But the cynical part, the abandoned mother who'd never felt his hands caress her belly or whisper words of encouragement when she'd felt ugly and scared, refused to care.

"I tried to tell him I was sorry, but he just stared at me." She stifled a sigh. "He's never acted this way before."

"We've given him a lot to handle. Give him some time to work it through."

"I'm trying, but he's making it difficult." Absently she wiped the beads of perspiration from her forehead. "He's not very...receptive."

Trevor ran a hand across his belly. There was still a trace of moisture over her upper lip. It would taste salty, he knew, and tantalize his palate like the finest wine. He swallowed hard, willing himself to stand still. "In other words, I'm not about to be welcomed with open arms."

"No." She sighed. "He claims he doesn't want a father, but I think he's just scared. Some of his friends, like Mike Cobb, don't have such great ones."

"Are you saying that I would be a good one?" Trevor was afraid to breathe.

"I don't know, Trevor," she said in a low, weary voice. "But I know that a battle between us could only hurt Jason."

He wasn't much for subtlety, so it took him a moment to figure out that she wasn't glaring at him anymore. Instead, she seemed...rigidly controlled. He wasn't sure he liked that any better. He exhaled slowly. "This time I won't let you down, Jill. I promise."

Jillian saw the memories come into his eyes, memories of her, of them together. She saw his lips curve upward at the corners, then part slowly. He stopped breathing, then started again, but this time slowly, as though each breath brought pain.

His gaze slowly warmed, then kindled into a strange light. Jillian couldn't look away. His eyes were filled with a hypnotic mixture of pleading and hunger that held hers. His lashes were still sandy blond and as thick on the bottom as they were on the top, and his brows were an intriguing mix of gray and blond.

"I was such a jerk." He said the words so softly that they sounded more like a tortured breath.

So slowly that it seemed to take forever, his hand came up to touch her cheek. His fingers were slightly raspy and very gentle as they traced the line of her cheekbone as though he were a blind man trying to see her face through his fingertips. His hand slid along her cheekbone and into her hair, and his thumb gently stroked the curve of her cheek.

Jillian couldn't make herself move away. She held her breath as his head tipped slowly to one side. Her lips tingled as his gaze lingered there, caressing her as potently as any touch. She tried not to react, but deep inside, in the part of her that had been cold and empty since his betrayal, a sweet warmth began to spread. Slowly his gaze lifted to her eyes, and she saw the question written in the shadowed pupils. He wanted to kiss her.

"Jill?"

"No, Trevor," she whispered.

Before he could release her, she heard a sound behind her. A split second later she heard Jason's voice.

"Mom? Are you all right? He's not going to hurt you, is he?"

Trevor's gaze jerked past her head, and his hand fell, then clenched into a fist. She twisted around, her cheeks on fire.

Jason was standing at the door to the kitchen, his face contorted and pale. His eyes were two copper circles full of some stormy, unrecognizable emotion, starkly outlined between wide open lashes.

Jillian twisted her hands together in front of her. "Of course he's not going to hurt me. This . . . this is Trevor. Your father."

Jason's face started to crumple, and for an instant Jillian saw the ravished features of the little boy he'd once been.

"I told you I didn't want him here," he mumbled, scuffling his feet.

"I knew you didn't really mean it, sweetie. Every boy wants to know his father. You've been hurt, I know, but I want you to try to put that aside, at least for today. Please. For. . . for my sake."

Jillian moved quickly to his side and touched his shoulder, but he jerked away from her and stumbled backward until he crashed into the kitchen table. The vase of giant mums in the center fell over with a loud explosion of breaking glass. Water spread over the table and onto the floor, but Jillian ignored the dripping mess.

"You never listen to me!" Jason shouted, his rubber soles crunching on the glass. "You pretend to listen, but you never do. I always have to do what you want. I never get to do what I want."

"Jase! That's not true. I always listen to you. And I try to do what pleases you, but sometimes I can't. Sometimes I have to do what's best, even if it's not what you want."

"Bull—"

"That's enough, Jason." Trevor's voice startled her, and she uttered a yelp of surprise.

Trevor moved silently to her side. "Your mother's right," he said quietly, but with a steely firmness that tightened Jillian's spine. "I'm here because we both love you. And because it's time for you to know your father."

"Yeah, sure," Jason sneered, his head snapping up defiantly. "That's why you're putting the make on my mother."

Trevor's violent intake of breath startled her. "That's enough talk like that," he said in flat, commanding voice. "Your mother doesn't deserve it, and I won't stand for it."

Surprise surfaced in Jason's glittering eyes. "You can't tell me what to do." His voice cracked, and his pale face flooded with color. He suddenly looked more frightened than angry.

"I can, and I will."

"Trevor, wait," Jillian said urgently, aching for her child. "Jason doesn't understand what you mean."

Trevor's face looked gaunt in the bright midday light, and the stillness was back in his eyes. "I'll handle this, Jillian," he said in an unyielding tone. "Jason and I need to come to an understanding."

Jillian braced herself. If Trevor said one wrong word, if he hurt her child, she would risk the embarrassment and go to court. There were other attorneys with fancy stationery and high-priced skills. She would mortgage everything she owned if she had to in order to protect her child.

"Be very careful," she told Trevor in cold warning.

Trevor heard the threat in her voice. He knew she would fight him with everything she had if he threatened her baby, and a deeply buried feeling of tenderness welled inside him. It was his child she was protecting so fiercely.

"Let's talk about this," he said to his son firmly. "Man to man."

Jason's brow furrowed. "Nothing to talk about," he muttered.

Jillian saw her son's hurt and indecision, and her heart lurched. Jason had been sheltered and protected all his life, and now, when he was the most vulnerable, all the years of stability and security had been ripped away, leaving him confused and angry and upset.

Guilt shuddered through her. If only she could take those lying words back. If only she'd had the foresight to know she'd been making a terrible mistake.

Jason's Adam's apple moved convulsively, and his hands balled into fists. "You'n'me got nothing to talk about," he told his father in a trembling voice.

"Then I'll talk, and you listen." Trevor moved away from her and toward their son. Jillian hugged herself, her eyes fixed on Jason's twisted face.

Trevor halted a foot away from Jason and shoved his hands into his pockets. "I'm the one who blew it, Jason," he said in a steady, slow voice. "Not your mother. I was the one who walked out on her, and on you. I didn't know about you, but that's no excuse. I should have known, but I wasn't around long enough for your mother to tell me." He inhaled deeply, then let the air out in a slow stream. "I wasn't much of a man in those days. I was mad at the world and bitter as hell. I didn't know if I'd ever walk without crutches again."

He glanced down at his feet, then back at Jason, who hadn't moved. "I'd just spent ten months in two godawful military hospitals, and the first civilian I saw when I got out called me a baby killer and told me I deserved to be a cripple for the rest of my life."

Jillian uttered a choked sound of protest. The long, sinewy muscles of Trevor's back rippled as though his body had clenched, but he didn't turn around.

His voice roughened. "I don't blame you for being mad, but take it out on me, not your mother. She was simply protecting you from a guy who would have made a lousy father."

Jason's shoulders jerked. "She could have told me the truth."

Trevor shook his head. "I don't think so, Jason. You needed a father to be proud of, not a spoiled, bitter excuse for a man who ran away from his problems." His shoulders were frozen, and his head didn't move as he added softly, "I'm sorry for hurting your mother, and I'm sorry for hurting you."

Jillian heard the rumble of sincerity in his voice, and the regret. She believed him, and maybe she even understood a little, but she would never forgive him for letting her stand there in her wedding dress, alone, waiting. He could have written, called, anything.

Jason's troubled gaze shifted to Jillian, and she forced the past from her mind. "I know this is hard to take in all at once, but give it time, okay?" she said softly.

The boy bit his lip, his eyes blinking rapidly, his posture drooping. He looked so sad, so vulnerable. Jillian started to go to him, but Trevor stopped her with a hard hand on her shoulder.

"Here's my bottom line, Jason," he said with a grave masculine gentleness that brought a lump to her throat. "You're my son, and I want to be a part of your life. I'm not demanding that you love me, or even like me. That's something that has to be earned, and I intend to do my damnedest to earn it. But I won't let you take this out on your mother. Do you understand what I'm saying, son?"

Jason's lips drooped into a sulky pout, but much of the anger was gone from his eyes. One shoulder lifted in a brief shrug.

Trevor's lips slanted in a wry smile. "Does that mean yes?"

Jason nodded.

"Then please apologize to your mother for upsetting her. She's given you a lot, more than you know, and she doesn't deserve to be hurt."

Jason hesitated, then dropped his gaze to the floor in front of him. "I'm sorry, Mom," he said in a barely audible voice.

"It's okay, sweetie," she said, fighting the urge to cry. "I know this is hard for you. It's . . . hard for all of us."

Trevor flexed his shoulders as though relieving a sudden cramp. "One more thing you need to know, son. I'm not walking out on you again. No matter what happens."

Jillian's face felt as though it were going to shatter. Why hadn't Trevor said that to *her*? Because it wasn't true, that was why, she realized instantly. He was here because of Jason, not her. And that was the way it would always be. Once Jason was grown and on his own, she doubted that she would ever see Trevor again, except at some function or other having to do with their son.

Ignoring the strange feeling of hurt spreading inside, she forced a smile for Jason. Right now she had to get through this day. They all had to get through it.

"Why don't you put on the new bathing suit I got you last week?" she told her son in a persuasive tone. "It's already scorching today, and the lake will be nice and cool."

"Okay," Jason said in a jerky voice, but the flush had receded from his cheeks, and the pain was gone from his eyes. He looked at his father one more time, then turned and headed toward his room.

Jillian waited until she heard his door close before allowing her shoulders to sag. With a muttered curse, Trevor pulled out a chair and pushed her down into it. She felt shaky, and her head was beginning to throb.

Trevor hesitated, then pulled out another chair and gingerly lowered himself into it. "Is he always like that?" he asked with raw intensity.

"What do you mean, like that?" she shot back, her nerves still on edge. "He was upset. He had a right to be."

"Sure, he had a right to be upset, but he was acting like a spoiled brat who wasn't getting his way. He had no right talking to you the way he did. If he'd been a few years younger, I would have turned him over my knee."

Jillian felt her control snap. No one criticized her son. No one. "Don't you ever touch him! I've never spanked Jason, and I never will." She looked around angrily. "This was a mistake. I can see that now. I should have let you take me to court. There were things I could have told the judge, too. Like how you asked me to marry you and then didn't have the guts to tell me in person that you'd changed your mind. What kind of an example is that for a boy?"

Beneath his skin, the thick muscles of his forearm slowly tightened into a hard potent bulge as he clenched his fist. "We're going to get past this, Jillian." Trevor raised his voice slightly. "Right now."

At his harsh command her gaze flew to his face, and alarm raced down her spine. His expression was hard, and his eyes were filled with some intense emotion she didn't dare analyze.

"Say what you have to say," he continued in a harsh voice. "All of it. Hit me if it will make you feel better, but get that damn poison out of your system." His fist slammed the table, and she jumped.

"Don't you dare tell me what to do. Don't you *dare*!" Her lips trembled and her stomach heaved. She felt scalded from head to toe, and it was his fault.

"Then back off, Jill! Damn it, give me a chance to show you that I'm sorry for what I did to you—and to our son." His eyes sparked with barely contained fury and something that looked like frustration.

"I am."

"The hell you are! Every chance you get, you aim one of your acid little remarks at my head."

"You deserve it."

"No, I do not," he said in an emphatic voice. "I've paid for what I did, Jill. More than you can ever imagine. And I'll be damned if I'll let you put me through any more hell for a mistake that neither of us can change. The past is finished. History. And that's the way it's going to stay."

Jillian gripped the edge of the table. "Get out of my house."

"No." His hand trapped her. "Look, Jill," he said, making a visible effort to control his temper. "We've both made mistakes. I hurt you badly. I know that. But how do you think I feel, knowing you deliberately denied me my son?"

His voice vibrated with anger, but his eyes were hollow. He'd been hurt, too.

"Even if I'd put your name on his birth certificate, it wouldn't have mattered. You made it very plain you didn't want to hear from me again—ever. I couldn't even have sent you a birth announcement, remember?"

His hand tightened, and she winced. "I told you why I did that. I wasn't in any shape to deal with ... problems."

Jillian inhaled swiftly. "You're absolutely right, Trevor. An illegitimate baby would certainly have been a problem."

His jaw colored. "That's not what I meant, and you know it."

"Do I?"

Trevor sighed. "This isn't getting us anywhere."

"I couldn't agree more. Let's drop the whole thing," Jillian said stiffly. "If you'll let go of my arm, I'll get the food."

She started to get up, but his big hand moved to her wrist and tugged her back into her seat. The chair was hard against her bare thighs, and her hand felt numb.

"Can we try to put all that behind us, Jill? Can we try to be friends, for our son's sake?"

Sharp, tingling shivers shot up her arm, and she tried to jerk away, but Trevor's fingers tightened around her wrist. He exerted just enough pressure to keep her from escaping.

Jillian stared in stony silence at the convoluted oak grain beneath the spot where he held her. Fifteen years of pride and anger and hurt tumbled in her brain, colliding with some new and as yet unnamed feeling.

"Please, Jill," he said in a gruff voice when she remained silent. His fingers slid past her wrist to capture her hand. His grip was warm and possessive.

"I don't know, Trevor," she answered as honestly as she could. "I just don't know what I'm thinking or feeling right now. So much has happened in a short time."

"Will you at least think about it?" His fingers tightened just enough to convey his urgency.

"Yes," she said, because she couldn't seem to help herself. "I'll think about it.

His jaw tightened, and he released her hand. They sat in strained silence for heartbeats before Trevor pushed himself to his feet and began picking up the jagged pieces of the shattered vase.

Chapter 7

The air was steaming hot. Jason had asked Trevor to lower the top of the convertible, and the sun beat directly down on their heads.

By the time Trevor had driven the twelve miles to the turn-off, Jillian's forehead was beaded with sweat beneath her visor, and the front of her playsuit was sticking to her skin.

"There's Big Pine Road. You turn to the right," she said as the Jaguar rounded another hairpin curve on the twisting mountain road.

Behind the aviator sunglasses, Trevor frowned. "It says Clayton Clinic on the sign."

"Miracle Lake is just past the clinic on the edge of that stand of Douglas fir. Addie—Dr. Franklin—built the clinic here because the water of the lake is supposed to have healing qualities."

Trevor glanced across the console, his brows lifting above the gold rims of his dark glasses. "Hence the name, Miracle Lake. Sounds like Dr. Franklin has a sense of humor."

Jillian nodded. "She claims it was only whimsy—and a good deal on the land. But Addie has a strong mystical streak in her, and I have a hunch she believes in the power of suggestion, if not in the waters themselves."

"She could be right. I've seen guys in the unit make remarkable progress once they finally believed it was possible."

Jillian stared at him. Once he'd told her that the only things he believed in were himself, the U.S. Navy and a strong left hook.

"Are you saying you believe in miracles?"

He flicked her a brief smile. "Yes, I do, but only as a result of a lot of damn hard work."

Silence fell between them. The tires hummed on the cracked pavement, and the scenery whipped by in a gray-green blur. She inhaled slowly, savoring the pungent smell of the mountain sage and pine.

The summer was nearly finished, and soon the tall trees lining the road would be bare. By Thanksgiving there would be snow halfway down the slopes, and by Christmas the streets of Clayton would be lined with dirty piles of plowed drifts.

Where would Trevor be at Christmas? she wondered, twisting restlessly in the low bucket seat. Where had he been for the past fifteen Christmases?

He wouldn't be here, that was one thing she knew for certain. She wouldn't be able to bear it. Even now, she could never listen to the familiar carols without feeling as though she were being torn apart inside. It was only because of Jason that she celebrated at all.

"Hey, look. There's Mike's dad in front of the clinic," Jason called suddenly from the back seat. He released the seat belt that Trevor had insisted he wear and leaned forward.

"Stop for a minute," Jillian said with a frown. "I think something's wrong."

Trevor gave her a quick glance, then flipped on the signal and pulled into the circular driveway leading to the clinic. The sheriff's black-and-white Blazer was parked in front of the wide glass doors. Mel stood behind it, one booted foot resting on the reinforced bumper, a small notebook balanced on his knee.

As Trevor pulled the convertible to a stop next to him, the sheriff looked up and scowled. His expression turned speculative when he caught sight of Jillian.

"What's wrong, Mel?" she asked quickly, absently clutching the edge of the door. The metal was blistering hot, and she snatched her hand away.

His lip curled into an ugly and strangely triumphant smile. "I'll tell you what's wrong," he muttered as the heel of his boot hit the pavement with a hard thump. "At approximately 4:00 a.m. this morning, two men wearing ski masks overpowered Mrs. Montoya, the night charge nurse, and took her keys to the drug cabinet. Cleaned it out. She's in shock, and Adrian says she might have a concussion."

Jillian gasped. "They hit her?"

"Hell, yes, they hit her! With a flashlight, she says." Mel closed his notebook and shoved it into his back pocket.

"How is she?"

Carmen Montoya was a friend, as well as a fellow officer in the Clayton High School PTA. Her son, Ramon, was in Jason's class.

"She has a hell of a headache, and she's sick to her stomach." The sheriff frowned. "I've been back three times to see her, but this was the first time she could remember anything. She's still pretty upset, so I didn't push her too hard."

"Does Mrs. Montoya know who they were?" Jason asked from the back seat. "I mean, do you have any, uh, suspects?"

He sounded boyishly eager, as though this were better than any TV show. Mel's expression softened marginally as he leaned over to cuff Jason's chin lightly with a meaty fist.

"Hey, sport, sounds like you and Mike are just alike," he said with a grin. "Always interested in hearing about the bad guys." His expression sobered. "Carmen says one was big and husky, and the other was taller and skinny. She thought they might be young, although it was hard to tell, because the one who talked disguised his voice." Mel grunted in disgust. "It don't take much detecting to figure out where they came from." He jerked his thumb in the direction of Wilderness Horizons.

"If you're implying the thieves came from Horizons, Sheriff, you're wrong." Trevor's voice was silky and far too calm, and it made the skin of Jillian's bare legs shiver. From the corner of her eye she could see Jason's head swivel toward his father.

"The odds say I'm not, Mr. Markus. There hasn't been a drug theft in Clayton since it was founded by old Josiah Clayton himself. Not one that's on the books, anyway. And then, all of a sudden, this so-called treatment center of yours comes to town and two weeks later the clinic's hit."

Cobb's angry blue gaze shifted from Trevor to Jillian. "We got us a problem here. I can feel it."

He tugged on the bill of his cap and hiked up his sagging trousers. He turned to go, but stopped when Trevor called his name in an icy voice.

"If you intend to charge anyone at Horizons, you'd better be damn sure you can back up any and all allegations you make, or I'll personally see to it that you're finished in this town or anyplace else."

Jillian could almost smell Mel's anger.

"Oh, yeah? Well, maybe I'd better do some checking up on you, hotshot. Maybe you got a few skeletons in your closet you don't want anybody to find."

Mel swung his attention to Jason, and his mouth twisted into a humorless smile. "Mike said you called this morning, sport. Something about your dead daddy showin' up alive?"

Jason looked sick. "I told him not to say nothing," he mumbled, twisting his seat belt over and over in his pale, bony fingers.

Jillian reached between the seats and covered his hand with hers. Jason flinched and jerked his hand away. "Leave me alone," he said in a strangled voice.

Trevor knew he was very close to smashing a quick left into Cobb's beefy face. He could almost hear the distinctive crack as the man's nose shattered, could almost smell the blood as it spurted.

He glanced down at the flattened knuckles of his left hand. From that first summer when he'd gone to work in the shipyard at sixteen, he'd had to fight. As the son of the owner and big for his age, he'd been a target for the rough, hard-bitten steelworkers who'd delighted in goading him into a brawl.

He'd taken their insults and their abuse for as long as he could, and then he'd learned to use his fists to shut them up. But he'd never learned to handle the rage behind his fists. It had taken a lot of hard living to teach him that, and it had been a long time since he'd used his fists to solve his problems.

But it was tempting.

"If that's your way of asking if Jason's my son, Cobb, he is, and I'm damn proud of it. And I'm . . . honored that Jillian is his mother."

Trevor sharpened his voice to a slicing edge. "Now, if you have a problem with me personally, we can go to the wall any time you want. But leave Jillian and Jason out of it, or I swear, you'll be working security in the city dump before I'm through with you." He never took an oath lightly, and he let the man see the truth in his eyes.

Mel took a step backward. "I'm not done with you yet, Markus. Not by a long shot." He set his jaw, then turned and climbed into his Blazer. The tires left black smears of rubber on the pavement as he roared off.

Shaken, Jillian stared down at her fingers. The crimson enamel on her nails shimmered like drops of blood in the sun. "You wanted to hit him, didn't you?" she asked in a hollow voice.

Trevor exhaled heavily. "Do you blame me?" He was visibly trying to calm down.

"No," she said emphatically. "Mel Cobb is a pig, in every sense of the word."

She glanced over her shoulder. Jason was staring at his father, his jaw slack, his eyes wide. She'd never seen him look so lost.

"Jason, Mike's dad was way out of line," she said in an urgent voice. "He's just . . . upset because he didn't want Horizons to come here, and the council overruled him. He's trying to take it out on all of us."

Jason's face closed up. "I don't wanna talk about it," he mumbled in a barely audible voice.

Jillian bit her lip, then nodded. "We'll drop it for now, Jase, but we have to talk about it sooner or later."

Jason slumped back against the seat and crossed his arms. He didn't look at her.

She and Trevor exchanged looks. Only the faint deepening of the lines fanning into his temple showed he was still angry.

"Don't let a redneck like Cobb bother you, Jason," he said, starting the car. "He's just a bully. He likes to hurt people because it makes him feel like more of a man, but inside he's weak and scared."

Trevor glanced in the mirror. Jason was staring straight ahead.

"He'll tell the whole town that . . . that I'm a bastard," the boy said in empty voice.

Jillian gasped and looked at Trevor.

"Legally, that's the truth," Trevor said matter-of-factly. "You can let it bother you, or you can shrug it off. Your choice." Jillian wasn't sure whether he was speaking to Jason or her, or to both of them.

Jason's mouth twisted. "I wish you'd hit him!"

Trevor sighed. "That wouldn't have changed the facts. And it would have landed me in jail for assault." A grim look that Jillian hadn't seen before flashed across his face, and the powerful car shot forward with a low-pitched growl. "Somehow I don't think that's the kind of example a father's supposed to set for his son. Do you?"

Jason slumped back against the seat. "How should I know?" he muttered. "I never had one before."

They ate in the shade of a lightning-scarred Douglas fir growing at the edge of the wide beach. Tiny flakes of mica sparkled in the sun, turning the sand black in spots.

The heat was oppressive, even in the shade, and the air was heavy with the kind of dense humidity Jillian had rarely experienced in the high country. She was acutely uncomfortable, but the weather was only part of the reason. She was still shaken by Jason's reaction to Mel's ugly attack.

Reuben Anderson had used that word once in her presence, and at that moment whatever love she'd felt for her stepfather had died. She'd kept his name as a courtesy to her mother, but she'd never again thought of Reuben as her father. She realized now that she'd even blamed Trevor for that. She'd blamed him for a lot of things.

Munching on a cookie, she rested her back against the cooler. She'd been too nervous to eat, and Jason had only picked at his fried chicken and potato salad. Trevor had been the only one whose appetite hadn't been affected by their run-in with Mel. In fact, he'd eaten his share and most of hers.

"*Beat the Rap* is a dud, a real downer album," Jason muttered, slashing the sand by the blanket with a plastic knife. "I don't like any of the songs. I don't know how you can say they're any good."

Jillian sensed he was being deliberately unpleasant, but she didn't have the heart to reprimand him, especially since Trevor seemed to be handling him just fine without her help.

He sat with one leg raised, his wide forearm balanced easily on his knee, his hand relaxed and open. But there was a restless aura surrounding him, as though he was having trouble sitting still, like a mountain cat she'd once seen in a game warden's cage.

"I don't suppose you liked *Dirty Dealings*, either." Trevor finished his Coke and crumpled the can in his fist before tossing it into the trash sack.

"It was bogus."

"You have to admire Glen Trapp's guitar work, though."

Trevor leaned forward and tugged off his shirt, exposing his muscular brown chest. An intricate silver medallion hung from a heavy chain around his neck, and his chest hair was the same mix of gray and blond as his eyebrows.

That soft masculine fur had been sun-bleached to blond when she'd given him his daily rubdown after the cast had come off. His muscles, then as now, had been as hard as seasoned oak, his skin slightly rough from his years of exposure to the sun and the sea. She looked away, concentrating on the jagged outline of the trees against the sky.

"Yeah, Glen's hot. I wish I could play like that." Jason stabbed the knife into the sand and broke it in two. He frowned in disgust and dug the point from the sand.

"I could teach you if you like."

"You can play the guitar?" Jason looked grudgingly impressed.

"Some. Part of my misspent youth was spent at the piano teacher's doing penance for my sins, so I can read music. I taught myself to play the guitar when I was in the hospital."

"You didn't mention that in your letters," Jillian blurted out.

Dusky color flooded his face, and she immediately regretted her words. She'd sounded as though she didn't believe him, when she'd only meant to convey surprise.

Trevor shrugged casually, but his jaw was tight. "I guess I didn't think it was important enough to mention."

She gave him a conciliatory smile. "It's just that I'm surprised, that's all."

Trevor nodded, but he didn't return her smile. "It kept my mind off a lot of things I didn't want to think about."

Like marrying me? she wondered.

Suddenly Jason looked around. "Mom, I need to go to the bathroom, okay?"

"Sure, okay." The public rest rooms were at the far end of the lake, half hidden by a cluster of young pines.

"I'll be back in a minute." Jason avoided looking at his father as he slid his sunglasses over his nose and picked up the black backpack that went with him wherever he went.

Jillian watched him go in silence. He was getting taller. In a few more months she'd be looking up at him.

Trevor folded both arms over his knees and watched Jason walk along the edge of the lake. The boy's head was down, and his shoulders were slumped. "Round one," he muttered with a sigh. "I think I lost."

"More like a draw," she said grudgingly. "The next time will be easier."

"I have a feeling I have a long way to go."

"What did you expect?" she asked out of curiosity, noticing the way he rubbed his thumb over his upper lip. He had done that in the hospital whenever he was having trouble expressing his feelings.

"Just about what I got, actually. I'm not exactly the prodigal dad, although—" he lifted his empty plate "—this has to have been as good as any fatted calf." His tone was so ironic that she had to laugh.

"Have another cookie. Chocolate chips are good for a bruised ego."

Trevor grunted, but he took her advice, devouring the crumbly cookie in two bites. "You're a good cook, Jill. Better than good."

"Actually, these came from the bakery next door."

Trevor's eyes cooled. "My mistake."

He leaned back against the rough trunk and closed his eyes. Sweat glistened on his forehead, and his hairline was damp. His face was wiped clean of expression, but there was a tiny pulse throbbing in his temple.

Jillian drew her legs to her chest and linked her arms around her shins. Above her head the leaves rustled gently. It was a lonely sound. "I'm . . . sorry, Trevor," she said stiffly. "The Santa Ana makes everyone uptight."

His thick, sandy lashes rose slowly. His eyes were still cool, but his lower lip relaxed into a wry curve. "Apology accepted."

He picked up an apple, looked at it and put it down again. He extended his leg and rested his palm against his thigh. The restlessness she'd seen in him earlier seemed more pronounced.

"Was Jason a good kid? Growing up, I mean," he asked suddenly, rubbing his knee with his palm.

"Not exactly. One day, when I was still in the Navy, I came home early to take him to his pediatrician for his checkup. I gave him his bath and dressed him in his best pair of shorts. I'd gotten him a new pair of shoes the day before, and they were still nice and white."

She glanced at Trevor to see if he was following her. He was listening intently, a half smile tugging at his mouth. "What happened then?"

She sighed. "While I was changing out of my uniform, Jason decided to go wading—in the john."

Trevor's jaw dropped. "The john? You mean the toilet?" He looked as though he couldn't believe what he'd just heard.

"Yes, that's exactly what I mean. He was having a wonderful time, splashing water all over the bathroom and himself. Of course, his brand-new, terribly expensive shoes were ruined."

Trevor laughed. "He sounds like he was a little terror." She could hear regret in his voice, and pain. He'd missed so much.

"He was, actually. By the time he was eighteen months he could climb anything in the house." Her expression softened. "But he was also very loving, and he loved to cuddle."

Trevor's brows wagged. "Good man."

Memory arched between them, and the sounds of the lake faded. Trevor had loved to cuddle, too, as often as he could talk her into climbing in next to him. His gaze flicked to her chest, and she knew he was remembering the nights when he'd fallen asleep with his cheek pillowed on her breast.

Damn you! she thought, feeling the welcome anger rise in her again. Damn you for saying you loved me when you didn't. Damn you for leaving me.

She took a shallow breath. Easy, Jill, she told herself. They were here because of Jason, and that was the only reason.

"What about you?" she asked coolly, deliberately changing the subject. "How come you're not the president of Markus Shipbuilding, the way you'd planned when you found out you couldn't fly again?"

"How do you know I'm not?"

Jillian removed her visor and wiped her brow with a paper napkin. "There was an article on you in the *Clayton Clarion*. It said you were an engineer."

Trevor shifted restlessly against the tree trunk. "After I resigned my commission, I found I had a problem staying in one place for more than a few months at a time. Since I had a degree in engineering from the Academy, I decided to find something that would let me do most of my work outdoors. My brother Brian runs the yard for Pop now."

"And Horizons?"

Silence stretched between them until she began to suspect he wasn't going to answer. Finally he sighed. "I, uh, told you about my brother Tim? That he was killed when his speedboat hit a log in the Sound and flipped?"

Jillian nodded. His resonant baritone had a hollow tone she'd never heard before.

"He was only nineteen, you said."

"Yeah. He had his whole life ahead of him, but Timmy never wanted to wait for anything. He lived for excitement, for the next high. He loved fast boats, faster cars, and even faster women. We were a lot alike."

His brief smile was bleak. "Then someone turned him on to uppers. Speed, they called it then. Timmy loved the irony of it. He wanted to go fast, he told me once, and he used speed to get him there. He thought that was funny as hell."

Jillian leaned forward, a sick feeling of surprise filling her. "Your brother used drugs?"

"As many as he could get."

"How terrible," she said sadly.

"Yeah, it was terrible, all right. He was high when he lost control of his boat and crashed. The coroner said the concussion killed him instantly."

Jillian thought of the methamphetamine on her shelves. These days the drug was rarely prescribed, and only in cases of extreme obesity.

"When I was in college, I lived on diet pills during finals," she said quietly. "Everyone did. In those days no one knew they were addictive, not even the doctors."

Trevor picked up a pinecone from the sand and, with one violent movement of his powerful arm, threw it toward the lake. It splashed into the water and sank.

"During training the doctor on the carrier passed them out like candy." He hesitated, then added flatly, "I never used them. They made me sick."

Jillian's mind flew back in time. Trevor had gotten violently ill the first time the doctor had prescribed a synthetic painkiller. Morphine, because it was derived from the poppy, had been the only drug that hadn't caused an allergic reaction in his system.

"So you started a drug treatment center because of your brother?"

Trevor shifted again. His face was tight, and the tiny pulse had started again in his temple. "Yes, because of Tim," he said. "And . . . because of the guys who came back from Nam hooked on one drug or another. Horizons can't help everyone, but we do what we can."

His voice carried a harsh note of finality that Jillian couldn't ignore. A moment ago his large hand had been open and relaxed on his heavy thigh. Now, however, it was clenched into a fist, and the tendons of his thick wrist bulged. She suspected that talking about his brother was something he didn't do very often or, for that matter, very easily.

"I'm sorry about your brother," she said softly. And she was. But she was also very worried. Involuntarily her gaze drifted toward the far side of the lake.

Jason, the red rims of his sunglasses a bright splotch of color against his pale face, was wading along the shore, kicking water high into the air the way he used to do as a small boy.

"Trevor, don't tell Jason about your brother until he gets a chance to know you better. Okay?"

"Why not?"

Jillian heard the deceptive note of calm in his voice, but she took a deep breath and plunged ahead. Protecting Jason was more important than sparing Trevor's feelings.

"He's going to have enough to handle, just getting used to the fact that his father wants to be a part of his life."

"And you think knowing his uncle was an addict would upset him?"

"Yes. It's only natural that he would want to be, well, proud of his new family."

Trevor stared at her impassively for several seconds. Then his big shoulders lifted in a shrug. "Whatever you say, Jill. I guess no one wants to admit he has a junkie in the family."

The raw note in his voice caused her exposed skin to prickle, but she knew she was right to insist. Jason was her only concern.

Silence fell between them. Because he was so big, he took up more than his share of the blanket. Consequently his thigh was only inches from hers, and his shoulder was less than a sigh away from touching hers.

Jillian could feel the tension rising in his body, and a sudden fear shot through her. He'd allowed her to set the rules for his visit this time. And maybe he'd let her call the shots the next time. But after that, she had a feeling Trevor Markus would begin to make his own rules.

We'll just see about that, she thought, frowning. She felt her chest rise and fall under the thin cotton of her outfit. She hadn't been so aware of her body in years.

She felt a sudden shiver, and she looked up to find him watching her with smoldering eyes. He wanted her. She couldn't have been more certain if he'd shouted the words in her face.

"How about a swim?" he asked brusquely. "It's damn hot." Without waiting for an answer, he stripped off his shoes and socks and stood up stiffly, arching his back slowly, one vertebra at a time, like the mountain cat he resembled.

He held out a hand. "Well?"

Jillian ignored his hand as she got to her feet. "Miracle Lake is always cold. You probably won't like it."

"I'll swim fast," he said with a trace of sarcasm.

Trevor stripped off the medallion and tucked it into a fold in his shirt, then reached for the top button of his fly.

"What do you think you're doing?" she asked quickly.

"Undressing," he drawled. He was angry at her, and she didn't know why. "It's customary when a guy goes swimming to shed his jeans first."

Jillian glanced up and down the beach nervously. There was a family of six about twenty yards further along the perimeter, and another group of children and adults across the lake. No one was paying attention to the two people by the scarred tree.

At her worried look, he relented. In spite of the heat, cold beads of sweat dotted his forehead, and his muscles were painfully tight. He couldn't sit still a minute longer. If she wouldn't swim with him, he'd swim alone. He was used to it.

"I wore my suit, if that's what you're worried about."

Her cheeks warmed. "So did I," she muttered, unzipping the front of her playsuit to expose her one-piece suit.

"So you did," he said in a dry voice, watching her intently.

Her swimsuit was white, with a slashing diagonal of emerald across one hip, and a strapless top. She'd bought it on a dare from Adrian one day when they'd been shopping in Sacramento, and today was the first time that she'd worn it.

Suddenly, as his eyes warmed into violet golden flames beneath his angry brows, she wished she'd stuck with her ratty old tank suit. At least it covered slightly more of her generous curves.

She didn't look at Trevor as she stepped out of the jumpsuit and slipped out of her sandals, but she could feel his gaze on her. Carefully she folded the crinkled cotton, lining up the seams with slow precision, listening for the sound of his zipper.

It didn't take long.

"Ready?" he said in a voice that sounded oddly rigid. She put her bundle next to his shirt and looked up. He was wearing black boxer trunks, and they were very tight, hiding little of his potent physique.

Something primitive and hot uncurled inside her. And then she saw his face. He was flushed with embarrassment.

"Pretty bad, huh?" he said grimly, glancing down at his legs. He rubbed his hand against his hip, as though it suddenly hurt. Both legs were brutally scarred from his hips to his shins, the puckered scar tissue very white against his tan.

Jillian forced her features into a nonchalant smile, but inside she was sick. Not because of the way he looked, but because of the grindingly hard hours she knew he'd put in just to make those battered legs work again.

"If you mean, are your legs pretty, no, they're not. But I was there when they choppered you in, remember, and I know that you almost lost those nice long legs."

He went very still. "I remember. You told me I'd walk again, even when the doctors said I wouldn't."

"Doctors only work with muscles and bone. Nurses work with people. I . . . I knew you'd make it."

"For a long time you were the only one."

If he touched her, Trevor thought, he'd touch her there, where the top of her suit met the soft swell of her creamy breasts. But if he touched her now, he'd never be able to stop.

A hot pain traveled through his gut to settle between his thighs. I hope to hell that water's as cold as she says it is, he thought with a hard, silent wince.

"Ready?" he asked.

"Ready."

Jillian's legs felt stiff, and the sand burned the soles of her feet, making her walk faster and faster until she was nearly running. She dropped her towel above the waterline and walked into the lake, which wasn't just cold; it was frigid. Jillian felt her teeth begin to chatter the moment the water closed over the top of her suit.

Trevor was walking beside her, a good three feet away. He was looking toward the far end of the lake, where Jason was lying in the shade of a stunted willow, staring at the sky.

"Doesn't he swim?" he asked, glancing over at her.

"Not much. As a little boy, he used to be afraid of the water. I tried, but I could never get him to put his face under."

Trevor nodded. "I was like that, until one day my dad pitched me off the deck of our house into the Sound. I hit bottom like a rock and had to fight my way to the surface."

Jillian stopped walking and stared at him. "That's a terrible thing for a father to do!"

Trevor glanced at Jason again. Fleetingly he wondered what his son was thinking. The boy was too quiet, too self-contained, almost morose at times. He needed to laugh more, but maybe that would come when he was used to having a father around periodically.

"Pop had tried everything else he could think of to get me to learn, but I'd refused to try. He was afraid I'd walk out on the deck and fall in, so he did what he had to do to keep me from drowning someday."

"So he was being cruel to be kind?"

"Exactly."

She shook her head. "That's not my way. Today is the first time I've ever forced Jason to do something against his will, and you saw how much he resented it. I'm still not sure it was for the best."

"I guess I look at the bottom line. I might be dead now if my dad hadn't thrown me off that pier." He gestured toward the diving raft in the middle of the lake. "Wanna race?" he said, lifting one brow in challenge.

Jillian felt a wicked stab of pleasure. Swimming was one of the few sports she did well, and she was going to enjoy beating him. "Loser cleans up?"

Trevor gave her a measuring look. "You're on."

Before he could seal the bet with a handshake, she lunged forward and began swimming away from him with long, graceful strokes.

"Hey," he shouted, then grinned. He'd been taken. The lady was a fighter, all right, and it looked as though she intended to beat the bejabbers out of him.

He dived forward and began to swim. It took half a dozen strokes before the muscles of his back began to loosen. And another half dozen to find a smooth stroke that didn't twist his spine. By then Jillian was far ahead.

He put his head down and pulled as hard as he could, but she touched the side of the raft a full stroke ahead of him. When he surfaced, she was holding on to the raft and gasping for air, water dripping from her tangled auburn curls.

"You lose," she said, laughing triumphantly.

Trevor watched the sun tip her lashes with pure gold as she gazed directly at him. In the bright light her eyes were a flawless apple-green, and filled with the sunny, innocently sensual glow he remembered so vividly.

"Uh-uh. You jumped the gun." He wiped the lake water from his face and enjoyed the look of mock indignation that wrinkled her freckled nose.

She crossed her arms and glared at him. "I did not!"

Her shoulders were tawny gold above the white suit and dappled with drops of water. The exertion had pulled the suit down a half inch or so, and the white skin below the tan line drew his gaze. His body stirred to life in spite of the cold.

Trevor managed to raise his gaze to her lips. They were slightly blue, and her teeth were beginning to chatter. "You'd better get out of the water," he said. "Here, I'll give you a boost."

Jillian didn't argue. The water was making the skin below the water numb, while above the surface, his heated gaze was making her steam.

His hands bracketed her waist, his fingers exerting just enough pressure to make her aware of his strength. Ignoring the flare of pleasure shooting along her skin under the wet suit, she put both hands on top of the raft and started to heave herself aboard. Unexpectedly the heavy structure lurched violently as she put her weight on it. Off balance, she toppled backward and fell hard against Trevor's chest. His hands splayed against her breasts as he grabbed for her again, and they both went under.

Wrapped together in a tangle of arms and legs they sank into the dark green void. Jillian opened her eyes and blinked against the stinging chill. The water was very clear, with black shadows below and sparkling diamonds of light above.

There was no sound.

The moment her gaze found his, Trevor's arms tightened convulsively, and his lips came down on hers. In spite of the cold, his mouth was hot and insistent, his tongue thrusting arrogantly between her lips.

Pleasure shot through her, filling her, and for an instant she wrapped her legs around his thighs and returned his kiss. His chest was hard, his arousal startling. She rubbed against him, feeling the rough warmth of his chest and legs. She was hot and cold and nearly breathless.

No, she thought. She didn't want this.

His hand tangled in her hair, and she felt a sharp tingle of pain. Her ears began to ring, and she pushed hard against his chest. He released her immediately, and she kicked toward the surface.

Trevor followed, furious with himself. He'd known better than to touch her. But when her soft body had slid against his, his resolve had weakened. And when she'd opened her eyes and looked at him underwater, he'd been lost.

"Don't ever do that again," she sputtered, gazing around angrily. Two bright spots of color dotted her cheekbones, and she was breathing hard. She'd wanted him, and she was furiously angry at herself for being a victim of her hormones. She knew better.

"The winner deserved a victory kiss." Trevor winced inwardly, but it was the best he could do. He was still feeling the impact of her breasts sliding down his bare chest and her thighs pressing against his.

Jillian's teeth were chattering so hard that she couldn't get out another word. Once he'd used that same teasing tone to order her to touch him, to run her fingers through the wiry thatch covering his wide chest, to play with his flat nipples, teasing them into hard little rocks under her fingertips. She'd loved the way she could make him groan before surrendering to the desire shaking her. And then his eyes would turn this same gold and he would wrap his strong arms around her so tightly that she couldn't breathe, just as he'd done a moment ago underwater.

She glared at him for a few seconds more, then began swimming furiously for the shore.

Damn, Trevor thought, watching her swim away from him. Over the years he'd learned to exercise rigorous control over his emotions. His only passion had been building bridges and skyscrapers and roads, each one carefully planned in meticulous detail, just like his days and nights.

But since Jill had come back into his life, he was having trouble handling anything but the most uncomplicated tasks. During the past two weeks it had taken a great deal of concentration on his part to keep from screwing up some very important projects.

Scowling, he muttered a harsh curse, followed by a little prayer for patience. It was going to be a long afternoon.

Jillian rested her head against the seat and closed her eyes. She was exhausted, and her head throbbed in rhythm with the tires droning monotonously on the rutted pavement. Even the thunder of Prokofiev playing on the Jaguar's tape deck sounded discordant filtered through the pain in her temples.

It was nearly five-thirty, but the sun was still warm, and the wind flowing through the open car stung her cheeks. She'd been a nervous wreck from the moment that Trevor had kissed her.

He hadn't been her first lover, but he'd been the first one to show her the difference between sex and making love. With him, she'd felt replenished. With him, she'd learned what it was like to give totally and completely and to receive that same devotion in return. She'd never felt that with any other man. And now she suspected she never would. The sense of loss that had started the night she'd reread his letters grew stronger.

"Is it okay to park here? It says loading zone."

Trevor's husky voice jerked her from her inner reverie. He swung the convertible to the curb behind her bright red mini-truck parked near the back door of the pharmacy.

She sat up, rubbing her eyes. "No problem. Mel's pretty lenient on weekends."

His lips tightened. "Don't kid yourself. He'd like nothing better than to slap a parking ticket on me. I'm the enemy, remember?"

Jillian sighed. "Clayton doesn't have enough deputies to enforce the parking laws, even though we lose money that way.

That's why we don't offer a free day on the meters. We figure it balances out.''

"Sounds like some of the countries where I've had to negotiate contracts.''

She glanced at the steps leading to her apartment. Trevor had carried the cooler down for her. He would expect to carry it back up. And then what?

"Mom, can I go to Mike's now?'' Jason asked from the back seat.

"Not now, Jason. And carry the cooler upstairs, okay?'' Jillian saw the frown form between Trevor's shaggy brows as he rested his arm on the wheel and watched her.

Jason unfastened his seat belt. "Can't Trevor do it? Me and Mike made plans to go to Truckee to play vids as soon as I got back.''

Jillian gathered her purse and her tote bag, avoiding Trevor's gaze. The tension between them had grown nearly unbearable. "Video games can wait. You have homework to do,'' she said firmly.

"It's done. I did it this morning.''

Jillian refrained from commenting on the kind of work he must have produced while that terrible music had blared. Instead she gave him a measuring look. His eyes were hidden behind his dark lenses, but he was smiling slightly. And he was bouncing back and forth on the seat like a little boy who'd been confined for too long.

"Okay, you can go, but carry that thing upstairs for me first,'' she said, relenting. The day had been difficult for all three of them, and Jason had tried to be congenial, at least for a while. When he'd returned from the far side of the lake, he'd been sullen and withdrawn, spending the rest of the afternoon dozing on the blanket.

"Great! I'm outta here.'' Jason opened the door and started to get out, but Trevor leaned through the opening between the seats and stopped him.

"The guys at Horizons are starting a soccer tournament tomorrow, and one of the teams is shorthanded,'' he said, keeping his hand on Jason's shoulder. "Your mom tells me you're a great goalie, and we could really use you to fill in.'' He grinned. "You can be on the team I'm coaching.''

Jason glanced away. "I have school.''

"The recreation period is from four to six, plenty of time for you to make it. I'll come and pick you up if you'd like."

Jason's blank gaze shifted to Jillian, and she smiled encouragingly. "I think it's a good idea, sweetie. Since you've quit the team, you're not getting nearly as much exercise as you should."

He shrugged. "I got better things to do with my time than hang around a bunch of dumb losers."

Jillian opened her mouth to reprimand him, but Trevor beat her to it.

"Pay attention, Jason, because I'm only going to say this once. I don't *ever* again want to hear you refer to the residents of Horizons as losers." He didn't raise his voice, but the flinty hardness was more frightening to Jillian than the loudest shout.

"They're boys like you who've made some bad mistakes and are trying the best way they can to put their lives back together again. And that's damn hard work, son, because every day they wake up with a craving in their belly that can't even be described. Every night they go to bed clean is a major victory."

He sighed, and Jillian could tell he was trying to contain his anger. "They don't deserve your contempt, or mine, or Sheriff Cobb's, and until you've been in the places where they've been and fought the same fight they're fighting, you don't have a right to judge."

Jason went completely white beneath his sunburn. He stared at Trevor in frozen silence. Suddenly, before Jillian could utter a word, he scrambled out of the car and took off running.

"Damn it to hell!" Trevor exclaimed into the stunned silence. "I guess I blew that royally."

He pounded his fist on the gearshift, and Jillian felt some of her anger dissipate.

"I can build a road that will last for a hundred years, but I can't seem to handle one fourteen-year-old kid." He narrowed his eyes and looked at her. "Go ahead. Say what you're thinking. This time I deserve it."

Jillian opened her mouth, then closed it again. How did he know what she was thinking?

"He's picked up that attitude about Horizons from Mel Cobb," she admitted grudgingly. "Mel's son, Mike, has become his best friend."

"Terrific."

Her temper flared again, and she glared at him. "If I forbid him to spend time with Mike, he'll just dig in harder."

Trevor ran his hand through his hair. The silver thickness had dried in a tousled cap that gleamed in the sun. "You're right. That's exactly what he'd do."

Jillian was having trouble staying mad. He seemed so discouraged, and he'd tried so hard.

"Sometimes, when I hear a statement like Jason's," he told her cynically, "I think we should just round up all the addicts in this country and shoot them. It would be kinder in the long run."

"He's just young. He doesn't understand about prejudice."

"Do you?" he shot back.

"Yes, Trevor, I do," she said angrily. "I'm an unwed mother, remember?"

Trevor took off his glasses and rubbed his stinging eyes. "Sorry, that question was out of line," he muttered, tossing the glasses onto the dashboard. "This hasn't been the easiest day I've ever had."

In the space of five minutes he'd managed to alienate his son and put the anger back in Jillian's eyes. Great going, Markus, he thought grimly. Keep this up, and neither one of them will ever speak to you again.

"C'mon," he told her brusquely, pushing open his door. "I'll help you with the picnic stuff."

Chapter 8

The living room was stifling and smelled musty. While Jillian hurried to open the windows, Trevor carried the cooler to the kitchen. After setting it on the floor by the sink, he rolled his shoulders to release the knots, then ran some water and splashed his hot face.

When he returned to the living room, Jillian was standing by the window overlooking the street. She was staring at the horizon, where the sun was dipping below the tree line like a brilliant orange balloon.

His body stirred, pushing insistently against the tight denim. He'd been without a woman for a long time. Too long.

And she was beautiful, standing there in the golden light. He wanted her. Now.

Violently. Possessively. Totally.

Trevor wiped the drops of water from his jaw, then jammed his hands into his pockets. His jeans tightened over his loins, and he stiffened at the surge of blood that shot through him.

He'd thought that he had this leftover ache handled. But he'd been wrong. He wanted to possess her, to manacle her to him until she let him into her bed again.

But he wanted more than her body. He wanted some of that inner fire, that special one-of-a-kind spirit that had stayed with him even when she'd drifted into a painful memory.

These days he kept his feelings on a short rein, just the way he ran his companies, and he never thought about love. It wasn't a word he used anymore. Not for fifteen years. Most likely he'd never use it again.

But this power that Jillian had over him was different. Special. He didn't quite understand it. He wasn't sure he wanted to understand. Mostly he just knew he *wanted*. With her, he was out of control, and he knew how dangerous that could be. It had nearly killed him once. But there didn't seem to be anything he could do about this gut-deep need she excited in him—except wait it out.

"You took a big chance, talking to Jason like that," Jillian said, turning to look at him. "He may refuse to see you again."

He ambled toward her. "How would you feel about that?"

"I haven't decided." She crossed her arms over her chest and watched his rangy body fill up her cozy living room. He seemed too restless and too powerful to be contained by four walls.

He glanced toward the sofa, but he didn't sit down. Jillian saw the pinched look around his eyes and realized his back must be bothering him. But she couldn't afford to care.

"Robin said you were a tough negotiator," he said with a lazy half smile.

"Is that a criticism?"

He moved closer, pushing into her private space. "No."

Jillian held her ground. "Then why did it sound like one?"

"Damned if I know."

He reached out and took her hand, and she stiffened.

"Are you afraid of me, Jill?" His voice was sheathed in warm steel.

"No." She resisted the powerful urge to pull her fingers from his. She couldn't show fear, not to this man.

Thoughtfully he rubbed her empty ring finger with his thumb. "You could have married. Given Jason a stepfather to be proud of."

"Yes." Tiny shivers of sweet pleasure began shooting up her arm, making it hard to concentrate. It had been a long time since she'd been so aroused by a man's touch.

"Does that mean you never . . . found anyone special?"

"No . . . no one special."

His head was bent, his attention focused on her hand, but she could see the slight lessening of the tension along his jaw. His fingers folded over hers, and his thumb moved to her wrist. "Your pulse is racing so fast your skin feels hot," he said in a husky voice. His thumb moved in a slow circle. "Tell me what you're thinking to make your heart pound like that."

Thinking? Jill blinked. Didn't he know? Couldn't he see the way he upset her every time he came near her? Couldn't he feel the heat in her body?

Inside the small, hot room, the atmosphere changed as the silence lengthened. Every breath she took seemed to heighten the tension building inside her. "I'm ... not thinking anything," she said.

His hand tightened around hers. "Shame on you, Jill. You should know better than to tell a lie when a man has his hand on your wrist." He slid his hand up her arm to her shoulder. "I've thought about you every day since I saw you on that dais. I thought about ... kissing you again." Maybe if he gave in, he thought, just once, he could purge the ache from his body—and his soul.

"Don't. I'm warning you."

In the square across the street the birds were beginning to gather in the trees, and the sound of their chirping reminded her of the tiny nest in Tokyo. Trevor had been the one to wipe the tears from her eyes when the frail little bird had lost his fight. And Trevor had been the one who'd turned the cool reserve inside her to fire, making her a woman.

She swallowed the thickness in her throat and stared at him helplessly. What did he want from her? What kind of game was he playing?

"Angel."

His lips were whisper-soft as they took hers. His kiss was tender, without passion. His strong hands slid along her cheekbones and into her hair, cherishing her with their gentleness, and yet she could feel his restraint as his thumbs gently stroked the curve of her cheek.

His lips moved, tasting, nibbling. His breath mingled with hers, warm and moist against her mouth. He tasted good, like the chocolate chip cookies he'd finished off before they left.

"Relax, Jill," he whispered against her lips. "Relax and let it happen."

Jillian stiffened, but her knees felt weak. Gradually, without wanting to, she allowed her body to mold against his. Her arms encircled his hard torso, and her skin tingled as she slid her palms along the hard ridge of his spine.

His body was warm, his shirt damp where it rested against his skin, his muscles hard. He was lean and angular and rugged, all the things a man should be.

Trevor groaned as her hands explored his back, his spine, his hips. The moment her fingers slid under the waistband of his jeans, his kiss grew hard and insistent, as though he'd been waiting for her response.

The pleasure of that realization was sweet, like a stroll through a sunlit meadow in the early morning. She felt her soul unfolding like a tightly furled bud, eager for the heat of the sun.

His kisses became hot, insistent, and she met his arrogant demand with an equal intensity. She could feel the ripple of his muscular back under her palms as he pulled her hard against him. His wide chest crushed her breasts, and the pressure excited a delicious ache in her nipples.

She moaned and opened her mouth to him. His tongue slid inside, tentative at first, and then, when she welcomed him with the tip of her own, his kiss became possessive. She was hot, eager.

A harsh groan shuddered through him. His breath was wonderfully moist against her skin as he trailed hot, urgent kisses along the curve of her cheekbone.

"So damn long," he whispered almost incoherently.

Too long, she echoed mindlessly. She wanted to forget the long, empty years. She wanted reality to fade until there was only Trevor. Only his hard body and demanding lips.

She wanted him, blindly, senselessly. Only him. She didn't want to remember. She wouldn't remember, not while his hands were cupping her buttocks and pulling her against him intimately.

His legs moved, his thigh pushing between hers. The rough pressure of the hard muscle beneath the two layers of cloth sent ripples of moist warmth deep into her center. She began to move, answering his primitive male call.

Glorious, she thought, running her hands over the magnificent width of his shoulders, loving the power there, and the strength. Her warrior knight, her lover. He was that and more.

Giddy with sensual memory, eager to feel all of him again, she clung to him, pressing her body hard against his. She could feel his instant hard response, his raw male need. He hadn't forgotten. He still wanted her.

Warmth spread along the tawny surface of her skin, softening the last of her resistance. His fingers combed her hair, tugging on her scalp, and the sensation was exquisite.

Under her hands she felt his muscles harden, and he jerked against her. Jillian let her hands relax, her palms stroking his biceps until they bulged like burled redwood.

"Take me to bed, angel," Trevor whispered hoarsely against her throat. "I can't take much more of this."

To bed?

To make love? Or to have sex?

Fleetingly Jillian remembered the way it had been between them. But this time it would be different. This was only physical. And it would ruin the special memory of their times together, the only memory he hadn't tarnished.

She couldn't bear it. He'd taken everything else. He couldn't have that, too.

"Let me go, Trevor," she said in a strangled voice. "I don't want this."

She struggled, breaking his hold, and withdrew her arms from around him. Her head was swimming, and her body felt leaden and hot.

"The hell you don't!" Trevor's face was flushed, and he was breathing hard. "What is this, Jill? Some kind of revenge?"

Jillian took a step backward and folded her arms over her quivering belly. Inside, shame was spreading through her like a virus, churning her stomach and chilling her to the bone. Hadn't she learned her lesson yet? Did she really have to be hurt all over again before she could get this man out of her system?

"I think you'd better go," she said stiffly.

A thunderous frown tightened his face, and his eyes seethed, his need raw and plain to see. Both hands were balled into fists at his sides, and his jeans bulged with his unslaked desire.

"I will—this time." His frown twisted into a hard smile. "But the next time I kiss you I won't leave. Remember that when you issue an invitation with those sexy green eyes of yours."

Jillian gasped. "Get out."

Trevor snapped her an exaggerated salute. "Yes, ma'am!" He spun on his heel and walked out, letting the door slam violently behind him.

"I hate you," she shouted after him. But even as she said the words, she knew that she lied. She didn't hate him.

Jillian crumpled onto the sofa behind her and buried her burning face in her hands. She loved him. God help her, she was still in love with Trevor Markus.

It was past midnight. Trevor and Hank sat alone in the cavernous kitchen tucked into the far end of Horizons' main building.

"Cobb's an imbecile," Trevor muttered in controlled fury. "Anyone with any sense at all could tell that damn mask and the bottle of Percodan were planted. The guys we get here are too streetwise to stash anything where it could be found so easily." He raised his foot and sent an empty chair skidding across the newly waxed linoleum to crash into the stainless-steel refrigerator.

"You know that, and I know that, but he's got a pretty good start on an indictment," Hank said with a grim half smile. "All he needs is a fingerprint match on that blasted bottle."

Trevor rubbed his upper lip with his thumb, feeling the whisker stubble scrape his skin. "Could he have planted the pills himself before he went to your office?"

Hank stood up and began pacing. "Not unless he climbed up the ravine and vaulted the fence. Hendricks was at the gate, and he logged him in and called me immediately. I was waiting for him when he got out of the car."

Cobb had arrived shortly after Trevor had returned. The sheriff had brought his two deputies and a search warrant signed by a local judge. In an empty gym locker one of the deputies had found a black ski mask wrapped around a bottle of high-potency painkillers. The clinic's label had been pasted on the small plastic vial.

As soon as the sheriff had left, taking the evidence with him, Trevor had called an emergency meeting of the staff, asking question after question and poring over files until both he and Hank were convinced none of the boys had been involved in the theft and assault. The other members of the staff had long since gone to bed. Only Trevor and Hank remained.

Trevor shifted his feet on the slick floor and tried to find a comfortable position, but the chair was too small and the molded plastic back too hard. As he'd had to do for years, he tried to ignore the clawing pain in his back, but even the shallowest breath hurt. He needed a long soak in a hot tub to relieve his tortured muscles.

"If all our guys were accounted for, someone else put that stuff in the gym, probably one of the guys who boosted the junk," he told Hank in a tired voice. "There's no other explanation."

Hank frowned, then perched on the end of the table, his booted foot swinging restlessly. "I agree. But how?"

Trevor shook his head. "Beats me. But I think you'd better have security check the perimeter again. We've got a lot of fence. Someone who knows the area could find a way to sneak in without being seen."

He stared at the dark residue in the bottom of the white mug. The cold coffee was like acid on his stomach. Or was it frustration that was eating at him?

Forget it, Markus, he told himself one more time. Jillian wasn't the only desirable woman in the world. She wasn't even the prettiest or, damn it, the sexiest. So why did she have him tied in knots?

For a long moment he allowed himself to think of her swimming to shore ahead of him, her long hair streaming in a vibrant cloud behind her, her luscious body neatly contained in that shimmering white suit that had been more provocative than the briefest bikini.

His body stirred again, and he cursed himself a dozen ways for being a fool. Jill didn't want him. She didn't even like him.

"I need a drink," he muttered, glowering at the foul-tasting coffee.

Hank's chuckle was without humor. "You know the rules. No booze, no drugs on the grounds—except in the infirmary."

Trevor glanced across the table. A bank of fluorescent lights illuminated the stark white area, giving the room a cold look.

"How long's it been since you had your last drink, Hank? Fifteen, sixteen years?" Trevor's long, blunt fingers wrapped around the heavy mug so tightly that the knuckles whitened.

"Fifteen years, six months and thirteen days," Hank said with a challenging look.

"You still want it, don't you?"

"Every day."

Hank had come back from two tours of duty as a field surgeon in Vietnam with a vicious hatred of war and an equally vicious drinking problem. Trevor had met the taciturn Texan at Balboa Naval Hospital, where Hank had been assigned to temporary duty after he'd gotten himself sober by camping out alone for six weeks in the mountains east of San Diego. After Trevor's release, they'd kept in touch, and when Trevor had started Horizons, Hank had been the first one he'd called. The two men shared a mutual regard and affection and had few secrets from each other.

Trevor shoved his cup away and rubbed his eyes. He was exhausted. "I'm calling it a night. Maybe things'll look better in the morning."

"We'll beat that bastard yet," Hank muttered, resting a booted foot on a chair and shoving his hand in his pockets.

Bastard . . .

Suddenly Trevor saw Jason's white face. And Jillian's stricken eyes. He flexed his battered left hand. He should have flattened the jerk when he had the chance. Hell, he had a good lawyer, and Cobb more than deserved it. Any judge would agree.

"Trev, what's with you? I haven't seen that look in years."

"What look?" Trevor asked impatiently, clenching his fist.

"Like you're fixing to take me apart. You got some kind of problem with me I don't know about, partner?" Hank dropped his foot and pulled his hands from his pockets.

He and Trevor had been through a lot, and Hank knew better than most how violent Trevor could be when he lost his temper. Once, in the hospital, he'd seen his friend so angry that he'd smashed his fist through the glass front of a drug cabinet and hadn't even flinched from the pain.

"Hell, it's not you, Hank. It's me." Trevor muttered a harsh obscenity, followed by a terse apology and a brief recounting of the sheriff's veiled insult and Jason's reaction.

Hank's braced body relaxed. "Cobb's the real bastard, not Jason," Hank drawled, kicking the leg of the table. "Don't let it get to you."

"Easy for you to say. You don't have to face the kid. Or his mother." His voice tightened. "Or the damn guilt."

He looked up to find Hank watching him speculatively, a frown on his angular face.

"You did the right thing fifteen years ago, Trev. You had no choice. None at all."

Trevor flexed his tired shoulders. "We always have choices, Hank. I made the wrong one, and that's pretty hard to live with right now."

Hank stood and slid his hands into his pockets. "Start over. Win her back."

"You know what the odds are against that? Too long to even count."

"The odds never bothered you before."

"It's more than that, and you know it. There's a lot she'd have to know, a lot I'd have to tell her. I'm not proud of the man I was in those days, Hank."

Trevor's gut tightened. He'd flown twenty-three missions over North Vietnam before the crash without feeling more than the usual preflight jitters, but now he broke into a cold sweat whenever he thought about that part of his life.

"And you think, if she knew, she'd hate you as much as you hated yourself for too many years?"

Trevor dropped his head, then slowly raised it. His expression was grim. "Right now I don't know what the hell I think. And at the moment I'm too tired to care."

He'd flown back from Thailand on Friday and driven all night to get to Clayton early on Saturday. He desperately needed a few hours of oblivion.

Hank's curt nod signaled his understanding. "I hear you." He ran a long brown hand down the thick neatness of his beard, then glanced at the clock on the wall. It was nearly one.

"I'd better get back to the infirmary. We've got a new admission who's going through detox."

"How's he doing?"

"Not good. It's never easy."

Trevor braced both palms on the slick surface of the table and pushed himself slowly to his feet. The frayed nerves in his back screamed in protest, and he held his breath, waiting for the pain to let up enough so that he could make it across the compound to the guest house.

"No," he said softly, thinking about Jillian's angry eyes and fragile smile, "it's never easy."

"Ouch!"

Jillian sucked her finger and glared at the chef's knife that had just sliced the tip. A splotch of blood glistened on the cutting board next to the celery she'd been dicing, and she grabbed a paper towel to mop it up.

She wrapped her finger in the towel and picked up her knife. She attacked the celery again, venting a tiny piece of her growing frustration with every slice.

It was Wednesday, her day off, and she was fixing an elaborate Chinese dinner for Jason and herself. Cooking had always soothed her nerves and helped her to think.

For the past three days, since the picnic, she'd been at the mercy of her flip-flopping emotions. For the first time since the wedding that never happened she found herself thinking of Trevor in a new way. For the first time she wondered what it had been like for him over the past fifteen years.

In many ways he was the same sexy, provocative man she'd loved, and yet he was different, too. In those long-ago months he'd been boyishly selfish and unabashedly conceited.

What he'd wanted, he'd gone after. At twenty-one and desperately smitten, she'd adored the single-mindedness with which he'd charmed her into his bed, and she'd reveled in the masterful way he'd convinced her to give up nursing and marry him.

"Hey, I've got plenty of money," he'd told her with his wicked grin. "We'll have a good time before we settle down and raise the next brood of Markuses."

Now, however, she sensed a depth in him that hadn't been there before, and a reserve that was somehow more appealing than the brash openness she remembered. And buried deeply in his sexy eyes was a quiet sorrow that was always there, even when he laughed.

Much to her surprise, he'd called early on Monday to tell her about Cobb's visit. But she'd already received a call from the sheriff himself, demanding that she convene a special meeting of the council to discuss the revocation of the lease.

Because she had no choice in the face of the evidence he'd found, she'd agreed. But she'd insisted upon waiting until Orrie Hughes returned from a two-week visit to his daughter in San Francisco to schedule the time and place. Mel had grumbled, but he hadn't challenged her decision.

"What do you think, Jill?" Trevor had asked in a tense tone after she'd told him what had transpired. "Could he have planted those pills himself to discredit us?"

Jillian had taken her time answering. Because she disliked Mel Cobb so intensely, she'd had to sort through her feelings before she could find an objective answer.

"I don't think so, Trevor," she'd answered slowly, but definitely. "I admit Mel is irrational about Horizons, but he's also afraid of losing his job. He's got a son to support, and, according to the things Mike has told Jason, a lot of debts to pay off. The man is a pig, but he's not stupid."

There had been a brief silence.

"So you have no idea who might have planted the so-called evidence on us?"

"Unfortunately, no."

He'd sighed and switched the conversation to Jason. Their son had been subdued and withdrawn when he'd returned at nine Sunday night, she'd admitted, and Trevor hadn't pushed her to explain further.

"Tell him I said hello," he'd said before they hung up.

He hadn't asked about her.

The sharp sound of the screen door banging shut drove the disquieting thoughts of Trevor from her mind, and she looked up quickly to see Jason stalking into the kitchen. His face was flushed, and his hair was disheveled and wild-looking.

"I hate this stinking place," he shouted, his eyes hidden behind the dark glasses he wore almost constantly now. "And I hate that stinking school. I'm not going back."

He threw his books at the wall and stalked out.

Jillian stood in frozen silence, the heavy knife gripped tightly in her hand. She stared at the textbooks piled in a heap against the baseboard. One of the books had gouged a deep chunk from the plasterboard, and white dust powdered the linoleum.

"My God," she whispered in a choked voice before her wits returned.

Throwing down the knife, she hurried after her son. His door was shut. She knocked, but the music blaring full blast from his stereo drowned out the sound. She took a deep breath, pushed open the door and walked in. Jason was lying facedown on his rumpled bed, his hands clenched around his pillow.

"Sweetie, what happened? What's wrong?"

He didn't answer.

Jillian winced as a metallic scream filled the room. Keeping her gaze fixed on Jason's tense form, she crossed the room and lowered the volume to a tinny whisper.

Sitting next to him, she stroked his hair. Her jerked away and sat up, his back pressed firmly against the wall. The springs squeaked as she moved closer to him.

"Jason, tell me what's wrong," she said again, this time more firmly.

"I've been suspended for a week. Mr. Grable's gonna call you."

Jillian blinked. "Why, Jase? Why is the principal going to call me?"

"Because he says I stole twenty bucks from a guy's locker during fifth period gym class." He crossed this arms over his chest and seemed to stare at her from behind the blank dark lenses.

Instinctively she reached out to grip his arm. "Did you take the money, Jason?" she asked in stern voice.

"No," he muttered, then dropped his chin so that he was no longer looking at her. "Not exactly."

Jillian's heart speeded up painfully. "What do you mean, not exactly?"

"Mike and the other guys said it was a test. To see if . . . if I was man enough to stay in the club."

She inhaled slowly, fighting the surge of anger that shook her. That damn Mike Cobb again! she thought, releasing her grip. Her instincts had been right. Mike was trouble.

"Did you explain all of this to Mr. Grable?" she asked, striving to keep her voice calm.

"Naw, he was too mad to listen."

"I see," she said, stalling for time. What should she do now? she wondered urgently. Call Mel Cobb and tell him what his son was up to? Or call Ed and see if she could get Jason reinstated in school so that he wouldn't fall behind?

Feeling as frightened and helpless as she'd felt when she'd given birth to him, Jillian slowly raised her hand and removed Jason's dark glasses. For her own peace of mind, she needed to see the truth in his eyes.

Tears shimmered in the copper depths, and his pupils were wide with fright, but he met her searching gaze squarely. Jillian exhaled in relief. There was no deceit mirrored there. None.

"What you did was wrong," she said sternly. "But I'm proud of you for telling me the truth."

His shoulders sagged forlornly against the garish poster of a grinning skull behind his back. "I was going to give it back, Mom. Honest."

"Oh, baby," she whispered, pulling him into her arms for an awkward hug. "It's okay. We'll get through this."

"I know it was a dumb thing to do," Jason said, his voice wobbling. "I'm not going to listen to Mike ever again. I promise."

"Good," she said, patting his arm. It was going to be all right. He'd learned his lesson. She was sure of it. "I think that's a wise idea."

Jason wiped his eyes with the back of his hand and dropped his gaze. "Are you mad?" he asked in a low voice, his hands fumbling with the comforter.

"No, I'm not mad, but I am disappointed. I thought you knew better."

He rubbed his back against the wall. "Are you gonna tell *him*?"

Jillian heard the quavering note in his voice and frowned. "Who?"

"You know. Trevor. My...father." He sounded nervous.

She wetted her lips, and glanced through the window toward the mountains. "He has to know."

"He'll just yell at me again," Jason mumbled, flopping down on his back and staring at the ceiling. "He doesn't like me." His voice lowered. "And I don't like him. He's always lookin' at me funny, like he keeps waiting for me to do something stupid."

"Jase, that's not true!"

"Yes, it is. You wait. He's out to get me. He'll be mad."

"Not if you explain—"

"You're not the same since he came here," he interrupted angrily. "Nothing I do anymore is right. You're on his side!"

"Jason, there aren't any *sides* here."

Jillian saw the stubborn set of his jaw and realized further discussion would be useless. He was feeling hurt and threatened, and she had to give him time to work through all the things that had happened to him in the past few days.

"I'll explain your side to your father," she said softly. "He'll understand." She hesitated, then added in a sterner voice,

"You're forbidden to see Mike Cobb, except at school, and you're no longer in that club."

His gaze jerked around the room. "Aw, Mom—"

"No arguments, Jason. I mean it." She forced a smile. "In the meantime, you rest. Dinner will be ready in half an hour. I'll call you."

She left the room and closed the door behind her. She went directly to her bedroom and sank down onto her bed, her legs shaking and her stomach churning. Inside her head a strident buzz echoed the music that once more blared from Jason's room.

I have to do something, she thought, wiping her clammy hands on the bedspread. But what? Dear God, how can I fix this? How can I make sure this never happens again?

She clenched her hands in frustration, and the nubby chenille bunched between her fingers.

"Trevor."

Suddenly she realized she'd called his name aloud, and her heart lurched. She had to tell him before he heard about it from someone else. She'd promised Jason she would.

Her hand shook as she reached for the phone by the bed. Breathing slowly through her mouth in an effort to calm her galloping heart, she punched out the number. But the line to the guest bungalow was busy.

"Damn," she muttered.

She hung up, her hand still resting on the receiver. Then, tightening her lips, she made another call. The principal answered on the second ring.

"I was going to call you, Jillian," Ed Grable said as soon as he heard her voice. "I knew you'd be upset."

"What happened, Ed? I couldn't get much out of Jason."

The principal's heavy sigh throbbed against her ear. "One of the other boys in Jason's gym class saw him taking money from a locker. It wasn't Jason's locker, and it wasn't his money."

Jillian cleared her throat. "He claimed he was going to give it back, that it was a prank, something to do with an initiation requirement for this . . . club he belongs to."

"I've heard rumors about that club, Jillian. Personally I don't like the idea of any group that wants to feel exclusive, and this one certainly seems to have gotten off to a bad start, at least where Jason is concerned."

Jillian heaved a sigh. "I agree. I've forbidden him to be a member."

"Good. In the meantime, a week away from his classes might shake him up enough to get him back on track."

Jillian bit her lip. "I, er, was wondering about that, Ed. You don't have to keep him out so long, do you? He's sure to fall behind."

There was a brief silence. "I have to make an example of him, Jillian. Too many other students saw what was going on. And he can keep up with his work at home. If you stop by to-morrow, I'll have a list of his assignments for the next five days."

"If that's the best you can do..."

"It is."

"I'll be by in the morning," she said, accepting defeat grudgingly.

Jillian sat stiffly on the edge of the hard mattress, the receiver pressed tightly to her ear. She was trying to make up her mind.

Finally she decided Jason's welfare as too important for her to let her pride stand in the way. "Ed, Jason's father has just come into his life for... for the first time. Do you think that might be affecting him badly?"

There was a lengthy silence, and then Ed cleared his throat. "It's very possible. Family upheaval can be very upsetting to a sensitive boy like Jason." He paused, then added, "Perhaps it would be a good idea if the boy's father came in for a conference. It might give Jason more confidence, knowing both his parents are concerned with his progress."

Jillian stared down at the oak floor beneath her sneakers. Her bedroom was under the eaves, and she could hear the wind rushing through the boughs of the tall aspen outside her window.

"I'll... mention it to... to Trevor." But she knew such a meeting would only solidify Jason's belief that she and Trevor were somehow conspiring against him.

Teenagers, she thought dejectedly. Who could understand them?

The principal cleared his throat. "If there's anything I can do, Jillian, please ask."

Jillian heard the sincerity in Ed's voice, and she felt slightly better. "Thanks for the offer, Ed. I'll make sure Jason doesn't give you any more trouble."

"Enough said," he told her, and they exchanged goodbyes.

Jillian hung up and stared at the phone. Jason's music was still pounding, and her head was still throbbing. Sighing, she dialed Trevor's number again.

His line was still busy.

Chapter 9

Evening, ma'am. Welcome to Wilderness Horizons.''

The burly guard leaned out of the small square box, a polite smile on his face. Middle-aged, with a deeply tanned face and graying sideburns, Ralph Hendricks was built like a tank, with wide shoulders and a thick torso that strained the seams of his dark blue uniform.

"Hello Mr. Hendricks. I'm here to see . . . Mr. Markus."

The guard did a double take. "Mayor Anderson! I didn't recognize you." His respectful smile bloomed into a friendly grin that lit his blue eyes and split his ruddy cheeks. "If you'll wait, Mayor, I'll call ahead and tell reception you're coming." His voice carried an unspoken apology. "It's routine."

"Of course."

Jillian fidgeted in the seat. She'd tried to reach Trevor again before dinner and twice after Jason had returned to his room. But the line had been busy each time. Finally, after nearly exhausting herself pacing, she'd decided to drive the nine miles to Horizons and speak with him there.

When she'd gone to tell Jason where she was going, she'd found him sprawled across his bed, asleep. After leaving him a note in case he woke up to find her gone, she'd taken a quick shower, reapplied her makeup and dressed in a new pair of white cotton slacks and a lavender shirt.

At least she felt somewhat rejuvenated, although the adrenaline was still prodding her heartbeat into an uncomfortable rhythm, and her stomach felt queasy.

"All set, ma'am," Hendricks said in a hearty voice that made her smile. "Mr. Markus's line is busy, but Dr. Stoneson said it was okay for you to go directly to the guest bungalow."

He handed her a laminated visitor's pass, which she clipped to her collar, and asked her to sign the log. He added the time and initialed the entry.

"Do you know the way?"

Jillian shook her head. She was beginning to have second thoughts. Trevor was a bachelor, after all. He might have simply unplugged his phone for privacy.

"When you get to the split in the driveway, take the right fork and drive all the way to the end. You can't miss it."

"Thanks a lot, Mr. Hendricks."

"My pleasure." He shoved his uniform cap to the back of his head. "If it hadn't been for you, I'd probably still be collecting unemployment instead of picking up a nice paycheck every Friday. This town owes you a lot."

Jillian felt a glow of pleasure that quickly faded as the memory of her conversation with Mel Cobb intruded. "I hope the town remembers that when we have the meeting on Horizons' future in two weeks."

Hendricks scowled. "I tried to tell Mel Cobb he was way off base, but he's like an old bulldog I once had. Once that mutt got his teeth into something, it took a hard rap on the head to make him let go."

Jillian laughed. "What happened to that dog?"

The guard scowled. "He turned plumb mean and chewed up my littlest girl pretty bad." His scowl deepened. "I shot him."

Jillian shuddered, then glanced at the brown gun belt encircling his thick belly. "Best keep your revolver at home if you attend the meeting."

"Yes, ma'am. I intend to. I'd hate to be tempted." His eyes twinkled for an instant before he saluted and stepped back inside the box.

The newly applied gravel crunched beneath the tires as she followed Ralph's directions. The road followed the fence line, and the metal links gleamed like chrome lace in the setting sun.

The guest house stood well away from the main compound and was built of the same redwood and glass as the other buildings. It had a sloped roof and large picture windows on the two sides she could see from the road. She couldn't see a door.

Trevor's convertible was parked about ten yards from the house under a towering sycamore, the top up and the windows closed. Jillian pulled in next to it and shut off the engine.

The silence was so complete that she could hear river frogs croaking at the bottom of the ravine. Above her a shaft of pale sunlight filtered through the trees to pattern the gravel like an expensive Persian carpet. Sighing, she grabbed her purse, left the truck and walked around the building.

The front of the bungalow had a redwood deck surrounded by a low railing. Trevor was sitting at a picnic table, dressed only in his black trunks, a cordless phone clamped between his ear and his bare shoulder. He was peering intently through a pair of tortoiseshell glasses at a set of blueprints spread out in front of him and writing on a legal tablet with his left hand.

Jillian faltered, then stopped, feeling like an intruder but unwilling to retreat now that she'd come so far. He was sure to finish soon, and then they could talk. It wouldn't take long to tell him about the theft and Jason's suspension, and then she would leave him to his work.

In the thick silence every word seemed amplified, and she couldn't help hearing. Trevor was asking questions in a brisk, no-nonsense tone that sent shivers up her spine, and it was obvious from the scowl on his face that he wasn't pleased with the answers.

"That's unacceptable, Nick. Five days ago you assured me you had this job under control. Now you tell me you have a problem with unexplained equipment breakdown. Either it's under control or it isn't. Which is it?"

He tossed his pen down in disgust and looked up at the trees, listening with half-closed eyes. He looked tired, and yet, Jillian decided with an odd little flurry in the pit of her stomach, powerfully sexy and very masculine.

"No, I have more important things to do here in Clayton, and I don't know when I can get away. You messed it up. Now you fix it." He riffled through a stack of papers in an open briefcase on the bench beside him. Raising a sheet of paper to the light, he quickly scanned it. "The penalty is two thousand a day American. I pay you top dollar to accept the responsibil-

ity for a mistake like this. If I'm forced to pay, it's coming out
of your bonus." He listened for a moment longer. "You do
that. Right. Goodbye."

He let the phone fall into his hand, then began punching out
another number. He was lifting the phone to his ear when he
suddenly looked up. "Jill."

He was clearly surprised to see her, but his face remained
carefully impassive as he put the phone down and slowly stood.
He leaned forward slightly, resting his hands on the papers in
front of him, and regarded her with steady eyes.

Jillian felt the impact of his copper gaze immediately. The
hard edge of surprise gave way to a guarded amber, and his
lashes dipped quickly, then rose slowly, as though he were
trying to take in all of her. The lazy once-over was definitely
intimate and very unsettling.

"I tried to phone," she said as she skirted the deck and
climbed the steps. His potent gaze followed every move. "It was
busy."

Trevor looked oddly sheepish. "Now you know one of my
darkest secrets. I'm a workaholic."

"At least that's a positive addiction." Her heels clattered
against the rough planks as she walked toward him.

"Somehow I think that's a contradiction in terms, but I'm
not about to argue with you. We've done enough of that." He
rested his hands on his hips and tilted his head to one side,
waiting.

Suddenly she didn't know where to begin. Three days of
thinking about him in new and disturbing ways had left her
oddly vulnerable. She didn't like the feeling.

"I thought engineers did most of their work in front of a
computer terminal nowadays," she said, glancing toward the
blueprints.

He shrugged. "That's only half of it," he said matter-of-
factly. "The other half is making sure the construction super-
visor brings the project in on time and within the budget. A
week ago I was in Thailand."

The silver medal on his wide brown chest caught her gaze.
"Is that where you got the medallion?" He was wearing the
same medal he'd worn on Sunday. It gleamed with dull light
against the sandy gray hair on which it rested.

The medallion was interesting in its uniqueness, but it was his
body that intrigued her more. She wanted to touch him, to trace

the tapering line of curly hair down the corded line of his belly. She curled her fingers into her palm and tried to concentrate on the silver chain.

Trevor glanced down at the heavy oval resting above his heart. It was thicker than most medals and was embossed in a bold masculine pattern that she liked.

"Actually, this was made by a guy in San Diego. There was a street fair in Balboa Park while I was in the hospital there, and I got to talking to this hippy who had antiwar slogans plastered all over his booth."

"Talking?" Jillian asked softly, noting the angry flash of his eyes.

His mouth slanted into a grim line. "I was still wearing braces on my legs, and he could tell right away I was a patient on furlough from the Navy hospital. Patients used to wander through the park a lot in those days."

He paused as though he were remembering, and Jillian could see the memory wasn't pleasant.

"Anyway, we got into this shouting match about the war— after I'd paid for this—" he slipped his hand under the medallion and lifted it toward her "—and a crowd gathered. Pretty soon everyone was shouting." His hand closed over the gleaming silver for an instant, as though to protect it.

"Who won?"

"No one ever wins an argument like that, but before I hobbled off he gave me the chain to go with the medal." He let the medallion fall back against his chest.

"Why did he do that?"

Trevor shrugged. "I suppose he felt sorry for me, or maybe he wanted me to know he didn't think I was personally responsible for the war he hated."

"Is that why you wear it?" she asked. "To remind you it wasn't your fault?"

"More to remind myself that I survived, and that I'd damn well better make the most of it."

"I . . . see."

The dense silence settled around them. Jillian began to feel foolish. She wasn't an impulsive person, but with Trevor she didn't seem capable of making rational decisions.

"I . . . am I interrupting anything important? I can come back—"

"My business can wait. What's wrong?"

The thread of subtle command in his voice jolted her from her train of thought. Didn't he ever relax? Did he always have to be in control?

She rubbed her arm with a nervous hand and darted a quick look behind him. The sliding door to the interior was partially open, and a classical guitar played softly somewhere inside. She hadn't noticed it before.

"I . . . are you alone?"

Trevor's brows arched. "Yes, I'm alone."

He'd been more or less alone for fifteen years, he thought with a cynical, imaginary shrug. None of the lovely and willing ladies he'd bedded over the years had touched him inside. Not the way Jillian had touched him. He'd just never let himself admit it—until now.

He glanced around, but he couldn't see her little red truck. "Is Jason with you?" he asked, trying to read the look in her eyes.

She shook her head. "Jason's the reason I drove out to see you, though."

Trevor hesitated, then removed his glasses and tossed them on top of the blueprints. "C'mon, let's go inside. I'll fix you some tea."

He slipped into a pair of Topsiders that had seen better days and grabbed a pale blue shirt that had been draped over the railing. He shrugged into the shirt and opened the door, stepping aside to let her precede him.

The interior was furnished simply with large, comfortable-looking furniture in restful shades of blue and rose. A thick cranberry rug covered the tiled floor. At one end of the living room was a freestanding metal fireplace, at the other a large picture window facing west, looking out over the deep ravine.

There was a small adjoining kitchen and breakfast area, and a hallway leading to what she took to be the bedroom and bath. In the corner by the dining area stood an acoustic guitar.

The music was coming from a large tape player on the coffee table. Trevor walked over and ejected the tape.

"Very nice," she said, smiling at him nervously.

He watched her wander around the cozy room, his curiosity increasing with every step she took. She was jittery, like a sleek red vixen scenting danger. Her small hands touched the furniture absently, as though her mind were on something else. But he'd learned patience over the years. He would give her all the time she needed.

"All the guest quarters look alike," he told her when she'd finished her inspection. "Once, visiting one of the units in the South, I forgot where I was, and I had to look at my pocket calendar to find out."

Jillian laughed. "Poor Trevor."

"Yeah, well, I manage." He crossed to the kitchen and opened one of the cupboards. "Looks like we have herbal and regular," he said, taking down two boxes of tea bags. "Your choice." He waited.

Jillian sat down on the sofa and tried to relax. "Actually, I'd . . . I'd rather have wine, if you have it."

Trevor tossed the boxes onto the counter. "Sorry, we don't allow any kind of alcohol on the grounds. How about hot chocolate instead? I can have someone bring it over from the cafeteria."

"No, nothing, thanks." She stared across the ravine to the horizon, where the first streaks of pink and orange were striping the low-lying clouds.

Trevor watched her in silence for several seconds. The light coming through the big window touched her skin with gold and set her hair aflame. God, how he wanted her, he thought. Right here, right now. On the table, on the floor. Anyplace.

He tried to ignore the sudden flare of heat in his groin, but it only grew hotter and more insistent. He fastened the two bottom buttons of his shirt, then walked over to one of the chairs placed at right angles to the sofa and sat down.

"So why don't you tell me what's wrong?"

His voice was surprisingly gentle, and for an instant Jillian was disoriented. The last time she'd been with Trevor he'd left in a towering rage. But here he was now, sitting calmly a few feet away, his hands open on his knees instead of clenched at his sides, the lines of his face relaxed instead of rigid with fury.

For the life of her she'd never be able to figure out what he was going to do next. Maybe that was why he made her so uneasy. She liked things organized and predictable.

She took a deep breath, feeling the oxygen expand her lungs. There was a slight breeze blowing through the open door, and the air felt cool against her face.

Say it, she told herself. Get it over with.

"Jason was caught taking twenty dollars from a gym locker this afternoon. There was a...witness." Her voice wavered, but her eyes were dry.

Trevor went completely still. "What does Jason say?" he asked carefully.

"He claims it was some kind of initiation ritual for this stupid club he belongs to." She felt her anger begin to build again. Swiftly, in short staccato sentences, she told him about the group of boys that met in Mike Cobb's garage. "I know it's Mike's fault," she concluded angrily. "Jason hasn't been himself since that kid came to town."

Trevor flattened his palms against his thighs and watched the indignation march into her green eyes. Her claws were sheathed now, but she was ready to fight.

"Jill, if Jason took the money," he said slowly, feeling his way carefully, "he's the one who's got to take the heat, not this Cobb kid or anyone else."

Jillian sighed impatiently. "But he's not really guilty! Not in any serious way, I mean."

Trevor raised one brow. "I don't understand. Did he take it or not?"

"Well, yes, but he was going to give it back." Stumbling over her words, she repeated what Jason had told her. "I can tell he's really sorry. I think he even cried himself to sleep."

Trevor ran a hand through hair that was already tousled. He knew exactly how guilty Jason felt, and it hurt to know that the boy he was beginning to care about was in torment. But that didn't change the fact that Jason had to accept the consequences of what he'd done. Trevor slid back against the cushions, bracing his back. He knew all about consequences.

"In the long run this may be a good thing for him, Jill. Getting suspended has to be humiliating, and it'll make him take school and a lot of other things in his life more seriously. There's nothing like being denied something to make you want it more."

Jillian heard the rough emotion in his voice, but she ignored it. He was wrong about Jason. Being humiliated this way was the worst possible thing for his fragile ego.

"I don't agree. All it will do is make Jason more rebellious. He's already talking about hating Clayton, and he's always loved living here."

She traced a random pattern on the rug with her toe. She felt awkward, sitting here fully dressed, while he wore only trunks and a half-buttoned shirt.

Trevor took a deep breath and leaned forward slightly, folding his hands between his knees. "Jill, Jason did wrong. Stealing is stealing, no matter what it's for, and he deserves to be punished for it." He hesitated, then added very gently, "Or he might do it again. Or try something worse."

Jillian's jaw dropped, and her blood pressure soared. "How *dare* you imply my son is some kind of . . . of criminal!" She stood up and began pacing the room, her arms flailing. "It's not as if he's anything like the boys here."

"But he could be."

"What! Are you calling my son a drug addict?" Jillian whirled around and faced him, her hands curled into fists, her cheeks hot.

Careful, Markus, he warned himself silently. Don't make her mad, or she'll never listen to you. Not that he'd ever been much good with words, but he had to try to make her understand.

"Of course not, Jill. I meant that major crimes can grow from little ones that go unpunished, or sometimes are even excused. It's easy to overlook a single incident, but I don't think that's wise."

"Wise?" she asked in a deceptively calm voice. There were all kinds of memories shooting around in her head. Things, *incidents*, in the past that she'd handled alone. She hadn't needed him then. She didn't need him now.

"Jill, don't look so upset, okay? I'm simply saying that you may be too close to Jason to see him clearly."

"Too close? Too *close*?"

The stress of the past few weeks was finally beginning to get to her, and something snapped inside. "Let me tell you about close, Trevor," she said in a chilled voice that vibrated with anger. "I was there night after night for four months when he had colic and screamed for hours on end in my arms. I was there through an endless series of ear infections when his fever spiked to a 103, and I had to sponge him constantly to keep him from going into convulsions. I was there when he cried all the way to kindergarten on the first day, and when Tiffany George broke his heart in the sixth grade, and I'm still there." She took a breath. "Where were you, Trevor?"

He made himself wait out the sharp swell of anger. He could tell her about the nights when *he'd* walked the floor, wanting her so much he'd had to keep his hands in his pockets to keep from reaching for the phone to beg for another chance. He could tell her about the Christmases he'd spent with a bottle of brandy and a lot of hurting memories. He could tell her a lot of things, but he wouldn't.

"You're right, Jillian. I wasn't there. But I'm trying my damnedest to be here for you now. And for Jason." His brows drew together in an accusing frown. "You're the one who keeps pushing me away."

"Then stop telling me I'm a rotten parent because Jason was caught stealing!" Her voice rose in a shrill crescendo, and her control crumpled. To her intense dismay, tears filled her eyes and cascaded down her cheeks.

"Damn," she muttered, looking around frantically for a tissue. She had to get out of here. Coming to see Trevor had been a mistake.

"Hold still." Trevor was suddenly beside her, his hand steady as he wiped away her tears with his fingers. "You're not a bad parent," he said in a rusty voice. "You're caring and dedicated and the best damn mother I've ever seen. When I found out about Jason, I wanted to get down on my knees to thank you for giving me such a great son."

Jillian blinked up at him, the tears still clinging to her long golden lashes in a sparkling row. Her lips trembled, and she gulped, trying to contain the sobs shaking her. "I just want him to be happy and safe," she whispered. "That's all I've ever wanted."

"I know." Trevor had trouble with his breathing. For too many years he'd told himself he would never have the right to touch her again, or comfort her or to love her. But at least now he could hold her and keep her safe for a few moments, if not a lifetime.

Very gently he pulled her into his arms. She stiffened, and he held his breath, desperately afraid she was going to pull away. If she did, he wasn't sure he could let her go. Not when his body was urging him to pull her even closer.

The moment passed, and she relaxed against him. His hand shook as he pressed her temple against his shoulder and rested his cheek on her silky head.

Suddenly Jillian was enfolded in warmth. His chest was solid, like the granite slopes surrounding the town, but wonderfully warm, as though the sun had heated the hard planes just for her.

She was confused and exhausted, but he held her against him, supporting her, comforting her. He was so strong. Nothing would happen to her while he held her.

"It's going to be okay, angel," he whispered. "We'll get through this together."

Jillian felt his chest rise and fall in a steady cadence. His bronzed skin smelled of soap, and radiated a masculine heat, sending tiny shivers of feminine awareness through her body.

A ray from the sinking sun caught the silver medallion, drawing her gaze. His wide chest was darker than it had been on Sunday, and gleamed like polished teak in the light. Involuntarily she licked her lips, and the muscles of his chest rippled.

"I can't seem to stop wanting you, Jill," he muttered against her hair. "Even when I knew I'd never see you again, I wanted you. The feel of you, the smell of you, you're inside me, and no matter what I do I can't get you out."

She held her breath as his fingers slid under her chin and raised her face to his. Her lips tingled as his gaze brushed them with molten heat. His eyes locked onto hers, pulling her deeply into those glowing depths. She'd never been able to resist, never been able to deny him anything when he looked at her so intently, as though he were trying to touch her soul.

"Kiss me, Jill," he whispered in ragged need, dropping his gaze to her lips. "Kiss me like you used to."

Jillian tried to resist, tried to tell herself she was a fool for even being here, but her body ignored the signal to stop. Trevor had taken control, and she was powerless to resist.

His lips were gentle as they took hers. A sweet warmth spread through her, and she allowed her body to mold against his. Tentatively, her fingers shaking, she ran her hands over the width of his shoulders, loving the power there, the strength.

Trevor shuddered as her hands touched the exposed skin at the back of his neck. His hands moved down her back, stroking, teasing, pressing her closer. The tips of his fingers slid over the rounded contours of her buttocks, and a wild, frantic yearning shook him to the marrow.

He hadn't expected to feel her against him again, not like this. He hadn't marshaled the defenses he needed to protect himself against the hold this woman had over him. He was helpless to restrain himself, powerless to hold himself away from her when she was responding to him with such fire.

This was Jillian, his woman, a part of him. Without her he felt truncated, a man alone. But with her he felt complete and . . . strong.

Trevor groaned, and Jillian smiled against his lips. Instantly his tongue traced the curving line, trailing warm moisture over her mouth. Parting her lips, she invited him closer, inhaling sharply as his tongue entered and began stroking hers. He tasted like good, strong coffee.

Her pleasure shifted, deepened, began to shake her. He caressed her lower lip with his tongue until she shivered, then began trailing moist, hot kisses along her jaw. When he reached the sensitive spot under her ear, she moaned and leaned against him.

Wrapping her arms around his broad torso, she explored the strong contours of his back, her fingers hesitating when they touched the faint indentation of his incision. Her fingertips stroked the hair-roughened hollow of his spine, then pushed past the low waistband of his trunks. Trevor inhaled swiftly, his chest scraping her breasts, and she could feel his hard arousal prodding her abdomen.

His kisses changed, becoming gentler, more persuasive, as though his fiery passion was too threatening, too abandoned, to maintain. He began to stroke her arms, slowly, yet with an arrogant intimacy, as though touching her were his right.

She pressed closer, loving the hard masculine feel of him against her breasts and belly and hips. Nothing had ever been better than this. Nothing.

A hot rush of raw need overpowered her, and she rose to her toes, taking him between her thighs. His arousal surged and throbbed, and Jillian squeezed hard, loving the feel of him. At this moment he was hers, this hard, strong, intensely masculine man with the stillness in his eyes.

She moaned softly, and she could feel him shudder. She felt his muscles bunch under her fingertips as though he were controlling himself. Tension flowed between them, static-charged and dangerous, heightening the savage need that drove her.

She hadn't been with a man in a long time, and never like this. Never with this feverish, primitive abandon. Her hands slid up his neck to tangle in his thick hair. It was silky but resilient and curled around her fingers as though drawn to her by some magnetic force.

"My God," he whispered against her lips as passion surged between them. "Stop me, Jill. Stop me now or I'll never stop." His voice was an agonized groan of sound, raspy and out of control.

"I can't. I want you, too."

He groaned and looked deep into her eyes. It was there again, that look of sweet, helpless need that used to fill him with such happiness. She wanted him.

Trevor led her into the bedroom slowly, not quite believing that the beautiful woman looking up at him with passion-softened eyes was real. Too many times, in his dreams, she'd drifted away before he could reach her.

Inside the small suite, the fiery glow from the setting sun turned the white walls to deepest gold and bathed the bed in warm light. The room was sun-warmed, and a faint breeze scented with pine and mountain sage came through the large open window and brushed his cheek as he slowly raised his hands to her shoulders and turned her toward him.

"Jill, I...don't want to make you pregnant again." His face was drawn, his gaze tortured.

Jillian felt a sweet warmth spread inside her. He was taking care of her. "It's okay. I . . . it's the wrong time."

"I want you so much," he whispered, his hand shaking as he reached for the top button of her blouse.

In the soft light her eyes held a beautiful glow that warmed all the lonely dark places inside him, and her tremulous smile filled him with the kind of tenderness he'd thought he would never feel again.

Jillian shivered as his hard fingers brushed against her breasts. She slid her hands up to his shoulders and pushed her way under his shirt. His skin was firm and smooth and so hot in places that it burned her fingertips.

Finished with the buttons, Trevor slid the silky shirt from her shoulders, and Jillian dropped her arms, letting the shirt fall to the floor.

Trevor's breathing grew louder and more labored as he stared at her. Beneath the lacy cup of her bra, her nipples were rosy

and erect, and her breasts cast crescent shadows on the pale
cream skin. He touched her gently, reverently, feeling tiny
shivers spread under his fingers as he removed her bra.

"Beautiful," he whispered in a strangled voice as he dropped
the scrap of lace and satin next to the shimmering shirt. "I
thought I remembered . . ."

He dropped his head and kissed each breast in turn, his ragged breath moistening her skin with delicious warmth. She
tangled her fingers in his thick hair, playing with the ends.

Her heart was pounding beneath the skin he was kissing, and
her knees felt watery. He was so big, so masculine, so demanding. She felt small and delicate and loved.

She bent her head and planted a kiss in the clean-smelling silk
of his hair, then pulled his head against her breast.

Groaning, he raised his head to give her a heated kiss, then
wrapped his arms around her waist. Holding her tightly against
him, he moved toward the bed. The edge of the mattress
pressed against the backs of her knees, and she felt suddenly
weak.

"Trevor," she whispered, "I—"

"Shh. Don't talk. Just feel."

His lips closed over hers, and Jillian shivered, feeling the
powerful need in his kiss and in his body. She was overwhelmed, enveloped in raw emotion that shook her to her toes.

His lips were demanding, his tongue aggressive as it plun-
dered the inside of her mouth. Helplessly, eagerly, her lips
softened against his, inviting the arrogant intrusion. It was
wonderful, it was terrifying, it was dangerous, but suddenly she
craved the wild feeling of freedom he was exciting in her.

The years fell away, and she was once more twenty-one, in
love for the first time in her life, and eager to taste all the exotic flavors of Trevor's passion.

She held on to his shoulders, her fingers digging into the
tempered steel hardness. She was shivering, but inside she was
hot, like a parched desert traveler desperate for water.

"Yes," she whispered thickly. "Yes, yes, yes."

Trevor stiffened, and his arms were like thick, unyielding
cables encircling her. "Oh, angel, I need you so much. I'll try
to be gentle, but I don't know if I can."

Jillian pushed against his chest, and he released her. Her eyes
never left his as she slid his shirt off his shoulders, smiling seductively as it joined the pile on the floor.

Trevor groaned and reached for the waistband of her slacks. Together they slid them down her legs to bunch around her feet. She kicked off her sandals and stepped clear.

In turn she helped him remove his trunks, her breathing shortened and labored, and in seconds they were both naked and lying together in the center of the bed.

Trevor's eyes rivaled the fiery sun outside the window as she leaned forward to kiss the hair-roughened skin surrounding one flat nipple. His hands clenched, and the muscles of his chest bulged as he let her work her way downward, using her tongue and her lips to excite him. When she got to the sensitive area around his navel, he stiffened and reached for her, rolling them over so that he was half lying, half leaning over her.

His hands tangled in her hair as he kissed her eyes, her nose, her lips. He moved lower, his hands caressing her breasts, her rib cage, her belly.

Jillian was inundated in a sea of sensation, feeling the need building with each kiss, each touch. Trevor was wrapping her in pleasure, his rough hands gentle and yet controlling, seeking the sensitive spots that made her moan, his eyes half closed against his own need, his hard face strained in the dying light.

Jillian writhed, helpless, her head tossing from side to side on the pillow. Trevor moved upward, his breathing raspy and nearly out of control. With a shaking hand he parted her thighs, caressing her, exploring her.

He shuddered as he slid inside her. She was warm and wet and ready for him. He was ready to explode, but he made himself rest quietly against her, letting the blood that throbbed hotly through him ebb slightly.

This was Jill, his special lady, the only woman he'd ever wanted for his wife. He wanted her like sweet hell, but he didn't want this to end. Too many of his dreams had ended with a sweat-drenched awakening that had left him feeling more empty than ever.

Jillian moaned softly and moved against him. She made a low, sultry sound deep in her throat, and his body responded instantly.

What little control he had disappeared instantly, and he drove into her, thrusting harder and harder, feeling the need build until it was exquisite torture, and still he held off. She wasn't with him. Not yet.

"I need you, angel," he urged hoarsely. "Stay with me."

Jillian whimpered as the scalding pleasure built inside her. She thrashed against his heavy thighs, trying to get closer, trying to release the tingling, searing pressure.

"Jill, baby, hurry." Trevor's voice was a tortured plea, and she arched upward, feeling the explosion burst inside her, lifting her higher and higher in wave after wave.

She clung to him, loving the power and the tenderness in him as he trapped his lower lip between his teeth and groaned out his release.

He rested his head next to hers on the pillow, his hand pressed over hers as it lay on the coverlet. She loved the heavy weight of his body and the musky scent of his sweat-dampened skin.

His breathing slowed gradually, and she smiled, stroking his thick, soft hair. Always before she'd had to make love to him. this time he'd made love to her.

His arms slid under her, and he rolled over to let her rest on top of him, their bodies still joined. She raised her head and looked into his eyes. His hard face was soft, relaxed, and there was a gentleness in his beautiful eyes that she'd never seen before.

"My sweet Lord, that was good," he said in a thick voice.

"Yes," she whispered, and smiled.

He traced the curve of her lips with his finger. "The next time it'll be better. I'm a little out of practice. It's been a long time for me."

His voice slurred, and his eyes closed. He tucked her head against his shoulder, and Jillian snuggled against him.

In a few minutes she would have to leave. In a few minutes she would have to return to the real world, where her problems with Jason and her own internal turmoil were waiting.

Her eyes drifted closed. Her body felt sated and buoyant, and her veins hummed with contentment.

Trevor's big chest rose and fell rhythmically, soothing her, and before she could find the strength for another rational thought, she was asleep.

Trevor came awake suddenly and knew he was in trouble. His back was one excruciating spasm. The muscles were locked in a rigid tension that wouldn't let go for hours, and it hurt so much that he felt an involuntary groan start in his throat.

He bit it back, but not before Jillian stirred against him. His arms tightened around her, and he buried his face in the fragrant tangle of her thick hair.

He couldn't let her leave him. Not yet. It was too soon. He needed to feel her against him, her head pillowed trustingly on his shoulder. He needed to pretend it would always be this way, for just a while longer.

It was dark outside, and the only illumination was the eerie blue glow from the security light outside the window. The room was still warm.

Jillian's leg slid against his, and she stretched. "What time is it?" Her question was muffled by his shoulder and ended in a yawn.

Trevor tried to look over her shoulder to see the clock radio, but the pain was relentless, leaving him nearly breathless. And the familiar sickness was spreading in his stomach. He was trapped, a prisoner of the mangled vertebrae that were punishing him for ignoring the warning twinges.

"I can't see the clock," he said in a taut voice. "You'll have to look."

Jillian raised her head, her eyes still cloudy with sleep. She looked at him questioningly, a half smile playing over her lips.

Trevor tried to return the smile, but it was a failure.

"What's wrong?" she asked instantly, sitting up.

The movement of the mattress sent a hot spur into his already straining muscles, and he gasped. He could feel the clammy sweat popping out on his forehead, and he grabbed the coverlet and held on.

"Spasm," he muttered between clenched teeth.

He hated to have her see him like this, helpless and impotent. He should be making love to her again, branding her with his body until she couldn't remember any man but him. Instead, he couldn't even move enough to kiss her the way he suddenly wanted to.

"Does this happen often?" she asked softly, recognizing the look of dark frustration in his eyes.

"No."

He was lying.

Jillian bit her lip and glanced down at their naked bodies. Her skin was rosy where it had rested against Trevor's skin.

A flare of desire ignited deep inside her as she remembered the way he'd loved her, but she quickly quelled it. "I ... we shouldn't have."

"Oh, yes, we should have," he shot back in a low, frustrated growl. "And damn it, we should again." He tried to touch her, but the pain defeated him, and he let his hand fall back against the mattress.

Jillian saw the ashen tinge spread along his jaw, saw the way he was breathing, short bursts that barely moved his chest, and she knew he was in agony. Becoming once more the efficient nurse, she shoved her tumbling feelings aside and began to dress. She fumbled slightly with the buttons in her haste, glancing over her shoulder to find Trevor watching her with turbulent eyes.

"It was more fun taking that off," he muttered, his voice thick with pain. He looked furious and rumpled and very sexy.

She smiled. "Behave yourself."

"Believe me, Jill," he said wryly, "at the moment I don't have a choice."

She chuckled. It sounded like old times, with her ordering him around and him making jokes to forget the pain.

As soon as she finished dressing she went into the bathroom, snapped on the light and opened the medicine cabinet. She found an assortment of male toiletries and a bottle of extra-strength aspirin, but no prescription pain pills.

"Trevor, where are your painkillers?" she asked from the doorway.

"Don't have any," he muttered, his eyes closed, his clenched fist pressed over his forehead.

"For heaven's sake," she retorted, knowing the kind of pain he was experiencing. "Why didn't you bring them with you?"

Trevor opened his eyes and glared at her. "They're only allowed in the infirmary."

"I'll call Hank—"

"Stop fussing and give me a kiss." He sounded angry and embarrassed.

"Lord save me from the male ego," she muttered as she returned to the bathroom. A minute later she returned with a bottle of hand lotion and a glass of water. In the pocket of her slacks she carried the aspirin.

She put the glass on the night table, and only then did she notice the folded heating pad. No doubt Trevor spent most nights with his back on that warm square.

A pang of guilt shot through her, but she forced herself to ignore it. It was almost ten. She had to get home soon in case Jason was awake and wondering what was keeping her.

But first she had to do what she could for Trevor.

"What's that?" he muttered, shifting his gaze to the bottle of lotion in her hand.

"It's hand lotion," she said with exaggerated patience. "I'm going to see if I can loosen some of those knots in your back."

"The hell you are!" he said loudly, trying to sit up.

His face drained of the little color that remained, and he fell back against the pillow. He muttered a rank obscenity and glared at her.

She shook out three aspirin and held them out to him. "Here, take these."

"What are they?" he asked again.

Jillian hung on to her temper with difficulty. Trevor was an impossible patient, but then he'd always been difficult. They'd had some royal battles when she'd been his nurse.

"These are aspirin, acetylsalicylic acid, commonly used to relieve pain," she said in a singsong that brought a bright spot of color to each of his pale cheeks.

"Very funny," he said with a growl, but he let her pop them into his mouth. She held his head while he drank, and he managed to get the aspirins down without gagging. "Thanks," he muttered, lying back.

"You're welcome. And now I'm going to help you turn over onto your stomach."

He exhaled very slowly. "Jillian, leave me alone, please. I feel like a jerk, lying here buck naked and totally helpless with a beautiful, sexy-as-hell woman in my bedroom. At least let me suffer the indignity in private."

His protest was choked off by a groan as she helped him ease to his side and then to his stomach. He lay shaking and gasping, his head buried in the snowy pillow, his hands clenched.

She uncapped the lotion and poured the creamy liquid into her palm, where she let it warm against her skin. Trevor gasped as she touched him, and she stopped. "Does that hurt?"

"Yes," he mumbled against the pillow, "but not the way you think."

She smiled and began massaging his shoulders. She worked slowly and methodically, using her thumbs and the heels of her palms to release the tension bunching his muscles.

He had a wide back, with clearly defined muscles and smooth, tanned skin. She could feel the power in those muscles as she worked, moving lower and lower until she reached the small of his back, where most of the damage had been done. Two long surgical scars, one on each side of his spinal column, reminded her of the precarious balance of those crushed and splintered disks.

He was lucky he could move at all.

Trevor groaned as he felt the pain slowly ease. Her hands were warm and magical. She was touching him skillfully, with the deftness of a professional.

In his dreams she'd touched him with love, with passion, and he wanted that now. He set his jaw, trying not to imagine what it would be like to have those long, slender fingers stroking him, petting him, caressing his body in the same way he'd caressed hers.

Raw hunger shuddered through him in spite of the spiking pain, and he wanted to pull her down beside him and bury himself so deeply inside her that she would never get away from him.

Lousy rotten back, he thought, rubbing his cheek against the pillow. It carried the same flowery scent as Jillian's hair, and he inhaled slowly, loving the sensual memory that shivered through him. Between his thighs his body stirred, but it was hopeless. He couldn't even move without feeling as though he were going to pass out.

Trevor was drowsy and mumbling into his pillow by the time Jillian felt the last of the spasms give way. She'd given him temporary relief, but as soon as he exerted himself at all, the spasms would return.

She turned on the heating pad and laid it next to him. "Help me, Trevor," she whispered, and he obediently let her roll him over onto the warm pad.

He looked exhausted, and his face was still very pale. He lay motionless, his eyes closed, his hands flung out to the sides. Jillian bit her lip as she gazed down at him.

He looked so much like the young flyer she'd loved so desperately. And yet he wasn't. And she was no longer that young nurse.

They'd just made glorious love, but that was transitory. What happens now? was the question she didn't want to ask.

Sighing, she looked around for the closet. On the top shelf, she found a folded wool blanket.

Trevor didn't stir as she unfolded it and spread it over his lean, very masculine body. He was still partially aroused, and an answering moistness warmed the spot between her legs. She would remember this night for a long time.

His breathing settled into a harsh rhythm, and his brow furrowed, but at least he was sleeping. For now, anyway. She hesitated, then decided to leave the light in the bathroom burning.

She moved closer to the bed, tears suddenly welling in her eyes. Carefully, so she wouldn't jar the mattress, she leaned over and kissed him gently on the lips.

His lashes fluttered, and a drowsy smile passed over his hard mouth. He turned his head toward her, as though seeking her warmth, but he didn't open his eyes. "Angel," he mumbled, his voice soft.

Clamping her lip between her teeth, she hurried from the room and closed the door firmly behind her.

Dawn was slipping down the steep slope of the mountain outside her window when Jillian woke up on Thursday morning. Her cheeks were wet, and her heart was pounding. Her body was tangled in the sheets, and her skin was so sensitive that it hurt to move.

The dream had been so vivid, so real. Trevor's eyes had glowed as he'd slid his body over hers.

She moaned and buried her face in the pillow, but the heat flooding her skin only increased. Her body was alive and yearning, eager for the release the dream had promised.

She writhed helplessly, trying to ease the heat stirring inside her. But the friction of the sheet against her breasts only increased the ache, and she turned onto her back.

In her dream she'd felt him, hot and hard against her, and his arms had been so strong. "I love you, angel," he'd whispered. "I love you."

As she fought the memory, her nipples hardened and pushed against the thin cotton of her short gown. "Oh, no," she whispered into the silence, crossing her arms over her chest as the remnants of the dream disappeared in the early-morning light.

She'd made a bad mistake.

Caught in the throes of a passion that had overwhelmed them both, she'd forgotten something very important. In the terse words of apology and regret he'd spoke to her, Trevor had never mentioned love.

The dream she'd just had was a mirror, showing her the way it should have been. He should have said the words. The instant before his body had thrust into hers had been the perfect opportunity, the moment when a man in love wants his woman to know what's in his heart as he makes them one.

But Trevor had said nothing.

Jillian ran her finger over her slightly swollen lower lip. Her body was sore, muscles that she hadn't used in a long time aching in a very special way. But the ache in her heart was worse. She loved him, and she couldn't have him, not in the way she needed him. She needed to come first in his heart, and that would never be.

He'd come back because of Jason, not her. She was simply Jason's mother, a woman who'd once loved him. He still wanted her. Maybe he even loved her a little, in a nostalgic, grateful way, but the powerful mystical feeling that made a man and a woman one heart was missing.

No, Trevor didn't love her, and she couldn't risk loving him.

She would offer him the friendship he'd asked her for, but that was all. For her own sanity she had to rebuild the barriers that had protected her so well for so long.

Jillian stared through the window at the new day. *One day at a time,* she thought. That was the motto she'd seen in Horizons' literature and on a small ceramic plaque in Trevor's bathroom, and that was the way she would manage to live without him.

She sighed and threw off the sheet. She still had Jason. At least he needed her.

Trevor slowly turned his head and looked at the clock. He'd slept until nearly midnight, then spent the rest of the night alternately cursing his back and missing Jillian.

He still couldn't believe she'd let him make love to her. And yet the bottle of lotion was still on the night table, and his clothes were still in a pile on the floor.

Hank, when he'd come by at six for a cup of coffee, had raised a speculative brow but said very little. He'd been more concerned with helping Trevor to the bathroom and making sure he didn't pass out while he was brushing his teeth.

Trevor ran a hand down his stubbled jaw. He needed a shave and a shower, but just raising his hand sent a searing pain down his spine and into his hips.

Muttering a few choice words he'd learned from a master chief on the *Ranger*, he struggled to reach the phone which Hank had retrieved from the deck and placed on the night table. Lying flat, he started to punch out Jillian's number, then cursed again as he realized she would be at work. He got the number of the pharmacy from information.

She answered on the fourth ring, and his heart began to pound. Just hearing her low, vibrant voice made him ache to feel her against him again.

"How could you just walk out like that on a man in pain?" he asked accusingly, feeling himself smile. They'd made a start on a new relationship, and in spite of the pain in his back, he felt terrific.

He heard her breath catch in her throat, and his smile grew. He hoped she was remembering the way their lovemaking had begun, not the way it had ended.

"You told me to go," she said, her voice sounding slightly breathless.

"I didn't mean it."

"Yes, you did. You're a rotten patient."

Trevor chuckled and glanced down at his nude body. Just talking with her on the phone was arousing him. "If I promise to be good, will you come and see me?" He closed his eyes and thought about her touching him again. Her fingers were supple and strong and very soothing. He wanted to feel them against his skin.

"No way." She was laughing, but there was an odd note in her voice that he didn't like.

"Jill, is something wrong?"

There was a brief silence. "I was going to call you in a few minutes. There's been another drug theft."

Trevor muttered a harsh expletive before he could stop himself. "At your place?" he asked curtly.

"No, at Addie's office. She called me about half an hour ago, and I've been on the phone with Mel for the past twenty minutes. Her receptionist walked into a mess when she opened up at nine."

"Anyone hurt?" Trevor asked quickly.

"No, it happened sometime in the night. Addie keeps her narcotics in a small safe, so all the thieves got were some syringes and a small amount of petty cash. But from what she told me, they pretty much wrecked the office."

Trevor closed his eyes. "And Cobb? I suppose he's claiming one of our guys did this, too?"

"Of course. I'm surprised he hasn't been out there by now."

"He might have been. I'm still in bed."

He sighed and rubbed his forehead. There was no way he could stay in bed now, but he wasn't sure how he was going to manage.

"Trevor, I'm sorry, but all of this has to come out in the council meeting. I hope you and Hank can make a good case for Horizons, because I've already had some calls. A lot of people are worried."

"Yeah, well, I'm pretty worried myself. I don't want to close this unit, Jill. If I do, these boys will have to go back into custody, and that would be a damn shame."

He ground his teeth at the thought. In the short time he'd been here, he'd come to know a lot of the residents fairly well. They were a tough bunch of guys, and most of them were trying hard to change.

"I . . . never thought of that," she said.

Trevor could almost see the compassion flood her eyes. She was the warmest, most caring woman he'd ever met. And she'd let him make love to her. He started to smile again. Damn, he felt good.

"Uh, Trevor, there's something else I want to talk with you about."

"What's that, angel?"

There was a sudden silence.

"Jill?"

"Uh, about last night—"

"Last night was hell on wheels," he said quickly. "I'm still high."

"That's just it. It never should have happened."

"The hell it shouldn't have! It should have happened sooner, on Sunday. It was what we both wanted. What we both still want."

"No. It can't happen again, Trevor. Ever. We made a mistake—"

"Not me, Jill. That was no mistake." Trevor's hand gripped the phone so tightly the plastic creaked.

"Then I made a mistake. Either way, it's not going to be repeated. You wanted friendship, you said, not an affair. And I think we'd better leave it at that."

Her voice sounded strained, but firm, and Trevor closed his eyes. The nausea had returned, and he was sweating again.

"It sounds as though you've made up your mind." His voice carried a bitter edge. "Thanks for the good time, and here's your hat. Is that about it?"

Jillian ushered a harsh denial. "Stop thinking about yourself and think about Jason for a change! The gossip about us has already started. How do you think he's going to feel if he finds out we've been . . . been—"

"Making love?" He held his breath. What was she trying to tell him?

"No, that's not what it was, and you know it. That's why it has to stop." He heard the sound of a ragged breath. "This won't affect your relationship with Jason," she added with formal courtesy. "You can see him any time you want."

She hung up.

Trevor stared at the phone in his hand for a heartbeat and then, with a vicious curse, threw it against the wall.

Chapter 10

This can't be right," Jillian muttered, staring at the three columns of figures on the ledger in front of her.

One represented the quantity of Class Two narcotics on her shelves, while the second showed the amount purchased since the last inventory. The third was a compilation of the prescriptions she'd filled for those stringently regulated drugs. According to the numbers, she had a big discrepancy, much more than the five percent variance allowed by the state. But that had to be wrong. In ten years she'd never been off more than a percentage point or two.

"I'll just have to do it over," she said in a disgusted voice, throwing down her pencil and rubbing her eyes.

It was Saturday, and she'd left her office in the town hall early in order to work on the inventory that had to be filed with the State Board of Pharmacy in two months. But for some reason she was having trouble concentrating.

She pushed aside the pile of prescription carbons and rested her chin in her hand, trying to summon the energy to start over. She was uncommonly tired, and she'd been on edge for days, since the night when she and Trevor had made love, she admitted grimly. The heat Trevor had kindled inside her was still there, and nothing she'd done had been able to douse it.

Yesterday, after she'd closed the store, she'd ridden her bicycle for miles along the twisting back roads, but the ache had only grown worse.

And the cold shower she'd taken when she'd returned home from her ride had cooled her skin but not her desire. Or her love.

An abrupt knock on the door to her tiny office interrupted her thoughts, and she glanced up to see Darcy Hammond peering around the doorframe, a look of anticipation on her round pixie face.

"Jillian, there's someone here to see you."

"Tell me it's not another salesman," Jillian said in a weary voice. "I'm not in the mood."

Darcy's eyes twinkled, and she lowered her voice into a sultry imitation of Mae West. "I think you'll be in the mood for this guy, honey. I certainly am, and I'm a happily married woman."

Jillian laughed, and some of the lines in her brow smoothed. "Did this paragon give a name?"

"Yup. In a very sexy baritone, I might add. Said his name was Trevor Markus."

Jillian stood up so fast that her chair rolled backward and hit the wall with a loud crack. "Uh, thanks, Darcy. I'll be right there."

"Don't take too long." Darcy's ruddy complexion grew even rosier. "That's one gorgeous man. And he has a sweet smile, too."

Sweet? Trevor? Darcy must need glasses. The man was arrogant and demanding and totally selfish, but he wasn't the least bit sweet.

Jillian watched Darcy leave, then exhaled slowly as she counted to ten, but she could still feel her heart pounding a painful tattoo in her chest. Trevor was probably here to see Jason, she decided after a moment's thought, but Jason had gone to the athletic field behind the high school to cheer for his old soccer team against a local rival.

No problem, she told herself with forced confidence as she tucked her short-sleeved turquoise shirt into the tight waistband of her gray slacks. She would give Trevor directions, and he could talk with Jason there. Her sneakers made little sound on the worn floor as she left the cubicle and headed down the center aisle. Trevor didn't hear her approach.

He was standing in front of the magazine rack by the front window, paging through the latest issue of a business weekly. He was wearing faded jeans and a red polo shirt, through which she could see the rigid contours of a back brace. His glasses were firmly settled on his straight, autocratic nose, and his hair had been carefully brushed, though it still curled slightly at the muscular nape of his neck. He needed a haircut.

"Jason isn't here," she said as she reached his side. His musky after-shave tantalized her nostrils, making her recall instantly the time they'd spent in his bed.

Trevor looked up from the page. "I know. I called earlier, and he said he was going to a soccer game. I came to see you."

He closed the magazine and carefully replaced it in the rack. Light from the front window tangled in his hair and splashed over his shoulders, making them look broader than ever.

"Me?"

Jillian tried not to notice the way his slow, lopsided grin erased years from his face, or the way her pulse was suddenly racing out of control, but she failed.

"Since it was Saturday, I looked for you in the town hall, Madam Mayor, but the place was locked up tight, so I came here."

"Very clever." She let a trace of sarcasm filter through her words.

Trevor's grin widened, creasing his cheeks with devilish amusement. "Hey, I'm not just a pretty face, you know. I occasionally have an intelligent thought."

"Humph." Jillian frowned. He was teasing her, and she wasn't sure she liked the warm glow of pleasure that was slowly spreading inside her.

She'd expected him to be angry with her. Or at least distant. After all, she'd told the man to get lost less than twenty-four hours after giving him her body, and a normal man would be nursing a very bruised ego.

But Trevor wasn't a normal man.

The trouble was, she had no idea what kind of man he was. She just knew he didn't love her.

"I'm busy, Trevor," she said, striving to maintain a cool distance. "What do you want?"

There was an instant connection, and Jillian knew he was remembering their lovemaking, just as she was. But his gaze never wavered. The man was more controlled than anyone she'd ever known.

But then his heart wasn't involved, she realized suddenly. He'd made love to her because he'd wanted her body, not her love. She'd been the one who wanted more. The emptiness inside her yawned wider.

"I came to ask your permission to take Jason on a river rafting trip," he said.

"With you?" she asked more sharply than she intended.

Stay calm, she told herself. He wasn't suggesting a lengthy trip to Seattle, or anything remotely like that. Or was he?

"With me and a group of boys from Horizons. Every three weeks the counselors take ten guys on some kind of outing. This time it's a trip down the Donner River by raft. Since Jason's out of school anyway, I thought it might be a good idea for him to have something to do besides brood." He hooked his thumbs through the loops of his jeans and regarded her gravely.

"Are you crazy, Trevor? You can't raft down the river with your back the way it is!" Her words brought an immediate flush to his stubborn jaw.

"It's a nice, easy trip, very little white water, or so they tell me," he said curtly.

"I'll bet."

Frustration flared in his eyes, and he frowned. "You're not my nurse now, Jill, so back off. I don't want your pity."

No, she thought dejectedly, and he didn't want her love, either. Only her body.

"Okay, okay. Be stubborn and suffer," she said, using sarcasm to cover the hurt that coursed through her.

His lips tightened, but he seemed determined to avoid an argument. "What about it, Jill? When we were at the lake the other day, Jason told me he likes camping, and this sounded like the perfect opportunity."

Jillian considered it. On the surface it sounded like a good plan—if she could get Jason to go.

His moods had been volatile since his suspension, swinging from insolence to indifference, and she'd given up trying to figure out what he was really thinking. Or feeling. She only knew he was hurting, and for the first time since he'd been born, she hadn't been able to help.

"When are you leaving?" she asked cautiously.

"Six a.m. tomorrow. The trip starts upstream, near Truckee, I think Hank said, and ends twenty miles below Clayton. It should take about two and half days to get to Clayton, and I thought we'd end our part of the trip at that point. That should be sometime Tuesday."

The thin, dark rims of his glasses gave him a studious look, but she knew that was deceptive. Trevor was a man of action. And determination.

"He might not want to go with you," she warned. "He's still very uptight about the suspension."

Trevor's face tightened. "Maybe you don't want him to go with me," he said in a low, taut voice. "Is that it, Jill? Are you afraid to trust me?"

"No, of course I'm not afraid." But I am, she thought suddenly. But not of Trevor. Of herself, and the feelings he was exciting in her.

He didn't look convinced. "So you'll come?"

Jillian blinked. "Me? You said Jason."

"He'll never go with me unless you're along. You heard how he feels about the guys at Horizons. A bunch of losers, I think he called us."

His voice deepened slightly, as though it hurt to say the words, and the subtle change touched something deep and caring inside her.

"He wasn't talking about you, Trevor," she said softly, impulsively laying a hand on his arm. At her touch, his brows jerked together as though he'd felt a sudden spasm of pain, and his arm stiffened.

Instantly she removed her hand, regretting the spontaneous gesture. Now that she'd told him she didn't intend to make love to him again, he didn't even want her to touch him.

"About the trip," she said with a smile that felt stiff on her lips. "If you can convince Jason to go with you, I think it would be a good idea."

At least it would keep him away from Mike Cobb for a few more days, she thought, and more importantly, it would give Trevor another chance to bond with his son.

"Once he knows you're going, he won't have a choice."

"But I'm not going," she said flatly, trying to remain calm in spite of the adrenaline flooding her system. "I'm not on vacation like you are."

She couldn't spend three days with Trevor in a small rubber raft. Just being in the same town with him was difficult enough.

Trevor glanced around the store until he spotted Darcy behind the soda fountain washing glasses. "Your assistant minds the store on Sunday, right?" There was the barest suggestion of masculine amusement in the crooked slant of his mouth.

Reluctantly Jillian nodded her head. "Yes, but—"

"Surely she could take your place for two more days."

Trevor wanted to kiss her long and hard until she had no breath left to say no, but he didn't dare touch her. He'd vowed to back off until she invited him closer again. But it was hard, especially when she looked so cute, with a smudge of ink on the small, rounded chin she was lifting so defiantly. Now that she'd given him her body, he wasn't going to give up until he had all of her.

"No, you need time alone with Jason," she said after a moment's hesitation. "I'd only be in the way."

Trevor prayed for patience and the right words. For two days he'd tried to figure out a way to start over with her, and this was the best thing he'd come up with. He took a deep breath that turned into a half gasp as pain knifed through his back. The brace helped, but his muscles were still stiff and tender, and would be for a few days more.

He saw sympathy soften her eyes, and he ground his teeth. "Jill, I need you to come. Being a dad feels...awkward to me right now, and I'm liable to make a real mess of things if you're not there to keep me on track. I...accept the fact that you don't want me for a lover, but I really do need your help as...as a friend. And as Jason's mom."

She was silent for so long that he was sure he'd lost. Her eyes were focused on some inner vision, and her lips were pursed into a frown that heated his blood almost as much as it worried him.

He glanced up at the ceiling where an old-fashioned fan was slowly stirring the air, and Jillian watched him from the corner of her eye. Deep down she knew he was right. He'd made a start on a relationship with Jason, but it was very tenuous. And Jason was particularly vulnerable at the moment.

Even if she managed to convince him to go, the trip would more than likely turn into a disaster. Jason was still convinced his father disliked him, in spite of all the talking she'd done to the contrary, and Trevor was more used to handling adolescents with serious problems than a normal boy like Jase.

"I'll come," she said, meeting his hooded gaze. "If Darcy can take over for me." Jason needed her, and so did Trevor, and at the moment she couldn't deny either of them.

Trevor had to clear his throat twice before he trusted himself to speak. "That's great. It'll be fun. There's a great bunch of guys going, and Hank will be there. You like Hank, don't you?" He wanted her to like his friend, but not too much.

"Yes, I like him." A sudden thought occurred to her, and she frowned. "Will I be the only woman?"

Trevor looked startled. "Uh, I don't know." His brows slid together. "This facility has several women counselors, but I don't know who's planning to make the trip. Is it important?"

Jillian didn't want to sound like some neurotic teenager, but the thought of being the only woman with all those men was strangely intimidating. Or maybe it was just the thought of being so close to Trevor for so long that was making her stomach flutter.

"I was just thinking about...about sleeping arrangements." She gave him a frank look. "I assume we're sleeping in tents."

Trevor didn't smile, but the hollows in his cheeks deepened slightly as though he wanted to. "Yes. If there aren't any other women going, you can have a tent all to yourself. I'll see to it personally."

"Fine." She rubbed her palms against her hips, but her skin was still unusually damp.

"If you don't have sleeping bags, we have extras." His voice was suddenly rusty and deep.

"Uh, we have bags."

"Good." Trevor's jaw clenched, and his lashes lowered until they rested for an instant on his cheeks. Slowly he opened his eyes and smiled briefly. "I, uh, better let you get back to work." His voice roughened slightly. "I'll pick you and Jason up at five-thirty tomorrow morning."

"Okay."

He didn't touch her, but suddenly Jillian felt as though he'd pulled her close and kissed her. Under the crisp twill of her slacks, her thighs tingled as though his hand slid against them, and beneath the lace of her bra and the soft knit of her shirt her nipples swelled into hard little buds, as though waiting for his lips to ease the hot ache.

Neither of them spoke as he took another step backward, then turned and walked away from her, his steps unnaturally shortened. At the door he turned and waved. His grin was so full of sensual promise that she began to shake inside.

"Dear God," she whispered into the store that suddenly felt much too hot after he'd walked out. "What have I done?"

The sunset was beautiful. Jillian had never seen such fiery streaks in the sky, and the air was like a warm hand against her skin.

Beyond the gently sloping bank where she sat on a large granite boulder, the river was a smooth golden ribbon, edged by lacy ripples that lapped in a soothing rhythm against the smooth pebbles bordering the wheat-colored grass.

She leaned back and raised her knees, linking her arms around her shins. Arching her neck, she let the slight breeze brush her thick hair away from her face. She'd just polished off a huge helping of steak and beans, and since the cleanup crew had refused her offer of help, she was trying to stay out of the way.

It had been a long day, and she was tired and tense. The current in the Donner had been strong enough to propel the six yellow rafts at a steady pace, but not fast enough to be dangerous. After the first hour she'd stopped worrying about Trevor's back and started worrying about her peace of mind.

The raft was large enough to accommodate three in relative comfort, but far too small for Trevor to fully stretch his long legs. Seated next to him, she'd been acutely aware of the hard brown thigh that now and then brushed hers whenever he moved. Under her life preserver her skin had tingled whenever his shoulder had bumped hers. By the time they'd stopped for the night she was wrung out, and so aware of Trevor that she found it hard to think of anything else.

"Having fun?" a deep voice close by drawled.

Jillian gasped in surprise, then grinned as Hank sank down on the rock next to her and extended his long, jean-clad legs in front of him. "You scared me half to death," she said, waiting for her heartbeat to return to normal.

"Sorry, I thought you heard me coming." He clicked the hard soles of his boots together, and Jillian giggled.

"Do you wear those to bed?" she asked with a shake of her head.

He gave her a sideways look. "Naw, not anymore. I've been around you Northerners so long I've gotten soft."

Jillian sneaked a look at his rangy, muscular body and decided there wasn't anything soft about him, unless it was his heart. "After this trip, I think I'll know just how soft I am," she said with frown.

"Problems?" he asked.

She glanced toward the shadowed spot where Jason sat alone, his back against a rock, earphones clamped over his head. He'd flatly refused to go on the trip, and she'd been forced to threaten him with the loss of his beloved stereo for a month in order to get him to change his mind.

"I was hoping this trip would bring Jason and Trevor closer together, but Jason just sits there, listening to his music. He barely spoke all day. I'm about ready to toss him overboard."

She dropped her gaze to her hands, which were pressed together tightly in her lap. Slowly she flexed her fingers, relieving the tension.

"Trev will handle him," Hank said in a surprisingly serious tone, watching her. "He knows how to be patient."

"He wasn't very patient with that boy who kept insisting he wasn't an addict."

Jillian thought about the group meeting that had been held before dinner. The boys had talked about their day and the things they were grateful for. Most were grateful because they weren't in prison, or because they were learning to handle the cravings inside them. But one short Hispanic boy refused to admit he was grateful for anything or anybody. Trevor ordered him to go off by himself and chop enough wood to last the night. "And while you're chopping, Carlos," Trevor had told him, "think about the things you've done that landed you here with us."

"Trev doesn't compromise, that's for sure," Hank said in a neutral tone. "The guys know he's hard-nosed, but they also know he's on their side. He's on Jason's side, too."

She drew her brows together. "Sometimes I wonder. He's been pretty tough on him."

Hank's wide shoulders hunched slightly. "That's the only way Trev knows how to be." He inhaled slowly. "He's one of the good guys, Jillian, one of the best I've ever known," he said quietly, but with a depth of feeling she couldn't question.

She bent down to pick up a twig and began to peel back the bark, strip by strip. "Hank, that first day when we met, I had the strangest feeling that you...knew me." She looked up quickly, catching surprise in his gray eyes. "You know about Trevor and me, don't you?"

Admiration darkened his eyes. "I met Trevor about three months after he'd...returned from Hawaii. It nearly killed him to leave you, Jillian. I think you should know that."

Jillian looked down at the crooked stick in her hand. "How much did he tell you?"

Hank's hand closed over hers, and he squeezed gently. She could feel the strength in his long fingers.

"He told me everything, and he wasn't very kind to himself in the telling. It wasn't a pretty story, and I have a good idea how badly he hurt you." He hesitated. "He was raw for a long time."

"I hated him," she said evenly, feeling the hard knot of anger form again inside her. But this time it melted away as quickly as it had come.

"He's come a long way since then, Jillian, a very long way. Maybe, someday, you'll know just how far." There was kindness in his eyes and a hard kernel of intelligence. But most of all there was a challenge.

She looked down at their joined hands. She wanted to ask him about Trevor's personal life, about the lovers he must have had over the years, but she didn't know how.

"Hey, you two. What's going on here?"

Jillian looked up to find Trevor standing a few feet away, holding two plastic cups of cider. He was wearing faded khaki shorts and a white T-shirt bearing the logo of the Seattle Seahawks. He was still wearing the brace that restricted his movements.

She returned his smile and took one of the drinks. Taking a sip she licked her lips. The cider was pleasantly warm and very tart.

Hank looked up and grinned. "Go away, Markus. The lady likes me."

"The hell she does." Trevor's voice was teasing, but there was a hard warning in the look he sent Hank.

Hank turned to her and winked. "Sorry, darlin'. The man pays my salary." He leaned over to kiss her cheek, then stood up.

"You're not overdoing it, are you, buddy?" he asked Trevor, his eyes narrowing. "I'd hate to have to carry you out of here if your back seizes up again."

Trevor scowled. "If you don't keep your hands off the mother of my son, you'll be the one who gets carried out of here."

The two men grinned at each other like bickering little boys, and Jillian couldn't help laughing. It was obvious there was a deep affection between the two. Hank punched Trevor lightly on the shoulder, then ambled off.

"What was that all about?" she asked Trevor, looking up at him.

"That?" He walked over and sat down. Unlike Hank, he sat stiffly, his knees flexed to take the strain off his back.

"That look you gave Hank. What were you asking him?"

Trevor shot her a quick glance. "You're dangerous, lady. I'm going to have to watch myself around you, or I won't have any secrets left."

His tone was light, even flirtatious, but there was something in the set of his jaw and the look in his eyes that was suddenly very unsettling. A pang of fear shot through her, and her heart began to pound. "Do you have secrets, Trevor?" she asked bluntly, her gaze fastened on his rugged profile.

He didn't move, but Trevor could feel him withdraw from her. Silently, unable to stop herself, she searched the hard planes of his face for a clue. But the stillness was in his eyes again, and his tanned face was wiped clean of all expression.

There was a part of Trevor that was closed off from her. It was as though, whenever she came too close, he withdrew to a place inside where she wasn't welcome to follow.

"Yes, I have secrets, just like everyone else. Only mine aren't very interesting." He took a sip of cider. "What about you? What were you and Hank talking about?"

"Not much. Mostly the day."

Jillian glanced toward the clearing beyond the tents where the boys who weren't cleaning up were playing a very rough game of touch football. "They're nice boys once you get to know them," she said, sighing. "I wish Jason would let himself like them."

Trevor glanced toward their son. Jason's eyes were shut, closing out the rest of the group. "I wish he'd let himself like *me*," Trevor said in a taut voice. "I must be losing my touch. My nephews like me a lot."

His grin flashed and then faded, but not before Jillian had a glimpse of the sensitive man she'd known in Tokyo. He was hurt because his son was pushing him away, and there was nothing she could do to help.

"He's never handled change very well. He just needs time."

"Has he always been so moody?" His thigh was only inches from hers, and she edged sideways, giving him more room.

"He's always been quiet," she said slowly, "but the intense highs and lows started just about the time he turned fourteen."

She frowned as she thought back over the past eight months. She'd had more trouble with him in that short span of time than in any other period of his life.

Trevor chuckled. "Mary Rose, my sister-in-law, says that adolescence is like an endless electrical storm, with lots of thunder and wind."

Jillian laughed. "That's perfect. She sounds like the mother of boys." She took another quick sip and tried not to notice the way his thigh muscles bulged as he leaned forward slightly.

"She's anxious to meet you and Jason," he said quietly. "Everyone is. My dad actually passed out cigars at the yacht club when he found out about his newest grandson, and my mom is already planning the first meal she's going to serve him."

Jillian felt a sadness deep inside. Trevor's parents sounded like nice people. Jason would like them.

"Maybe someday," she said noncommittally, studying the last inch of cider in the plastic cup. She would never meet Trevor's family. It would be too hard to be the outsider, the one who would always be a guest, invited because of her son.

Trevor watched the distant look return to her eyes, and he felt like smashing his fist into the rock beneath him. Whatever he'd said to her had been wrong. Maybe it would always be wrong.

"Mr. Markus?" called a voice from across the campsite. "The fire's all made."

Trevor looked up quickly to see one of the older boys standing by the flickering fire, holding his guitar. A ragged chorus of encouragement rose from the group, and Trevor groaned in silent frustration. How could he spend time with Jillian when he was surrounded by ten raucous teenagers?

"Your public calls," Jillian murmured, a look of frank curiosity displacing the wary look he hated.

"Yeah, but it's what they're gonna call me after I play that has me worried."

Jillian laughed at the look of mock terror on his face. These boys treated Trevor with obvious respect, bordering on affection, suggesting that in many ways he was acting as a surrogate father to them.

"You'll do fine," she said with a catch in her voice.

Trevor squeezed her hand. "Save my place," he said in a husky voice as he pushed himself to his feet.

As he walked over to the circle, Trevor felt his face grow warm and his stomach tighten. He liked to play, but as he took the guitar from the boy and sat down on an upended storage box, he was suddenly nervous, knowing that Jillian would be listening.

"Okay, guys. What do you want to hear first?" He strummed a chord, adjusting one of the pegs until the guitar was in tune.

Listening to the shouts and the good-natured banter as Trevor and the boys settled on a song, Jillian found herself watching him. In the glow of the fire the lines and shadows of his face were softened, and he looked like the sexy light-hearted youth he must once have been. Like Jason would someday be.

Slipping off the rock, she went over to sit next to her son. She touched his arm, and he jerked upright, his eyes wide with shock. Smiling, she removed his earphones and pointed toward Trevor.

Jason scowled, but he turned off the tape player clipped to his belt and watched his father with sullen eyes. Jillian wanted to shake him, but she restrained herself. She had to give him time to adjust.

Trevor was good. He took every request and did his best with it. Even when he didn't know a song all the way through, he improvised well enough to please his highly vocal audience.

Gradually, as he played and the light faded from the sky, the requests became more mellow. Jillian was lulled into a peaceful mood as Trevor played more and more ballads, and the boys' banter died to an occasional murmur.

Finally, when the sky was a deep cinnamon overhead, Trevor called a halt. "That's it, guys. I've had it."

"Just one more," the boys called in rough chorus. He shook his head firmly and started to prop the guitar against a large rock.

"One more," Jillian called impulsively, drawing his startled gaze.

"Okay," he said, holding up his hand to stop the shouted requests. "This one's for the lady. What's your pleasure, ma'am?" There was a strained edge to his voice that she'd never heard before.

Instantly curious faces turned her way, and she felt herself blushing. "Uh, let me see...."

Frantically, wishing she hadn't given in to impulse, Jillian searched her mind for a song he hadn't already played. Suddenly she remembered one that had been popular during her college days, one she'd hummed often on the ward in Tokyo to distract herself from the daily horror. She called out the name, which was followed by an immediate buzz of comment. Not one of the boys had heard of the bittersweet ballad.

But Trevor knew it. He'd played it countless times in the privacy of his hospital room in San Diego. Sometimes he'd played it over and over until the desperate anger and loneliness torturing him had lessened, and he'd been able to sleep. He closed his eyes and summoned the image of Jillian's beautiful laughing face that had always been with him whenever he'd played this song.

Jillian sat motionless, listening to the power and beauty of the music. Without words, the melody was hauntingly lovely, and Trevor played it with a depth of feeling that stunned her. It was as though he was trying to tell her something so powerful and sublime that he had no words. Her defenses crumbled, and in the deepening twilight she let the music sweep her into a fantasy world where there was only Trevor, where he loved her and she loved him until the end of time.

It was ethereal. It was passionate. It was a lie.

Trevor came to the end of the song and let the notes fade into the silence. He was breathing hard, and sweat dotted his forehead. Slowly, ignoring the applause and shouts from the boys, he opened his eyes and looked at Jillian.

She was gone.

Trevor glanced around apprehensively, looking for her bright yellow shirt. He spotted her far downstream, walking along the bank, her head down, her shoulders hunched. As he watched, she disappeared behind a pile of large granite boulders that bordered the river.

"Damn," he muttered under his breath as he handed his guitar to one of the boys and stood up. He had to find out what she was thinking.

The sharp pebbles on the bank crunched under his soles as he took off after her, walking as fast as the pain in his back would allow. The sounds of the boy's voices faded as he gradually drew closer to her.

She was walking rapidly, etching narrow footprints into the wet clay, and her arms were crossed tightly over her chest. It was obvious from her jerky stride that she was upset.

"Jill, wait," he called, frustration and uncertainty making his voice harsher than he'd intended.

Her shoulders jerked, and her head came up as she whirled around to face him. Her eyes were dark with pain, and her cheeks were wet. She was crying.

A sharp pain bit deeply into his gut. "Don't cry, Jill," he whispered hoarsely, balling his hands into fists at his sides. "I know you're worried, but Jason's a good kid at heart, and you've done all the right things." He didn't know what else to say.

She swallowed a sob and tried to turn away, but Trevor reached for her, pulling her roughly into his arms. Jillian pushed her face into the hollow of his throat and gulped back the tears.

"I'm getting your shirt all wet," she mumbled, her hands bunching the soft cotton knit where she clung.

"That's okay. I've got plenty of shirts."

She felt him rub his cheek against the top of her head, and she bit her lips to keep from sobbing. Her tears made her vulnerable, and that was something she couldn't risk.

"I'm fine," she muttered, pushing against his chest. He linked his arms around her back to keep her from escaping.

"Sure?" He didn't look convinced.

She nodded, sniffling.

His hard features eased into an indulgent smile as he reached into his back pocket and pulled out a snowy handkerchief. His hand shook slightly as he wiped the tears from her cheeks.

"I know I'm a better engineer than I am a musician, but I've never had my audience in tears before."

"You play beautifully," she said in a voice she knew sounded thin. "I'm just . . . tired."

"Are you sure you're not dredging up old hurts? I wouldn't blame you if you were." He returned the handkerchief to his pocket, then rested both hands on his hips.

"Maybe I am," she admitted, knowing intuitively that the past and the present were all mixed up in her love for him. "I had the past slotted away neat and tidy in my mind, and suddenly, just when I thought my life was in perfect balance, you showed up. And then . . ." She gestured helplessly and fell silent.

"And then?" His voice carried a cutting edge.

Damn that song, anyway, she thought as she stared into his shadowed eyes. The stillness was there, hiding his thoughts from her.

"And then my carefully constructed present blew up in my face, and now I feel as though I'm ... wading through rubble." She gave him an angry look. "I hate it."

Trevor turned away and glanced toward the sharp peaks that were starkly outlined against the orange sky. "No, you hate me. Isn't that what you really mean?"

He turned back to accept the truth he knew he'd see in her eyes. Maybe once she'd said the words it would be easier to convince her to let go of the bitter feelings.

"No," she said in a sad voice. "I don't hate you. I'm not sure I ever did. I think I was just so ... hurt that I told myself I despised you."

She didn't look at him. Instead she watched the river surge past a half-buried log. The pressure of the water had wiped the large branch clean of bark, leaving the wood satiny smooth.

"I'm tired of thinking," she said softly.

He moved closer, feeling the subtle warmth of her body touch his skin. "I think about you," he said, telling her the truth. "All the time. I have for years."

He saw the disbelief in her eyes, and it hurt. "Sometimes it was only a fleeting thought when I caught a glimpse of a woman who reminded me of you. And sometimes your presence was so strong I had to swim laps for hours to get you out of my head."

"Trevor, please—"

He silenced her by putting two fingers against her lips. "Shh, just listen, okay?"

Her eyes widened until they were almost golden and glowed with uncertainty.

He dropped a quick kiss on her forehead and wrapped his hands over her shoulders. "I'm asking you to forgive me, Jill. I don't deserve it, I know, but I'm asking anyway. I want a chance to win you back."

Jillian's heart began to pound, but he didn't say the words she longed to hear. But maybe it was too soon.

"Because of Jason?" She searched his face for the truth. She had to know.

Trevor heard the tremor in her voice and cursed his clumsiness. "No, because of me."

Give him a blueprint and he could build anything, but trying to open himself up to her, to anyone, was damn near impossible.

"I've lived with my mistake for so long." His voice grew harsh with feeling. "I'd rather die than hurt you again."

Jillian couldn't breathe. "For a long time I thought you would come back," she said in a shaky voice. "Late at night I'd read your letters aloud so that your child would know his father. I told him his daddy would be so pleased..."

Her voice broke, and she clamped her trembling lip between her teeth as tears welled in her eyes again. She started to turn away, but Trevor wouldn't let her go.

"I'm sorry, Jill. So sorry." His voice was thick.

Without saying a word, he pulled her closer, as though he were trying to pull himself inside her. His arms were strong, and his body was powerful, but inside he was the same sensitive man she'd fallen in love with so long ago. He'd suffered then because his bombs had fallen on innocent victims, and he was suffering now because she'd forced him to share her pain.

They stood that way for a long time. The night grew purple above them, then black. The stars were bright, twinkling with steady light, and a yellow harvest moon began its slow climb across the jagged peaks in front of them.

Finally Trevor raised his head and looked at her. He kissed her so gently that at first she thought it was the wind brushing her lips. She sighed, and he caught the slight sound with his mouth. His hands bracketed her head as he deepened the kiss. His lips were cool, but his breath was moist and inviting and just as delicious as the cider he'd brought her.

Jillian let the pleasure flow over her, just as the water rippled over the rocks a few feet away. He nibbled at her lips. pushing the tip of his tongue into the corner of her mouth, then withdrawing it, teasing her, tantalizing her, giving her time to resist.

But she couldn't pull away. Not while it felt so good to be held like this. Not while he was stroking her with such absorbing care, letting his fingers trail along her jawline, the inside of her arms, the thin skin covering her wrists.

She liked the feel of his big, hard body rubbing slowly against hers, caressing her, provoking her, and she loved the feel of his hands on her bare arms, gentling her, petting her, inviting her to put those arms around his neck.

He groaned as her hands slid over his shoulders and linked behind his head. He nuzzled her neck with his face, then kissed the tender area below her earlobe before tracing the delicate whorls of her ear with the tip of his tongue.

Heat rocketed through her, and she rubbed against him, letting the friction of his hard chest abrade her nipples until the tiny peaks pushed hard against her shirt.

"My angel," he murmured against her lips as his arms slid around her waist. With masculine insistence, he pulled her closer, letting her feel his need. She knew he wanted her. She had power over this strong, enigmatic man who had tried so hard to hide the caring person inside.

That knowledge put an edge on her desire, making her want him more. As though he could sense her feelings, Trevor slid a hair-roughened thigh between hers and rubbed, sending an electric current deep inside her that made her gasp aloud.

Her body began to hum, and then to vibrate with a primitive force, and she ran her hands over his shoulders and down his arms, pulling him closer, closer.

He took her lips, plunging his tongue between them until she was sucking on him, loving the taste and feel and wetness of him inside her mouth. She moaned helplessly.

Trevor stiffened, then broke off the kiss and slid his hands down to her buttocks. He lifted her to her toes, then began rotating her against him. She could feel the instant response of his large, hard body, and an answering wetness erupted inside her.

"Angel, let me love you," he whispered in a husky, choked voice.

Jillian was lost in a haze of need. She should tell him no, but she couldn't. "Yes," she answered in a low, throbbing voice. At this moment she belonged to him, no matter what happened in the future.

He groaned hoarsely and buried his face in the curve of her neck. A ragged breath shuddered through him, and his arms tightened convulsively.

"Here. Now," he whispered, more a demand than a question.

Jillian knew he would stop if she insisted, but he would suffer for it. And so would she.

"Now," she answered, and he exhaled slowly, as though he'd been holding his breath.

Silently Trevor took her hand and led her into the shelter of the massive rocks. In the private niche the coarse grass was thick and green and smelled of the summer sun. Moonlight cast shadows on the steep walls surrounding them, and chips of mica and quartz sparkled in the light as Trevor drew her down onto the soft natural blanket.

She lay on her back, her legs flexed, her eyes on his face. He looked slightly dangerous in the moonlight, and an involuntary thrill skipped along her veins. He would never take her against her will, but he could, easily.

Slowly Trevor unbuttoned her blouse and opened her bra, letting her breasts spill into his palms. The air was cool on her skin, but his lips were warm as he kissed first one hard nipple, then the other. She reached for him, and her fingers brushed against the hard edge of his brace. She stiffened and started to protest, but he stopped her with a hard, thorough kiss that left her lips tingling and full.

She gasped as his fingers slid along her sides, warm and intimate. She loved the rough feel of his skin and the hard demand of his hands as he pushed the elastic waistband of her shorts down over her thighs.

He was directing her, controlling her, using his hands and his lips to send her soaring. Using only the strength in his arms, he lifted her off the ground and against his chest. He kissed her over and over, finding her lips, her eyelids, her earlobe, trailing fire behind him.

She'd never been so consumed, so masterfully excited. He was totally dedicated to her pleasure, stroking, squeezing, kneading, bringing her to the brink of release over and over until she was moaning his name in helpless urgent need.

"Now," she pleaded in a pleasure-drugged whisper, her fingers digging into the hard expanse of his shoulders. "Inside me, now."

She'd never been so demanding, and yet Trevor was a man who wasn't afraid of her demands, a man who could meet the strongest command with equal strength.

She could unleash the wildest passion, and he would follow. She could soar, and he would climb the heights with her.

She was shaking with need, and her breath was strained to a whimper as he unzipped his shorts and slid them down his strong, hard legs, kicking them aside impatiently, as though he was as eager as she was to join them together.

He kissed her with potent need, then straddled her, his shins pressed against her thighs. She arched against him, feeling him hard and hot and ready for her. He filled her completely, with exquisite tenderness, as he moved slowly, letting her set the rhythm. She clutched his forearms, desperate to feel all of him, and he thrust harder, his face intense in the silver light, his dark gaze focused on her face.

She twisted under him, moaning with throbbing need deep in her throat. He leaned forward, filling her, stroking, thrusting, until she was dizzy, knowing only Trevor and his loving.

Their rasping breaths mingled with the love call of the river frogs, filling the intimate space within the confines of the rocks with the song of loving.

Jillian gasped as he plunged deeply within her, melding them together, promising, fulfilling, sending her over the edge into a mindless state of sublime ecstasy. She clung to him, sobbing in release and love.

Trevor was dripping with sweat and breathing harshly as he slowly extended his legs alongside hers and lay next to her, his body still joined with hers. He buried his face against her shoulder and kissed the hollow of her neck. Jillian was replete and sated, and her body was drugged and heavy, and yet she felt as though she were floating far above the fragrant grass.

Inside, she was smiling, but her lips were trembling and vulnerable as she pressed them against Trevor's tousled hair. He smelled clean, and the tangled pewter mass was slightly damp.

He stroked her arm, bringing her back into her body slowly, and she reveled in the sensation. She stretched languidly, then froze as she realized he was still hot and hard inside her. He hadn't followed her into the heights.

"Trevor?" she whispered, her voice a sultry, sated wave of sound.

He moved, firing her with instant heat, and she gasped. He rocked gently inside her, sending little rockets of instant pleasure shooting into the velvet sheath that contained him.

This time he brought her to the peak slowly, thoroughly, his own need building along with hers. He loved the little sounds she made with each thrust, and the feel of her thighs against his drove him steadily toward the limit of his control. He'd wanted to make it perfect for her, to wrap her in so much passion that she would never escape, but once he'd entered her he'd had to fight his own powerful need.

She was perfection, this lovely woman who had once loved him. And he would never deny her anything again.

Trevor felt the heat building, driving him, consuming him. She cradled him perfectly, enticingly, her skin like warm satin, her hair a silken tangle around his fingers, her breasts ready for kissing.

He called her name over and over in his head as he felt the intimate contractions throbbing against him. He let himself rush over the edge, feeling the hot, violent eruption spill into her. She moaned, her hand grasping the neckline of his shirt, and the material gave way with a soft, ripping sound, exposing the heavy silver chain.

He smiled as he collapsed against her. This woman would always demand his best, and he would give it for as long as she let him.

Jillian tried to smile as Trevor rested his head on her shoulder and sighed. But she was too drowsy with pleasure.

Trevor let her heartbeat settle into a normal rhythm. They had to get back soon, or they would be missed. And he didn't want Jason to worry about his mother.

He nuzzled Jillian's soft curls and inhaled the seductive scent of her. He wanted to keep her here forever, just the two of them alone, with no past behind them and no future to face. But that wasn't possible.

He closed his eyes and thought about the night when he'd asked her to marry him. He'd thought then that he had it all together. Hell, he was rich. His father was ready to hand him a plush job once he was on his feet again. A beautiful, sexy, intelligent woman wanted to be his wife.

Damn straight, Trevor Markus had it all. He could handle anything. But he'd been dead wrong. He hadn't handled anything. His life had come crashing down around him, and he'd run away.

He pulled her tighter, letting the feel of her gentle the harsh, dark thoughts he knew were coming. He'd done terrible things, things that even now made him cringe inside, things he didn't want to admit to anyone, ever.

A dozen times since he'd seen Jillian again he'd told himself he was a different man now. That he'd changed, grown up, learned his lesson.

But before he could believe that, she had to know the truth about the man he'd been. And he had to tell her. But not yet. Not until she'd come to know the man he was now. Not until she'd come to trust him.

Jillian sighed and nestled closer, her breathing becoming more regular. She fit perfectly against him, her lush body tantalizing his even as he tried to gather the strength to sit up.

The familiar restlessness pushed through his exhaustion to torment him. He needed to move, to work through the terrible tension building inside him, but he didn't want to leave her. Sighing, he dropped a kiss on her nose. "Wake up, Jill," he whispered. "It's getting late."

Jillian stirred, a satisfied smile blooming on her lips. "I don't want to move," she murmured.

Trevor groaned and answered the seductive invitation with a kiss before he rolled away. The air was cold on his damp skin, and he reached for his shorts. He pulled them on, then looked around for Jillian's. They were in a crumpled heap by her feet.

"Sweetheart," he murmured, tracing her lips with his finger, "you need to get dressed."

Jillian kissed the tip of his finger and opened her eyes. She would remember this night forever. On the nights when she missed him the most, she would let the memory of his loving soothe her empty soul, and when her heart ached for him in the quiet time before dawn, she would cling to this night.

"I suppose you're going to say you're still out of practice," she said in a throaty voice as she let him pull her to a sitting position.

He laughed, and she felt the infectious, boyish sound bounce off the rocks. He sounded...nervous. "I could use a few more sessions like this," he said, helping her with her bra. His fingers were warm against the tender skin around her nipples, and she sighed in pleasure.

She wiggled into her panties and shorts, then looked around for her shirt. She'd been lying on it.

"Jill, before we go, you need to know that I meant what I said." He smoothed her hair away from her cheek and kissed her lightly, then set her away from him firmly. "I want us to start over, to try to make it work between us again. I'll do anything you say, take it slow, court you, anything you want."

Jillian's heart began to pound, and her mouth went suddenly dry. "Court me?"

"Yes, if that's what you want. We could date. You could come visit me in Seattle, go sailing with me." His grin flashed. "I'm pretty rusty in the romance department, but I'll give it my best shot."

Jillian glanced around their private cubbyhole. It was shadowy and dark, but Trevor's lovemaking had made it seem as though it were filled with light. But could he do that with her life?

Jillian tried to summon a smile but failed. She was too shaken. If only he'd said that he loved her...

"I don't know what to say."

He stroked her thigh. "Think about it. Okay?"

"Okay," she said in a hushed voice. She had to fight hard to keep the tears from forming in her eyes again.

Dressing in silence, she felt Trevor's eyes on her. But he said nothing as she finished. He simply took her in his arms and kissed her with tenderness, but without passion. It was the kind of kiss a husband gives his wife at the end of a long day.

Chapter 11

"Wake up, Jill."

Jillian fought through the soft gray fog surrounding her. The voice calling her name was husky and deep and wonderfully warm.

Firm lips brushed hers, leaving the taste of minty toothpaste behind, and she smiled. This time the dream of Trevor was so real that she could smell the clean scent of shaving soap on his skin.

"C'mon, sleepyhead. Open your pretty green eyes and look at me."

"Mmm." Jillian rubbed her cheek against the flannel lining of her sleeping bag and kept her eyes firmly closed. She didn't want the dream to end.

"Jill, sweetheart, don't tempt me like this. I'm trying to be a good guy here."

Hard fingers brushed her jaw, and she nuzzled a large, warm palm. Her cheek rubbed a damp cotton sleeve that smelled of woodsmoke, and she wrinkled her nose in surprise.

This is not a dream, she thought, opening her eyes slowly to the hazy light of false dawn. In the shadowed gloom Trevor was watching her. His cheeks were red from the cold, and the collar of his foul-weather jacket was pulled up against his strong throat.

"Morning," she murmured, stretching. Her body was stiff, and there was a tingling soreness deep inside her. Last night he'd made love to her so thoroughly that she was still delightfully aware.

Heat spread upward from the space between her breasts to gather in her cheeks as she remembered the tumultuous way he'd taken her. "Uh, what time is it?" Her voice was thick with sleep, and her head felt fuzzy.

He brushed the tumbled hair away from her cheek before he bent closer. "It's a few minutes before six." His voice was almost as husky as hers.

He knelt beside her, his head bent to avoid the top of the nylon tent. The black jeans that stretched over his powerful thighs had faded to a soft pearly gray, and the neck of his plain gray sweatshirt was torn. His hair was rumpled, and his shoes were covered with mud.

"You look very...earthy this morning. Sexy."

She saw the heat come into his eyes as he slid his hand into the down bag to cup her breast. Her nipple pearled, and he caught it between his thumb and forefinger.

"I feel...sexy when I'm around you. And a lot of other things, too." He cupped her breast intimately, then withdrew his hand and drew the thick covering close to her neck. "You want some coffee?" His voice was a frustrated growl.

She ran her hand down is forearm, wrinkling the thick material covering his wide wrist. "Not necessarily," she teased, her voice low and sultry. She eased herself to a sitting position, and Trevor's gaze fell to the soft swell of her body under her purple sweatshirt. A jagged star of frustration flashed in his copper eyes.

"You're enjoying this!" His voice was low and threatening.

"That's true. It isn't often I have you in my power."

His expression became deadly serious. "Do you want me in your power, Jill?"

"I'm not sure that's possible," she answered, equally serious.

"It's possible. I'm must not sure I want you to know how possible." Before Jillian could answer, he leaned forward to give her a swift, possessive kiss. Her hands encircled his neck trapping him. "Don't tempt me," he said with a harsh groan.

"Why not?"

"Because there's a hell of a storm coming, and we have to get an early start." Gently he removed her arms from his neck and held her hands in his.

"A storm? You mean with lightning and thunder?"

"Looks like. The wind's from the right direction, and it's picked up at least ten knots in the past hour." He released her hands and reached for her tote bag. "If the rain does come, Hank's decided to end the trip as soon as we can find a place to go ashore. Do you have any suggestions?"

Her eyes focused on his drawn face, finding the worry lines furrowing his brows. She unzipped the side of her sleeping bag, and cool air hit her with a shivering rush. She inhaled sharply and reached for the tote bag he held out to her.

"Let me think a minute," she told him through chattering teeth. "There's some pretty wild country between here and town." As she rummaged through the jumble of spare clothing, she traced the river's course in her mind. "The best spot would probably be an old ferry landing about five miles above town. There's still a pier of sorts there, and a road leading to the main highway. It would serve in an emergency."

She pulled out her jacket and started to shrug into the sleeves, but Trevor took it from her cold hands and helped her into the fleece-lined canvas. His fingers were possessive and warm as he lifted her thick hair from the back of her neck and planted a quick kiss on her skin before adjusting the collar for her.

"Okay, I'll tell Hank," he told her with a lazy grin. He started to back out of the tent, then stopped suddenly, his jaw clenching.

"You should be wearing your brace," she admonished instinctively, watching the color drain from his tanned skin.

"Damn thing itches. I'm fine without it."

Trevor met her defiant gaze squarely. "And you wouldn't tell me if you weren't," she said in a good imitation of his brusque tone.

He scowled, then started to laugh. "No, I wouldn't, Miss Smarty." Before she could blink, he rocked forward on his hands and kissed her hard and thoroughly. "By the way, you look sexy as hell in that purple thing," he said with a pleased grin as he left her.

Jillian glanced down at the top of her running suit. Just for that she would keep it on all day.

The storm came in at noon. The sky turned from gray to black, and the wind skimmed the river in furious gusts, bringing the scent of rain long before the first big drop hit.

"Wind's got to be thirty knots, at least," Trevor said with a scowl as he pulled Jillian closer to his side and glared up at the sky. On Puget Sound he'd raced a twelve-meter in stronger winds than this, but that had been a far more seaworthy craft than the flimsy raft.

"I don't know about knots," Jillian muttered, rubbing her hands together, "but I know it's a lot colder than it was when we started." She huddled under the hood of her jacket and watched the rafts ahead of them rocket from side to side in the churning rapids.

They were in the most dangerous part of the river. The water was well over a man's head, and the current was swift. Both banks were lined with large, jagged boulders that dotted the riverbed in a ragged line, creating a turbulence that could flip a raft in rough weather.

"Some fun, huh, Mom?" Jason called sarcastically from the front of the raft. His expression was petulant, and his eyes were sullen and angry.

Jillian inhaled sharply and sent her son a warning look. "I've had it with your complaints, Jason Gregory. No one can predict the weather."

Overhead, lightning sliced a white line through the towering clouds, and thunder clapped loudly in counterpoint.

Jason looked up with an exaggerated expression of disbelief. "Oh, yeah? I thought you knew everything, like how great this family togetherness stuff was going to be. Just you and me and *him*."

"That's enough, Jason," Trevor told him with quiet firmness. "This was my idea, not your mother's."

Something was wrong with the kid, he thought, watching his son closely. His eyes were dull, and his face was very pale. All morning he'd been jumpy as hell. Trevor was surprised that

Jillian hadn't noticed, but maybe that was just as well. She had enough to worry about at the moment.

"Right, *Daddy*," the boy muttered under his breath.

Trevor froze, and he felt Jillian stiffen against his side.

"Cut it out, Jase," she warned, avoiding Trevor's eye. "One more smart-aleck remark like that and you'll be grounded for a month."

Jason shrugged and huddled farther into the pointed bow. The bill of his baseball cap dripped water and beneath the orange life preserver his down-filled parka stuck to his body like scarlet skin. "I hate camping," he muttered into his collar. Suddenly he looked up and glared across the raft at his father.

And I hate you.

Trevor heard the words as clearly if if Jason had shouted them into the howling wind. He felt the muscles of his throat tighten as he swallowed the sharp, angry words that came immediately to mind. His son needed a good spanking, but he would never touch him, not that way. He didn't trust himself to be gentle enough.

"There's the pier," Jillian said, her voice heavy with relief. "See, near that oak hanging out over the water?"

"I see it." Trevor shifted his gaze to the lead raft, where one of the boys was pointing toward the sagging structure. All but one of the rafts ahead were clear of the rapids and in calmer water.

"Looks like Hank sees it, too. It won't be long now." Ten minutes, he calculated.

Suddenly, without warning, the raft lurched crazily to the left, throwing Jillian on top of him. "What the—"

Jason was leaning halfway over the side, vomiting violently into the turbulent water.

"Jason!" Jillian cried, scrambling toward her son.

Trevor reached for her, catching her by the tail of her jacket, but it was too late. The point of the overbalanced craft hit a partially submerged rock, and Jason tumbled over the side. His forehead hit the rock, and blood spurted over his red curls and into the water as he floated faceup, his life preserver supporting him.

"*Jason!*" Jillian's scream was turned into a sob by the wind, and the spray from the boiling river stung her face. Her eyes were wild as she fought Trevor's hold. "He can't swim. He—"

"Stay here! I'll get him," Trevor shouted, pushing her back against the opposite side of the pitching raft.

He went over the side feetfirst and held on long enough to push the raft away from the rocks, then put his head down and kicked as hard as he could. Jason was already a good five yards ahead of him, carried along by the current.

"Watch out! That rock."

Jillian's cry was splintered by the driving wind, and she scrambled frantically toward the front of the raft. Her feet tangled in the oars, and she sprawled in the sloshing water.

Trevor saw the boulder ahead, a wet gray wall barely inches from Jason's bobbing head. Lunging forward, he grabbed the boy's collar and pulled him backward, away from the rock face.

The raft rocketed by, lurching wildly, and Trevor had a glimpse of Jillian's white face before she sped by him. She was screaming, trying to draw the attention of the others as she paddled awkwardly, slowly wrestling the pitching raft toward shore.

Tightening his grip on the back of Jason's life preserver, Trevor kicked for the center of the river. Without warning, a foaming wave caught him full in the face, and he went under. As he came up coughing, his lungs stinging, his back crashed against the sharp point of a partially submerged rock, sending jagged shards of agony down his spine and into his thighs.

He felt sick, and a familiar light-headedness threatened to overwhelm him, but he fought it off and swam a clumsy side-stroke at an angle toward the shore, pulling Jason behind him. By the time his feet touched the rocky bottom and he was able to drag Jason between the rocks to shore, he was breathing hard, and his legs were numb.

He lay facedown, his arm around Jason's waist, trying to find the strength to move. The pain came in waves, one after the other, punishing him for every gasping breath he took.

Hank reached him first, followed by Jillian and several of the boys. Hank's harsh drawl and Jillian's worried cry blended into a rumble of sound. Trevor felt his hand being lifted from Jason, and he muttered a protest.

"Jason?" He tried not to groan, but it hurt to move.

"Let go, Trev. He's okay. Jason's okay. You got to him in time."

Hank's rough Texas twang cut through the noise. Hank would handle everything. Trevor allowed himself to sink into the clawing gray haze. Jason was okay. His son hadn't drowned.

"Trevor, can you hear me?" Jillian's voice was calm and soothing, just as he remembered. "One of the boys has gone for help. We're taking you and Jason to the clinic."

"No clinic," Trevor whispered hoarsely, opening his eyes and searching for Hank.

Hank knelt down and gripped his arm. "Don't worry, Trev," he said in rough voice. "I'll take you back to Horizons. I'll take care of you."

Trevor nodded and tried to relax. He felt soft fingertips stroking his face, gentle and warm. Jillian was with him, just as she'd always been.

Biting back a groan, he fought for consciousness, but the welcoming grayness beckoned seductively. "Don't let go," he whispered as he reached for her hand and held on tight.

"I won't, darling. I'm here."

Then his eyes closed and the gray turned to black.

"I'm not going! You can't make me." Jason's angry voice grated on Jillian's nerves, but she forced herself to remain calm.

Adrian had wanted him to stay one more day in the clinic, but Jason had adamantly refused. He'd been restless and irritable in the three-bed ward, the only space that had been available, and Jillian had finally relented.

Taking the day off, she'd made him stay in bed most of the morning so that she could watch over him. Every hour she'd checked his vital signs, looking for signs of a concussion, but he seemed fine.

His stomach was still upset, and he was pale, but after a short nap his disposition had greatly improved. For the past two hours, since lunchtime, he'd been pushing her to let him visit his friends. When she'd suggested a visit to Trevor, who was still in the Horizons' infirmary, instead, he'd exploded.

"Jason, your father saved your life. The least you can do is spend a few minutes with him while he's still confined to bed."

Jason flopped on the rumpled blanket and glared at her. "Why? He didn't come to see me."

Jillian inhaled slowly and counted the beats she could hear pounding in her head. When she reached twenty, she felt calm enough to answer. "I've told you this once, but in case you've forgotten, your father didn't come to see you because he twisted a disk in his back pulling you out of the river. Dr. Stoneson put him in traction."

Jason's face turned red, and he dropped his gaze, but she could see the stubborn resistance in the rigid line of his thin shoulders. "You didn't go to see him, either," he mumbled.

"That's because Dr. Stoneson wanted him to rest. Besides, he was probably so doped on painkillers he wouldn't have known whether I was there or not."

"So what's the big deal about today?"

"Today he asked Dr. Stoneson to call and tell me that he was lonely and wanted to see us. Both of us."

"Yeah, I bet."

Jillian bit her lip and reached for the battered black knapsack half hidden under the unmade bed. She needed something to occupy her hands and her mind. The past few days had stretched her patience to the limit.

"What are you doing?" Jason's voice rose sharply, and Jillian looked up in surprise.

"I'm going to do a load of laundry before I drive out to Horizons." She unzipped the top and started pulling out dirty clothes still left from their trip. She would give Jason time to reconsider.

"I'll do it."

"What?"

Jason slid off the bed and stood up. "I'll do it, Mom. It's time I learned." He rocked from side to side, and his eyes darted from her face to the bag in her hands.

Jillian stared at him. "You're offering to do the laundry?" she asked incredulously, and he nodded. A nervous smile spread over his pale face, and Jillian felt a sharp prickle of suspicion. "What do you have in here that you don't want me to see?" She held the nylon bag in her hand, searching his face for a sign of guilt.

His eyes flickered for an instant, then held steady on hers.

"Do you have something you want to tell me, Jason?" she asked, letting her tone become stern. He was hiding something.

"You don't trust me," he said in a harsh voice, his face mirroring a deep hurt. "Mike said you'd be bummed because of the club stuff. He said you'd be like his dad, always snooping in his room." He glared at her, and his lips stretched into an angry line.

What would make him so defensive all of a sudden? Jillian wondered, casting her mind back over the past few weeks. "Did you take more money, Jason?" she asked with forced calm. "From one of the boys on the trip? Or from your father?"

He dropped his gaze to the open flap of the satchel. "I told you I wouldn't do that again. Don't you believe me?"

Jillian went cold inside. His expression, the tone of his voice, even the tense lines of his thin body, suggested guilt.

"I want to, Jase, but I have to know for sure. Otherwise I wouldn't be much of a parent, would I?"

With a sense of growing dread she upended the bag and shook it hard. Rumpled shirts and underwear fell at her feet, landing with a soft plop on the toes of her sneakers. On top of the jumble, twisted into a cellophane wad, lay a sandwich bag.

Nausea pushed at her throat as she bent over and slowly picked up the small parcel. Her hand shook as she opened the bag. Inside were six yellow pills.

"This is Percodan," she said, raising her gaze to Jason's face. "Isn't it?" Her throat was so tight that she could barely get the words out.

The skin around his mouth pinched into a frown, and his gaze slid away from hers. "I don't know what it is," he mumbled, turning his back on her.

Jillian was afraid to move. *Narcotics,* she thought, her mind screaming in resistance. Drugs, used illegally. Potential poison.

Not Jason, she told herself in staunch denial. Not her little boy. It wasn't possible.

She glanced down at the small round pills. She'd filled countless prescriptions for this very potent analgesic. She'd even taken it herself when she'd fallen on the ice one winter and sprained her ankle.

But she didn't keep it in the house. And Jason wasn't allowed to go into the glass cubicle where this and other drugs were stored.

She thought about the numbers that didn't match, and her stomach lurched in sick panic.

Her fingers bit into the bony flesh of his shoulders, and he jerked beneath her hand as she spun him around to face her. Putting her shaking hand under his chin, she forced him to look at her. "Jason, I want the truth. Did you take these from downstairs?"

Jason tried to wrench his head away, but she tightened her grip. He winced in pain, but she refused to let him go.

"Tell me, Jason. Where did you get these pills?"

"Some guy on the trip gave 'em to me," he mumbled. He bit his lip, and his shoulders drooped. Suddenly he looked like a scared little boy bracing for a scolding.

"Which guy?" she asked him urgently. She was shaking uncontrollably, and her voice sounded hollow.

"The black dude with the scar. Raymond." Jason's face was scarlet from his chin to his hairline, and his tongue kept running over his bottom lip as though his mouth were dry. "He...he said he got 'em from the clinic. He said he'd be busted back to jail if they found the...the pills on him." His eyes flashed wildly. "He made me take 'em, Mom. I was afraid he'd hurt me if I didn't."

Jillian looked for the subtle signs that had always betrayed him when he was lying—the averted glance, the pinched nostrils, the nervous hands.

She saw none of them. He simply looked frightened.

"Stay here," she said sternly, pushing Jason down onto the bed. "Don't move until I get back."

Naked panic flared in his copper eyes. "What're you gonna do?" His voice was high-pitched and wavering.

"I'm going to make a phone call, and then you and I are going to have a very serious talk." She started to leave his room, but his anguished cry stopped her.

"You're not going to tell T-Trevor, are you?" His jaw hung open, and he was breathing hard.

"Yes," she said slowly and distinctly, "but first I'm going to call Sheriff Cobb."

Trevor found Hank in his office. The bearded director was leaning back in his chair, his eyes closed, his feet encased in scuffed boots propped on an open desk drawer. He was smoking a cigar, and the smoke hung like a blue wreath around his head.

As soon as Trevor crossed the threshold, Hank opened one eye and squinted at him. "You should be in bed, partner," he said accusingly. "You ripped that disk pretty good. If you put too much strain on it before it's completely healed, you could end up in a wheelchair again—this time permanently." The heels of his boots thudded loudly against the polished linoleum as he stood up.

"I'll be okay," Trevor muttered, glancing down the length of his own body. His gray sweats were loose-fitting and comfortable but even the slightest brush of fabric against his spine hurt. "I'm going crazy tied to that blasted bed, not knowing what the hell's going on in here."

Impatiently he shoved the sleeves of his sweatshirt past his elbows and perched on the edge of the desk. He'd managed to shower after Jillian called, but shaving had been beyond him. It had hurt too much to raise his arm.

Hank puffed on his cigar, then stubbed it out in the ashtray on his desk. "The guard at the gate called about two minutes ago. Jillian and the sheriff are on their way." He began rolling up the sleeves of his red plaid shirt. "Jason's with them."

"Poor kid. I bet he's scared to death." Trevor ran his hand over his thigh as he watched Hank pour coffee from an oversize thermos into two large mugs.

"Raymond's down in the lab being tested." Hank handed him one of the mugs, then returned to his chair and sat down. "This smells wrong, Trev. If it had been anyone but Raymond—" Hank broke off to mutter a blunt obscenity. "I hate to think I've been wrong about him."

Trevor took a greedy sip of the hot coffee. It was strong enough to strip the whiskers from his jaw. "We'll find out soon enough. Sounds like they're here." He put the mug on the desk and waited.

Hank's chair squeaked as he leaned back against the wall and fixed his hard gray gaze on the open doorway. "That man stomps the ground like a mangy old bull we used to have," he muttered, his brows lowered, his eyes narrowed to slits.

Trevor heard only Jillian's light feminine tread. He hadn't seen her in three days, and he was hungry for the sight of her.

Mel Cobb was the first one to enter. He was dressed in full uniform, with his hat pulled low over his forehead, his thick belt sagging under the weight of his gun and cartridge pouch. He slapped his thigh with a heavy black nightstick as he walked.

Jillian followed a half step behind. She was dressed in the same purple sweat suit she'd worn that last day on the river, only this time it was dry and unrumpled and, Trevor noticed, still sexy as hell.

She walked with her head up, her chin out, and she had her arm around Jason's shoulders in a protective embrace. Her hair was piled on top of her head, exposing the deceptively fragile line of her throat.

As soon as she saw Trevor, her face drained of the little color it possessed. "I didn't expect to see you out of bed," she told him softly. "Are you okay?"

Trevor heard the low tremor in her voice, and wondered what she was feeling. "I'm fine, just a little sore." He needed to hold her, but this wasn't the time.

Tamping down his frustration, he shifted his attention to his son. Jason stood shoulder to shoulder with his mother, dressed in worn jeans and a plain green sweater. The left side of his forehead was purple, and three neat stitches closed an inch-long gash that touched his hairline.

"Hello, Jason," Trevor said, forcing the boy to look at him. "How are you feeling?"

"Okay," Jason mumbled, not quite meeting Trevor's eyes.

"Good. I was worried about you."

Jillian watched Trevor's taut expression grow more strained, and she felt sick. She wanted to tell him that this meeting was Mel's idea, but that wasn't quite the truth. After Jason's confession, she was as concerned about Horizons as the sheriff. But before she could find the right words to express her worry, Mel interrupted.

"That's enough chitchat," he said in a coarse growl. "I came to get me a thief, and that's what I intend to do." His smug gaze swept the room, then locked with Trevor's. "This time I got you, hotshot." His voice was an oily stream of triumph that brought a scowl to Hank's face and a look of sharp anguish to Jason's.

Trevor's hands balled into fists, and he struggled to hold down the instant fury. If he moved, he knew he might not be able to stop himself from beating the man's face to a bloody pulp.

"Dr. Stoneson? I have the test results you wanted." The voice that interrupted was tentative, as though the woman at the door could feel the volatile tension in the big office. She was small and blond and nearly hidden by the large black youth standing next to her.

Raymond Williams was dressed in faded black cords and a black sweatshirt, hacked off at the shoulders to reveal massive upper arms. One side of his smooth black face sported a jagged scar that pulled his mouth up into a sardonic half smile.

Ralph Hendricks stood to one side, his hand on the boy's shoulder, his eyes alert. At Hank's nod the security chief removed his hand and stepped back to take up a post in the corridor.

Jillian resisted the urge to shiver as the youth ambled into the room. His narrowed brown eyes raked Jason with contempt as he passed, and Jillian pulled her son closer. His shoulders jerked under her arm, but he didn't pull away.

Hank took the one-page printout from the woman, thanked her warmly before dismissing her, then briefly recounted the testing procedure as the sound of her footsteps slowly faded. "In order to prevent cheating, Mr. Hendricks was with Raymond at all times during the test. Isn't that right, Ralph?"

Hendricks took a firm step forward and nodded. "Yes, sir, Dr. Stoneson. I can swear to that." His gaze hardened as he directed it toward the sheriff.

Cobb scowled, then held out a beefy hand. Hank scanned the report, then let the sheriff take it. Jillian held her breath as the sheriff quickly read off the results.

"Negative, my butt," he said, the words exploding from him in an angry burst. "I don't believe it. The kid's as dirty as they come."

He gestured with a meaty hand toward Jillian and Jason. "Tell these folks what you told your mom and me, Jase," he ordered. "Tell 'em how this sleaze said he stole the Percs from the clinic, then threatened to hurt you if you told on him."

Jason's head jerked, and his gaze flew to his mother's face. Jillian saw the fright in his eyes, and the helplessness. She glanced toward Raymond who looked ready to explode.

"Go ahead," she said, wishing she could spare him this. But he had to face up to the truth. He'd made a bad mistake, accepting the drugs and not telling anyone, but Raymond Williams had made a worse one. Even Trevor would have to admit that.

Jason wetted his lips and slid his frightened gaze toward his father. Trevor had an immediate sense of déjà vu. Timmy, he thought. Jason looked just like his brother, Tim, when he'd been fourteen. And Tim had died at nineteen.

"Tell the sheriff the truth, Jason," Trevor said as calmly as he could. "All of it."

Jason's face crumpled, and he dropped his gaze. "He said he needed to hide them from...from Trevor and Dr. Stoneson. He said no one could know."

"Liar!" Raymond's voice was a strangled roar, filling the room with waves of violent sound.

Jillian saw the muscles in Raymond's arms bunch a split second before he moved. Her heart leaped, and the acid taste of nausea stung her throat as she jumped in front of Jason's shaking body.

"Raymond, stop!" Trevor shouted.

Hank tackled the boy in midstride, and the two of them went down. Raymond fought to free himself, twisting and bucking like a wild bronco, but Hank held on, his back muscles straining with maximum effort as he kept the larger, heavier youth from escaping.

Hendricks rushed into the room and tried to grab Raymond's kicking feet, but the burly young man caught him on the side of the jaw with the toe of his shoe, and the guard sprawled backward.

"Freeze, sucker, or you're dead," Cobb shouted, reaching for his gun. His face was fiery red, and his hand was shaking so violently that he had trouble unsnapping the flap of the holster.

"Mel, *no!*" Jillian shoved Jason toward the open door, feeling his terror as Raymond Williams cursed his name. Her legs started to shake as she rushed toward Mel. She had to stop this insanity before someone got hurt.

Trevor reached the sheriff before she did. With one hand he grabbed Mel's plain black tie, twisting the sturdy cotton hard against the constricting collar to compress the man's windpipe while the other clamped around the sheriff's thick wrist, keeping him from drawing the .44 Magnum.

With a feral cry Raymond escaped Hank's hold and surged to his feet, his body braced. Cobb's eyes bulged, and he struggled against the choke hold, but Trevor held on. *"Think, man!"* he shouted. "This is no place to start shooting."

Mel froze, his face a distorted mask of hatred, but the fight had gone out of him. Trevor released his hold and took a step backward. His back was knotted and throbbing, and he felt sick to his stomach.

"Let's all calm down here and start making sense," Trevor ordered as quietly as he could manage. He could still feel the fury pounding in his head.

Breathing hard, he glanced at Raymond, who was standing with his legs apart and his fists knotted. "Sit down, Ray. You're in enough trouble," he ordered brusquely, raking his hand through his hair. "And keep your temper buttoned up tight."

The black youth scowled, but he backed up warily until the backs of his knees collided with one of the chairs lined up against the wall. He sat down and braced his big, scarred hands on his knees. His eyes were filled with turbulent fire and a desperate fear.

Turning back, Trevor saw the confusion and fright in Jillian's eyes. Her life was safe and comfortable and predictable. In her world people were solid and responsible. They worked hard and took care of their families. He couldn't expect her to understand the dark side of human nature, where a boy like Raymond had to fight for every scrap of self-respect he possessed.

Where he lived with a gut-twisting craving every hour of every day and always would. Where one slip could kill him.

"You want sense?" Cobb asked with a sneer. "I'll give you sense, Markus. I'm arresting this boy here for the theft at the Clayton Clinic and the assault on Mrs. Montoya." He pulled out a card and began reading Raymond his rights.

"It's a damn lie," Raymond shouted, his dark, wild eyes clinging to Trevor's. "I didn't take no pills. I swear." His voice choked, and his face twisted. "You gotta believe me, Mr. Markus. Your son there, he's lying."

Trevor stared into Raymond's pleading eyes. He saw terror there and a terrible helplessness. He'd seen that look before—in his own eyes. He knew what it was like to feel alone and scared and desperate for someone to believe in him.

He had to choose, the son he'd just found or this desperate boy. Either way he was going to lose. He took a deep breath and allowed himself a brief look at Jillian's white face. Damn, they needed more time.

Shoving his hands into his pockets to keep from reaching for her, he straightened his shoulders and looked Raymond straight in the eye. "I believe you, Raymond," he told the anguished boy in a strong voice. "Jason is the one who's lying."

Chapter 12

Trevor saw the shock shudder into Jillian's eyes, and he ground his teeth so hard that he felt something shift in his jaw. He'd never felt so helpless in his life, not even when he'd known his plane was going down and that he wouldn't be able to eject in time.

"What...what did you say?" Jillian stared at him, her body frozen.

"He said your son's a liar, Mayor," Mel Cobb told her with a snort. "Talk about a liar. He's the biggest one in the whole damn room. He'd do anything to save this sleazy place."

Jillian's face went white, and her eyes grew huge in her head. "Trevor," she asked in a pleading voice, "are you saying Jason's lying?"

Trevor swore silently and thoroughly as all the eyes in the room swung toward him. His back was one hard spasm of hot pain, and his legs were growing numb again. But he couldn't pass out now. Not when Jillian was looking at him with such horror in her eyes. He needed a few more minutes. Just a few more minutes.

"Jill," he said softly, moving toward her, each step agony. "We need to talk—"

"Answer me. Are you accusing your son of lying?" Her voice was flat, lifeless.

He was losing her; he could feel it happening as plainly as if she'd slammed a door in his face. He wanted to hold her, to beg her to understand, to love her, but he couldn't do any of those things.

His throat closed up. Angel, he begged silently, give me a chance.

"Yes, Jill," he said, hating every word he knew he had to say. "I think he brought those pills with him on the trip, and I think he's hooked on them."

Jillian heard someone gasp, then realized the harsh sound had come from her own throat.

The room was deadly still for the space of a shattered breath, and then it exploded into sound. Both Mel and Hank began shouting at once, angry, ugly words. But none were as ugly as the ones Trevor had just uttered with such harsh certainty.

"I told you he hated me," Jason muttered from somewhere behind her.

In slow motion Jillian turned to link her arm with Jason's. "Tell him you didn't mean it," she told Trevor, her voice stiff. "Tell him, Trevor. Now."

"I meant it, Jill. I wish I didn't." Trevor forced himself to wait. To let her decide.

She would never know what it cost him to accuse his own son, especially in front of a man like Mel Cobb. But he'd had no damn choice.

He'd watched Jason change on the river trip. He'd seen the mood swings, the growing agitation, the signs of narcotics withdrawal, and he'd tried his best to ignore them. But now he knew with cold certainty he'd been right. His son was an addict.

If he compromised here, if he didn't force Jason to face the consequences of his actions, his whole life for the past fifteen years would be a lie.

"You...you can't believe that Jason is...is an addict." Jillian's low voice was a wounded whisper.

Trevor watched the pained disbelief twist her face, and he felt as though he'd been laid open by that same pain. He was used to hurting, and he would gladly have taken her pain from her if he could. But he didn't know how.

"There's one way to find out," he said quietly, glancing toward the printout lying on the desk. "Have him tested. If he's using, it'll show up."

Jason flinched. With a choked cry he jerked away from his mother and bolted from the office, his sneakers pounding the linoleum as he ran for the front door.

Jillian felt the eyes of the others on her, but she saw only Trevor. His eyes were as shadowed and bleak as the gaping hole opening inside her. He'd known exactly how much his words would hurt her. How could he not have known?

"What kind of a man are you?" she whispered, raking him with her eyes.

Trevor met her fierce gaze steadily. "The only kind I know how to be," he said quietly.

She couldn't trust herself to stay in the same room with him. She wanted to scream at him. She wanted to rake his face with her nails for making her feel this unbearable pain all over again.

"Excuse me," she said with careful courtesy. "My son needs me."

Walking mechanically, feeling as though her body were made of thin, brittle glass, she left the office. By the time she reached the front door she was trembling so hard that she was afraid she would stumble and fall.

Clutching the door handle, she hunched over, drawing in great gulps of air. She closed her eyes and waited for her legs to stop trembling.

"Jill, please don't do this to yourself."

Trevor was standing a foot away, watching her closely, every muscle of his body radiating tension held in rigid check, like a man preparing for a bare-knuckles fight. She hadn't heard him following her.

"Do what? Hate myself because I was beginning to trust you? Because I was beginning to love you again?"

Trevor took a slow, careful breath. He didn't like the dead look in her eyes. "And how do you feel now?" he asked softly.

"Now I know that I was a fool." Her voice wobbled. "You asked me to forgive you, but how can I when you're deliberately hurting your own son?"

Frustration ripped at him, and he dropped his gaze to the floor, struggling for control. She's said that she loved him. And she was leaving him.

He'd longed to hear those words again, fought to earn the right to hear them. He felt as though he were bleeding to death. "What do you want from me, Jill? I've tried to show you that I care about you and Jason. I've tried to be a good father. I've tried to make it up to you for . . . walking out on you when you needed me. What else can I do?"

"You can tell me that you believe your son. And you can walk outside with me right now and tell Jason the same thing."

Trevor broke out in a cold sweat. From the first he'd known it was a long shot. But he'd fought for her as hard as he knew how. If he backed off, if he told her he trusted Jason, he might still have a chance.

And, dear God, more than his life, he wanted that chance.

"I can't, Jill. In my gut I know Jason is in bad trouble."

Trevor watched the denial pinch her brow beneath the soft bangs. She'd made up her mind, and he wasn't going to change it. Not without a lot more proof, anyway, which at the moment he didn't have.

"No, Trevor. Raymond's the one in trouble, and Horizons, but not Jason. He told the truth."

A sick, desolate feeling settled inside him. He'd walked away from Jillian once when he should have faced the truth, and they'd both paid a terrible price. He couldn't live with himself if he walked away from his son when Jason needed him the most.

Trevor cleared his throat. He wouldn't let himself feel. Not anything.

"Let me tell you what it's going to be like for him." His voice was flat. "I think he's maintaining now, just barely. Soon, though, he'll need more and more just to keep from getting the shakes. If he can't get it from your shelves or from the clinic, he'll steal the money, from you if he has to, and buy it from his friendly neighborhood pusher."

Jillian uttered a soft, hurt cry, but Trevor wouldn't let himself quit. If what he suspected was true, she was in for a very rough time. He'd do anything, *anything*, to save her from that kind of pain.

"He won't care where he gets the money or how he gets it. He won't care about you or his friends or anything except that filth he has to put into his body to keep from hurting. And he won't stop until he's in prison or dead."

"No!" Jillian backed away from him instinctively, her arms wrapped over her womb.

"Yes, Jill, *yes.* If he's hooked, he's living a nightmare. And someday he'll hate himself for the things he's doing now. He might even wish he were dead. Is that what you really want?"

"How can you even ask me that?" she gasped in a shredded voice, her face haunted. "I'd do anything for Jason. Fight for him. Die for him."

"I'm fighting for him," Trevor shot back, balling his fists impotently. "As hard as I know how. The only way I know how."

"Are you sure, Trevor? Or are you trying to save Horizons by putting the blame on Jason? We both know this will lead to the revocation of the lease."

Blotchy red stained his cheeks, and sweat darkened the ribbed neck of his sweatshirt as he stared down at her, his copper eyes glinting dangerously. "Horizons is important to me, Jill," he said in a voice so controlled that it was steely smooth. "But I'd *never* do what you're suggesting."

"Then what *are* you doing?" she cried, her voice rising as the anguish built inside her.

Trevor fought desperately for control. The violence that was always inside him was very close to erupting, and he couldn't let that happen. Not with Jill.

"I'm trying to save my son's life."

"By branding him a liar and a . . . a junkie?"

"I didn't have a choice."

"Of course you had a choice," Jillian said impatiently. "We both had choices, and I chose to believe my son instead of a . . . a thief. Because I love him."

"Love shouldn't blind you to the truth, Jill."

"Maybe you really believe Jason is capable of lying and letting an innocent person go to prison. But you're wrong, terribly, terribly wrong. And I don't think Jason will ever get over this . . . this betrayal."

But she'd been wrong, too. She'd believed Trevor when he'd said he wanted to start over. Like the fool she'd sworn never to be again, she'd let him seduce her with his hands and his lips and the promises in his eyes.

"Jill, please try to understand. This isn't easy for me. I hate like hell to think he's hooked on pills. Or anything else."

"He's not."

"Have him tested. Prove me wrong."

Jillian inhaled swiftly, and she stared at him in disbelief. "Are you crazy? He'd think I didn't trust him."

"I'll do it, then," he said in a hard voice. "I'll take the flak, and you can stay out of it completely. But I'll need your written permission."

Jillian felt her temper rise, and her cheeks began to burn. "I told you that Jason was just like all the other teenagers in town, for heaven's sake. Maybe he's a bit moodier sometimes, and we've had our moments, I admit, but that doesn't make him an addict. I mean—" Her words began to tumble angrily, and she stopped short. She was breathing hard.

Surely it wasn't possible, she thought. Surely not.

Jillian's throat worked convulsively. "No," she whispered. "A test like that would only humiliate him more. I can't do that to Jase. Not after today. He needs to know I believe him. He needs me, Trevor."

He saw the rejection come into her eyes again, and he knew it was over. But he couldn't give up. He couldn't lose her. Not when he was so damn close to having everything he'd thought he'd given up forever.

"I need you, too," he said quietly. He'd never said those words to anyone before in his life, not even her. "More than you can imagine."

"No, Trevor," she said sadly, shaking her head. "You want to make love to me."

Trevor gritted his teeth against the hot slash of pain in his spine. "I want to make love to you, and live with you, and grow old with you." Trevor felt his face grow hot, and he knew he was close to the end of his endurance. He would try one more time. "I love you, Jill. I never really stopped."

Jillian stared at him, a blinding joy blurring her vision. *He loved her!* Her heart pounded, but even as she began to smile, the joy faded.

He couldn't love her and do what he'd just done to their son. The man she needed wouldn't sacrifice someone he loved to save a . . . a thing, even something as valuable as Horizons. Because she knew that was exactly what he was doing, whether he believed it or not.

An icy cold settled over her, and she wrapped her arms around herself, trying to stay warm. She felt vulnerable, exposed, alone. So terribly alone.

"I think it would be best if you never saw Jason again. If you never saw either of us again," she said evenly.

"Don't do this, Jill."

He sounded almost as though he were begging her. But that was nonsense, Jillian assured herself. Trevor would never beg. He hadn't once begged in the hospital. He wouldn't beg for her now, a woman he didn't love.

"Goodbye, Trevor."

Trevor didn't move. In his hard face his eyes went completely blank. Only the subtle tightening of his lips into a thin white line showed he was feeling anything at all.

"I love you," he said quietly. "No matter what you think."

"Maybe you do, in your own way. But I don't want your kind of love."

Feeling as cold as death, she pushed open the door and walked out into the sunshine. It felt like the coldest day in winter.

She was a dream, a vision in white satin, floating gracefully toward him past the vivid clusters of exotic flowers. Her long hair was a silk flame in the bright sunlight, cascading in gold-tipped curls over her creamy throat. Her lips were slightly parted in enticing promise, and her green eyes were filled with vibrant joy. In her dainty white hands she held roses, bright red velvet buds with long green stems.

He stood transfixed, watching her smile curve sweetly just for him. Her lovely, beguiling face was softened by the love she felt for him, and her skin glowed with a rare sensual beauty that brought tears to his eyes. She was his light, his life, his bride.

From this day forward they would be one for all eternity.

"My love," she whispered as she placed her dainty hand in his. "You make me so happy. I will always love you."

She gazed up at him shyly, her shimmering green eyes shining with trust and love. And expectation. She was waiting for him to say the words. Those hard, terrible words.

He struggled, feeling the clawing need inside him. "No," he shouted. *"No!"*

The love in her eyes shattered, turning to glittering emerald hatred. Her smile hardened, shuddered, turned to contempt. Her slender hand flew out, sending his head whipping back, jolting his spine.

"No...no...*No!*"

Trevor jerked awake, the sound of his pounding heart filling the dark room. He balled his fists under the corners of his pillow and waited, his eyes closed, for the dream to leave him. It had been months, years, since he'd awakened in this same cold sweat, his heart racing, his body rigid.

It was cool in the bedroom, but Trevor was drenched. The sheet beneath his body was clammy, and the one covering his thighs was twisted and wet.

Outside the wind hissed through the trees and pushed at the curtain covering the open window. Somewhere nearby a screech owl hooted, and from the shallow ravine below came the sound of churning rapids.

The dream was always so real. He could almost feel Jill in his arms, her soft womanly curves gentling the hard, rough angles of his scarred body, filling him with peace.

She would be fragile and delicate, like a lacy pink flower he'd once seen growing in the thin air on the highest slopes of Mount Rainier. But, like that flower, under the gentleness she was tenacious and strong and determined to survive.

Trevor slowly flexed his legs, feeling some of the tension ease. He opened his eyes and stared at the swooping gray shadows above him on the ceiling.

None of the other women in his life had been like her. None of them ever listened, really listened, with her eyes and her mind and her heart, when he'd talked.

He knew he was good-looking. Hell, women had told him that all his life. But no one had really wanted to know the man behind the face—until Jillian.

For some reason he'd never been able to think of her as just another attractive, willing lady the way he'd thought of the other women he'd bedded.

She'd always been special.

And she'd made him feel special. Because she'd thought he was brave, he'd been able to stand the pain a little better. Because she'd thought he was kindhearted, he'd fought to contain his quick temper. And because she'd believed in him, he'd managed to believe in himself.

He'd tried his damnedest to be the kind of man she'd needed in that terrible hospital. And he wanted with all of his heart to be the kind of man she needed now.

But he didn't know how. Damn it, he didn't even know how to begin.

Holding his breath against the spasm in his back, he slowly pushed himself to a sitting position. Sweat ran down his face and dripped onto his bare chest, and his head swam.

After Cobb had left with Raymond, in handcuffs and under arrest, Hank had slapped him back into traction. He'd stuck it out for three days. Three days of thinking of her and wanting her and worrying about her. Three days of hell. Then he hadn't been able to take it any longer, and he'd made Hank let him get up.

Slowly, carefully, he turned on the light and reached for his wallet. From an inner pocket he took out a folded sheet of thin blue paper. His hands shook as he carefully unfolded the letter. He didn't need his glasses to read these words. He knew them by heart.

Someday, my darling Trevor, I'll tell our children how bravely you fought to live. How you laughed instead of cried. And how you gave me some of your strength when I needed it the most. Maybe they'll need some of that strength, too, someday. And you'll be there. That's why I'll always love you.

His fingers were stiff as he refolded the letter and tucked it away again. But she didn't love him. Not anymore.

He felt the familiar ache of loneliness settle inside his hurting body. He would give all he owned or hoped to own if he could live that Christmas over.

He should have fought for her then, the way he'd tried to fight for her now. But life wasn't like that. He'd made a mistake, and he'd paid for it. He was still paying.

He'd tried as hard as he knew how to become the man she'd thought him to be.

He'd tried to be there for Jason. He'd tried to love his son. He'd tried to love her.

He didn't know what the hell else to do.

Jillian groaned and turned over onto her back. Her bare legs found a cool spot on the sheet, and she shivered. She couldn't sleep.

She kept thinking of Trevor and the look on his face when she'd walked away from him. He'd looked stunned, like a man who'd just received a mortal wound.

But she'd been right to say the things she'd said. Hadn't she?

She stared at the ceiling, longing for the feel of Trevor's strong, sheltering arms. He'd been in pain; she'd seen it in the lines of his face. He shouldn't have been out of bed. But had he been there for her, or for Horizons?

I love you.

His words haunted her. Paradoxically, in spite of the anger she still felt, she wanted to believe him. But if she believed those words, she had to believe the other, terrible, words, too.

And she couldn't.

Jason wasn't a liar, and he wasn't an addict. For three days and nights she'd watched him. She'd looked for signs, for clues, anything that would show her Trevor had cause for alarm.

Jason had been withdrawn and nervous when they'd come home. He'd spent most of the weekend listening to music in his room. None of his friends had called, but she'd heard him on the phone often, talking with someone.

His appetite had been poor, and he was pale and complained of stomach cramps. This evening, after dinner, he'd thrown up. She'd put him to bed with two aspirins and a hot water bottle. When she'd checked at ten, he'd been sleeping soundly.

But Trevor's words wouldn't leave her head. "Living a nightmare," he'd said, and he'd sounded so...haunted when he'd said it.

Groaning, Jillian threw off the covers. The cool air hit her bare skin, and she shivered. Shrugging into her robe, she hurried down the hall to Jason's room. She needed to make sure he was all right, for her own peace of mind.

Jason's door was closed. Without bothering to knock, she pushed it open and snapped on the light by the bed. She reached out to touch his forehead, but he wasn't there. The sheets were rumpled, and his pillow was bunched against the headboard, but the bed was empty.

Whirling, she raced to the bathroom at the end of the hall. He wasn't there. Calling his name, she ran through the rooms, becoming more and more worried. He wasn't anywhere in the apartment. Wrenching open the front door, she ran out onto the balcony, but he wasn't there. Nor was he anywhere in sight.

Her heart pounding painfully, she returned to his room and searched his closet. As far as she could tell, none of his clothes were missing. Feeling more and more frantic, she searched through his drawers. Where was he? Was he running away? Or only hiding until he could face his friends at school again?

But where would he go? she thought frantically, pulling open the last drawer. She tugged too hard, and the heavy drawer slid free of the runners and fell onto the floor.

"Oh, my God," Jillian whispered in horror. "No, please, no."

Taped to the back was a long white envelope that bulged open. It was filled with pills and capsules, a rainbow array of deadly Class Two drugs. Slowly she pulled it free and shook some of the contents into her palm.

Percodan. Thorazine. Codeine. Narcotics, all of them. Controlled substances.

The pills spilled from her hand into the thick rug, scattering without a sound around her bare feet. Jillian slowly sank to the floor, fighting for control. As though everything were magnified, she could see the lint on the rug and the smudges on the wall. The shadows seemed to take on life, mocking her.

Her son was an addict.

Trevor had been right. Jason, her dear little boy, was just like those hard-faced criminals she'd seen that first day in front of the platform.

In a white haze of pain Jillian ran her hand over the scattered tablets, feeling the different shapes against her palm. Unlike most parents, she knew exactly what effect each of these chemicals had on the human body. She could recite the properties and reactions by rote. She knew why each was used and in what dosage. And she knew exactly and in terrible detail the kind of damage each could do if abused.

Brain trauma, coma, death, all were possible. No, she thought, crushing a handful of pills in her fist. Probable.

And Trevor had known all of those things, too.

"What have I done?" Her voice seemed to come from far away, like a long, tortured groan.

She hadn't been talking about Jason at all that day at Horizons. She'd been talking about herself. Sure, she'd told herself she was defending her son, but in reality she'd been thinking only of herself and her needs.

It was her pain, her needs, her wants, that had driven her to lash out at Trevor. And she'd been oh-so-self-righteous, brutally condemning him for not loving her enough. Or for not loving her the way she thought she should be loved.

But what about her? Her kind of love? Since he'd been back in her life, she'd made him fight for every scrap of affection she'd given him. She'd offered him her body, but withheld her love, even when she'd felt it inside her. She'd demanded he prove himself over and over, that he atone, that he beg....

Suddenly it was all so clear.

She'd wanted to humiliate him, just as she'd been humiliated. She'd wanted him to pay and pay and pay. She'd wanted him to earn her love.

But love couldn't be earned, she realized now. It could only be freely given, or it wasn't really love. Given freely and without strings, just as Trevor had given his love to Jason, with no real hope of having it returned. Just as he'd continued to give it to him by trying to make Jason face the truth about himself, knowing his son would hate him for it. That she would hate him.

Trevor hadn't been trying to humiliate Jason. He'd been trying to save him. And he'd gone on trying, even after she'd ripped into him.

I don't want your kind of love.

But she did. Desperately.

She wanted the kind of love that gave her hope when she needed it. That told her the truth when it had to be told. That wrapped her in a protective embrace when she was lonely or sad or scared.

Jillian's hand began to shake, and she pulled it back against her stomach. She'd told him it wasn't enough. She'd rejected him.

Jillian stared blindly at the shadowy room. The familiar furniture wavered in front of her eyes, coming closer, moving away. An icy gray mist began to blanket the room and seep into her bones. She was so cold, so empty.

Her tongue was thick and sluggish. Her eyes refused to focus, and there was a strange heaviness spreading through her. From a great distance she heard a voice calling her name, saying something, but she couldn't make out the words.

"Put your head down and take deep breaths. In. Out. That's good, Jill. Keep breathing."

The hand rubbing her neck was warm and comforting, and the deep velvet voice was soothing. She was so scared.

"I'm here, Jill. We'll beat this, I promise."

In. Out. Breathe.

Slowly the giddiness passed, and she opened her eyes. "I'm okay now." She raised her head and tried to smile, but her lips were numb.

"Sure?"

Trevor was kneeling stiffly beside her, still rubbing her back. His face was drawn, and his eyes were filled with pity. He knew.

"Why didn't I see?" she asked in a tortured voice, turning to look at him.

"It's called denial," he said quietly. "I haven't met a parent yet who didn't have it to one degree or another."

"You knew."

"Not at first. But when Jason threw up on the river, I started to worry. If things hadn't gotten out of hand so fast, you might have gotten suspicious, too."

Jillian's eyes stung as she shook her head slowly from side to side. He was being kind. Her face burned as she lifted her chin. She didn't want his pity.

"Jill, this isn't your fault," he said in a low, strong voice. "If you never believe another thing I tell you, I want you to believe that."

His face was stiff, and his eyes were wary, as though he expected her to lash out at him.

"Yes, it is," she whispered through stiff, cold lips. "I should have protected him from this. I'm his m-mother."

She'd been so sure she'd given her son everything he'd needed. She'd read the books and done all the right things. She was a good mother. She just hadn't been good enough.

"You're also human, Jill. And you love Jason. Sometimes love makes us look the other way without our even knowing it."

She nodded slowly. He was trying to make her feel better, but they both knew how badly she'd failed Jason. And a small, sad part of her wondered if Trevor would ever forgive her.

"I'm sorry," she said in a faint, weary voice. "I should have believed you."

She raised her head and looked at him, trying to see his thoughts in his eyes. But tears blurred her vision. She blinked, and teardrops spilled from her lashes.

Without a word Trevor reached for her hand, and together they stood up. Gently he gathered her into his strong arms. He held her securely, without passion, making no demands.

"You've had a bad shock," he murmured against her temple, "but you'll get over it. You're too strong to let this throw you."

Jillian let his words flow over her. Words that were meant to comfort. Words uttered in the husky, deep voice she loved.

Her body shook from the cold and from shock, but he held her against him, supporting her, comforting her. He was so strong. Nothing would happen to her while he held her.

She pressed her face against his wide shoulder, feeling the smooth coolness of his leather jacket. She inhaled slowly, letting his masculine scent fill her nostrils. Clean-smelling soap, musky after-shave, good leather, and maybe a hint of cigar smoke. Trevor.

Wrapping her arms around him, she tried to draw on his comforting strength.

"Better now?"

Jillian nodded silently, then raised her head and looked at his face. With a sinking heart she saw there was no fire in his eyes, no passion in his expression, no tautness in his body. No love.

He no longer wanted her. And she couldn't blame him.

"We need to find Jason," he told her gently. "Has he ever run away before?"

Pressed so closely to his chest, she could feel his words as well as hear them. "No," she mumbled. "It's never happened before. Not ever."

His brow furrowed. "Okay. We'll start with his friends. You'd better call, since you know their parents."

Jillian had heard that tone before. Trevor was talking to her in the same commanding way he'd used with the man named Nick. Taking charge. Issuing orders. Relegating her to the same importance in his life. She swallowed the rest of her tears and moved out of his arms. She had a feeling he would never hold her again.

"I'll use the phone in the bedroom," she told him evenly. "My book is in there."

Twenty minutes later Jillian had worked her way through the names of Jason's friends, even the ones she hadn't seen in months. But no one knew where he was.

It had been awkward, deflecting the anxious questions of the sleepy mothers and fathers who'd answered. But she'd simply told them she and Jason had quarreled, and that he'd run out in a fit of temper.

Most of the voices on the other end of the wire had immediately warmed with sympathy. These parents had teenagers, too.

With a heavy sigh she dialed Mike Cobb's number. He was her last hope, but Mike's phone was busy. Anxiously she glanced at the clock. It was a quarter to two.

"No answer?" Trevor asked tersely.

He leaned forward in the small padded chair in front of her grandmother's dressing table, his expression remote. The curved mirror reflected the tired lines of his back and the weary slump of his shoulders. The lamplight silvered his hair and deepened the lines of his face.

Jillian felt a pang of guilt. He looked exhausted. And it was her fault. If she'd believed him, Jason would be safe in bed.

"It's busy." She hung up and dialed again. It was still busy. She put down the phone.

Trevor pressed his palms against his knees. "Looks like we'll have to go look for him." He caught her gaze, and he smiled wearily. "I'll drive, if you tell me where to go. This isn't a very big place. He might be ... walking."

"Or he might be sick. Or hurt. Or—"

His smile became a bleak, warning frown. "Jill, stop it! You'll just make yourself crazy, and it won't help Jason."

Her guilt intensified. He was right. She was behaving badly. A wry smile curved her lips. How many times, as a critical care nurse, had she counseled frantic waiting relatives in that same calm way?

Too many times to be acting so irrationally, was the answer.

She pushed herself to her feet. She'd decorated this room herself. She'd wanted soothing colors, ivory and beige and cream, around her. And soft, sensuous fabrics to touch. This was her haven, her corner of serenity and peace away from her hectic, stressful life. But now this room was contaminated by the dark fear that filled her.

"Jill, it'll be okay." Trevor stood and came over to her. He took her hand and pressed it between his, warming her cold fingers.

He looked controlled and distant, the way he'd looked that first morning on the platform. Only his eyes had changed. The stillness that shadowed them seemed deeper, more a part of him than ever.

She summoned a smile. "Why did you come here tonight, Trevor? You never said."

His answering smile was surprisingly gentle. "Let's just say I came and let it go at that."

"You must have had a reason," she persisted. Deep down she was hoping he'd come to try again. That he hadn't been able to stay away. That, maybe, he still loved her.

"I came to try to convince you to have Jason tested. I had to try one more time before I left." There was a finality in his voice, and her hopes collapsed. She tugged her hand from his grasp.

"I'll go change. I won't be a minute."

Trevor shoved his hands into the pockets of his jeans. In the lamplight his eyes were the color of molten copper, but without the heat.

"I'll wait on the porch."

Chapter 13

The Jaguar was parked in the loading zone, just beyond the rectangle of grainy light spilling from the back window of the pharmacy.

Jillian huddled into the warmth of her fur-lined suede jacket and waited for Trevor to unlock the passenger door. The moon was sliding toward the west like a cold silver ball, and the air carried the harsh bite of frost. It was a lonely night.

"Do you have someone come in at night to clean up the store?" Trevor asked in a low voice next to her ear.

"No. I clean up before I open. Why?"

"Because there's someone in there."

Jillian's heart began to race as she stared into the dimly lit interior of the pharmacy. As a rule, she kept one light burning over the cash register, another in the rear where the prescription drugs were kept. Both lights were still lit.

"I don't see anyone," she murmured, her eyes straining. Everything looked perfectly normal.

"Someone's there, in the back behind that glass partition." His hand closed over her arm, holding her close.

"Do you think it's Jason?"

Her throat went dry, and her hands were shaking. The streets surrounding the square were empty and dark. They were alone.

"Does he have a key?" Trevor moved slightly, putting his body between her and the window.

"No. Only Darcy and I have keys. And Mel. As sheriff, he has keys to all the businesses in town."

"What about an alarm? You have one, don't you?"

"Of course. I set it myself before I locked up. Darcy and Mel have keys for that, too."

Trevor cast a quick glance around the area. "Okay. You go upstairs and call Cobb. Take off your shoes so you don't make any noise on the stairs. Tell him the guy is big, over six feet, and bulky. And he's wearing dark clothes. I don't know if he's armed."

Jillian strained to see the expression in his eyes, but the light was too dim. "What are you going to do?" Fear pounded in her temples, and her skin was clammy beneath the warm clothes.

"Nothing, unless the guy inside tries to leave. Then I'll stop him."

Jillian clung to his arm, feeling the power in the thick muscles beneath the leather. Trevor was brave, and he was strong, but his injured back made him vulnerable.

"What if he has a gun?"

"Then I'll duck." His voice was thin with impatience. "Enough questions. Go make your call." He gave her a little shove.

Heart pounding, Jillian quickly bent down to remove her sneakers, then hurried to the stairs and began to climb. She didn't want to leave him, but he was right. Mel should handle this.

Five minutes later she returned to find Trevor leaning against the front fender, his arms folded over his chest.

"Mel's on his way. He said not to do anything until he got here." She sat down and put on her shoes, tying the laces haphazardly before she got to her feet again.

"He would."

Jillian brushed the dirt from her jeans, then shoved her hands into the pockets of her jacket and stared at the window. Inside, she could see the tidy shelves and the spotless soda fountain. The long mirror behind the counter seemed to shimmer in the gloom.

"There he is," she whispered excitedly, her hand going to her throat. "I saw him in the mirror. He's as big as you are, and he's wearing dark clothes and carrying something—"

Mel appeared from the shadows, interrupting her. He was bareheaded and looked extra-bulky in his dark wool jacket. "Is the guy still in there?" he whispered when he came abreast of them.

"Yes," Trevor answered. "Jill just saw him. He might be armed."

Cobb drew his gun and clicked a round into the chamber. "Okay, I'm going in. You two stay here. When Howie and Arnold get here, tell them to be careful coming in. I don't want to get shot by my own men."

"Jill can tell them," Trevor said immediately. "I'm going with you."

Cobb whirled on him, his pale blue eyes glinting in the dim light. "No way, hotshot!"

Trevor's voice was flinty. "Don't argue, Cobb. According to your theory, the person inside there is from Horizons. If he is, I want to make sure he doesn't suddenly show up dead."

Jillian felt the sheriff's fury. He wasn't going to back down, and neither was Trevor.

She caught Mel's arm. "Stop arguing, you two. That's my stuff the guy's stealing. While you two fight it out, he could get away with my entire inventory."

The two men looked at her for a long second. Then Mel muttered a crude obscenity and jerked away. "Suit yourself, Markus," he said in furious growl. "But stay the hell out of my way."

Trevor grunted, then turned to Jillian. "Go back upstairs and wait," he ordered, grasping her by the shoulders. "When you see the deputies arrive, you can come back down."

"No. You might need me."

"Damn it, Jill, I—"

"You comin' or not?" Cobb interrupted impatiently. "'Cause I'm goin' in. Now."

Trevor's hands tightened on her arms, then suddenly dropped away. "Get behind the car, then, and stay down," he ordered as he followed the sheriff to the door.

Jillian hesitated. As long as she kept in the shadows, she would be safe. Walking as silently as she could, she followed the two men, taking care to stay in the dark patch by the steps. She heard the faint metallic click as Cobb tried the door, then saw the tiny triangle of light pattern the sidewalk as he eased it open.

The sheriff entered soundlessly, his gun pointed toward the ceiling, with Trevor right behind him. "Hold it right there!" Mel shouted. He and Trevor crouched side by side behind a display table a few feet away from the prescription counter.

Jillian ran closer, hesitating on the threshold. Inside, two men in dark clothes and ski masks stood frozen in the rear. One of the men clutched a black plastic garbage bag in his hand, while the other, tall and muscular, held a lethal-looking hunting knife.

"Run!" shouted the man with the knife as he sprang toward the front. His hip crashed into a large basket of Halloween candy, sending it flying, and his feet slipped on the slick wrappers littering the floor.

"Freeze, sucker, or you're dead!" Mel lowered his gun and took aim.

"Wait!" Trevor yelled, but it was too late.

The sound of the pistol blasted Jillian's eardrums and reverberated like thunder off the high ceiling. She cried out, and Trevor spun around.

"Get the hell out of here, now!" he shouted, but she shook her head. If the thief was wounded, she had to help.

The second man stood frozen, his hand extended toward a bottle of pills on the shelf. Jillian glanced quickly in his direction, then followed Mel toward the front. Trevor's large, powerful body was between the robber and the back door. He wouldn't get away.

The thief lay in a crumpled heap near the front, blood pooling on the floor beneath his leg. He was moaning harshly and trying to move as Mel handcuffed his hands in front of him. It looked as though the bullet had gone through the fleshly part of his thigh.

"Lie still," Jillian ordered, bending over him. "I'm a nurse."

The man's pale blue eyes watched her through the slits in the mask. The dilated pupils were filled with panic and pain.

"You're going to be okay," she said, gently pulling the mask from his head. He began to sob.

Mel's brutal cry of disbelief echoed her own. The thief was Mike Cobb.

"No, oh, no," Jillian whispered, dropping the mask and stumbling to her feet. Shaking uncontrollably, she turned and stared toward the cubicle in the rear.

Her gaze collided with Trevor's. He was standing next to the second thief, a large black flashlight in his hand. Carmen Montoya had been hit with a flashlight.

Please, no, she thought. But she knew. Dear God, she knew. It had to be Jason under the mask. If she'd been close enough to see his eyes, she would have known immediately.

Jillian forced herself to move forward. Her legs felt disconnected from her body, and she was icy cold.

Trevor waited until she was only a few feet away. Then, with a deep sigh, he reached out and pulled the mask from Jason's head. Their son stood under the light, his face so pale it seemed transparent. His bright curls seemed to flame around his head, and his freckles stood out like dark teardrops against his skin. He stood transfixed, a look of fear on his face as he stared into his father's eyes.

"Where'd you get the key, Jason?" Trevor asked in a harsh voice. "From your mother?"

"Mike got it from his old man," Jason mumbled, glancing toward his sobbing friend.

"What about the clinic and Dr. Franklin's office?"

Jason shrugged. "Mike got us in."

Jillian didn't know what to say, what to feel. This was worse than anything she could possibly have imagined. She felt helpless, adrift, unable to believe her eyes.

"Why, Jase?" she asked in a strangled voice. "Why would you do this terrible thing to yourself?"

His faced changed, and suddenly he was a stranger, a grim, defiant half-grown boy with the eyes of a pain-crazed animal caught in a trap. "Everyone does it," he mumbled, his voice sullen. "Just like you drink wine. It's no big deal."

Trevor glanced at the bottles of Percodan that littered the floor by their feet. He could smell the cloying scent of medicine, and he wanted to gag. He hated the thought of his son putting that stuff into his young, strong body.

Slowly he raised his gaze to Jillian's face. She looked frozen, like a beautiful ice statue, but her eyes were filled with glittering green lights of pain. He'd tried like hell to spare her this, but he'd failed.

"No...no big deal?" she whispered, her voice rising. "No big deal? You stole, and you lied. You...you hit Mrs. Montoya, and you call it no big deal?"

Her voice shook uncontrollably, and in her mind she had an image of Jason lying there on the floor, bleeding, dying. "You could be dead now, do you hear me? Dead!"

"You wouldn't care if I was. You've got him now." Jason's lips twisted as he glared at his father.

Jillian inhaled swiftly, fighting for calm. She'd get through this somehow. She had no choice. "I care. But I hate the thought of the things you've done because of this...this madness. It's not like you didn't know what this stuff could do to you. I've told you over and over."

"Yeah, yeah, I know." His voice cracked, and his lips clamped together.

Jillian felt as though he'd just plunged a knife into her stomach and was twisting the blade. "Jason, I'll help you," she said in hoarse voice. "Together we'll—"

"I don't want your help!" he snarled, his face splotched with crimson. "You're always *helping*, always smothering me, always nagging. There's nothing wrong with me, nothing. So get the hell outta my face and leave me alone."

He spun away, his body braced to run, but Trevor grabbed his arm and jerked him around to face them. "No more running, Jason." Trevor's voice was hard and unyielding as iron. "It ends here. Now. All of it."

"You can't make me quit," Jason shouted. "No one can."

"You didn't hear me, son," Trevor said calmly. "It's over. No more lies. No more stealing. No more hiding."

Some of the bravado left Jason's face. "I...I tried to quit, but...but you don't know what it's like. No one knows what it's like. It's *awful*."

Trevor exhaled slowly. "You're right. It's hell, but I'll help you, Jason. We'll do it together."

Jason dropped his head to his chest. His silky red curls were only inches from Trevor's strong, square chin. "I can't do it."

"You can do anything if you want to badly enough." Trevor forced Jason's chin up and waited until his son met his gaze. "You'll do it, Jason, or you'll die."

Jason stared at him for a long moment. Then, with a deep, wrenching sigh, he buried his face against his father's shoulder.

Cold, stinging rain blew in vicious torrents against the window, rattling the panes. Jillian stood alone in a small waiting room tucked into a corner of the Horizons infirmary. It was like every waiting room in every hospital she'd ever been in. It was nearly twelve-thirty in the morning, almost two full days since she and Trevor had brought Jason here. He was in withdrawal.

Shivering, she huddled in the warm cotton blanket the nurse had given her and watched her breath fog the chilled pane. Inside, she felt as cold and lonely as the black void outside.

During the long endless hours she'd watched Jason slip farther and farther into a nervous, agitated state, his eyes growing more and more desperate as the craving inside him built. She wanted to scream in protest and denial and fury, but she forced herself to simply wait.

Trevor was with him. And Hank.

"Mayor?"

Jillian turned and say Raymond Williams standing just inside the door. He was dressed in wrinkled flannel pajamas and a robe, with black high-topped sneakers on his feet instead of slippers. Mel had released him from custody as soon as the ambulance had taken Mike to the clinic.

Jillian had heard from Adrian that Mel was a shattered man. Faced with his own words and actions, he'd refused to let Adrian transfer Mike to Horizons. Instead, he'd taken him down to Sacramento to a treatment center where his son was undergoing the same hell as Jason. Technically both boys were under arrest, charged with breaking and entering and assault.

"What are you doing up so late, Raymond?" Jillian asked with a weary smile.

"I wanted to see how the kid was doing," Raymond told her in a gruff voice. "He's hangin' in there real good."

Jillian leaned against the wall, her leg muscles rigid, holding her erect. "It's very generous of you to care. After what Jason tried to do to you, I mean. I . . . appreciate it."

"Got ya covered, Mayor," he said with a shrug. He hunched his shoulders and looked around the spare room. "Us junkies got to stick together. As Doc Stoneson says, it's hard enough stayin' clean, even with the help of your friends. Without it, it's a crapshoot."

Jillian tugged the blanket tighter. "I . . . did you go through what Jason's going through now?"

Raymond's face twisted, and his scar looked very white against his dark skin. "Yeah, ain't no other way. Course, it's not as bad as it used to be. Now they got drugs, clonidine, stuff like that, that helps some, but used to be, a junkie had to go cold turkey." He shuddered. "Guys would bang their heads on the floor, trying to knock themselves out."

Jillian shivered. She could only nod.

"Well, I best be gettin' myself back to the dorm. Counselor only gave me leave to be gone twenty minutes." He gave her an almost shy smile. "You hang in there, hear?"

Jillian pushed herself away from the wall and walked over to him. "Thank you, Raymond. You hang in there, too." She opened her arms and hugged him.

Raymond returned the hug like a clumsy grizzly, then turned and jogged away as though he were embarrassed.

Jillian returned to her spot by the window. The storm had intensified. Lightning zigzagged a wicked pattern across the sky, and the thunder rumbled almost continuously.

"How're you doing?"

Jillian looked up to see Hank standing where Raymond had been, a starched white coat looking strangely out of place on his lanky body. His face was shadowed, and he looked tired.

"I'm doing lousy," she told him bluntly. "I need to see him again, Hank. I'm going crazy waiting here like this."

"It's almost over, Jill. Then you can see him."

"Take me to him now. He's my baby. I should be with him."

Hank hesitated, then sighed. "Okay, but just for a minute."

Jillian unwrapped the blanket and dropped it onto the drab brown sofa. In silence she walked with Hank to the closed door at the end of the corridor.

Before she could go in, he stopped her. "This isn't going to be pretty, Jillian," he said soberly. "He's in the acute stage now, when he can't keep anything down, and his muscles are screaming. Even with the medication we can give him to help, his body is fighting him."

Jillian nodded woodenly. "I've seen patients in withdrawal," she said. But only in the early stages, before they'd been transferred to the detox ward. And none of those patients had been her fourteen-year-old son.

Hank's arm circled her shoulder for a brief hug. "Ready?"

"Ready."

They stepped into the room together and stood near the bed. The air reeked of sweat and vomit, and the sheets on the bed were rumpled and damp.

A plump nurse with blunt Oriental features and somber black eyes sat in the only chair. She gave Jillian a sympathetic smile as she entered, and Jillian tried to smile back. Her lips trembled, and she bit down hard.

Trevor and Jason were on the bed, both wearing wrinkled green hospital scrubs and white socks. The back of the bed had been raised, and Jason huddled against Trevor's chest, groaning in an exhausted voice, his face contorted with pain.

Trevor's cheek rested on Jason's sweat-soaked head. His eyes were closed, his face as wet as Jason's. He was rocking his son back and forth as though he were a child.

"Make it stop," Jason pleaded, his voice a mere thread. "*Please*, Trevor. I can't stand it."

Trevor stroked his back, his big hand dark against the gown. "Yes, you can, son," he told him with firm conviction. "You're doing great. Just a little longer and it'll be all over."

Jillian wanted to go to her son, to hold him and rock him and tell him she would make it better, just as she'd done when he'd stubbed his toe or skinned his knee. But she couldn't heal this hurt with a Band-Aid and a kiss.

Oblivious to her presence, Jason burrowed his face against Trevor's wide chest, like a baby seeking comfort. He thrashed violently, his feet pushing at the blanket.

"Please, please make it stop. It hurts," he repeated over and over, sounding more and more frantic.

Trevor glanced up then and saw her. He wasn't wearing his glasses, and his face had a surprisingly naked look. His gaze held hers, but she saw nothing there but exhaustion.

"Are you okay?" he asked in a raspy voice.

"I'm managing. How... how are you?"

His face relaxed for an instant. "I've had better days."

She wanted to tell him how sorry she was, and how much she loved him. She wanted to beg him not to go away and leave her alone again. But the words stuck in her throat.

Her smile was shaky, and his answering one was brief.

Thunder crashed overhead, and Jason moaned again, his hand twisting the sweat-stained neck of Trevor's smock. The boy's clutching fingers tangled in the hair covering Trevor's chest, and he winced.

"Here, hang on to this," he told Jason. Trevor slipped the medallion from his neck and placed it in his son's hand. "Squeeze hard."

Jason's knuckles whitened as his hand clutched the silver medal. His breathing was raspy, and his head bobbed back and forth endlessly. Suddenly his eyes opened, and he saw Jillian.

"I didn't mean it, Mama," he cried. "I'll tell the truth about the pills, I promise. Just get me out of here." His voice was high-pitched and scared, his expression wild and pleading. "I didn't mean to lie. I... was scared you'd hate me."

"I could never do that," she whispered, seeing the guilt and anger and desperation all mixed up together in his wonderful copper eyes. Her beautiful baby boy, an addict and a liar. And a thief.

"Then you'll take me home?" His face twisted. "Right now, huh, Mom? I won't use anything ever again. I promise."

She swallowed hard, forcing herself to maintain a calm expression. "You need professional help, sweetie. I know that now."

Hatred flashed into Jason's eyes, and she pressed her hands tightly together in front of her.

"You don't know nothin'!" Jason shouted, his voice suddenly strident. "You hate me, just like they do!"

"No, Jase. No. I love you. We all love you."

He gagged, then moaned. "I'm going to be sick again."

His thin chest heaved, and he leaned over, vomiting water, the only thing he'd been given since he'd arrived, into the shiny bowl tucked against the bed railing. Trevor waited until the boy had finished, then reached for the damp cloth hanging from the bed rail and gently wiped Jason's white face. "You're doing fine, Jason. Just fine."

Jason began to whisper. Trevor gave her a brief glance, then ducked his head and began soothing the boy with the same endless litany.

Jillian pressed her trembling fingers to her lips and clutched Hank's arm. A clammy cold spread through her, and her head felt as though it were filled with soggy cotton. "How . . . how much longer?"

"Hard to say. At least a few hours more," he said in a low voice. "C'mon, I'll buy you a cup of coffee."

Jillian shook her head. "I'm not leaving him." A shudder ripped through her, and she hugged herself for warmth.

Trevor lifted his head and blinked at her. There was a smear of blood on the side of his neck where Jason's nail had raked his skin. "Jill, please," he said in an exhausted voice. "Don't argue. Hank knows best."

She started to refuse again, but Hank's rough drawl stopped her. "You'll be doing more for the boy by giving him privacy," he said in a terse professional tone. "Besides, he's going to need you in good shape and not as exhausted as he is when this is over."

Jillian nodded woodenly. Hank was right. She would only be in the way.

Six hours later Trevor stood by the bed and looked down at the face of his sleeping son. The boy's skin was pasty white beneath the freckles, and his features were contorted into an exhausted frown.

Sleep, son, he thought. Sleep while you can. He bent over stiffly and kissed Jason's damp forehead.

"He'll be out for a while now," Hank murmured, taking the boy's pulse. "I'll stay with him. You and Jillian have things to talk about."

"Where is she?"

Trevor's eyes stung with tiredness, and his back throbbed with the kind of deep ache that would invariably end in a spasm if he didn't rest his strained muscles soon.

"In the waiting room. I made her drink some soup at about four, and she promised to lie down for a while."

With a sigh Trevor removed the medallion from Jason's hand and slipped it over his neck. "Take good care of my son, okay? I've done about all I can do for now."

"Don't worry. He's tough, like his dad."

"Yeah, I'm tough, all right."

Hank gave him a thoughtful look. "Trev, she's class all the way. She can take the truth."

"Yeah, but can I handle telling it to her?"

He held his breath against the pain and pulled the sweat-soaked smock over his head. He threw it onto the end of the bed, took the fresh one Mrs. Sung held out to him and pulled it over his tired body.

He needed a shower and a shave and at least eighteen hours of uninterrupted sleep, but first he had to face Jillian. These three days and nights with Jason had taken everything he had, but he'd rather go through them all over again then live through the next few minutes.

Trevor found her in the waiting room where Hank had said she'd be. She was stretched out on the sofa, asleep.

It was dawn, and the storm was over. The rising sun filtered through the window, caressing her face with pale color. She was wearing some kind of fuzzy white sweater that looked soft against her skin, and her bare toes peeped out from beneath the edge of the blanket.

Trevor stood motionless, staring down at her. He longed to rest his head on her breast and pull her warmth and sweetness over him like that same soft blanket she was clutching so tightly. He needed her strength and her fire. And more than anything he needed her to smile for him one more time before he left.

But he hated to wake her. She looked so fragile, with her thick, long hair tousled into dark red ringlets against her pale cheeks, and her slender wrist draped over her eyes.

But his lady was no shrinking violet, for all her daintiness. She was strong and feisty and every damn thing a man could want in a woman.

His lady, he thought with a silent sigh. But only in his dreams. She didn't want his kind of love, and it was the only kind he had to give.

Gritting his teeth against the hot ache in his lower back, Trevor lowered himself onto the sturdy oak coffee table in front of her. His hand shook as he brushed a thick curl away from her forehead. Her skin felt like warm satin, and he let his hand rest against her cheek for a heartbeat, knowing it might be the last time he'd be allowed to touch her.

He squeezed his eyes closed, then sighed and dropped his hand. "Jill, wake up. It's morning." His voice was hoarse, and his throat hurt.

"Mmm."

Her lashes fluttered, and she opened her eyes. Trevor saw the pinched strain around her mouth and the bruised shadows under her eyes as she stared at him in drowsy confusion.

"Is it over?" she asked in the sleep-husky voice he loved.

"For now, yes. He's sleeping."

Jillian blinked, trying to force some life into her leaden limbs.

Trevor looked terrible. Under the gray stubble darkening his jaw, his skin was ashen, and his gaunt cheeks were drawn and shadowed. Beneath his furrowed brow, his eyes were bloodshot and rimmed in red. This was the man she'd accused of not caring enough, she thought, feeling the guilt and the anguish fill her.

She'd been such a fool.

"He's okay," Trevor said in a worn-out voice that hurt her to hear. "He's got guts."

Like his father, she thought.

Aloud, she asked softly, "But when he wakes up, he's still going to be an addict, isn't he?"

Moving carefully, she sat up and swung her legs over the edge of the couch. Ever since she'd left Jason's bedside she'd tried to push the horror from her mind, but she hadn't succeeded.

"Yes," Trevor said in a weary voice. "He'll always be an addict. It doesn't go away. Ever."

He rubbed his hands over his knees. He knew what she was going through, but he couldn't help her. She had to fight this out on her own.

"I could have stopped it," she said. "If I'd seen what was happening, I could have gotten him help."

"Maybe. But that hardly matters now."

"Of course it matters! I failed him."

The helpless tremor in her voice shook him badly. They were in the same room, sharing the same pain, yet they were miles apart. He knew now they always would be.

"Jill," he said wearily, forcing himself to concentrate, "Jason needs you now more than ever. It's not going to do any good to think about what you did or didn't do. He just needs you to love him and forgive him."

"I do. Of course I do," she said, fighting the tears. Last night she'd thought she would never cry again, but she couldn't seem to help herself. "But I can't make this go…go away. All…all his life he'll have to fight this…this awful battle, and the books say that sooner or later most addicts lose the fight and use again."

"Some don't."

She raised tortured eyes to his. "My baby's only fourteen, and his life is ruined."

Trevor's patience gave out. "If he wants to make it, he will. If he doesn't, he won't." He didn't bother to search for gentle words. He was too whipped for tact. "That's the bottom line, no matter what the damn books say. And you're not helping him by feeling sorry for yourself, or for him, either."

Jillian gaped at him. "How can you say that? You don't know what it's going to be like for him."

"Don't I?" His voice roughened. "When he's tired, or depressed, or sometimes for no damn reason at all, he'll remember the sweet euphoria and the blessed numbness. His veins will burn, and his muscles will tighten until he can't sit still. If he doesn't find something to distract himself, he'll go looking for a fix. But the choice is still his."

"Stop it! I don't want to hear that!"

"But you need to hear it. He'll want it, Jill. For the rest of his life. Every morning when he wakes up, it'll be waiting for him, this monster in his gut. So he'll fight, one day at a time.

And he'll win that same way." Trevor ran his hands down his thighs, trying to release the tension building inside him. "He can do it."

"What if he can't?"

"Then he'll die."

She inhaled swiftly, and the air hurt her throat. "No, no, Trevor. Don't say that. I don't want him to die. I...I don't want him to be an addict."

Trevor took a deep breath, wanting more than anything to have these next few minutes behind him. "I know, angel. I don't want this kind of a future for my son. I don't want him to be an addict, either. But he is. And...so am I."

Jillian stared at him, her pupils slowly dilating in horror. "No...no," she whispered. "I don't believe you."

Now that he'd started, he would tell her all of it, just as he should have told her weeks ago. It didn't matter now. He'd offered her all the love he had, and she'd rejected him.

A deep sadness settled inside him. He had a lot of empty days and nights ahead of him before he would stop missing her.

"It's true. I'm a junkie, Jill. For a long time, years, I woke up every morning with my gut screaming for a fix." He forced himself to accept the horror in her eyes. "I was hooked, Jill. On that same morphine you used to give me. That the doctors prescribed to keep me alive. By the time they decided I'd had too much for too long, it was too late. I needed it, I craved it, I'd do anything for it. I tried a dozen times to quit, but I couldn't."

Jillian saw the naked truth in the eyes she adored and knew that if she moved, she would start screaming and screaming and never stop.

"Your letters, you...you said everything was fine. You said you were getting better." Her lips were dry and moved woodenly, as though framing each word in slow motion.

"I lied." His attempt at a smile was a failure. "That's one of the things addicts do, Jill. They lie. They do other things, too. Stupid, senseless, shameful things, like...like betraying the ones they love the most."

Jillian shivered. Now it all made sense. Terrible, shocking sense. He'd lied when he said he'd be there at the wedding.

When he saw she wasn't going to say anything, Trevor forced himself to tell her the rest. "You asked me how I knew what Jason was doing. I knew because I'd been there, Jill. I spent all of my money buying black-market morphine. And when it was gone, I lied to my father and got more. When that was gone, I got it from my mother. I told her you needed it for your family. Something about your mother being terminally ill."

Jillian uttered a small cry, and his face twisted. The scalding guilt came back to him, making him relive the nightmare he'd tried so hard to put behind him, and he shuddered. "The night before I flew to Honolulu, I went to the hospital to buy the stuff from an orderly there. When he tried to hold out on me, I hit him and took it. I'm not proud of what I did, Jill, but I can't change it, either."

Jillian groped for the hard cushion behind her. "You...you never said..."

Trevor saw the pictures in his head, the blurred, shameful images of the things he'd done in those terrible, black months. He'd fought back, one day at a time, slowly regaining the trust of his family, gradually paying off his debts and regaining his self-respect by building the best damn roads and bridges he could. He'd driven himself relentlessly to change his life, to change himself, but it had been years before he'd been able to forgive himself.

"I was there, Jill. At the Royal Hawaiian. I stood there in front of that pretty outdoor chapel you'd made for us, and I started to cry. Everything was so clean and white, so...so decent. I wanted to be with you so much. More than I can make you know. It nearly killed me to walk away without you."

"Why...why didn't you tell me? Why didn't you let me help you?" Jillian felt as though she were choking. She struggled to swallow the lump in her throat, but it wouldn't budge.

Trevor saw the terrible anguish in her, and he wanted to cry. But he hadn't cried in years, not since that first Christmas without her.

"Because I was dirty, Jill. Inside and out. I hated the things I did to get the drugs I craved, and I hated myself because I didn't have the guts to quit. I would have done anything to get it, Jill, even...even lie to you so that you'd get it for me. I loved you too much to put you through that."

Trevor was intensely aware of every breath Jillian took. She looked stricken, as though he'd slapped her hard across the face. But he was afraid to move. Afraid to touch her.

He looked up at the ceiling. "I hit bottom after that. I was broke, my family was disgusted with me, I'd lost all of my self-respect." His voice was thick and tortured. "I'd lost you."

Slowly he dropped his gaze until it rested gently on her face. "One day I woke up in a strange bed with a strange woman, and I knew I would either have to get help or walk off the end of a pier."

Jillian wanted to touch him. To smooth the exhaustion from his face and gentle the bleak look of self-contempt in his eyes. But she was afraid. "What . . . what did you do?"

"I thought about you, about the things you'd said to me when I was half out of my mind in Tokyo. You told me to fight back, to dig down deep inside and find the guts to live."

He took a slow, deep breath. "Somehow I made it to the VA hospital and checked myself into the special program they'd set up for guys like me. That's where I met Hank. He was in charge of the program. He got me through withdrawal somehow. I still can't remember those first few weeks." He sighed heavily and ran his hand through his sweat-damp hair. "Hank tells me I should be glad I can't."

"Cold turkey," she whispered, her hand at her throat.

"Yeah, some name, huh? I still hate the sound of it."

He dropped his gaze. He couldn't look at her. He wasn't ready to see the revulsion in her eyes. He wanted to remember the way she'd looked at him on the river for just a little longer.

Jillian twisted the blanket in her lap. "I don't know what to say," she whispered, staring into his tired face. "All these years I thought you'd left me because you hadn't loved me. But you did, didn't you? Just like you love Jason."

Trevor braced his shoulders and slowly raised his gaze. She knew it all now, except for one last thing.

Her eyes were shadowed and dark, darker than he'd ever seen them. But she was watching him with wariness, not contempt. His heart began to pound, but he wouldn't let himself hope.

His hand shook as he pulled the silver medallion from its place against his skin. It dangled from his fingers, swinging gently in the dim light.

"I was ashamed to tell you the truth when I saw you again, Jill. I wanted you to get to know me the way I am now before . . . before I had to tell you about the loser I was before."

Jillian stared at him as he pressed a tiny latch on the side, and the top sprung open, spilling a wide golden band studded with diamonds into his hand.

"The first thing I did when I got on my feet was buy this for you," he said in a rough whisper, taking her hand and putting the ring carefully into her palm. "Before I quit using, I sold everything else, but I could never give this up, even when I knew you'd never wear it."

Jillian stared at the wedding band she'd never worn. All those years he'd kept it next to his heart, this man who'd said he loved her. Tears spilled from her eyes and trickled down her cheeks.

"Oh, Trevor, I wish . . . I wish you'd come to me. We could have fought this . . . this battle together." Her voice was sad.

"My life was so ugly. I didn't want it to soil you."

He touched her face. One last, sweet touch. He'd had years and years of wanting and not having, only to come so close. So damn close. His eyes burned with tiredness.

How? he thought wearily. How the hell was he ever going to make it without her? Somehow he would have to try, but it was going to be so hard.

She tilted her hand so that the diamonds caught the light. "It's a beautiful ring."

"When I was shipped stateside I felt as though we were already married," he said, touching the gold band with the blunt tip of his finger. "I felt that the ceremony would only be a formality. I—I never really stopped feeling that way."

He closed her fingers over the wedding band, then bent to kiss her hand. Jillian felt the brush of his lips, and she shivered. His firm lips were as cold as her skin.

"Keep the ring, Jill. It's always been yours." His hand tightened over hers. "I'll always love you, angel."

Jillian heard the sigh of goodbye in his voice, and she started to shake.

"Then why . . . why didn't you come looking for me, after . . . after you quit?"

Trevor felt the thickness clogging his throat. "It took me a long time to fight my way out of the pit I'd put myself into, Jill. I . . . I was sure you would have found someone else by then."

He wanted to wipe the tears from her face, but he knew he couldn't touch her. He had to get used to being alone again.

"There was never anyone but you. Not in my heart. There never will be. It's you I want. I love you."

Trevor stared at her helplessly. He'd never learned to pray. He wasn't sure prayers were even heard. But he knew there was a part of him that wanted to believe. Silently he breathed a plea that her love was strong enough to accept the flawed man he would always be.

"I can't make you any promises, Jill," he told her, needing to tell it all. "I can only handle one day at a time."

Jillian felt the lump in her throat dissolve, and a strange peace came over her, as though her life had gone full circle and returned to the place where she and Trevor had started.

"All I want is for you to keep the promise you already made me."

He frowned, and his eyes grew wary. "What promise?"

"A wedding. With champagne and roses."

Her face softened into a beautiful smile as she gazed down at the ring in her palm. "I can put it on now, but I'd rather you gave it to me in front of the chaplain, with Jason and Hank and Addie watching." She held her breath, letting her eyes and her smile tell him how much she loved him.

Trevor stared at her, his face tight. Slowly his eyes warmed until they were the beautiful molten copper she loved. "You'll marry me?"

He sounded shocked, and just a little scared. Jillian touched the tiny dimple that appeared at the corner of his mouth whenever he frowned. "Any time, any place." Her fingers brushed the rumpled locks away from his damp forehead, and a coarse tremor shook him.

Trevor wanted to crush her to him, but he was afraid to move. "I'm still a junkie. And I still want it, Jillian, especially when my back is giving me fits and all I can have is aspirin." He took a slow breath. "Sometimes I . . . I can be hard to live with. Sometimes I just have to . . . go off by myself and fight it through. I never know when that's going to happen, or how long it'll take. Sometimes it's months before I can handle a normal life . . . the kind you deserve."

She caressed his face with warm, loving hands. "Are you trying to warn me off? Because I have to tell you that it won't work. I can be just as tough as you, Trevor Markus."

Trevor felt something hard and mean give way inside him. She meant it. She wasn't afraid. Not of him, or his addiction, or the future.

Sweet, hot joy rushed through his body, more potent than any drug he'd ever craved, and he started to shake. He didn't need anything but her.

Trevor groaned and pulled her onto his lap. Through the double layer of soft cotton he could feel her heart pounding against his chest. His own heart was galloping so fast that he couldn't tell when one beat ended and the other began.

With a grateful sigh he buried his face in her thick hair and gave in to the one craving he would never have to fight. "Christmas Eve," he whispered hoarsely. "On the grounds of the Royal Hawaiian. I'll bring the champagne."

"And the roses. Lots of red roses."

Trevor closed his tired eyes and crushed her to him. He couldn't seem to stop shaking.

Jillian snuggled against his hard, tired body and knew nothing would defeat them ever again. Each had been through hell and survived. Together they could face anything.

"Don't let go, my darling," she begged, her eyes filling with tears. "Don't ever let go."

And Trevor knew he never would.

Epilogue

She was a slender goddess in ivory, floating gracefully toward him past the pink and orange clusters of exotic flowers. Her long hair was a silk flame in the bright sunlight, cascading in gold-tipped curls over her lovely throat. Her lips were slightly parted in enticing promise, and her green eyes were filled with vibrant joy. In her dainty white hands she held roses, bright red velvet buds with long green stems.

He reached for her, his hand folding over hers. Her smile curved, bloomed, warmed, just for him, and her lovely, ethereal face turned up toward his.

Love radiated from her eyes as she said the words, sweet wonderful promises that bonded them together forever. His heart swelled, and tears pressed his eyes, as her wide emerald eyes drew him closer, asking, promising, waiting for him to say the words. Those hard, terrible words.

He struggled, feeling the clawing need inside him. "No," he cried in agony. "No more."

Hurting, he reached for her, feeling the warmth of her light fill him, and the ache began to ease. "My angel," he whispered. "I love you."

The love in her eyes shimmered, grew brighter, soothed him. He bent his head to kiss her, but she floated away, lost to him. He'd waited too long....

"No, no, *no!*"

"Darling, wake up. Trevor, it's just a dream."

Trevor woke up in a cold sweat, his heart pounding, his body rigid. He was breathing hard, and harsh sound filled the bridal suite. Not again, he thought in a haze of pain. He couldn't make it without her.

"Darling, I'm here. It's all right." Her voice was soothing, sweet, and it took him a minute to realize she was really here, the woman he'd longed for for so long. His angel. Jillian.

"Jill," he whispered, feeling his heart throb in his throat. He reached for her, pulling her close so that he could feel her against him, soft and clean-smelling and sweet.

"I'm here, Trevor. Right next to you."

He closed his eyes, feeling the silk of her hair caress his neck. Her skin was warm and smooth, and she smelled of roses and sunshine.

"I was dreaming of the wedding," he whispered, feeling the catch in his throat. "I thought I'd lost you again."

He buried his face in her hair, suddenly ashamed of the need for her love that filled him more and more every day. She was his whole life, but he couldn't tell her. He was still afraid to accept the happiness she was offering with such sweet generosity.

And sometimes he was afraid he wouldn't be able to fight hard enough against the demons that sometimes haunted him, afraid that he would let her down again.

"You'll never lose me," she murmured, pressing her lips against his throat. She could feel the terrible tension in him, straining his powerful muscles against his skin.

A few hours ago they'd made glorious love for the first time as husband and wife. He'd whispered sweet, loving words of longing and need in her ear, and for the first time she'd known how very much he loved her.

Silently she lay against him, stroking his muscular chest with a gentle hand, soothing him, letting him feel her love. Gradually he relaxed, and his breathing gentled.

Over the past weeks she'd discovered that Trevor was a terribly complex man, warm and giving, but also moody and introspective. He drove himself hard, and he rarely allowed himself to relax.

From Hank she'd heard of those wretched hours when the morphine was slowly leaching from his body, the hours when Trevor had screamed her name in agony and pleading. And she'd cried when Hank had told her about the medallion containing her ring. Trevor had held it in his hand, too, just as Jason had. Only they'd had to pry it from Trevor's clenched fist after he'd finally passed out.

At the altar in the same familiar corner of the Royal Hawaiian grounds, watching the painful memories flicker in his eyes as he'd said his vows to her, she'd made a silent vow of her own. Somehow she would take the shadows from his eyes and replace the stillness with the kind of happiness she could feel in her own eyes. That would be her special wedding gift to the husband she loved with all her heart.

Trevor sighed and pulled her closer. "How do you like your wedding day so far?" he whispered, stroking her arm. Most of the tension was gone, and a pleased smile curved his lips.

"So far it's perfect." She inhaled slowly, filling her lungs with the seductive perfume filling the room. "Where did you get all the red roses? There must be a hundred."

"I went to the same florist. I think I had to put all the ghosts behind me, Jill. I loved our wedding, but in a lot of ways it's been hard for me. I had to face a lot of bad memories all over again."

His hand shook as he stroked her hair.

"Me, too, but having Addie and Hank here helped." She laughed, deliberately banishing the past to some far corner of her mind.

There was a soft, comfortable silence. Jillian listened to the quiet beating of Trevor's heart and thought about the weeks following Jason's arrest. He'd been at Horizons the entire time, learning how to deal with the things he'd done to himself.

Trevor had been forced to spend time in Seattle and abroad, but he'd called often and returned for brief visits as often as he could.

Every time he'd returned there had been a silent question in his eyes for the first few moments. He still couldn't believe she'd accepted him, but he would.

Jillian smiled. This was the first full night they'd ever spent together, and she wanted to savor every second.

The soft hair on his chest tickled her nose as she turned her head to peek at the clock. It was a few minutes past midnight. Christmas.

She stretched slowly, feeling the sleek sheets under her bare legs. The bridal suite of the elegant old hotel was huge, big enough for three couples, but she needed only this bed and the man beside her.

"Merry Christmas," she murmured.

Trevor groaned and lifted her face for a warm, loving kiss. "This is the first time in years I haven't been blind drunk by this time," he told her with a rueful chuckle. "I like this better."

"Me, too."

Jillian sighed in slumberous pleasure and traced the strong curve of his shoulder with her fingers. "Jason looked especially handsome today, don't you think?"

Trevor's chuckle was a sexy rumble in the darkened room. "I don't know about handsome, but when he called me Dad, I nearly lost it right there in front of the minister and everyone."

Jillian felt his chest rise and fall with a deep sigh, and tears pushed at her throat. "He's come a long way in two months. I'm so grateful."

Trevor stroked her back. "Me, too. For a lot of things, but especially for you. I still can't believe you're mine."

"You'll believe it when we move into that terrific house you're building for us. I intend to go crazy decorating."

Trevor laughed, and she felt shivers run up her spine. He laughed a lot now, but each time was a special gift.

"You can do anything you want, angel. I've never really had a home before, just a house on the lake. I don't care what you do to it, as long as we spend every night in the same bed."

"I know it was silly, making you stay out at Horizons, but—"

"Not silly. Frustrating, maybe. But you, my dearest wife, are a role model in my adopted hometown. I hated leaving you every night, but I'm proud of you, too.'' His hand combed her thick hair, spreading the silken strands over her shoulders in a warm fan.

"Do you believe Mel actually asked to have Mike sentenced to Horizons?" she asked incredulously. She still couldn't believe the change in the man.

The sheriff was still obnoxious at times, but his attitude toward Trevor and the others at Horizons had completely changed. He'd even wished the two of them well on their marriage.

"The judge was very generous to both boys," Trevor answered, his voice suddenly serious. "It'll be an incentive for them to stay clean, knowing he'll expunge their records when they're eighteen if there are no more incidents."

"Mmm. We've been so lucky."

He groaned and slid his big hands down to her shoulders. His thumbs stroked the fragile hollow of her neck, exciting her, pleasuring her. His leg slid against hers, and she felt the heat shoot upward, spreading into every part of her. She wanted him—again. And he wanted her.

"No, I've been the lucky one," he murmured. "I don't deserve your love, but I'll take it, because I can't live without you. Not anymore."

She traced the curve of his lips with her finger. "So what do you want for Christmas?"

He swallowed. "I have everything I've ever wanted, Jill. You, here in my bed, wearing my ring, and a son who's finally accepted me as his father. I have it all." His voice was thick with feeling.

Jillian's eyes softened, and a tremulous smile curved her lips. Her hand shook as she took his hand from her face and placed it on her warm belly.

"How about an autumn baby?" she whispered adoringly. "Maybe a little girl this time? With her daddy's beautiful eyes?"

Trevor stiffened. Slowly, gently, his hand pressed against her belly. "A baby? You want another baby?"

He sounded awestruck, as though the thought had never occurred to him.

"I want your baby," she whispered.

A hard tremor passed through his big, strong body. His eyes closed for an instant, then slowly opened, and he looked at her, happiness flaring in those beautiful copper depths.

"I love you, angel," he whispered in a tortured voice. "So much. So damn much."

She moved upward to kiss him. But first, very gently, very lovingly, she wiped the tears from his face.

* * * * *

Silhouette Intimate Moments®

COMING IN OCTOBER!
A FRESH LOOK FOR
Silhouette Intimate Moments!

Silhouette Intimate Moments has always brought you the perfect combination of love and excitement, and now they're about to get a new cover design that's just as exciting as the stories inside.

Over the years we've brought you stories that combined romance with something a little bit different, like adventure or suspense. We've brought you longtime favorite authors like Nora Roberts and Linda Howard. We've brought you exciting new talents like Patricia Gardner Evans and Marilyn Pappano. Now let us bring you a new cover design guaranteed to catch your eye just as our heroes and heroines catch your heart.

Look for it in October—
Only from Silhouette Intimate Moments!

Silhouette Romance®

AWARD OF EXCELLENCE

LONG, TALL TEXANS

Diana Palmer brings you the second Award of Excellence title

SUTTON'S WAY

In Diana Palmer's bestselling Long, Tall Texans trilogy, you had a mesmerizing glimpse of Quinn Sutton—a mean, lean Wyoming wildcat of a man, with a disposition to match.

Now, in September, Quinn's back with a story of his own. Set in the Wyoming wilderness, he learns a few things about women from snowbound beauty Amanda Callaway—and a lot more about love.

He's a Texan at heart . . . who soon has a Wyoming wedding in mind!

The Award of Excellence is given to one specially selected title per month. Spend September discovering *Sutton's Way* #670 . . . only in Silhouette Romance.

RS670-1R

ANOTHER BRIDE FOR A BRANIGAN BROTHER!

Branigan's Touch
by Leslie Davis Guccione

Available in October 1989

You've written in asking for more about the Branigan brothers, so we decided to give you Jody's story—from *his* perspective.

Look for Mr. October—*Branigan's Touch*—a *Man of the Month*, coming from Silhouette Desire.

Following #311 *Bittersweet Harvest*, #353 *Still Waters* and #376 *Something in Common*, *Branigan's Touch* still stands on its own. You'll enjoy the warmth and charm of the Branigan clan— and watch the sparks fly when another Branigan man meets his match with an O'Connor woman!

SD523-1

COMING SOON...

Indulge a Little
Give a Lot

An irresistible opportunity to pamper
yourself with free* gifts and help a
great cause, Big Brothers/Big Sisters
Programs and Services.

*With proofs-of-purchase plus postage and handling.

Watch for it in October!

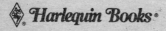
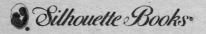
IND